The little girl flung up her arms and locked them around Nikki's neck, pulling her down.

Nikki felt incredible pain everywhere that Kirsten touched her. Strands of her hair ignited and burned with incredible speed. Tiny wisps of smoke rose into the air. She felt as if someone had strapped a blazing collar around her neck.

The flesh seared black in seconds. Welts appeared, became blisters, then burst, spilling their pus on to flesh that was already charcoal.

Reed tried to pull the little girl's hands away but he too was burned as he touched her skin, both palms turning a vivid red.

A choking acrid stench filled the room and grey smoke formed a shroud-like pall over the two grappling figures.

# Hell To Pay

## Shaun Hutson

TIME WARNER
BOOKS

TIME WARNER BOOKS

First published in Great Britain in 2003
by Time Warner Books
This edition published in 2004 by Time Warner Paperbacks
Reprinted by Time Warner Books 2006

A CIP catalogue record for this book
is available from the British Library

ISBN-13: 978-0-7515-3587-7
ISBN-10: 0-7515-3587-7

Typeset by Palimpsest Book Production Limited,
Polmont, Stirlingshire
Printed and bound in Great Britain by Clays Ltd, St Ives plc

Time Warner Books
An imprint of
Time Warner Book Group UK
Brettenham House
Lancaster Place
London WC2E 7EN

www.twbg.co.uk

This book is dedicated to Steve Lucas.
He shares my obsessions. He shares my
unsociability and we both shared frostbite
one afternoon at Elland Road.
Artist, film fan, Reds fanatic and bloody student.
This one's for you, mate.

# ACKNOWLEDGEMENTS

Right, then. Here's the usual list of people, places, things and meaningless drivel that you've all come to know and love.

I'd like to say, straight off, that this novel was a little easier to write than the last one. No, sorry, I'll rephrase that. It was a hell of a lot easier. Don't get me wrong, bits of it were, as I've said before, in the technical jargon, 'a bastard' but, for the most part, I got through it without too many explosions, uproar and smashed furniture . . .

So, to the thank yous. It's the usual suspects . . .

Many thanks to my publishers for their continuing support, especially Barbara Boote, Andy Edwards, Carol Donnelly, Sarah Shrubb, Kirsteen Brace and everyone else who makes me feel so at home. Extra special thanks to the superb sales team who never cease to amaze me.

Thanks to Sara Fisher, to Zena, Dee, Julie and Andy, Nicky, Terri, Becky and Rachel. To Jack, Tom, Barbara, Karen and Jim at the Clydesdale in Piccadilly.

To my accountant, Peter Nichols, and everyone at Chancery for their incredible work. Thanks to Margaret for the picture she painted me. It hangs with pride.

Many thanks, as always, to James Whale, Melinda (and Frisbee) and, as ever, to Ash.

Special thanks to Sanctuary Music.

On the subject of music, I know a lot of you are interested where the 'music' comes from in my books (well, the lyrics anyway . . . I'm making myself sound like Andrew Lloyd Webber here . . .). Well, there are lots of lyrics used in *Hell To Pay* and they were taken from Nickelback, Back Yard Babies, Great White and Lasgo (yeah, all right, that last one isn't what you'd normally find in one of my books but it fitted with the scene. I hope I'm forgiven . . .). They were probably also taken from a number of other sources but I can't think of any more off the top of my head. But thanks to all those bands anyway.

My usual thanks to my friend Martin 'gooner' Phillips. To Ian Austin.

To Claire at Centurion. To Ted and Molly.

To Nike football boots, to Yamaha Drums, Zildjian Cymbals and Pro-Mark sticks (yes, I'm back to beating the crap out of my drum kit again every now and then) and also to Aria guitars (on which *I'm* crap . . .).

A special thank you to all the staff and management at Cineworld in Milton Keynes. Must say, I'm not too impressed with that new coffee machine though, as you all know by now . . .

Thanks, as ever, to Graeme Sayer and Callum Hughes for all their work on www.shaunhutson.com. Many thanks to all those who've visited or contacted the site.

Some of my most meaningful thank yous go to two men who I miss as if they'd been my closest friends. They are the men of genius who were Sam Peckinpah and Bill Hicks.

As ever, I thank Liverpool Football Club. A source of such great pride to me for so many years. Even more so now. Thanks to all in the Bob Paisley suite. Also to Steve Lucas (searcher for 'extras' and a man, thankfully, as unsociable as I am . . . hard to believe I know) and Paul Garner (whose fairness is matched only by *my* fury). To the mighty Reds, I raise a glass. To SKY I raise two fingers.

My love and thanks, as always, to my Mum and Dad.

A special thank you to my wife, Belinda. She never ceases to amaze me and thanks is much too inadequate a word to express the extent of my gratitude to her for continuing to put up with me (especially when I'm talking to council workers . . .).

There is, of course, another girl in my life (the one who loves

Jerzy Dudek but always gets me to put a pound on John Arne Riise) and, my wonderful daughter, when you get older, you'll realise that everything I do is for you (I think you've got a pretty good idea already).

Finally, as always, the last thank you goes to you lot. My readers. Old and new.

Let's go.

Shaun Hutson

'Often the fear of one evil leads us into a worse.'
Nicholas Boileau

# MONDAY, MARCH 3<sup>RD</sup>

# 6.02 A.M.

Blue and red emergency lights turned silently atop the ambulances and police cars parked on the road and the verges that flanked it. Uniformed figures moved about in the gloom like shadows that had detached themselves from the half-light.

The sky was still dark. Not surprising considering the banks of slate-grey rain clouds moving across the heavens in unyielding masses. The reservoir too looked like liquid granite. The whole landscape was dark grey. A page from a manic depressive's colouring book.

As Detective Inspector Alan Fielding brought the Mondeo to a halt close to an ambulance, a few drops of rain hit his windscreen and he shook his head wearily. He took one last sip of strong coffee from his styrofoam cup then swung himself out of the car, glancing around.

To his right lay farmland. Beyond, the town of Kingsfield. Most of its inhabitants, he fancied, still tucked up warm in their beds.

*Lucky bastards.*

A number, of course, would already be making their way to work. Many to London. The capital lay just thirty miles south of Kingsfield. The town was firmly embedded in the commuter belt.

Ahead of Fielding, the narrow road stretched away between two high hedges. To his left, down a narrow slope, lay Kingsfield Reservoir. As the DI made his way towards the top of the slope he could feel a cold wind blowing in off the water. He pulled up the collar of his coat and muttered something under his breath as he began the descent on ground made slippery by two days of heavy rain. Today looked like following the same pattern.

He glanced briefly up at the sky once more and then concentrated on reaching the bottom of the incline without falling arse over head in the mud.

A number of uniformed policemen were attaching strips of blue and white ribbon to metal rods that had been pushed into the earth. They tied them off tightly and Fielding saw the words POLICE LINE DO NOT CROSS printed on the tape.

He ducked beneath one of the makeshift barriers and walked slowly towards a huddle of figures gathered close to the shore. He could hear the sound of the water lapping against the banks. He noticed some discarded newspaper floating on its surface, bobbing about as the wind blew.

Fielding dug in his pocket for his cigarettes, pulled one out and lit it, shielding the lighter from a particularly strong gust of wind. He puffed on the B&H and continued towards the group of figures now less than ten yards from him.

There were four of them. One in uniform, the other three dressed casually. They all looked frozen. Fielding recognised the plain clothes individuals, and, as he drew nearer, one of them turned and nodded a greeting in his direction.

At thirty-five, Detective Sergeant Rob Young was three years younger than Fielding. He gestured in the direction of the ground, at something the others were gazing down at.

It was a rubber sheet. Black, like everything else about the morning. Draped over something that lay less than six feet from the water's edge.

Fielding nodded to the others then turned his full attention to the sheet and what lay beneath.

'Let's have a look,' he said quietly, taking a drag on his cigarette.

Young pulled back the cover.

'Shit,' murmured Fielding.

# 6.03 A.M.

The body was naked. It lay on its left side, one arm twisted beneath it, the eyes peering sightlessly into the mud.

'He's about seven or eight,' said a female voice to Fielding's right.

Donna Thompson was kneeling beside the body, running her expert eye over it.

'Same as the others,' Fielding said flatly.

'Same m.o.,' Donna told him. 'No signs of violence. There's not a mark on him. Except these.' She took a biro from inside her coat and used the end to indicate two small puncture marks in the crook of the dead boy's left arm.

'Hypodermic?' Fielding asked.

Donna nodded.

'I need a full autopsy report by ten,' Fielding said, raising his eyebrows.

'No problem,' Donna told him.

'Anything at all?' the DI continued. 'Physical evidence? Prints?'

'Too early,' Young told him. 'Forensics are going over the ground from here to the road with a fine-tooth comb but they won't be able to see much until it's light. There are a few footprints but it's going to take time, you know that.'

Fielding nodded. 'Who found the body?' he wanted to know.

'Some guy was driving to work, his car was playing up,' Young said. 'He stopped up there at the top of the slope to check his engine, looked this way and bingo. He called it in on his mobile. There was no attempt made to hide the body.'

'Just like the others,' Fielding mused. 'Left in plain view, like he doesn't give a fuck if we find them or not.' The DI walked slowly around the corpse, his gaze straying time and again back to the open eyes.

'There are tyre tracks on both sides of the road,' Young offered. 'We're having casts made of them.'

'Probably a waste of time,' Fielding said. 'People drive up here all the time. Park up, go for a walk by the water, take their dogs for a run.' He took another puff on his cigarette, the smoke clouding around him for a second before it was blown away by another strong gust of wind. 'Whoever dumped the body would know that.' He looked at Donna. 'How long before you can give me positive i.d.?'

'Within an hour of getting the body back to the lab,' she said.

'And then all we have to do is tell the poor little bastard's parents,' Fielding said wearily. He turned his back on the corpse and wandered to the edge of the water, gazing out across the black expanse.

Donna Thompson replaced the sheet.

Young wandered across to join his superior.

'Three in two months,' Fielding said, staring at the reservoir as if expecting to find some answers in the deep, freezing water. 'All aged between six and nine. No physical or sexual abuse. It doesn't add up.'

'Since when does *anything* to do with killing kids add up, guv?'

'Killers who take kids do it for sexual pleasure, you know that, Rob. But not this bastard. All he does is pump them full of heroin.'

'Perhaps that's what he gets off on? Watching them die?'

Fielding shook his head. 'No. He'd wank off over the corpse or something if that was the case. He'd want to leave some trace on the body. Mark it. Like a dog marks its fucking territory.'

'He leaves the needle marks on them.'

Fielding ignored the remark. 'What the fuck does he do with them when he's got them? Why does he take them?'

'Perhaps the autopsy on this one will tell us a bit more,' Young said, none too hopefully.

Fielding took a final drag on his cigarette. 'I wouldn't hold your breath,' he muttered.

# 6.38 A.M.

The wind whistled around the Mondeo, the stronger gusts shaking the car. Fielding drummed his fingers slowly on the steering wheel and gazed out of the windscreen, watching as two uniformed men carried the body of the dead boy towards a waiting ambulance.

'What are we missing, Rob?' the DI asked, his gaze never leaving the mournful procession.

Young could only shrug. 'There's no obvious link between the three victims,' he said, glancing at his superior. 'We've even run it through the computer. No physical evidence from the killer. So far. No motive even.'

'Then either he's clever, lucky, or we're missing something.'

'If he's lucky then his luck'll run out.'

'And how many more kids have to die before that happens?'

There was a heavy silence in the car, finally broken by Fielding as he watched the boy's corpse being loaded, with as much care as possible, into the back of the ambulance. 'There's a motive here somewhere. There always is.'

'You said yourself that most child killers take kids for sexual reasons. None of the victims has shown any signs of abuse. Christ, they haven't even had cuts or bruises.'

'So, they've gone with him willingly. Right?' Fielding said.

'Seems like it,' Young replied.

'No signs of a struggle. They weren't snatched off streets, bundled into a car and tied up. So, what do we make of *that*?'

'They knew him?'

'It's possible but . . .' Fielding allowed the sentence to trail off.

8

'Kids of that age are trusting, guv. Any adult who's good to them, they like.'

'Enough to get in a car with them? Enough to go against what their parents should have told them about not talking to strangers? Yeah, kids of that age are trusting, Rob, but they're not stupid. You wait and see.' Fielding finally looked at his companion. 'When's it due?'

Young exhaled deeply and managed a smile. 'Two weeks,' he said, looking up as the doors of the ambulance were slammed shut. The emergency vehicle, its lights turning, headed off up the narrow road.

'How's Jenny?' Fielding wanted to know.

'Moaning about cramp.' Young smiled. 'Moaning about her back aching. Moaning about her feet swelling up like balloons. Other than that she's fine. She looks great. Pregnancy agrees with her.'

'Moaning, eh? That's what you get for marrying a police-woman, Rob.'

'She said you should come round for dinner some time. While she can still get near enough to the oven to cook.'

'Tell her thanks but she's got enough to think about at the moment. I'll come and see her when she's had the baby.'

'There's a friend of hers she'd like you to meet.'

'Tell your missus to stop trying to fix me up, will you? I'm fine the way I am. I've been on my own for nearly two years now. I like my own company.'

Fielding returned to gazing out of the windscreen. 'What's the point in looking for someone else anyway, Rob?' he murmured. 'I'm never going to find another woman like Kate. There couldn't be two like *her*.' His expression darkened. 'Do you remember what the judge gave that cunt who killed her? Eighteen months. He was three times over the limit when he was arrested.' The knot of muscles at the side of his jaw pulsed angrily. 'A year and a half. I got a fucking life sentence. I should have killed him. Got pissed, like he was when he hit Kate, and driven a fucking car over *him*. Do you think they'd have let *me* walk with a lousy eighteen months?'

He started the engine of the Mondeo and jammed it into gear. The back wheels spun for a moment as he stepped on the accelerator, geysers of mud spewing up. Then the tyres caught and the car moved off.

The rain that had been threatening finally began to fall.

# 8.56 A.M.

Fielding knocked once on the door marked PATHOLOGY then walked in, DS Young just behind him.

The smell of disinfectant was strong but he didn't react, merely closed the door behind him and glanced across the room.

There were three metal-topped work benches glinting in the cold, white light cast by the overhead fluorescents. Beside each were small trolleys covered with gleaming surgical instruments. Above the trio of tables were weighing scales and a small microphone, which poked out like an accusatory finger.

Fielding and Young walked towards the third table where Donna Thompson sat, dressed in her familiar white overall, scribbling on a piece of paper fastened to a clipboard. The pathologist glanced briefly at them then continued writing.

On the table before her lay the body of the boy they had found earlier that morning. The corpse looked like a Madame Tussaud's effigy, sporting the waxen-skinned sheen of the newly dead. The two detectives regarded it without expression as Donna completed her notes.

'I'll be with you in a minute,' she said, starting another sentence in her neat hand.

'No rush,' said Fielding.

Donna finally finished and pushed her pen into the pocket of her white lab coat. 'Jonathan Ridley,' she said flatly. 'Aged seven. Cause of death: heroin overdose.'

'Is that a positive i.d.?' asked Fielding.

She nodded. 'His parents are due within the hour to confirm, just for the record, but it's academic. The dental records are enough.'

'What else?' Fielding wanted to know, walking slowly around the autopsy table.

'He'd been dead for just over twelve hours when he was found,' Donna continued. She waved a hand in the direction of the body. 'As you can see, there are no external signs of violence other than the two puncture wounds in the right arm where the heroin was injected. Very minor bruising around one wrist but I'd say that was where the killer held his arm to inject him.'

Fielding continued walking around the table. 'But he doesn't touch them when he's got them,' he said. 'At least not that we can see.' He ran his eyes again over the body of Jonathan Ridley. It was perfect. Unspoiled. 'No prints on the body?'

'Nothing. He must wear gloves at all times. Even the slight bruising around the wrist doesn't show any prints.'

'Bastard,' whispered Young.

'No panic. No rush. Cool and calm,' Fielding said, still pacing slowly around the body. 'No discernible motive. No connection between the victims.'

'Apart from the fact that they were all local,' Young reminded him.

.'That doesn't mean the killer is though. He could be miles away by now,' said Fielding, finally stopping his pacing.

'Do you think he is?' Young asked.

Fielding shrugged. 'The only thing I'm sure of at the moment is that unless we get a break, this poor little bastard won't be the last kid on that slab.'

# 8.57 A.M.

Roma Todd turned down the volume on the CD player.

'Oh, Mum,' a small voice from beside her complained.

'I don't think we need to have S Club at quite such deafening levels, do you?' said Roma, glancing across to the passenger seat of the Range Rover where her daughter sat glowering at her.

'What is it Dad always says?' the small girl said defiantly. 'If you're too old then it's too loud.'

Roma smiled. 'If it's too loud you're too old,' she chuckled. 'Yes, that's what your dad always says.'

'Perhaps you're too old then,' said Kirsten, looking out of the side window as if reluctant to meet her mother's eye any longer.

Roma again glanced at her six-year-old and shook her head. 'Less of your cheek, young lady,' she said, good humouredly. 'Unless you want to walk the rest of the way to school.'

Kirsten didn't answer. She merely contented herself with picking at a thread on the sleeve of her dark-blue blazer then pulling at the long, light-brown plaits that framed her face.

'Did they have radio in Ireland, Mum, when you were a little girl?' Kirsten wanted to know.

'Yes, we had radio,' laughed Roma. 'We're not backward in Ireland, you know.'

'I know, but it was a long time ago.'

'It was only thirty-five years, young lady.'

'That's quite a long time.'

Roma reached out with one hand and tickled her daughter. The little girl squealed gleefully and squirmed in her seat.

'So, who did you listen to when you were a little girl, Mum?'

13

'People *you've* never heard of.'

'Like who?'

'Pink Floyd, the Beatles, the Rolling Stones.'

'Who?'

'See, I told you you wouldn't have heard of them.'

'Are any of them on Dad's label?'

'No. They're all too big to be on your dad's label.'

'I thought Dad owned a big record company.'

'He owns a successful record company but he hasn't got anyone as big as *those* bands on it.'

'Chloe said that she saw Dad in the paper the other day. He was having his picture taken with someone.'

'He's just signed a new band to his label. That'd be it, I would think.'

'Is that why he's been working late this week?'

'Your dad works late *every* week,' Roma said, a slight edge to her voice. She ran a hand through her shoulder-length light-brown hair and brought the Range Rover to a halt at a set of traffic lights.

A car drew up alongside them and Kirsten banged excitedly on the window, pointing at the occupants.

'Mum, look, it's Daisy and Bobbi,' she said, waving at two other girls her age, both dressed the same as her. Dark-blue blazer, white shirt, dark-blue tie, black skirt and black tights: the distinctive uniform of St Margaret's School. It was one of two private schools in Kingsfield. Both had easily recognisable colours and impressively high fees.

As the lights changed to green, Roma stayed close to the other car all the way to the gates of St Margaret's where a fleet of cars and people carriers was busily disgorging other pupils. Children as young as four were being shepherded towards the large building by mothers or childminders. Some of the girls ran eagerly, while others walked dejectedly alone or in groups.

Kirsten kissed her mother and scurried off to join the two girls from the other car.

Its driver, Louise Barton, smiled at Roma and blew out a weary breath. 'A few hours' peace and quiet,' she said grinning.

Louise was married to a cardiologist who had recently returned from a three-month spell working in Dubai. Money, as was the case with the majority of parents whose children attended St Margaret's, was not a problem.

Roma nodded. 'For some,' she said.

'Are you lecturing today, Roma?'

'Four hours. I don't start until twelve.'

'Do you fancy a coffee or something?'

Roma looked at her watch. 'Tomorrow, maybe,' she said, reluctantly. 'I've got some stuff to do this morning. Sorry, Louise.'

'Tomorrow. Right, I'll hold you to that.'

They said their goodbyes and climbed back into their respective vehicles.

Roma waited until Louise had driven away, ensuring the car was out of sight, then she checked her watch once more and started the engine of the Range Rover.

Her heart, she noticed, was beating a little bit faster as she drove off.

# 9.26 A.M.

Roma Todd eased her foot off the accelerator and reached for the ringing mobile, wondering, as she always did, if it was the school, telling her that Kirsten had been involved in an accident.

*Parental paranoia.*

'Roma, it's me,' said the voice on the other end of the line. She recognised it immediately as her husband.

'Everything OK?' David Todd wanted to know.

'Yeah, it's grand. Why shouldn't it be?'

'I just asked. Was Kirsten all right when you dropped her off?'

'Fine.'

'Look, I can't remember if I told you but I'm going to be late back tonight. I might not even make it home.'

'I hadn't forgotten.'

'We've got this party for the new band and Christ knows how long it'll go on for.'

'Don't worry about it, David. You never usually do.'

'I just thought I'd warn you. I was trying to be considerate. The least you could do is acknowledge that.'

'I'm supposed to be grateful because my husband rings to tell me he might not be coming home tonight?'

'You knew about the party.'

'Yes, I knew.'

'It's just the way things are. I've got no choice. It's important.'

'It always is, David.'

'I'm head of the fucking label, what do you expect me to do?'

'You go to your party. Take care of your new band. Make sure your little empire ticks over.'

16

'Fuck you, Roma.'

'You're never home long enough to do *that*, David.'

'Very funny.'

'Where are you staying if you can't get back?'

'The Athenaeum, as usual. You've got the number, haven't you?'

'I should think so. I've had to use it enough times before.'

'Are you on your way to the college now?'

'I don't start until this afternoon. In case you'd forgotten,' she added spikily.

There was a moment's silence then Todd spoke again.

'Give Kirsten a kiss from me,' he said. 'Tell her I'll see her tomorrow.'

'Are you sure you will?'

'I'll get home if I can,' Todd said wearily.

'Don't trouble yourself, David. We'll manage. Just make sure you're back by Saturday. You know what's happening.'

Another heavy silence. Then, 'I hadn't forgotten,' Todd said, his voice fainter.

'It has to be done, David. You know that.'

'That's two days away, for Christ's sake. I'll be home tomorrow,' he snapped.

'I don't like it any more than you but—'

'I'll speak to you later,' said Todd, cutting her short.

'See you,' said Roma, irritably and pressed Call End. She dropped the mobile back on to the passenger seat and glared at it for a moment. Then she swung the Range Rover around the corner and found a parking space opposite the house she sought.

She switched off the engine and regarded the building across the street. It was a terraced house, converted into bedsits and flats. Like so many other buildings along this street, the owner had not been slow to take advantage of the need for student quarters in this part of Kingsfield. The college was less than fifteen minutes' bus ride from the main campus.

Roma checked her reflection in the rear-view mirror,

17

smoothing down her hair, tutting under her breath as she saw the redness beneath her jade-green eyes. She hadn't slept well the previous night.

She wiped some fluff from her tightly fitting Levi's then finally climbed out of the Range Rover, pulling her jacket around herself. The wind was still cold.

She walked purposefully towards the door of number 12 Western Way, her heart thudding hard. It was like an accompaniment to the loud clicking of her boot heels on the concrete.

Roma waited a moment, studying the half dozen buzzers on the panel outside the main door. Next to each was a small paper strip bearing a name. Some were covered with Sellotape to protect them from the elements. One was blank. It was the buzzer beside that one which she pressed.

She had to wait only a second before a voice she recognised spoke through the metal grille of the intercom.

'It's me,' she answered, her voice shaking slightly.

There was a loud electronic buzz and the front door opened.

Roma stepped inside.

# 9.47 A.M.

Nikki Reed sat up when she heard the banging on the door.

Dragged from sleep by the sudden eruption of noise, she blinked hard, trying to gather her thoughts as she swung herself out of bed. She pushed the curly blond hair from her face and shivered as she felt the chill inside the bedroom.

The banging continued.

Nikki padded across to the bedroom door listening to the thunderous impacts on the wood, then, clad only in a T-shirt, she hurried down the narrow staircase.

Through the frosted glass in the door she could see the dark outline of a male figure standing in the small porch.

She hesitated for a moment, wondering whether or not to retreat back up the stairs as the barrage ceased momentarily.

*If you can see* him, *can* he *see* you?

She took a step back but then froze when the banging resumed with renewed ferocity.

'All right, all right,' she called, crossing to the door and placing one shaking hand on the handle. She eased it open until the chain went taut, and peered through the gap at the figure on the porch.

Luke Hamilton was a powerfully built man with a thick neck and close-cropped hair. He looked as if he'd been shoe-horned into his leather jacket. He ran appraising eyes over Nikki who pulled at the neck of her T-shirt trying to raise it to her chin. As she did, she exposed more of her slim thighs.

Hamilton regarded her impassively for a second. 'Open the door, love,' he said cheerily.

19

Nikki swallowed hard, her hand hovering over the chain.

'Look, do you want the fucking front door in pieces?' Hamilton persisted. 'Because if you don't, then take the chain off and let us in.'

She did as she was instructed, stepping back to allow Hamilton and his companion into the small hallway.

Tony Casey was leaner and sallow faced, his hair tied tightly back in a pony tail. Like Hamilton, he was also wearing a leather jacket over his T-shirt. He sported new trainers and tracksuit bottoms.

He looked first at Nikki's legs then at her breasts, barely covered by the thin material of the T-shirt, and smiled broadly, displaying a set of gleaming white teeth.

Nikki shut the door and followed them into the living room.

Casey sat down in one of the armchairs, Hamilton remained standing, close to the large television that occupied one corner of the small room. There was a DVD player beneath it and several films lined up alongside. Hamilton looked down at them and nodded approvingly. '*The French Connection*,' he mused. 'Good film that. And *Gladiator*. Not so sure about fucking *Notting Hill* though. Or fucking *Bridget Jones's Diary*. Who picked *them?* You?'

She perched nervously on the edge of the sofa and looked at Hamilton.

'Bit of a romantic are you, sweetheart?' Hamilton persisted, his face still unmoved.

Casey chuckled and noticed a PlayStation 2 close by. There was also a new sound system on the small MFI unit beneath the bay window.

'You've been shopping, haven't you?' he said, again running his gaze over her legs. 'Did you buy some clothes, too? What sort of things did you get? Those high-heeled shoes – you know, the ones with loads of straps?' He looked down at her carefully pedicured feet. 'Tight jeans? Short skirts? Sexy undies?' He laughed. It was a dry, rattling sound, devoid of humour.

'Where is he?' said Hamilton. 'Upstairs? Still in bed?'

'Waiting for you to come back?' Casey added, still grinning. He ran a hand over his groin and winked at Nikki.

'He's not here,' she said, clearing her throat.

Hamilton held her gaze. 'It won't take me a minute to check, you know,' he said.

'Go and look. He's not here,' Nikki insisted.

'Then where the fuck is he?' Hamilton demanded.

'Down the bookies again?' Casey offered, looking around the room. He ran his index finger over the wallpaper, digging the nail beneath a piece and pulling it slightly away from the wall. The ripping sound seemed to echo inside the small living room.

'Leave that,' Nikki said, with as much defiance as she could muster.

Casey looked at her and smiled. 'Or what?' he wanted to know.

'Look, Jeff's not here,' she said. 'He went out early this morning. He didn't say when he'd be back.'

'We'll wait,' Hamilton announced.

'No, fuck that, the cunt could be gone all morning,' Casey protested.

Hamilton looked straight at him. 'We'll wait,' he repeated.

Casey exhaled wearily. 'At least make us a cup of fucking tea while we're here then,' he snapped, looking in Nikki's direction. His gaze settled on her nipples. 'You look cold,' he said grinning, still staring at the stiffened buds. 'It's a pity you didn't buy some fucking heating for this shithole.'

She got to her feet and walked towards the kitchen. As she passed, Casey slid one hand up her T-shirt, along the outside of her thigh.

She jumped away from him, turning angrily. 'Keep your fucking hands off me,' she snarled.

'Leave it, Tony,' Hamilton said quietly, looking around the room.

'If you want any help out there, just call,' Casey said, as Nikki disappeared into the kitchen. 'Are you joining us? You look like you could do with something hot inside you.' He laughed that dry, humourless laugh once again.

'Just leave it, eh?' Hamilton repeated, still standing sentinel beside the television set.

'Cracking bit of cunt that,' Casey mused, gazing in the direction of the kitchen. 'She's wasted on that prick Reed.'

Hamilton didn't answer. He was still looking around the room, making a mental inventory of everything within.

'They've spent a lot of money,' he said, digging his hands into the pockets of his jacket.

His right hand brushed the hilt of the flick knife.

# 10.17 A.M.

She felt his tongue flicking gently across the lobe of her left ear, felt him take that fleshy nub between his teeth and gnaw so gently.

Roma Todd moaned softly as he moved slowly to her neck, nipping and nibbling the skin with incredible gentleness. He paused to kiss her, their tongues entwining briefly before he licked across her moist lips then kissed his way down to her breasts.

He stroked first one then the other with practised hands while his tongue played over each nipple in turn, wetting the swollen buds. He drew them between his teeth and she shuddered at the renewed pleasure, gasping as she felt his tongue glide down her flat belly towards her pubic mound.

She opened her legs wider, encouraging him to explore the moist wetness that awaited him. Roma opened her eyes briefly and looked down at him as his head moved gently between her thighs, his tongue and fingers gliding over her clitoris. He pushed one, then two fingers half an inch inside her, and she arched her back off the bed, pushing her pelvis towards his face, desperate for the pleasure to increase.

When he knelt between her thighs, looking down at her flushed body, she sighed, her gaze straying to his erection. Then he took his weight on his hands and gently brushed the tip of his penis against her slippery cleft.

She nodded and raised herself up to kiss him, again thrusting her pelvis towards him, trying to force him to slip his stiffness into her but he resisted, allowing just the tip of his organ to penetrate her sex.

Roma reached down and tried to grip his manhood but again he withdrew, allowing her to close her fist around it instead as she sat up. She moved her hand slowly up and down his shaft as they kissed and she could hear his breathing becoming more ragged. She knew that he needed release as badly as she did. And now it was he who let out a gasp as she gently squeezed, watching as the thick veins throbbed beneath her slender fingers. She raked his testicles gently with her nails and felt them contract.

She smiled at him, her hair damp with perspiration. Droplets of moisture ran between her breasts and, as she released his penis and turned away from him, he saw more glistening between her shoulder blades.

Roma arched her back and felt him move behind her, felt the glorious pleasure as he slid slowly into her. She gripped the sheets more tightly as he began to move gently backwards and forwards inside her, one hand holding her hip, the other gliding softly down the curve of her spine. He collected some of her perspiration on the pad of one of his index fingers and offered it to her. She drew the tip of the digit into her mouth with the relish of a suckling baby, her eyes now closed again as the pleasure mounted. He gripped her hips with both hands, his pace increasing as he drew nearer to his own climax.

She thrust back against his every movement, her body shuddering when she felt one of his hands slide to the wetness between her legs. He stroked her clitoris expertly as he moved inside her and the combined attention pushed her to the release she sought.

Roma arched her back once more, then, with a series of low whimpers, she surrendered herself to this ultimate pleasure. Her whole body shook as the orgasm surged through her. As the sensations began to lessen she was aware of his liquid release deep inside her and that new feeling brought fresh pleasure.

She felt him pull free of her, was aware of him lying down beside her but she remained on all fours, feeling some of his sticky warmth dribbling from between her legs. Roma slowly lowered herself down, rolling over on to her back, her chest heaving as she sucked in deep lungfuls of air.

Michael Harper kissed her tenderly on the lips and brushed a stray hair from her face.

Roma, her breath still coming in gasps, regarded him evenly. 'What are you smiling at?' she wanted to know.

Harper shrugged. 'I was just wondering if this constitutes a breach of ethics,' he said. 'A lecturer sleeping with one of her students.'

'Who cares?' she said flatly.

# 10.49 A.M.

All three of them heard the key in the lock.

Nikki Reed got to her feet, looking anxiously towards the sound, but Luke Hamilton shook his head and gestured for her to sit once more.

She did so, aware of Casey's unceasing gaze on her.

The door of the living room opened and Jeff Reed walked in. He froze as he saw Hamilton and Casey, thought for one brief second about turning and running back out of the house then merely pushed the door closed behind him. He looked across at Nikki who was still clad only in her T-shirt.

'All right?' said Reed, as nonchalantly as possible, looking first at his wife then at Hamilton and Casey.

'Where the fuck have you been?' Casey wanted to know.

'I had some stuff to do,' Reed said vaguely.

'Where? At Ladbrokes?' Hamilton chided.

Reed crossed to his wife and sat down beside her. 'What do you want?' he asked the two men.

'Fuck off, you *know* what we want,' hissed Casey getting to his feet.

'We . . . I haven't got it yet,' Reed stammered.

'You're two months behind with your fucking payments,' Casey snarled.

'We'll get the money,' Reed insisted.

'What, if the long shot in the 3.15 at Cheltenham comes in?' Hamilton said.

'We'll get it,' Reed insisted.

'You should have had it two months ago,' Hamilton persisted.

'Try putting your missus on the street,' said Casey. 'You'd have the cash in no time.'

'Fuck you,' hissed Nikki.

'Anytime,' Casey smiled.

'Look, we'll get the money, right,' Reed protested. 'We just need more time.'

'You haven't *got* any more fucking time,' Hamilton assured him. 'Max isn't a patient man. You should know that, you've borrowed off him before. You knew how much you had to pay back and you knew when you had to have it.'

'Look at all this shit,' said Casey, jabbing an accusatory finger at the DVD, the sound system and the PS2. 'You used the money to buy *this*, didn't you?'

Nikki held her husband's hand more tightly.

'You should have used it to do something with *this* fucking dump,' Casey continued.

'Listen, I swear I'll have some of the money by the end of the week,' Reed protested.

'No, not *some* of it, *all* of it,' Hamilton insisted. 'This is your last chance. I swear to Christ, if Max hasn't got his cash by the end of the week, you'll be pissing into a bag for the rest of your life. Both of you.'

He stepped forward and pulled the flick knife from his pocket. The swish click of the blade sounded deafening within the confines of the room.

Reed saw it and realised what was going to happen, but Hamilton moved with such speed that his victim was powerless to prevent his actions.

The blade caught Reed across the right cheek, hacking easily through flesh from the base of his ear to his nostril.

Nikki screamed as Reed clapped a hand to his face, blood streaming through his fingers.

'Get the money,' Hamilton said, cleaning the blade with a tissue and dropping the bloodied rag on the floor.

Casey grabbed Nikki and dragged her upright, pulling her

close to him. 'We'll cut you too,' he said softly, his forehead practically pressed to hers. 'I'll slice you a new cunt. But first, I'll make use of the one you've already got.' He shoved her violently away from him. She sprawled on the sofa for a moment then dropped, sobbing, to her knees beside her husband, who was still trying to staunch the flow of blood from his gashed cheek.

'Of course, there is one way of buying yourselves a bit of time,' Hamilton said, almost as an afterthought. He looked directly at Nikki. 'Max has always had a bit of a soft spot for you, darling. Perhaps you should go and see him.' He winked.

'Fuck off,' Nikki snarled.

'Just a thought,' Hamilton said, turning to leave. 'See you at the end of the week.'

He stepped through the door, followed by Casey who turned and smiled at the distraught couple.

'Take care,' he grinned.

They both heard the front door slam shut.

# 11.06 A.M.

'We should go to the hospital, Jeff.'

Nikki Reed winced as she looked more closely at the gash across her husband's cheek.

Reed peered at the cut in the bathroom mirror and shook his head. 'No, it doesn't need stitches. I'll be OK,' he said, trying to convince himself as much as Nikki.

She dampened some cotton wool with Dettol and pressed it gently to the wound.

Reed hissed in pain as she cleaned it, wiping away the blood that had now dried dark brown around the cut. He pressed his tongue carefully against the inside of his lip, fearing for a moment, that the rent would open and his tongue would burst through the laceration. It didn't.

'If he'd wanted to cut me deeper, he would have,' Reed said, wincing again as Nikki cleaned more congealed blood from his cheek.

'And next time he will. We've got to get away from here, Jeff.'

'And where are we going to go, Nik?'

'Just away. Another town. We could go to London.'

'And live on what? How the fuck are we supposed to survive with no money? That's why we're in this mess now, because we've got no fucking money.'

'Because we owe a loan shark, you mean.'

'And why do we owe it? Because we blew what we borrowed on shit.'

He exhaled deeply and sat down on the edge of the bath. 'Look at us, Nik. We're in our late twenties. We live in a council house and can't afford the rent. Neither of us have got jobs. We've both got form. The only fucking income we've got is from the dole. We haven't had much of a past, and we sure as fuck haven't got a future. Not if Max Tate's got anything to do with it.'

'Answer me one question,' Nikki said quietly. 'Did you blow the money we borrowed on the horses?'

'Horses. Dogs. Does it make a difference?'

'All I ever wanted when I was little was a nice house and some money. I didn't want to struggle like my mum and dad and everyone else on this estate. I wanted a decent standard of living. I'm sick of opening the paper every day and seeing celebrities showing off how much fucking money they've got. Why can't *we* have some of that, Jeff? Why can't we have a bit of *good* luck for a change?'

She opened the medicine cabinet over the sink and took out a large plaster. 'How are we going to get that money before the end of the week?' she wanted to know, peeling it open.

Reed could only shake his head.

'Keep still,' Nikki told him, pressing the plaster gently into place over the cut.

He touched the Elastoplast with his fingertips. 'Would your brother help us?' he wanted to know. 'He always seems to have money.'

'I can ring him,' Nikki said.

'I don't know what else we can do.' Reed sighed. 'Go back to nicking? Neither of us were very good at that, were we? We both got caught.' He attempted a smile.

She leaned forward and kissed him tenderly on the lips.

'I could go and see Max Tate,' she said softly. 'Like Hamilton said.'

'And do what? Plead with him?'

'I could . . .' She stopped as if finishing the sentence was abhorrent.

'No fucking way,' Reed snapped, as if he knew what she was

thinking. 'I'd let them kill me before I let that bastard touch *you*.' He got angrily to his feet. 'Anyway, do you think that Tate would be satisfied with just once?'

'If it gets him off our backs, even for a couple more weeks—'

'No,' he cried, cutting her short. 'We'll get the money. He's not putting his fucking hands anywhere near you while I'm still breathing. Ring your brother. Do it now.'

'And what if *he* can't help us?' Nikki wanted to know.

Reed didn't answer.

# 11.24 A.M.

When Roma Todd and Michael Harper stepped beneath the cleansing jets of the shower, she coaxed him back to stiffness and took him in her mouth.

Afterwards, she rested her back against the tiles and hooked one leg around the small of his back as he penetrated her. After he had filled her with his fluid once again she had washed slowly, running soapy hands over her body while he left the shower and made tea.

She finally wandered into the small kitchen wrapped in his bathrobe, her damp hair cascading over her shoulders.

They sat on opposite sides of the table, Harper wearing just his jeans.

Roma studied the contours of his body as she sipped her drink. At twenty-two, there were thirteen years between them. The attraction was a purely physical one. Neither of them was deluded enough to imagine otherwise.

'You should think about decorating,' she said smiling. 'I know it's only temporary but . . .' She let the sentence trail off.

'All the student flats look the same around here,' he told her. 'Well, the ones *I* lease do anyway.'

'Your little empire is still flourishing then?' She smiled.

'If anyone wants a place to rent, they come and see me.'

Her smile faded slightly. 'Mike, do any of your friends know about us?'

'What do you mean? Have I been bragging about fucking one of my lecturers? Give me some credit, Roma. Your husband doesn't know, does he?'

'What do you think?'

There was a long silence.

'Why are you doing this?' Harper asked.

'Does there have to be a reason? Other than the most obvious one that I enjoy it.'

'You've got more to lose than I have. You've got a family. A kid. A rich husband. A good job. If anyone found out about us, you'd be in more trouble than me.'

'Then we'd better make sure no one finds out, hadn't we?'

She sipped her tea.

'I don't come here for intellectual conversation, Mike,' she told him.

'Thanks,' he said indignantly.

'You know what I mean. And don't tell me you're not getting a kick out of knowing you're having sex with one of your lecturers.'

'Well, it does add a certain *frisson* to lessons,' he chuckled. 'Let's say I'd be the subject of envious looks if the others knew what we get up to. I'm not the only one who thinks you're sexy, Roma. Most of the guys you lecture would fuck you if they got the chance.'

'You have such a charming way with words, Mike.' She grinned, secretly buoyed up by the knowledge. 'Why haven't you got a girlfriend your own age? Some of the girls at the college are gorgeous.'

'I know, I've noticed. Are you trying to tell me something.'

'Like what?'

'That I should be looking for someone else? That this thing between us is coming to an end.'

'I never said that.'

'Roma, you teach psychology. I take your classes. One of the first things you ever told us was to learn how to read between the lines of conversation. That people don't always consciously say what they mean.'

'I'm flattered you remember.' She smiled again. 'No, I'm not trying to tell you something, Mike. The way things are between us suits me. No strings. No complications.'

'Unless anyone finds out.'

'They won't. Not if we're careful.'

She got to her feet, kissed him lightly on the top of his head then moved through into the small bedroom where she'd left her clothes. She dressed quickly, inspecting her reflection in the mirror.

'The lecture's at one,' she reminded him. 'Are you coming in?'

'I'll be there,' he told her. 'Keeping the carefully prescribed distance and showing the requisite lack of interest. What's the subject?'

She grinned broadly at him. 'Witchcraft.'

# 11.31 A.M.

There was no answer when DS Rob Young knocked on the door of his superior's office.

The younger man waited a moment then knocked again, finally peering around the door as he heard a muffled grunt from inside. He saw Fielding seated behind his desk gazing raptly at his computer screen.

'Am I disturbing you, guv?' Young wanted to know.

'Looking for clues,' murmured Fielding, smiling humourlessly. His eyes remained fixed on the screen.

'Found anything?'

'Nothing to help *us*,' the DI said. 'Have a look.'

Young walked in and perched on the edge of his superior's desk.

'Child killers,' said Fielding, indicating the list of names on the screen. 'Hundreds of them. Stretching back to some geezer called Gilles De Rais in the fifteenth century.'

'I recognise some of those names,' said Young. 'Brady and Hindley.'

'Yeah, it comes right up to date. This one here, Ronald Frank Cooper, was executed in South Africa in 1978. In his diary he wrote that he wanted to kill thirty boys. Four of them were to be used as human sacrifices.'

'Fuck. How many did he get?'

'Just one. He attacked and molested three others.'

'What about that one? Klaus Grabowski?'

'Strangled a seven-year-old girl in Germany in 1980. The bastard was shot and killed in court by the kid's mother.'

'That's what you call justice,' chuckled Young.

'A lot of these are parents who've been sent down for killing their own kids,' Fielding continued. 'Abuse cases that got out of hand. That kind of thing. Kids burned with fags. Beaten to death. Swung round by the foot and slammed into walls. Punched so hard their intestines ruptured. Kicked so badly their skulls split. The usual sort of thing.' The knot of muscles at the side of his jaw pulsed angrily.

'What about Raymond Leslie Morris?'

'The Cannock Chase Murderer. Killed four kids in the 1960s. Molested Christ knows how many more.'

Young looked at the list of names then at his superior. 'So, what has this lot told you, guv?' he asked.

'Every single one of them used physical violence against the kids. The murders were either done before, during or after some kind of abuse, usually rape. Even the ones who weren't sexually abused were assaulted.'

'What's your point?'

'Over two hundred child murderers listed, Rob, and every single one of them got their rocks off by hurting their victims. Sexual gratification was achieved by rape or abuse. That hasn't happened with the three kids we've found. Whoever's taken them hasn't murdered them for sexual pleasure.'

'So why take them?'

Fielding could only shrug.

'There must be something he's doing to them that we haven't discovered yet,' Young persisted.

'It would have shown up in the autopsies.'

'Then he's getting some kind of psychological kick out of holding them prisoner. Is there any clue as to how long each one's held before he kills them?'

'I checked that. From the time that Marie Walker, the first kiddie, was taken, to us finding the body was two days. Callum Hughes, the second one, was missing for less than eighteen hours before his body was discovered. The last one, the Ridley boy, was gone for about a day. Whatever he does, he does it quick.' Fielding glanced at the files that lay on his desk, then flicked through them, looking briefly at the photos of the murdered children.

'Any link as to where they were snatched *from*?' Young asked.

'No. The first one was walking home from school. The second was playing in fields on the other side of Kingsfield. The Ridley boy disappeared from outside a cinema in the middle of town. All the abductions happened within a five-mile radius of Kingsfield town centre and all the bodies were found within that same area. Chances are the next one will follow the same pattern.'

'What pattern? There *is* no fucking pattern.'

'Like I said before, Rob, this bastard is either very clever or very lucky. I'm more inclined to think he's clever and that makes him even more dangerous.'

'We can put uniformed men outside every school in town. That might frighten him off.'

'I doubt it. He doesn't pick them up from the school gates. Besides, it'll just cause more panic among the kids and parents. If everyone thinks that their kid's a potential victim this could get right out of hand.' Fielding sighed. 'What we need to know is why the kids don't put up a struggle when he approaches them. Why do they feel inclined to trust him?'

Fielding looked back at the computer screen and the disquietingly long list of killers. 'How long before *his* fucking name goes on here?' rasped the DI.

# 11.57 A.M.

The playing fields and playgrounds of St Margaret's School were enclosed by high and perfectly manicured hedges. It was as if the barrier emphasised the exclusivity of the establishment, which had been founded more than a hundred years ago.

The buildings themselves were of weathered stone but everything else about the school was strikingly modern. From the state and sheer volume of technology available to the children, to the youth of the teachers, the majority of whom were in their late twenties to early thirties. Only the headmaster and his deputy had reached beyond their fifties. There was a fairly even split between male and female teachers, all faced with classes which, in some cases, numbered no more than twelve pupils. Money didn't buy happiness, so the saying said, but, when it came to education, it bought smaller classes and first-rate facilities.

Pupils entered the school aged four and remained (provided the fees were paid on time) until they were eighteen, when more than ninety per cent left for higher education.

Kirsten Todd had already decided that she didn't want to go to university when she left school in eleven years' time. She wanted, she had told her parents, to be a vet, a singer, a supermodel or a fashion designer. Not necessarily in that order or simultaneously.

She didn't want to get married and she didn't want children. She was seven and she had decided. And when Kirsten Todd, like most children her age, made up her mind about something, she had no intention of changing it.

Just as this morning, as she raced happily about the playground, past groups of other children and watchful teachers, nothing was going to divert her from her decision. She was going to tell Chloe Barton that Chloe could stay at her house for a night, even though Kirsten had yet to ask permission of either her mother or father.

Roma and David both liked Chloe, they didn't even object to her habits of eating with her knife and wiping her nose on her sleeve. But the last time she had stayed, she'd spent a fitful night arguing with Kirsten about who was best: Westlife or Boyzone. The argument had led to a telling off by Kirsten's mother (her dad, as he so often was, had been away for the night) then a prolonged silence the following morning, not helped when Chloe accidentally broke the arm of one of Kirsten's Barbies.

This time, however, Kirsten was convinced it would be different.

She could see Chloe just ahead of her as she ran. The gap between them was narrowing. Another few yards and she would be caught.

Chloe turned and saw her and both girls giggled, racing out on to the thick grass that surrounded the paved area of the playground. They ran up and down the grassy mounds where other children were playing their own games.

It was a bright, crisp morning, the sun having finally fought its way from behind some menacing-looking banks of cloud. The air smelled of damp grass and wet earth.

Kirsten saw Chloe turn and mouth something at her, then wave.

Then the first wave of nausea swept over her.

Kirsten stumbled, her head suddenly throbbing. She touched a hand to her forehead. She felt dizzy.

Chloe had stopped running away and was now hurrying back towards her.

Kirsten tried to speak but the words would not come. The world was suddenly turning too fast. It was, she imagined, like being inside a giant spinning top.

Then she blacked out.

# 12.03 P.M.

Roma was parking the Range Rover outside the college when her mobile rang. She muttered under her breath and ignored it for a moment.

*Probably David telling her that there was absolutely no chance he'd be home that night.*

With the vehicle finally parked, she fumbled in her handbag and pressed the phone to her ear.

'Hello,' she said curtly, glancing into the back seat for her briefcase and a couple of text books that were lying there.

'Mrs Todd?' asked the disembodied voice at the other end of the line.

'Yes,' Roma answered, not recognising it.

'This is Claire Stevens, Kirsten's teacher, I—'

'What's wrong?' Roma asked, a sudden urgency in her voice.

'It's nothing to worry about,' the teacher told her.

'Has there been an accident?'

'No. Kirsten's fine. She's here in the nurse's office.'

'I can be there in ten minutes.'

'There's really no need, Mrs Todd. She just fainted, that's all.'

'When did this happen?'

'About ten minutes ago. I wanted to wait until Kirsten was feeling better before I rang you. I didn't want you to worry.'

'Can I speak to her, please?'

'Of course.'

Roma heard muttering in the background then the familiar voice of her daughter sounding her usual cheerful self.

'Hello, Mum,' Kirsten said, as if the entire episode had been one enormous adventure.

'Are you OK?' Roma asked anxiously.

'I got a headache. Then I fainted. I'm fine now.'

Roma closed her eyes for a second. 'What did you tell them?' she said evenly.

'I just fainted, Mum. That was all.'

'Tell me *exactly* what happened.'

'We were playing in the playground, running around, and I started to feel dizzy. I had a headache then I fainted. I told you that.'

'Have they given you anything?'

'What do you mean?'

'Any tablets? You know you're not supposed to take other tablets with your own, don't you?'

'Mum, I know that. I'm fine.'

Roma sucked in a deep breath, her heart thudding with anxiety. 'If you want me to pick you up, I will,' she said.

'No, I'm better now. Thanks.'

'Let me speak to Miss Stevens again, darling.'

'All right. See you later, Mum.'

More muttering on the end of the line.

'We think it's OK for her to stay until the end of school, Mrs Todd,' said the teacher. 'And Kirsten says she feels better.'

'I know, she told me,' Roma said, a little sharply. 'But you are aware that she has a medical condition, aren't you?'

'It's all here in her records, Mrs Todd. She really does look fine though and she seems well enough.'

Roma didn't answer.

There was a hiss of static on the line.

'Mrs Todd,' said the teacher.

'Yes, I'm still here,' Roma said.

'If you want to pick her up then please feel free to do so.'

'No, it's all right. If she says she feels better then I believe her.' Roma attempted a laugh but it came out more like a grunt.

'Call me immediately if there's any change though, won't you?'

The teacher was about to answer when Roma pressed End Call on the phone. She sat in the Range Rover for what seemed like an eternity, gazing from the building to the phone. She finally dropped the mobile back into her handbag, got out of the car and strode across the tarmac to the main entrance of the building.

Her heart was still beating hard and, as she pushed open the main doors, she noticed her hand was shaking.

'Now, are you sure you feel all right, Kirsten?'

The question came from Maureen Wagstaff, the resident nurse at St Margaret's. She eyed the girl challengingly, watching as she sat up on the leather couch and nodded, putting down the glass of water she'd been given.

'I am, honest, Mrs Wagstaff,' said Kirsten, getting to her feet.

Claire Stevens looked on with a faint smile. 'You go off back to class then, Kirsten,' she said, watching as the girl hurried out into the corridor beyond. 'And don't run.' She heard the footsteps receding away more slowly.

Maureen Wagstaff got to her feet and crossed to a window, her nose slightly wrinkled. 'Can you smell that?' she said, pushing open the impeccably painted frame.

Claire Stevens inhaled and nodded. 'Smells like burned paper,' she said, looking around. 'You haven't left a cigarette burning have you, Maureen?' She grinned and made for the door, ignoring the withering gaze her colleague shot her.

Claire paused in the corridor and drew in another breath. The smell of burning was noticeable in the air there too.

# 12.17 P.M.

Nikki Reed pressed End Call on the phone and exhaled wearily. 'There's no answer from John's home number or his mobile,' she said, jabbing the digits once more. In hope rather than expectation.

Reed paced the small living room agitatedly. 'Where the fuck is he?' he snapped angrily.

'If I knew that, Jeff, I'd call him there, wouldn't I?' Nikki said, the phone still pressed to her ear.

Reed glanced around the room. 'We could sell some of this stuff, I suppose,' he mused. 'We'd get a few quid for the DVD, and the PlayStation.'

'A hundred quid, if that,' she said mournfully. 'What good would it do?'

'It might get Tate off our backs for a few more days.'

'Jeff, we owe him nearly twenty thousand. A couple of hundred isn't going to help, is it?'

Reed continued pacing for a moment longer then stopped, shook his head and sat down heavily.

'I keep getting John's voicemail,' Nikki said forlornly.

'Then leave him a fucking message. Tell him to get back to us as quick as he can.'

'What do you think he's going to do for us, Jeff? Give us the twenty grand?'

'He's always got money, Nik, you know that.'

'But not twenty grand.'

'We don't know *what* he's got. Fuck's sake, we don't know

43

where he gets it so how the hell are we supposed to know how much he can give us?'

They regarded each other silently for a moment.

'Even if he's got the money, there's no guarantee he'll help us,' Nikki offered.

'Look, you're his younger sister, he's not going to see you in the shit if he can help it, is he? He's helped us out before.'

'Yeah, but not with twenty grand.'

'Just try him again, Nik.'

She did as Reed asked. 'John, it's Nikki,' she said, when she reached the voicemail. 'Call me back as soon as you can. This is very important. Thanks.'

'So now we sit and wait for him to get back to us,' Reed murmured, 'or we do something ourselves.'

'Like what, Jeff? Nip down to Ladbrokes and put our last tenner on a long shot?'

'What the fuck are you talking about?'

'That's where most of the money we borrowed went, wasn't it? You pissed it away on horses?'

He glared at her. 'The reason we're always short of money, Nik, is because you're too fond of spending it. You always want fucking clothes or new carpets or something.'

'I want the house to look nice. I want us to have good things.'

'It's a fucking council house on a run-down estate. How much do we have to spend to make it the way you want it? Have a look around, Nik. This is our life.' He made an expansive gesture with his hand. 'It always has been and it always will be.'

'It doesn't have to be.'

'It does when we're borrowing money from a fucking leg breaker like Max Tate just to put food on the table,' he snarled.

'Well, if you stayed out of the bookies we wouldn't be in this mess now, would we, Jeff? How much did you lose? Five? Ten?'

'Twelve thousand,' he said, quietly.

'Jesus Christ,' she exploded. 'And you've got the nerve to have a go at *me* about buying clothes?'

44

'It's not just the fucking clothes,' he snarled. 'It's the carpets, the curtains, the furniture. Everything. You've filled this house with stuff trying to make it something that it's never going to be. It's a shitheap, Nik. We live in a shitheap and we always will. No amount of money's going to change that. People like us don't have a choice. We never have.'

A heavy silence descended, finally broken by Reed. 'I'm going out,' he said, striding towards the hall door.

'You can't run away, Jeff, there's nowhere to go,' Nikki shouted after him.

She heard the front door slam as he left the house. Nikki looked down at the phone, willing it to ring.

# 12.38 P.M.

Roma Todd sat down in one corner of the room and pulled the mobile from her handbag. She glanced around at the other lecturers either chatting or, like herself, sitting alone. Some were preparing work, others, who had just completed lectures, were packing away the paraphernalia of learning: books, pens, files and paper.

It was a large, square room in need of decoration. The worst sections of peeling paintwork were covered with posters or flyers. Even a map. Roma gazed around for a moment longer before dialling the number she wanted.

There was a slight delay then a female voice told her that she had reached the office of David Todd.

'I need to speak to him, please,' said Roma.

The voice at the other end said he was busy.

'Tell him it's his wife,' Roma insisted.

There was a buzz then she heard the female voice once more. Could Roma call back?

'No, I can't call back,' she snapped. 'Put me through now, please.'

She shifted irritably in her seat then, after what seemed an eternity, she heard her husband's voice.

'Did you tell your secretary to ask me to ring back, David?' Roma demanded.

'Look, Roma, things are fucking crazy here at the moment,' Todd said. 'I'm due out in about five. I've got to be at the restaurant for—'

'Don't worry, I won't keep you. It's nothing too important. Just your daughter. Remember her?'

'I haven't got time for this shit, Roma.'

'You've never got time, David. That's your problem.'

'You told me earlier what happened. She fainted at school but she's fine.'

'You know where we have to take her this weekend.'

'I know.' His voice sounded positively icy now.

'You *are* going to be able to make it, aren't you?' Roma persisted.

'The appointment's at eleven on Saturday morning, right? I'll be there. What the hell do you take me for?'

'I'm not sure sometimes, David. I just wanted to make sure that your business wasn't going to get in the way again. Like it is tonight.'

'You know what my work entails, Roma. You always have. Tonight is big news for us, for the label. You and Kirsten will benefit too, you always do.'

'Yeah, I know. More money. More holidays. More toys for Kirsten. More designer clothes for me.'

'You could at least sound a little grateful.'

'I'll be grateful when Saturday's over and our little girl is OK. Perhaps we just have different priorities, David.'

'Look, why are you telling me this now? There's another four days before we have to take her to the clinic . . .' He allowed the sentence to trail off.

'Are you home tomorrow night?' Roma wanted to know.

'Yes, of course.'

'Unless something comes up?'

'I'll be home tomorrow night. I'll see you both then.'

'Kirsten misses you when you're not there.'

'I miss *her* too,' he said quickly. 'Listen, Roma, I've got to go. You're supposed to be teaching now anyway, aren't you?'

'Lecturing,' she corrected him.

'Whatever. I'll see you tomorrow.'

'David, don't ever tell your fucking secretary to ask me to ring back again.'

'See you, Roma.'

She pressed End Call hard and dropped the mobile back into her handbag.

There was a large clock, usually five minutes slow, on the wall above the door and Roma glanced at it then consulted her watch. She got to her feet, exchanging niceties and smiling efficiently at several of her colleagues as she made her way to the door.

The corridor beyond was virtually deserted. She made her way quickly towards the room she sought.

# 12.49 P.M.

When DI Fielding entered, he saw that there were close to twenty officers in the small room inside Kingsfield police station.

Both uniformed and plain clothes, they stood, sat or perched on the edges of desks as their superior entered, followed by Young. The babble of conversation that had filled the room stopped instantly, and all eyes turned in Fielding's direction. Several coughs punctuated the relative silence and Fielding looked around at his colleagues.

'I'll keep this short,' he said. 'You all know why you're here. There's no need for me to run over stuff we've already covered.' He turned to the noticeboard behind him where three photographs smiled out at the waiting throng.

Marie Walker. Callum Hughes. Jonathan Ridley.

'Three dead kids,' Fielding continued. 'The same m.o. in all three cases. No known motive. No physical evidence. No known suspects. In short, we've got fuck all and it just seems like a matter of time before whoever did these three does another one.'

'Didn't forensics turn up anything, guv?' asked a plain-clothes man seated near the front.

Fielding shook his head. 'For all the evidence the bastard's leaving behind he might as well be a ghost.'

'What are the chances he's already left the area?' another voice enquired.

'It's possible,' Fielding mused. 'But I'd say it's unlikely. Why *should* he leave? He's taking kids at will and there's nothing we can do to stop him, it seems. He must be thinking he's got one over on us, and that's good because he might get careless.'

'Do you really believe that, guv?' asked another man near the back.

'Truthfully, no,' Fielding answered wearily. 'But there's always a chance. And we've got to cling to that. Because at the moment it's all we've got.'

Another heavy silence descended, finally broken by Fielding. 'Now, I find it hard to believe that nobody knows *anything* about these dead kiddies. Someone, somewhere knows something and I want them found.'

'But we've asked all the usual sources, guv,' a uniformed man protested.

'Then ask the *un*usual,' snapped Fielding. 'All the nonce cases, the fucking school cruisers. The lot. If you've interviewed them once then pull them in and interview them again.'

There was a collective groan from the room.

'I mean it,' Fielding continued. 'Anybody with form in this area, I want them questioned again. Here or at their home, I couldn't give a fuck. And I'll tell you something else: question close family members too. Anyone connected with those three kids, I don't care how tenuous the link is, I want them questioned.'

Another collective exhalation greeted his remark.

'It's your job,' he persisted. 'All of you. So just do it. The only good thing so far is that we've been able to keep the press at arm's length. But if this bastard takes another kid then I guarantee you there'll be newspapers and film crews on us like flies on fresh shit and none of us want that. So, get out there and get talking. Or, more importantly, get the right people talking. And keep me informed at all times.' He paused for a moment. 'One other thing. Don't be fooled by this bastard. We're not looking for a certain *type* in this case. All the evidence points to a different kind of killer.'

'What do you mean, sir?' a uniformed policewoman wanted to know.

'The fact that he abducts and murders kids points to someone with a background in this sort of thing,' Fielding continued. 'Someone who might have graduated from molesting kids to this, but the problem is that as far as we can see, and forensics and pathology back this up, he has no sexual contact with the victims at any time while he has them with him. That's why I say it's a different kind of killer. What he wants from these kids, or what he *gets* from them, is different to your average nonce case. It's entirely possible that the geezer doesn't even *have* any form. Not in this field anyway. So don't narrow your range of suspects too much. Everyone's telling me they've spoken to the same old faces. Well try some *new* ones too. Got it?'

There were murmurs from around the room.

'The funeral of the Ridley boy is in two days, I want men there,' he said. 'Keep your distance but keep your eyes open for anything unusual. Anyone watching the ceremony who shouldn't be there, that kind of thing. Check the list of people attending with the parents.' He looked around the room at the rows of faces. 'Now, unless anyone has any pearls of wisdom to add, I suggest you all get moving.'

There were more mutterings then the officers began filing out of the room, leaving just Fielding and Young.

The DI looked at the three photos pinned to the noticeboard. They smiled back at him.

'We'll get him, guv,' Young said.

Fielding nodded almost imperceptibly. 'I wish I had your faith, Rob,' he said quietly.

# 1.02 P.M.

Roma wrote one word on the board in the lecture theatre then turned to face her students. Some, she noticed with a smile, were chuckling.

Even Michael Harper, seated about four rows from the back of the small auditorium, was smiling.

'Come on then,' Roma said. 'Why the laughs?'

She looked again at the single word she had written.

WITCHCRAFT

'The idea of witchcraft isn't confined to movies like *Rosemary's Baby*, *The Devil Rides Out* and *The Omen*. It's a very relevant area of psychology. Most of the great witchcraft trials of the sixteenth, seventeenth and eighteenth centuries have their roots not in black magic but in psychology. Or, more to the point, psychosis. Mass hysteria. Schizophrenia. Paranoia.'

'What about *The Exorcist*?' someone called out.

There were more chuckles around the room.

'*The Exorcist* is a good example of how supposedly supernatural happenings actually had a basis in reality. All the symptoms manifested by the possessed girl in the film, or boy, as it was in real life, were actually diagnosed as psychosomatic to begin with.'

'What about her head turning round?' another voice called.

There was more laughter. Roma raised a hand for quiet.

'All right, I know that in the film she was eventually proved to be possessed but in ninety-nine per cent of reported cases of so called demonic possession, there are psychiatric answers to what appear to be supernatural questions.'

She looked around at her students in silence for a moment before continuing.

'Incidents of so-called black magic took place at Louviers in France in 1647, at Aix-en-Provence in 1611 and at Loudun in 1634. Some of you might recognise the last one.' She grinned. 'Aldous Huxley wrote a book about the incident called *The Devils of Loudun* and Ken Russell made a film about it with Oliver Reed called *The Devils*. Has anyone seen it?'

A couple of hands were raised.

'The priest who was burned alive for bewitching some nuns was called Grandier,' Roma continued. 'It has become apparent, over the years, that he was the centre of a political plot and yet more than sixty witnesses were found to testify that he was responsible for using black magic against the nuns of the convent in Loudun. Some of them his spurned mistresses.'

*Was Harper looking?*

'Wasn't the power of the church the thing that made people confess?' someone asked.

'Well, usually it was torture,' Roma said. 'But it isn't the nature of the confessions, or how they were extracted, that's our concern. It's the fact that so many people actually believed themselves to be possessed or touched by the Devil that should be interesting to any would-be psychologists.'

She turned back to the board for a moment and wrote once more: MASS HYSTERIA.

'The convents where these three famous cases took place were filled with teenage girls,' Roma continued. 'Most from rich families. Many had led very sheltered lives. They were impressionable. Easily led. If instructed, or threatened, to feign possession they would do so. If told to implicate a certain person they would do so. Once one of the nuns began to act as if possessed, it was a relatively simple step for the others to imitate her. They actually believed that they were possessed. A situation doubtless helped by their surroundings.

'Once possession had been established then it was merely a

matter of getting them to name names. Those who'd bewitched them. Usually priests. More often than not their lovers. The clergy weren't renowned for their ability to resist the temptations of the flesh.' There was more laughter. 'The interrogators would then move in. The torture of suspects would begin. More often than not, the interrogators were as ignorant as their informants. There was no understanding of paranoia or hysteria in those days. Everything that could not be understood was seen as the work of the Devil.'

'But what about things like the Spanish Inquisition?' another interested voice enquired.

'The principle was the same,' Roma explained. 'The inquisition was thought to have been responsible for the deaths of over thirty thousand people in its time but most of the men, women and children it burned were victims of ignorance, not divine justice. Back in the fifteenth and sixteenth centuries, the church was as powerful as any sovereign state and it used its influence to the full. It ruled by terror, and the fear of witchcraft was a perfect weapon for it. No one wanted to be different. Anyone who stood out from the crowd, voiced opinions not in keeping with the norm or acted in what was considered an unacceptable way was thought to be either a witch or bewitched. Society hasn't changed that much if you think about it. Even these days, we're all a bit wary of anyone different. Anyone who expresses an opinion a little too strongly. Mankind seems to have a built-in mistrust of anything it can't understand. That includes psychiatric and psychological problems. Witchcraft was nothing more than an affliction of the mind. Many of those executed suffered from what we now know as depression, psychosis and schizophrenia. In those days they would have been condemned as conjurers or maniacs.'

'So are you saying that witchcraft never existed?' someone wanted to know.

'Not in the way that it's portrayed,' Roma said. 'No old women in pointy hats flying off to orgies with cats on their broomsticks.'

A ripple of laughter ran around the room.

'You said the Inquisition killed thirty thousand and there were thousands more around Europe who were burned as witches,' said a young dark-haired woman in the front row. 'Surely they can't *all* have been suffering from undiagnosed psychological conditions.'

Roma smiled. 'Are you telling me you believe they were *real* black magicians?' she said.

'I don't know but I don't think you can dismiss it all as ignorance,' said the young woman.

'Perhaps you're right. I'm just offering the alternative possibility.'

'Would you dismiss the idea of witchcraft completely?' a tall student near the back wanted to know.

'Define witchcraft,' Roma said challengingly.

There was an uneasy silence. Some faces turned towards the questioner. Others remained fixed on Roma.

*Michael Harper was looking at her.*

The tall student thought for a moment then raised his hands as if in surrender. 'Well, you read about witchcraft and witchcraft murders in the Sunday papers, don't you?' he said limply.

'It depends which Sunday papers you read.' Roma smiled.

There was more laughter.

'So would you say that there's no such thing as witchcraft?' asked the young woman at the front of the room.

'It may well exist as a religion,' Roma conceded. 'But I can't, and you shouldn't either, be prepared to accept it as something other than superstition, misunderstanding and ignorance.'

## 1.36 P.M.

The Oak Apple was the largest pub on the Walton Grange Estate. A characterless building, in keeping with the houses that surrounded it, the venue had replaced all the traditional qualities of a good pub with the multi-purpose themes of so many creations like it around the country.

It boasted a dizzying array of mediocre food, a jukebox that seemed fixed at a deafening volume and the obligatory satellite television. The Oak Apple was busy most nights but on the evenings when football was being shown on the large screen, it was virtually impossible to get into the place.

Jeff Reed sat at the bar nursing a pint of Carlsberg between his hands and glancing around at the faces inside the pub. He recognised many of them and was on nodding terms with most. He spoke to half a dozen as he did his best to make the pint last. He sipped from it slowly, barely wetting his lips, his eyes constantly scanning the crowded bar.

As ever, the jukebox was thundering away in one corner.

*'I've been wrong, I've been down, been to the bottom of every bottle.'*

Reed took another tentative sip of his drink.

*'These five words in my head scream, "Are we having fun yet?"'*

'What did you say you did to your face?'

He turned as he heard the voice beside him.

The barman, Maurice, a rotund man with a balding head, was drying some glasses. He was gazing alternately at Reed and two youths who were playing one of the fruit machines, trying to shake a jackpot out of it.

'Jeff,' the barman persisted. 'I said—'

'Yeah, I heard,' Reed said without looking at him. 'Your missus closed her legs too quick.'

Maurice chuckled. 'If *my* missus had closed her legs too quick, she'd have taken your head off.' He grinned.

Reed continued his appraisal of the other customers.

'Where's *your* other half?' Maurice wanted to know. 'I haven't seen her for a while.'

'She's all right. She's at home.'

'Shouldn't you be there with her instead of propping up my bar with a pint you've made last for half an hour.'

'If I want advice, Maurice, I'll ask for it, right. I'm looking for somebody.'

'Who?'

'Paul Macken. Does he still come in here?'

'Yeah, the little cunt still comes in. Mostly in the evenings but I've seen him in here during the day. I barred him twice but . . .' He allowed the sentence to trail off. 'What do you want with *that* little shit anyway?'

'I need to talk to him.'

The barman shook his head, replaced another dried glass and wandered down the bar to serve a new customer.

Reed returned to his vigil. It was another fifteen minutes before he spotted the face he sought.

Paul Macken was twenty-two. A tall, slender man with his dark hair tied in a pony tail. He had two silver rings in his right eyebrow, another in his left nostril. He was wearing a dark-blue Tommy Hilfiger jacket, a T-shirt and jeans.

Reed watched as he chatted animatedly to two men. They were roughly the same age. Reed thought they looked nervous.

One of them bought Macken a drink and Reed watched as he sipped at it, chewing on one of the broken pieces of ice he'd sucked from the glass.

'Look at the little bastard,' hissed Maurice, returning with more clean glasses. 'He walks around like he owns the place. He's rolling in it.'

57

Reed didn't answer.

Another five minutes and Macken got to his feet and headed for the gents' toilet.

Reed slipped off his barstool and followed him. As he reached the door a man burst through it with a pained expression. 'How fucking hard is it to flush a toilet?' he gasped, as if expecting Reed to answer him, then he blundered back into the bar.

The stench inside the lavatory was, as usual, appalling. Reed walked in, catching a glimpse of his reflection in a cracked mirror. He moved to one of the urinals and began relieving himself.

There was no sign of Macken but he heard movement from inside one of the cubicles behind him.

Reed remained where he was for a moment longer until he heard the door open.

Macken stepped out and crossed to one of the sinks at the far end of the room where he washed his hands.

As he turned to leave, Reed zipped up and stepped away from the urinal. 'You got a minute?' he asked.

Macken looked him up and down. 'Do I know you?' he said, wiping one nostril with his index finger and sniffing loudly. He had a high, whining voice that reminded Reed of an even more than usually dense David Beckham.

'No, but *I* know *you*. I just wanted a word,' Reed told him.

'About what?'

'Something I need.'

Macken looked him up and down again. 'If you're filth, man, you've got to tell me, you know?' said the younger man.

'Do I look like a fucking copper?'

Macken didn't answer.

'Now do you want to do business or not?' Reed persisted.

'I don't know what you're talking about.'

'I need something, somebody told me you might have it.'

'Who told you?'

'Everybody in that fucking bar knows what you sell, so let's stop pissing about.'

Macken took a step back. 'What you after?' he wanted to know.

'What have you got?'

Macken smiled. 'I ain't got anything on me except some skunk and a bit of whizz,' he said.

'What about Charlie?'

'Fuck off. I don't carry *that* unless I know I'm going to shift it. If you want it you have to place an order, innit?'

'What else can you get?'

'You tell me what you want, I'll fucking get it, right? There ain't nothing I can't get my hands on if the price is right.'

Reed held Macken's gaze for a moment longer then nodded. 'You in here tomorrow night?' he wanted to know.

'I can be.'

Reed stepped aside to allow Macken access to the exit. 'I'll see you then,' he murmured.

The younger man paused by the door. 'Tomorrow night,' he said. 'What time?'

'About ten.'

'It's cash upfront, right?' Macken said. 'No fucking about. I ain't got time for that.'

He left.

Reed watched as the door swung shut behind him. Then he looked at his distorted reflection in the cracked mirror again. From inside the bar the jukebox thundered on.

*'These five words in my head scream, "Are we having fun yet?"'*

# 2.04 P.M.

'What about voodoo?' Again the question was from the dark-haired girl in the front row of the lecture theatre. She was looking at Roma as if demanding an answer.

'It's the same principle,' Roma told her. 'In places like Haiti, where voodoo is most prevalent, it's viewed very much as a religion. Just the same as Catholicism was in Europe during the witch-hunts of the fourteenth and fifteenth centuries.'

'I've seen films about voodoo,' someone near the back called. The remark was greeted with a smattering of laughter.

'There've been a few,' Roma said. 'Everything from *I Walked with a Zombie* through to *The Serpent and the Rainbow*.'

'That was crap,' called the tall student.

'We're here to discuss witchcraft and psychology, not audition as film reviewers.' Roma smiled. 'But you're right, it *was* crap.'

More laughter.

Michael Harper watched her evenly, his face impassive.

'We've talked about the reaction to those accused of witchcraft,' she continued finally. 'Reactions made without the benefit of any psychiatric or psychological knowledge. It's only right that we examine the psychology of those who believed themselves to be witches and practitioners of black magic itself. Or at least possessed. There are very few examples of men or women freely admitting they were what we call witches. Obviously, because of the terrible punishments that went with such an admission. However, that again raises the question of validity. If these people believed themselves to be possessed of a certain power then why didn't they use it against their accusers?'

Roma waited, as if expecting an answer.

'The only assumption we can make is that, obviously, they *had* no power,' she continued. 'If you look at the most recent cases of self-proclaimed witches, men like Anton Le Vey and Aleister Crowley, then it's difficult to see beyond their desire to use witchcraft as an excuse for sexual excess. That was particularly true of Crowley. His orgies were said to be in the name of the Devil but they were just drug-fuelled sex parties. Nothing more.'

'That sounds like a good idea,' someone called from the back.

Laughter filled the room once again.

'But didn't they offer human sacrifices too?' asked the dark-haired girl.

'Human and animal. But then that was the case in pagan countries thousands of years ago. Animals were sacrificed to ensure things like a good harvest. If animals didn't do the job a human would be used. Most of you must have seen *The Wicker Man*.'

There were murmurs of confirmation.

'That's a good example of the representation of paganism,' Roma said, 'although slightly different to what we're examining here.'

'But the Ancient Britons, the Greeks, the Incas, the Egyptians and even the Romans all sacrificed people in the name of their gods. Isn't that the same kind of thing?' the girl insisted.

'Yes. And those sacrifices were made in ignorance too. An ignorance of the elements. Not to further power in a so-called religion.'

'How were sacrifices chosen?' the girl asked.

'Sometimes, in witchcraft cases, they'd be members of the coven itself. Chosen by the high priest. Sometimes they'd be willing volunteers. If not, then victims were taken from wherever they could be found.'

'What about kids?' she persisted. 'They sacrificed children mainly, didn't they?'

'Children and babies were the most sought after offerings. Their purity was thought to make them more acceptable to the Devil.'

# 2.26 P.M.

Detective Inspector Fielding took a final drag on his cigarette then tossed it out of the open window of the car. He loosened his tie slightly and reached forward to adjust the temperature inside the Renault.

Beside him, DS Young continued to gaze out of the windscreen, scanning the sparsely populated streets of the Westview Estate. The estate was comprised originally of 1930s houses built close together, each with its own front garden and short drive, interspersed with small clutches of shops. Now the skyline was dominated by blocks of council flats that thrust upwards into the bright blue sky as if stretching towards the thin wisps of white cloud that drifted across the heavens.

Through a combination of council neglect and general malaise, the estate had deteriorated during the past twenty years and now boasted the highest crime rate in Kingsfield. Its three schools vied for the title of worst attended, and Fielding saw several young kids scurrying across the road ahead, chasing a football. They disappeared down an alleyway between two of the red brick houses.

'Jenny's sister used to go out with a bloke from around here,' Young murmured, glancing around at the houses.

'I hope she kept her hand on her purse when she was with him,' Fielding muttered.

'It's weird, isn't it? On one side of the town we've got company directors and Christ knows what else. People who've got more money than they know what to do with, living in houses so big they could get lost in them, and then we've got this.' He gestured at the buildings around them.

'Every town's the same, Rob, you know that. Good areas and bad areas.'

'People on this estate don't have much to look forward to though, do they?'

'How old are you?' Fielding asked, a slight smile hovering on his lips.

'Thirty-five. Why?'

'You're too old to start developing a social conscience,' Fielding chuckled. 'Just drive the fucking car.'

Young shrugged. 'Where are we going again?' he enquired, scanning street names.

'Robson Court. Number 56.' He pointed to one of the tower blocks looming up ahead of them. 'I want a chat with an old friend of mine.' There was no expression in his voice when he spoke. His gaze was fixed on the high-rise.

'Who is it?'

'Clive Fowler. If I had a fiver for every time I'd arrested the bastard, I could retire.'

'And you think he might know something about what's been going on?'

'Not much happens in this part of town that he *doesn't* know about.'

Young brought the car to a halt on a wide concrete forecourt close to the main entrance of the block and both policemen climbed out. Young glanced around, saw one or two curious faces peering down at them from the walkways that ran along the front of the flats above. A dog was barking. Probably locked in. There was graffiti sprayed on the walls of the ground-floor flats, some of it even on the doors.

'This is no way for people to live,' Young murmured. 'Dog shit on the doorstep . . .'

'I told you, leave your social conscience in the car,' said Fielding, and he set off towards the main doors of the building.

They were made of bevelled, reinforced glass but still they were cracked. As the two men walked into the main entrance they were both struck by the stench of stale urine. There were lifts ahead. Young crossed to them and jabbed the Lift Call button. The doors opened almost reluctantly and the DS stepped inside.

More graffiti on the walls.

## MAN UNITED ARE CUNTS

in large red letters. There was a plastic bag in one corner. Young saw a hypodermic needle in it.

Fielding stepped in beside him and pressed the button marked '5'. The lift remained stationary. He tried again. The doors slid together a couple of inches then stopped.

'Looks like we're walking up,' the DI said. He wandered across to the stone staircase and began to climb.

Young followed, both of the policemen moving at an even pace up the precipitous steps, pausing slightly at each landing. The walls on both sides of them were a patchwork of peeling paint, graffiti and stains. Fielding could hear loud music coming from one of the flats, the steady thump of the bass reverberating around the concrete monolith. The barking dog was like an accompaniment.

They finally reached the fifth floor and emerged on the walkway. Fielding glanced over the metal parapet, down at the car seventy feet below. Then he looked in the direction of the town. From their high vantage point, both policemen could see the shopping centre and the dome of the large multiplex cinema that dominated it. The structure was topped by a huge red star that seemed to glow no matter what time of the day or night.

Kingsfield lay in a hollow surrounded on all sides by low hills but a view such as this could be gained only from such a towering perspective. The town and the houses that surrounded it looked so small from where the men now stood. The conurbation seemed still and untroubled.

Not the place where three children had been murdered in the last few months.

The DI sucked in a deep breath and turned to look at the flats. Many of the empty ones had their windows boarded up. Those still inhabited sported net curtains in all shades from white to unwashed grey. There was broken glass scattered across the concrete walkway and the paint was peeling from most of the front doors and window ledges.

He followed the numbers to 56 then knocked hard on the green door.

There was no reply.

'Perhaps he's out,' said Young, glancing over the parapet then at his superior.

Fielding didn't answer. He merely hammered on the door again and waited.

Finally there was movement from inside and the sound of bolts sliding back. The door opened a fraction, a chain across the gap.

The face that peered out from inside was pale with large, inquisitive eyes.

'This is Detective Sergeant Young,' said Fielding. 'You know me. Let us in, Clive.' The detective edged his foot across the threshold.

'I haven't done anything,' Clive Fowler protested.

'Then you won't mind letting us in, will you?' Fielding persisted.

'You can't harass me. I know my rights. You need a warrant.'

'Let us in, Clive.' Fielding's voice was low but full of menace.

'Look, if any of my friends see me talking to you . . .'

'You haven't got any fucking friends,' sneered Fielding, leaning closer. 'Now let us in before I take this door off the hinges.'

Fowler hesitated a moment longer then slipped the chain and stood back to allow the policemen into his flat.

'I said I haven't done anything,' he said.

Fielding slammed the door behind him as he walked in.

## 2.41 P.M.

'Why are you here?' Clive Fowler looked from one policeman to the other, his large eyes darting back and forth in their sockets. He reminded Fielding of a chameleon.

The DI looked around the flat. It was sparsely furnished and what pieces there were had seen better days. The sofa and chairs were worn. An arm was missing from one of the chairs. There was a small coffee table in the centre of the room, scratched and covered by rings of dried moisture. The only item in the whole place that looked new was the computer perched on a chipped desk in one corner of the small sitting room.

'Look, I haven't done anything,' Fowler said again, watching as Young wandered through into the kitchen.

It was in a similarly wretched state. A formica-topped table, complete with breakfast bowl, half-empty bottle of milk and a packet of cornflakes, was wedged in one corner. The walls, those not seething with black mould from skirting board to ceiling, were peeling and cracked like old skin. The dull surfaces of the worktops, particularly around the sink, didn't look as though they'd been cleaned for some considerable time. One of the taps was dripping constantly.

Young crossed to it and, almost without thinking, tried to turn it off. The drips continued.

'Sit down, Clive,' said Fielding, as Young walked through into the single bedroom beyond.

'Where's he going?' Fowler protested, jabbing a finger in the direction of the DS. 'You can't do this without a warrant.'

'Do what?' Fielding wanted to know. 'We're just having a look round. I just want a little chat with you. I don't need a warrant for *that*.'

Fowler remained on his feet, his large eyes still darting back and forth agitatedly.

Fielding took out a packet of cigarettes, lit one for himself and offered another to Fowler, who hesitated a second then took it, also accepting the light the policeman offered.

'Sit down, Clive,' Fielding repeated and Fowler finally parked himself on one end of the sofa. 'I'll make this as quick as I can. We've got other things to do. So, the more help you give us, the faster we're gone. Got it?'

Fowler sucked on the cigarette and nodded.

Young rejoined them in the living room, shook his head almost imperceptibly at Fielding and took up a position a couple of steps from his superior.

'I need some information, Clive,' the DI said. 'I think you might be the one to give it to me.'

'What sort of information? The bird three doors down is on the game. There's geezers going in and out of there all the time—'

'Information about kids,' said Fielding, cutting him short.

'Oh, fuck off. Why are you asking *me*?'

'Because you're a convicted paedophile, that's why. You've been picked up for flashing at little kids. Cruising schools. Downloading kiddie porn from the Internet.' Fielding nodded towards the new computer. 'Is that why you've upgraded? Better quality prints?' He spoke through clenched teeth.

'That was a one off and the stuff wasn't for me.'

'Right, it was for Gary fucking Glitter. Don't fuck me around, Clive. If I was to check that computer now, what would I find?'

Fowler's eyes began moving at even greater speed. Fielding was waiting for them to spin round completely like the reels on a fruit machine.

'What have you heard about the three kids who have been killed in Kingsfield?' the DI snapped. 'And no bullshit.'

'I haven't heard anything.'

Fielding took a step towards him. 'I said, don't fuck me around. We're not talking some bastard touching them up. We're talking murder. Three fucking murders.'

'What do you think I know? Who killed them?'

'Maybe. I want to know if any of your mates have heard anything. Any of the other school-run brigade.' There was sneering contempt in his voice.

'I haven't heard anything.'

'Then use your fucking ears,' snarled the DI. 'And then, use your finger to dial my number.' He pulled a card from his jacket pocket and tossed it at Fowler. 'I want some information before the end of the week, Clive.' Both policemen turned towards the door. 'If I don't get it, I'll be back to talk to you again, and if I'm *still* not happy then you *and* your new computer are going over that fucking parapet outside.' Fielding paused as he reached the door. 'Don't even think about doing a runner.'

'I haven't heard a fucking thing,' Fowler protested. 'If I had I'd tell you.'

Fielding tapped his ears. 'Use them, Clive,' he said. 'Otherwise you'll be wearing them as a necklace. Along with your bollocks.'

He slammed the door.

Pausing outside Fowler's flat he dropped his cigarette butt and ground it out beneath his foot.

'What do you reckon?' Young asked.

'Maybe he knows something, maybe not. I doubt if he's the killer. That's not his style. Besides, he's too fucking incompetent to kill three kids without leaving any evidence. He's small time. A fucking nonce. That's it. But if *he* doesn't know anything, I'd bet a pound to a pinch of shit he knows someone who does. Either way, we're coming back here before Friday.'

# 2.57 P.M.

Jeff Reed looked at his wife, waiting for her answer as eagerly as a child waits for affirmation of good behaviour.

Nikki exhaled deeply. 'It'll never work,' she said finally.

'Of course it will,' Reed insisted. 'Macken supplies most of the estate and probably half of fucking Kingsfield with gear. By the time I meet him tomorrow night he'll be loaded.'

'I doubt if he carries his money around with him.'

'Then I'll follow him. Find out where he keeps it. He might have a couple of thousand on him by the time I take him out.'

Again Nikki sighed. 'Even if it does work, Jeff, it's still only a couple of thousand,' she said dispiritedly.

'It's better than nothing,' he snapped.

'It won't be enough for Max Tate. You know that.'

'Have you got any better fucking suggestions?' he snarled, a note of desperation in his voice.

She watched him as he paced the small living room.

'Now, are you going to help me or not?' he asked.

She looked down at the worn carpet as if seeking inspiration in the threadbare warp and weft. 'All right,' she said finally.

Reed smiled. 'It'll work,' he assured her. 'Macken can't report the robbery to the police. Even if I have to . . .' He allowed the sentence to trail off.

Nikki looked suddenly concerned.

'If I have to hurt him, I will,' Reed said. She nodded. 'Just be careful, Jeff,' she urged. 'Please.'

He lit another cigarette and puffed on it. 'Everything'll be all right,' he told her.

'I hope so.'

'Still no word from your brother?'

'Nothing. I've left more messages on his mobile. I don't know where the hell he is. I thought he would have answered by now.'

'We can't rely on him, Nik. That's why we've got to help ourselves. Turning Macken over's our best chance.'

'And what if Tate won't accept the money we get from Macken? What do we do then? Who do we rob next, Jeff?'

'Look, if we give Tate *some* money it shows that we're co-operating with him. *Trying* to pay him back. It's better than nothing.'

Nikki nodded hesitantly. 'Are you sure Macken'll be at the pub tomorrow night?' she wanted to know.

'He thinks he's going to earn some money, he's not going to miss out on that.'

'What if he's got people with him?'

'Like who? Bodyguards? He's a fucking drug dealer on an estate in Kingsfield, not some Colombian coke baron.'

Nikki chewed on a fingernail. 'Ten o'clock?' she muttered.

Reed nodded. 'Once we've got the money, we take it straight to Max Tate. He won't give a fuck where it's come from.'

'No, he'll just want the rest before the end of the week,' Nikki murmured.

'We'll get through this, Nik. Somehow.' Reed wasn't sure who he was trying to reassure. His wife or himself. 'But we've got to stick together. Otherwise we're fucked.'

Nikki held his gaze. She said nothing.

# 3.01 P.M.

Roma brought the Range Rover to a halt about twenty yards from the main entrance of St Margaret's School and climbed out from behind the steering wheel.

All around her, other vehicles were pulling up, or moving away with their cargo of children. Roma nodded or waved greetings to many of the other parents.

She saw Louise Barton driving off with her own daughter and two other children, and she waved at the other woman who sounded her hooter in return.

The children, looking somewhat less than immaculate after the schoolday, continued to pour from the school and Roma finally saw the figure she sought.

Kirsten was talking to another of her friends, Megan Brown, a small child with short brown hair and large front teeth. When Roma saw her daughter she began walking towards her.

*She looks OK.*

Kirsten saw her mother and broke away from Megan who waved and wandered off to find her father. Kirsten ran towards her and hugged her.

'Are you all right?' Roma asked, looking into Kirsten's eyes.

'I just feel a bit tired,' the little girl admitted, taking Roma's hand and wandering back towards the waiting Range Rover.

Roma helped her up into the passenger seat and strapped her in, then she clambered into the vehicle and started the engine, guiding the Range Rover back down the driveway towards the road.

'You look a bit pasty,' Roma remarked, glancing at her daughter.

'I'm fine,' Kirsten said, gazing out of the windscreen. 'Mum, Megan's having a party on Saturday and she's invited me and—'

Roma cut her short. 'Not *this* Saturday, Kirsten,' she said.

'But—'

'You know why.'

Kirsten sighed and nodded gently.

'Are you sure you're feeling better?' Roma persisted, reaching out to feel her daughter's brow. 'I should have come and picked you up as soon as they called me.'

'Mum, I just felt a bit sick. That's all. I said I'm fine now.'

There was a pallor to Kirsten's skin that left Roma somewhat sceptical.

'Mrs Wagstaff said I was all right. *And* Miss Stevens.'

'Miss Stevens is a teacher, not a nurse.'

Kirsten sucked in another weary breath and reached for the On switch of the CD player.

'No, leave it,' Roma said.

'But why?'

'It won't hurt you to have a bit of peace and quiet, and when we get home, I want you to rest for a while. OK?'

Kirsten looked out of the side window.

'Are you listening to me?' Roma snapped.

'But I wanted to play in the garden.'

'You can. But I want you to rest for a little while first. Do you understand?'

'Yes,' the girl intoned, her voice one note from insolence.

Roma looked at her daughter once more and pressed down on the accelerator that little bit harder.

The quicker they got home the better.

# 3.32 P.M.

'Take a right here, will you, Rob?' said DI Fielding, massaging his neck. The beginnings of a headache were gnawing at the base of his skull.

'I thought we were going back,' Young noted, swinging the car around as he'd been instructed.

'*You* are. There's something I want to do.'

Young realised where they were.

Golden Hill Cemetery was a very large expanse of ground befitting an expanding town such as Kingsfield. It was ringed by a high privet hedge that made the neatly kept rows of graves invisible to passers-by. One side of it, the part occupied by older resting places, was somewhat darker due to the tall and very old oak trees that rose above it. In the summer they blocked out the sun and in the autumn they scattered their leaves across graves already long neglected.

Gravel paths cut across the necropolis in several places. They were barely wide enough for two people to walk along them side by side.

The new side of the cemetery was separated from the old by a wide tarmac drive that bisected Golden Hill and drew a line between the dead of one generation and those of another.

Few people who visited graves in the older part were younger than sixty. Many of those buried there, Fielding realised, had now been joined by the members of their families who for so long had visited.

In time he knew he too would join his own wife in the same plot.

Sometimes he felt the sooner that happened the better.

'Just drop me at the main gates,' he said to Young who brought the car to a halt and glanced across at his superior.

'Do you want me to wait for you?' asked the DS. 'Run you back?'

'No thanks, Rob. I'll walk. I'm not going back to the office. Being away from there for a couple of hours might help me think straight. It's only twenty minutes to my place from here. The fresh air might clear my head a bit.'

He hauled himself out of the car and turned to his colleague. 'See if anyone else has turned up anything. Any leads. Any clues. See who's talking and who isn't. Call me later.' He turned and walked off towards the main entrance of the cemetery.

Young watched him go then reversed out on to the main road, glanced once more in the direction of the cemetery then headed back towards the centre of Kingsfield.

Fielding walked briskly along the central tarmac drive of the cemetery until he came to one of the gravel paths that led off to the right. He took it, walked past the area of the graveyard reserved for those who'd been cremated, then made his way towards a row of new graves.

He passed the first two then stopped and looked at the inscription on the gleaming white marble headstone.

### KATHERINE DANIELLE FIELDING

### BELOVED WIFE

### THE BRIGHTEST FLAME BURNS QUICKEST

Fielding stood before the grave and smiled weakly. 'Hello, darling,' he said quietly.

The policeman knelt and removed the dead flowers from the metal pot on the plinth. He gave the headstone a quick wipe over with his handkerchief then moved back slightly, still crouching close to the stone.

A light breeze gusted across the cemetery, ruffling his hair. He took a deep breath, turning the stem of one dead flower between his thumb and forefinger.

'Where do I start?' he murmured, smiling to himself. 'You'd probably know, wouldn't you? You'd know what was bothering me even if I didn't tell you. You'd know what I was feeling even if I couldn't put it into words. How helpless I feel. How fucking angry I feel.' He sucked in a deep breath and held it for a moment before exhaling wearily. 'The bastard's killed another kid. A little boy this time. And I'm still no closer to catching him.'

Fielding got to his feet but didn't stray more than a foot from the headstone. 'It used to be easier than this, Kate; I'm sure it did. Or perhaps having you around just made it feel easier. Now everything I see I keep locked up in here.' He tapped his temple with one index finger. 'You always listened to me. No matter what I wanted to say. I used to think I was wrong for telling you some of the things I'd seen. I had no right to talk about the car-crash victims, the suicides, the dead babies. But you still listened. You helped. Just by being there you helped.' He smiled.

'Perhaps I really *can't* cope without you. Not now. Not with a case like this . . .' He allowed the sentence to trail off then looked down at the polished headstone, his eyes focusing on the name.

When he spoke again, his voice cracked slightly. 'I miss you,' he whispered. 'So much.'

A bird took flight from a tree near the grave and Fielding watched as it soared up into the heavens.

'I'll see you soon,' he murmured.

He finally turned from the grave, dug his hands into his pockets and headed back towards the tarmac drive that led to the main gates of the cemetery.

# 4.37 P.M.

'Shit.' Roma hissed in pain and jerked her hand away from the overflowing saucepan.

Some hot water had splashed over the rim and landed on her. She hastily pushed her hand beneath the tap and spun the cold conduit, wincing as she saw the flesh turning pink. She let the cold water cascade on it for a moment longer, her eyes straying to the leaded window before her.

From where she stood she could see out into the large garden. Kirsten, now dressed in leggings, trainers and T-shirt, was swinging happily back and forth on the large climbing frame set up at the bottom of the garden. When she tired of the swing she clambered up the steps of the slide and laughed happily as she descended.

Roma finally turned off the cold tap and dried her hands, still watching Kirsten who had now returned to the swing. Kirsten was moving backwards and forwards, her long hair swirling around her.

*Not a care in the world.*

Roma sighed and continued preparing their dinner. The flesh on the back of her hand stung but the discomfort would pass. She hadn't scalded it badly.

*No scars.*

She spooned uncooked rice into the boiling water and looked into the bubbling pan, momentarily hypnotised by it.

The spell was broken when she heard a shout from outside.

'Kirsten,' she murmured, looking out of the window once more.

*What if she'd fallen or . . .*

There was no damage done. The shout had been one of pure delight.

As Roma watched, her daughter swung herself into the air once more then, when the swing was at its highest, she leapt from the plastic seat and landed assuredly on the grass below. Again she called out joyfully as she rolled across the immaculately cut lawn.

Roma wondered for a second if she should stop the child. Prevent her from hurling herself about so recklessly. Dissuade her from . . .

*From what? Putting herself in even more danger?*

Roma moved to the back door, wondering whether to call Kirsten in now.

She hesitated, relieved to see that her daughter had returned to the more sedate diversions offered by the slide, then returned to the cooker. She remained ever watchful, however. Every minute or two her eyes strayed back to the window and the garden beyond.

*Back to Kirsten.*

The small sound system that stood on one of the worktops was on, music spilling from the speakers:

'. . . *So many years to go by, so many tears to fill your eyes . . .*'

She stirred the rice and looked out once more at Kirsten.

'*So many fears to lock behind the door . . .*'

Another five minutes, Roma decided, and she would call her daughter.

Inside she was safe.

# 6.02 P.M.

LONDON:

The man moved quickly and easily among the crowd. This part of Soho was always busy around this time. Choked with people making their way home. Clogged with tourists. He glanced at few faces as he made his way among them.

They were of no interest to him.

He stepped into the road, holding up a hand as if to halt an oncoming taxi. The driver braked hard and scowled at him from behind the wheel but he merely walked on, past the rubbish piled high at the end of Berwick Street. A legacy of the market that filled that thriving thoroughfare every day. The man could smell rotting vegetables and fruit.

An older man dressed in a filthy brown overcoat was rummaging through the piles. Finding nothing, he turned his attention to the bin nearby and dug out a half-eaten quarter-pounder. He brushed some pieces of polystyrene from it and took a bite before moving off.

On both sides of the street neon signs, barely visible during the day, were beginning to flicker into life over shops, restaurants and boutiques.

As the man walked purposefully along the road he looked at the diners in a seafood restaurant.

Next door two men in their early twenties were gazing wistfully into the window of an Ann Summers shop, edging gradually towards the entrance but not, it seemed, willing to take that final step inside.

He passed a vivid red sign proclaiming: FANTASY CABARET. A woman wearing far too much make-up and teetering on precipitous heels tossed her long black hair and smiled at him. She said something but he ignored her and continued on his way.

A flickering blue sign across a blacked-out window spelled out: PLEASURELAND. He pushed his way through the strips of plastic that constituted a doorway and stepped into the shop.

Music was blaring out.

'. . . Well, I've heard it a million times, now it's payback time.'

There were three customers inside. All browsing. One, a man in his late forties who had been engrossed in the gay section, hurriedly put back the magazine he'd been flicking through and walked out.

Behind the counter a man was leafing through a copy of that night's *Evening Standard*. He looked up as the newcomer entered, a wave of recognition crossing his face.

'How you doing?' Devon West asked, almost reverentially. 'You here to see Jake?'

The newcomer nodded and stepped back as another man approached the counter with three cellophane-wrapped magazines in his hand. He paid for them quickly, never making eye contact with West who slipped the magazines into a plain brown bag and pushed them back across the counter with the punter's change on top. He dropped some of it as he made to leave but made no effort to retrieve it.

Devon walked around the counter, glanced down at the dropped money and scooped up a couple of pound coins, which he pushed into the pocket of his jeans.

'Jake's upstairs in the office,' he said. 'You can go up if you want.'

The newcomer nodded, patted Devon on the shoulder and disappeared through a door behind the counter.

Beyond it was a narrow staircase. There were posters on the walls. Jenna Jameson, Pamela Anderson, Silvia Saint and Stephanie

Swift, all naked, smiled out at him as he climbed. So too, for reasons at which he could only guess, did a poster of West Ham Football Club. Fortunately the players were all fully clothed.

There were three doors at the top of the small landing and he knocked on the one in the middle.

A voice from inside told him to come in.

Jake Fox looked up from the paperwork on his desk and smiled at his visitor. 'Hello, mate,' he said, sitting back in his chair. 'How's it going?'

He gestured to the paperwork and wiped a hand across his forehead. 'Before we had a licence I didn't have any of this fucking shit to do,' Fox said, wearily. 'But now everything has to be in order, in case the law want to have a look. Every fucking video and DVD listed, catalogued and rated. Rated! Can you fucking believe that? They'll be checking the length of our fucking vibrators next. See if they're of a universal standard.' He smiled.

So did the newcomer.

'Good job not *everything* has to be catalogued, isn't it?' Fox grinned. He motioned for the visitor to sit down. 'What have you got for me this time?'

# 7.38 P.M.

With the evening had come a chill wind. Roma could hear it whipping past the window as she sat beside Kirsten's bed, the book from which she'd been reading held open in one hand.

'Right,' Roma said, with an air of finality. 'We'll read some more tomorrow.'

'Oh, Mum, just another page,' Kirsten protested.

'Tomorrow,' Roma told her. 'It's late. You'll be tired for school in the morning.'

Roma got to her feet and replaced the book on the shelf, glancing at the myriad stuffed toys arrayed around the room. There was a small doll's house in one corner, sandwiched between a wardrobe and a chest of drawers. Above it more shelves groaned under the weight of more books, toys and games.

'Are you sure you feel OK, now?' Roma asked, bending over Kirsten's bed and tucking in the edges of the Disney duvet.

'Fine,' Kirsten said.

Roma looked at her for a moment as if doubting the truth of her answer then she bent forward and kissed her daughter first on the forehead, then the tip of the nose and finally on the lips.

'Mum. Do you think Dad might read to me tomorrow night?'

Roma hesitated.

*If he's here.*

'Of course he will,' she said. 'Ask him when you see him tomorrow.'

'If he's not too busy.'

82

'What do you mean?' Roma said, sitting on the edge of the bed.

'Well, Dad's busy a lot, isn't he?'

'He thinks his company can't run without him.'

'I like it when he's here.'

'Me too.'

'I like it when he takes me to the pictures on a Saturday morning.'

Roma nodded.

*When he's got the time.*

'You ask him tomorrow and he'll read to you,' Roma said.

'I could leave him a note for when he gets in, couldn't I?'

'Good idea. Now, settle down, sweetie.'

Again she got to her feet and this time made it as far as the bedroom door.

'Mum,' the small voice called again.

'Yes,' Roma said, feigning impatience.

'What shall I dream about, Mum?' Kirsten asked sleepily.

'Dream about Dad.'

Kirsten giggled. 'I'll dream about us going on holiday,' she said.

'You do that. Goodnight, darling. See you in the morning.' She made for the stairs.

'Goodnight, Mum. I love you.'

'I love you too.'

'I'll write the note for Dad when I get up.'

'OK,' Roma called back, now halfway down the stairs. 'You settle down now.'

'I will, Mum. Goodnight.'

Roma wandered into the kitchen and made herself a cup of tea which she then carried into the sitting room. She seated herself at one end of the sofa and gazed blankly at the television. She reached for the remote and channel hopped for a moment or two. It was the usual stuff. Soaps, nature programmes, gardening and cookery.

She sighed and turned down the volume, her gaze still directed towards the TV but not at the screen. She was looking at the photo of Kirsten perched on top of it.

It had been taken six months ago. Roma regarded the impish grin, the sparkling eyes. The hair tied in two long pig-tails. A typical photo of a typical little schoolgirl.

Except, she thought, Kirsten was anything *but* typical.

As she studied the photo, she was surprised at how quickly her tears came. The sobs racked her entire body so hard she feared they would never stop.

# 8.02 P.M.

He ate in the kitchen most of the time now. There was a small dining table there, usually covered in a snow-white cloth.

Kate had always been very particular about things like that. Clean tablecloth and usually a vase of fresh flowers as a centrepiece.

He had dispensed with the flowers since her death. But he kept up the ritual of the clean cloth.

Fielding put his microwaved beef stroganoff and rice on to the place mat, poured himself a glass of red wine and sat down in the silent kitchen.

There was a small portable television and also a midi-hi-fi system in the room but he didn't feel like watching or listening while he ate. The silence, though not always welcome, might give him a chance to think.

His mobile phone lay on the table close by. He would finish his meal and then ring Young. Just to check. See if anyone had come up with any leads. Even a microscopic bit of fucking evidence that might point them down the right road.

Fielding ate slowly, chewing each mouthful like a gourmet relishing the labours of a three-star Michelin chef but he barely tasted the food. He hadn't felt hungry despite the fact that he'd eaten very little all day. He'd have been just as happy to sit and drink the bottle of wine and to hell with the food.

*Kate wouldn't have approved of that, would she?*

He took another mouthful.

During the two years since her death he'd found that loneliness had been a less frequent visitor than he'd expected it would be. There were times (and he sometimes felt ashamed of it) when he thought only briefly of his deceased wife. It was easier, of course, when he was working, and one of the reasons he hadn't taken a day off for the last eighteen months. But even at night, alone in the house where they had shared all their married life, he had only occasionally suffered the soul-crushing desolation that comes when someone so close has been taken.

It had been worse at the beginning. The first three months had been almost intolerable. But it wasn't the loneliness that he'd feared might destroy him. It was as if a part of his soul had been torn away and buried with her. Something inside *him* had died. Killed as effectively as Kate had been by the head-on impact with the drunken driver's car.

Fielding pushed more food into his mouth and realised that the feeling that had consumed him during those initial months had not been despair but rage.

Rage at the bastard who had caused her death. Rage that the thing he had loved most in life had been taken from him and, above all, rage that he could do nothing to ease the pain.

More than once he'd thought about killing the driver responsible. Perhaps that would be his only salvation. The only way to cure the ache. Take the life of the man who had robbed him of his only true love.

*Simple.*

Fielding took a sip from his wine glass, looked at the half-eaten meal and wondered if he could force down another few mouthfuls. He elected to refill his glass instead.

When he had told the parents of the three dead children that he knew what they were feeling, he was telling the truth. He *did* know. He was only too aware of how a hole opened up in the lives of those who had loved ones taken from them so suddenly and so needlessly. When he had looked into the eyes of those distraught parents, he had seen mirrored there the same despair he had been forced to confront after Kate died.

*Very philosophical.*

But true. He knew that feeling of ultimate pain. Of irreplaceable loss.

Perhaps by finding the killer of those children he could, by proxy, release some of the rage he would be forced to carry within himself for the rest of his life. For DI Fielding finding this man was not just a matter of justice but a matter of exorcism. The cleansing of some of his *own* demons.

He took another sip from his wine glass then reached for the phone.

## 8.11 P.M.

The smell of the Chinese takeaway was strong in the small living room. It seemed to cling to the wallpaper and carpets.

Jeff Reed sipped from his can of Carlsberg and looked across at Nikki who was picking disinterestedly at her chicken chow mein.

'Perhaps I should have cooked something instead of us spending money we haven't got,' she said wearily.

Reed pushed a forkful of rice and pork into his mouth and chewed thoughtfully. 'We'll have some money tomorrow night,' he said.

'But we *won't* will we, Jeff? Even if we *do* manage to get some cash from Macken, it still won't be *ours*, will it? It'll belong to Max Tate. Just like everything else in this fucking house.' She pushed her plate away and reached for her cigarettes.

'I told you, we'll get through it. You've got to believe me, Nik.'

'I don't know *what* to believe any more,' she told him, sucking hard on her cigarette.

'Let's see what happens tomorrow night with Macken,' he insisted.

Nikki nodded and ran a hand through her hair. 'God, I feel so helpless,' she murmured.

'At least we're *trying*.'

'And you think Max Tate is going to be impressed with that, Jeff? "Sorry we couldn't pay your money back, Max, but at least we tried."' She shook her head.

'There's no other way.'

'Yes there is and you know it.'

He understood. 'I've told you before. No fucking way. You stay away from him, Nik.'

'I'm the only thing we've got that he wants.'

Reed glared at her. 'You'd be willing to sleep with Max Tate,' he rasped.

'If that was what it took to get us more time then yes.'

The silence that descended was almost palpable. Reed could see the tears in her eyes.

The stillness was broken by the ringing of the phone. For what seemed like an eternity, neither of them moved then, finally, Nikki got to her feet and answered it.

'Hello,' she said.

Reed saw a slight smile crease her lips.

'Where are you?' she asked the caller. 'Did you get my messages?'

Reed got to his feet and took a step towards her. 'Is that your brother?' he asked. 'Let me talk to him.'

Nikki raised a hand to silence him.

He saw her nodding then she replaced the receiver.

'*Was* it him?' Reed persisted.

'He said he'll be here on Wednesday.'

# 10.46 P.M.

Roma yawned, stretched and finally got to her feet. Sleep was closing in on her as surely as the zip being drawn shut on a body bag.

She had already drifted off twice during the evening, bored by the lack of quality television, and unimpressed by the book she was trying to read.

She moved around the sitting room quickly, switching off lights, ensuring windows were secure. She repeated the procedure in the kitchen then made her way upstairs.

As she reached the landing, she paused. There was soft whimpering coming from Kirsten's room.

Roma hurried across to the open door and listened more intently.

'Mum.' The voice that filtered through the darkness sounded weak and fearful.

Roma strode in and found her daughter struggling free of the confines of her duvet. She sat up as Roma entered and there were tears glistening on her cheeks.

'What's wrong, sweetie?' Roma wanted to know, sitting on the edge of the bed.

'I had a bad dream,' Kirsten said, sniffing back more tears.

Roma embraced her, feeling the child warm against her.

'It's OK,' she whispered. 'It's all gone now.'

She held on to Kirsten for a moment longer then gently wiped the tears from the little girl's cheeks and handed her the beaker of juice that stood on her bedside table.

Kirsten took it and sipped at it while Roma tucked her in again.

'What was the dream about?' she asked.

'I can't really remember now.'

'See, I told you. Bad dreams never stay in your memory very long.'

'I can remember something about a man. A big man. But I couldn't see his face. He was chasing me through the trees and . . .' The words faded.

'You settle down now. I'm coming to bed too. I'll just be across the landing if you need me.'

Kirsten snuggled back beneath her duvet and smiled up at her mother.

'Is Dad back yet?' she asked.

'I told you, he won't be back until tomorrow,' Roma said, a little too sharply. 'You go back to sleep.'

She kissed Kirsten on the forehead, nose and lips then turned and headed for the bedroom door.

'Goodnight, Mum,' Kirsten called, her voice thick with sleep.

'Goodnight, sweetie. See you in the morning.'

'What time will it be morning?'

'Quarter past seven.'

'Is that soon?'

'Very soon. Good night.'

Roma made her way across the wide landing into her own room where she undressed quickly and slipped on a white T-shirt. She combed her hair rapidly, studying her reflection in the dressing-table mirror. What little make-up she wore she also removed then, after brushing her teeth, she slid beneath the covers with just the light of the bedside lamp illuminating the room with its dull yellow glow.

She glanced down at the phone on the bedside table, waited a moment then dialled the number she sought.

After a moment it was answered. 'Athenaeum Hotel, Lucy speaking, may I help you?' said the voice.

'Can you put me through to Mr David Todd's room, please,' Roma asked.

There was a hiss of static on the line then she heard more ringing.

And ringing.

No answer.

The robotic tones of the voicemail finally cut in and invited her to leave a message.

Roma hung up.

*Still enjoying your party, David?*

She lay down and was about to reach across to switch off the bedside lamp when her gaze settled upon the phone once again.

Roma sat up and reached for it. She swallowed hard then dialled another number.

This time there was no answerphone. She recognised the man's voice immediately.

# TUESDAY, MARCH 4TH

# 10.23 A.M.

There were eleven black-and-white ten-by-eights Blu-Tacked to the board at the front of the room. Faces of men ranging in age from twenty-five to sixty-three stared back at the uniformed and plain-clothes men and women gathered in the smoky room inside Kingsfield Police Station.

On the other side of the board the three smaller photos of Marie Walker, Callum Hughes and Jonathan Ridley also looked out at the law-enforcement officials.

If there was defiance on the faces of the men in the black-and-whites then there was pleading in the eyes of the three children.

That, at least, was what DI Fielding thought as he regarded the shots carefully.

'I told you all at the beginning of this investigation not to concentrate on a particular *type* of villain,' Fielding said, still looking at the photos. 'But I'm assuming all that lot have got form.' He nodded towards the monochrome shots.

Most he recognised. A number he himself had arrested over the years for crimes encompassing everything from indecent exposure, theft (usually of underwear from clothes lines) and possession of illegal pornography, to drug use, drug sale and, in at least three cases, assault.

There was a photo of Clive Fowler among them.

'Right,' said Fielding, turning to face his companions. 'What have we got – and somebody give me some *good* news, eh?'

'Most of them were willing to talk, guv,' said a plain-clothes man near the front. 'But what they gave us didn't amount to much. Not in relation to the deaths of these three youngsters anyway.'

'So what *did* they talk about?' Fielding wanted to know.

'Their "hobby",' said another plain-clothes man. 'That's what they call the kids. They can talk openly about them then, without attracting too much attention.'

'Their *hobby*,' Fielding muttered. 'If they call them that it depersonalises them. Stops them seeing the kids as real people.' He shook his head. 'Bastards.'

'The suspects up there have all been convicted of crimes concerning kids, sir,' said a WPC. 'Everything from making indecent images of children to distribution and indecent assault.'

'Have any done time?' Fielding enquired.

'Three of them,' the WPC told him. 'None longer than three years though.'

'All of them have been found in possession of indecent material relating to kids,' another officer added. 'Some had drawings done by kids.'

'What kind of drawings?'

The officer consulted his notebook. 'One of them had twenty-seven pictures drawn by kids aged from five to eight. They were titled things like "Blond fuckers", "Fingering", "First sex drawing", that kind of thing.'

'So the kids did the drawings on the say so of the paedophile?' Fielding asked.

The officer nodded.

'Any links as to where the others got their material?' Fielding asked. 'I know these fuckers work in rings but on the whole they're solitary.'

'Nearly all of them admitted to using the Internet to download stuff,' said a uniformed man. 'Everything from stills to videos.'

'We confiscated computers from all of them,' said a plain-clothes man. 'The stuff's being downloaded and checked now.'

'How long's that going to take?' Fielding asked.

'It could take days,' the officer told him. 'It all depends on how much stuff they've got on disk.'

'Right, well when it's done, I want to see everything. And I mean *everything*. I want every single picture looked at and compared.'

There were audible sighs around the room.

'Yeah, I know it's going to be a big job,' Fielding continued. 'No one said it's going to be easy but at least when the fucking papers ask us if we've got any leads we'll be able to tell them that we have. What we won't tell them is that we've got about twenty thousand leads.'

There was some muted laughter around the room.

'Some of the bastards use Internet chat rooms to attract kids too,' Young interjected.

'See if any of the dead kids had been into computer chat rooms,' said the DI. 'Check with their parents. I know they were young and it's a long shot but do it anyway. Whoever killed them might have got to them that way initially. That might be why there was no struggle when he took them. They might have known their killer.'

Fielding looked around at the sea of faces once more then shrugged. 'Let's get on with it. I want this fucker caught before he chalks up number four.'

The officers began to file out of the room.

DS Young remained with Fielding, studying the black-and-white photos pinned to the action board. 'I was looking through some of their files last night,' he said. 'It doesn't make sense does it?'

'What?'

'How a grown man can get any pleasure from looking at sexual pictures of little kids. Or from touching them.'

'How long have you been a copper, Rob? Twelve years? Since when did *anything* in this fucking game make sense?'

'They're sick.'

'They're also clever. As much as I despise them, they aren't usually stupid. They're well organised and they know their business. That's the problem. If they were all stupid they'd be easier to catch.'

He sat on the edge of the table and looked at the array of ten-by-eights. 'Bastards,' he muttered through clenched teeth.

# 10.27 A.M.

Roma felt her heart gradually slowing down.

It had been thudding madly only minutes earlier as she and Michael Harper had both reached their peaks of pleasure. Now, like Roma, he lay on his back on the bed inside his flat getting his breath back.

She stretched, feeling the liquid warmth between her thighs. Some of his oily fluid was already seeping from between the swollen lips of her slippery cleft. Roma let out a contented sigh and rolled over to face her lover.

Harper smiled up at her, watching as she traced patterns on his chest with her carefully manicured nails. He allowed one hand to brush against her thigh, the probing digits gliding over the smooth skin until they came to rest against her tightly curled pubic hair. He felt the moisture on the tip of his index finger.

Roma leaned forward and kissed him. For long, pleasurable minutes, they remained locked together, and Harper groaned as he felt her hand envelope his penis. She squeezed gently, trying to coax the stiffness back into it. She finally released him and moved back slightly, that smile still on her face.

'Not yet,' he said wearily, raising his eyebrows.

She returned to running her nails over his chest.

'Are you lecturing today?' Harper asked.

She shook her head. 'No. You're spared,' she told him.

Harper smiled. 'So, what are you doing for the rest of the day?' he wanted to know.

'Does it matter?'

'I'm curious.'

'Don't be. What I do when I'm not with you isn't important.'

'Don't you ever wonder what I'm doing when we're not together?'

'I wonder if you're still expanding your business empire here. Wondering where you get the money to buy these properties that you rent out to other poor, downtrodden students.'

'That would be telling,' Harper said smiling.

'Other than that, no, I don't think about you when we're not together,' she said flatly, and he saw a coldness in her eyes he'd not noticed before. 'Because it's none of my business. We fuck, Mike. That's all we do. When the sweat dries, there's nothing else between us.'

Harper looked at her warily.

Roma saw his expression and smiled thinly. 'Listen, when you have an affair, you have to play by the rules,' she told him.

'Whose rules? Yours?'

'*The* rules,' she told him. 'Keep your distance emotionally. Never let your feelings get out of control. Never discuss your other life.'

'You know them well then. How many other times have you done this kind of thing?'

'It's not important.'

'*I* might think it is, Roma. You see, no one told *me* the fucking rules.' His tone had taken on a hard edge.

'What did you want from this?' she asked. 'From you and me. What did you expect when it began? That I was going to leave my husband and child for you?'

'No, of course not. I never wanted that.'

'What *did* you want? A quick fuck? That's what you get, isn't it? That's what we both get. We both get what we want from this arrangement.'

'Arrangement? Can't you even dignify it by calling it a relationship? You make it sound like some kind of fucking business deal.'

She swung herself up and on to the edge of the bed. 'I'd better go,' she said.

'Where? Back to your husband and kid? How can you look them in the eye when you've been doing this with me?'

She didn't turn to face him. 'I'm not hurting them, Mike,' Roma said quietly. 'I never would. And I don't need a lesson in morality from you.'

'Would you hurt *me*, Roma?'

'Not intentionally. And if you play by the rules you won't get hurt.'

'Fuck your rules, Roma,' he hissed. 'This is all just one big laugh to you, isn't it?'

'And what is it to you, Mike?' she said, finally turning to face him. 'A big love affair?'

'No. I just don't want to feel like another accessory in your life. Like your Louis Vuitton handbag or your Gucci shoes. I don't want to be just one more thing that your husband's money can buy.'

She shook her head and got to her feet. Harper watched her as she padded across the bedroom and began to dress.

'So, is this it? Is this how it ends?' he wanted to know.

'Only if you want it to. I never said anything about ending it, Mike.'

She pulled on her jeans and began tucking her black T-shirt into them.

Harper clambered out of bed and walked across to her, still naked.

Roma stepped into her shoes then looked at him.

'I don't want it to end,' he said. 'And by the way, when we're not together, I sometimes go to London. Visit friends. Surf the net . . .' He smiled.

Roma returned the gesture but it never touched her eyes.

He took her in his arms and embraced her. A moment later she held him too. But not quite as tightly.

# 10.43 A.M.

He counted the money again. Just short of three grand.

The notes were a combination of crisp new fifties and filthy, wrinkled twenties but that didn't matter. It wasn't what the money looked like, it was what it bought.

He pushed the wedge back into the thick manilla envelope, sealed it and pushed it into his inside pocket. If anyone else in the café in Eversholt Street had seen him count it then they certainly hadn't made it obvious.

It was quiet in the eatery. A couple of cab drivers in the back room were talking noisily about fares from Heathrow while the small portable TV lodged high up in one corner of the room spewed out the daily diet of morning programmes.

The man glanced up at it and watched as an expert (good looking tart with long blond hair and a tight-fitting white jumper and black jeans) gave tips on how to complete the best pedicure.

The man watched as she crouched over the shapely feet of the patient model while the two presenters (a Scottish geezer and some fat bird) hung around her like flies around shit.

He sipped his tea and glanced across at the two women serving behind the counter.

Both in their late twenties, they were babbling away in some foreign language (it was a harsh accent, Czech or something like that, he guessed) until one wandered over to the door and lit up a cigarette. She stood in the doorway puffing on the B&H,

occasionally smiling at passers-by as if to tempt them inside.

The man ordered another tea and some more toast from the girl behind the counter, pushing his plate away from him. She dutifully collected it and scuttled off to get his order.

He took a drag on his cigarette and slid a hand inside his jacket, just brushing the envelope with the tips of his fingers. It was as if he were ensuring that it had not somehow magically moved. He'd taken fifty quid from the total, which he'd use to pay for his breakfast and whatever else he needed during the remainder of the day.

He spread the newspaper out before him on the formica-topped table and flicked through it.

Increases in street crime. Some politician caught up in a sleaze scandal. Local elections. An earthquake in Turkey. The rest of it was bullshit about fucking celebrities.

*It always was.*

He turned the pages slowly, his gaze finally coming to rest on a photo halfway down page nine.

He looked at the caption: DAVID TODD, OWNER OF NEMESIS RECORDS.

There was another picture of some long-haired twats standing around him. Apparently Todd had just signed some American band called Stonethrower to his label. Two more pictures on the other side of the column were captioned ROMA TODD and KIRSTEN TODD.

*Good looking woman. Nice kid.*

He saw the words *multi-millionaire* then flipped the paper over to the back page to look at the sport.

His reading was interrupted by the arrival of his tea and toast. He thanked the girl with a smile, ate his fill then paid. He left a small tip on the table.

Before he squeezed past the girl smoking the cigarette in the doorway, he tapped the envelope inside his jacket once again.

He was in no hurry. He had all day. His train didn't leave until eleven that night.

# 11.01 A.M.

KINGSFIELD:

The bike chain felt heavy in his hand.

Jeff Reed closed one gloved fist tightly around it and swung the lethal implement hard. It slammed into the trunk of the tree, gouging away small pieces of bark. Reed drew several inches of the metal back into his hand, shortening the reach of the weapon. Then he swung again.

He smiled as the chain thudded into the trunk again. It was much more effective used short like that. He held it for a moment longer then dropped it back into the plastic bag and pushed the whole package into his jacket pocket. Then he lit a cigarette and wandered across the disused playground to the rusty slide.

Reed sat on the bottom of the ramp and looked around, the chilly wind whipping at him. He pulled up the collar of his jacket and sat immobile, puffing away on his cigarette.

The playground, surrounded by high hedges, was approachable by two paths. One to his left, the other ahead of him. Both paths ran between and around terraces of the same kind of fifties' style house in which he and Nikki lived. He could see their roofs from where he sat. There were also allotments nearby. He'd seen a couple of old men working on them when he'd arrived.

Not that he need concern himself about being disturbed. The kids that the playground had been built for were in school (*some* of them at least) and others who frequented it didn't usually show up until after dark. From where he sat, Reed could see a hypodermic needle and a bloodstained handkerchief lying beneath a bush. A used condom had been hung on the rusted climbing frame like bizarre bunting.

No one used this area for its original purpose.

All that remained of what had once been swings was the large rusted frame. All the paint had peeled off like leprous skin. Pieces of chain hung from the crossbar and the filthy remains of a rotted, wooden seat dangled uselessly from one.

There was a roundabout near him. It too was broken. Graffiti had been sprayed on it and part of it was blackened like the remains of one of the benches at the far end of the playground.

*Someone had been playing with matches.*

There were coiled dog turds all over the grass and the tarmac. Some fresh, some decayed. Reed thought how appropriate that was. The entire playground had become little more than a toilet. It mirrored the degeneration of the estate that it had been built upon. Once new and fresh. Now desolate and wasted.

Reed shook his head, hawked and spat. He got to his feet and crossed to the remains of the roundabout. He pulled off a piece of rusted metal about twelve inches long and two inches thick. It felt comfortingly heavy. He drew his arm back and brought the makeshift cosh down with thunderous power on to the rotting wood of the roundabout.

It cracked in several places. Reed smiled and struck it again, striking until he'd loosened a sliver of wood. He proceeded to smash it to splinters then stepped back, his breath coming in gasps, his eyes wide.

He wrapped the piece of metal in another plastic bag, but he carried that by his side as he turned and walked back down one of the paths that led to the street beyond.

She stood naked before the wardrobe gazing at the clothes hanging within. Jackets, blouses, jeans, skirts. Some of them crammed on to one hanger. T-shirts were folded and piled on the shelves of the large piece of furniture. Other items of clothing were stuffed into drawers. At the bottom were shoes, boots and trainers. Some still in boxes.

Nikki Reed reached into one of the drawers and pulled out a black thong. She slipped it on, sliding it up her slim thighs, adjusting the thin material between her shapely buttocks. Then she lifted a bra from the same drawer, gazed at it for a moment and discarded it.

She took a white blouse from its hanger and slipped it on. The cool silk made her nipples stiffen and she turned to look at herself in the mirror, noticing that the hardened buds were straining against the flimsy material.

In the background, the music from the ghetto blaster filled the room.

*'Cherry stem in her mouth she could tie in a knot . . .'*

Nikki buttoned the blouse quickly then selected a tight, black, leather skirt and slipped that on too. The hem finished three inches above her knees, showing her shapely legs off to perfection.

*'Favourite trick she does, one of ten that she's got . . .'*

Again she examined her reflection, unbuttoning the blouse slightly so that each time she moved she revealed a tantalising glimpse of her breasts.

*'Makin' friends, setting trends hardly having to try . . .'*

She glanced at the array of shoes and finally chose a pair of high-heeled black sandals into which she slid her feet before carefully fastening the straps around her ankles. She flexed her toes then moved back to the dressing-table mirror and sat down.

*'All her looks, by the book, best that money can buy . . .'*

She applied eyeliner, mascara then lipstick. All with practised care. Her blond hair, freshly washed an hour earlier, was already brushed and styled but she ran her hands through it lightly once more and studied with pride the face that stared back at her.

Satisfied with her make-up, she returned to the wardrobe and slipped on a short, black, leather jacket then, yet again, she turned to the full-length mirror and ran appraising eyes over herself from her perfectly coiffured hair down to her immaculatly pedicured toes.

*'Look what your money bought . . .'*

The music roared around her.

'Do you want to touch me?' she whispered.

*'It's all that she's got . . .'*

'You want to fuck me, don't you?' Nikki smiled, her lips glistening. 'If you want to, you can.'

For what seemed like an eternity, she stood staring at herself then, as if some kind of spell had been broken, she crossed to the ghetto blaster and switched it off.

Silence descended.

Nikki slipped off the jacket then sat down before the dressing-table mirror again.

She began to remove her make-up, scrubbing it away as if it were some immovable stain.

Long before she began to scour away the mascara, tears had begun to course down her cheeks.

# 11.17 A.M.

'What time did you get back?' Roma stood in the doorway of the sitting room looking across at her husband.

David Todd was seated in one of the large armchairs looking at a selection of newspapers spread out on the coffee table before him. Beside him was a steaming mug of tea from which he sipped as he scanned the mass of material.

'I wasn't expecting you until tonight,' Roma continued, placing her car keys in the small china dish on top of the heavily polished antique sideboard nearby.

'I got back about an hour ago. I thought I'd surprise you,' Todd said, getting to his feet. He crossed to Roma and took her in his arms.

She kissed him briefly and ran a hand through her hair.

*Could he smell it on her? The scent of another man?*

Roma sat down opposite him, her cheeks slightly flushed.

'I thought you'd have been here when I got home,' Todd said, returning his attention to the papers.

'I had to go into Kingsfield to get a few things after I dropped Kirsten off,' she lied. 'The party obviously went all right; I saw photos in the papers. What happened?'

'The usual stuff. The band got drunk. Two of them had to be carried into the limo that took them back to their hotel. Another one of them tried to pull Dawn. You know, my assistant.'

'Yeah, I know Dawn.'

Todd caught the slight edge in her voice and looked up briefly.

'What time did you get back to the hotel last night?' Roma persisted.

'About two. I didn't think there was any point ringing you at that time.'

'No. No point.'

'I just wanted to get home. It was all a bit hectic last night. Perhaps I'm getting too old for all this.'

'I'm surprised you left the office unattended for the day.'

'They can manage without me once in a while.'

'So, we get the pleasure of your company instead.'

'How's Kirsten?' he said, without looking up.

'That used to be the *first* thing you asked.'

Todd exhaled wearily. 'Oh, come on, Roma, give me a break,' he sighed.

'I know. You're tired.'

They regarded each other venomously for a moment then Todd spoke again. 'So, how is she?' he wanted to know.

Roma swallowed hard. 'She's getting worse,' she told him quietly.

'Did the doctors tell you that?'

'They don't have to, David.'

'She's due more treatment at the end of the week. She—'

'I don't think it can wait until the end of the week.'

'Then book her into the clinic for tomorrow. If she needs help, Roma, then she's got to have it.'

'You think I don't know that? David, it doesn't matter how much help she gets. How much medication they give her. Not in the end it doesn't.'

A heavy silence descended.

Roma said, 'She's going to die, David. *You* know that. *I* know it, and so do the doctors.' She felt tears welling up and she tried to sniff them back but it was useless. 'Our daughter is going to die and all the money in the world can't help her.'

Todd got to his feet and crossed to Roma, snaking his arm around her shoulders. He pulled her close and she responded, her body shaking.

'We'll take her to the clinic tomorrow,' he said. 'The school know the situation, don't they? They know . . .'

109

'About her condition?' Roma said, her voice cracking. She wiped her face with her hands and sniffed. 'They know as much as they need to know.'

'Has Kirsten said that she feels worse?'

Roma shook her head.

'It might not be as bad as you think, Roma.'

She got to her feet. 'I want to show you something, David,' she said. She turned and walked out of the room.

Todd followed her, through the spacious hallway and up the stairs to the first floor. Across the landing to the white door that bore the name plaque: KIRSTEN.

Roma opened the door and stepped across the threshold. She crossed to a pile of stuffed toys at the bottom of the bed and picked up a large cuddly polar bear. She handed it to Todd who swallowed hard.

'She was playing with that last night,' Roma said.

Todd turned the bear over in his hands. There were several dark scorch marks on the toy.

They were in the shape of a child's hand.

For interminable moments, as if hypnotised by the sight of the singed toy, Todd simply stared at the burn marks.

He finally dropped the stuffed bear on to Kirsten's bed, wiping his hands on his trousers as if he'd just touched something vile or diseased.

'Is there anything else?' he asked quietly, looking around the room.

'No,' Roma told him. 'Just that. Isn't it enough?'

'Call the clinic now. Tell them.'

'Tell them what, David? That Kirsten's condition is getting worse. I think they already know that.'

'Is she taking her medication? You know what kids are like, they sometimes forget.'

'I always check. If you were here in the mornings you'd know that.'

Todd regarded his wife irritably for a moment then turned and walked out of the room. He crossed the landing to their bedroom and began unpacking his overnight bag, laying his clothes on the bed before hanging them up in one of the large wardrobes that lined the room.

Roma sat on the end of the bed, one leg drawn up beneath her.

'Does Kirsten know her condition's deteriorating?' Todd wanted to know.

'She says she feels fine. Do you want me to spell it out for her? Tell her how ill she really is?'

Todd shot Roma an almost frightened look. 'When it was

111

first diagnosed, the doctors said they had no idea how long she had, didn't they?'

Roma nodded. 'Anywhere between five and ten years they told us,' she murmured. 'At least that's what they thought. No one knows enough about her condition, David. There aren't any experts. *We* know as much as they do.'

Todd exhaled deeply, almost painfully. 'So, we just sit around and wait for her to die,' he said flatly, and the words came out as a statement rather than a question.

'When she's had the treatment again, she'll be . . .' Roma let the words trail off.

'She'll be OK for another four weeks, Roma, and that's it. She's living from month to month.'

'We *all* are.'

'But we're not the ones who are going to die, are we?'

'As the condition becomes more advanced, she'll need increased medication. Treatment more often,' Roma said.

'She shouldn't be at school with other kids. She might be a danger to them.'

'She's not a monster, David. What she's got isn't contagious. She's not Kingsfield's answer to Typhoid Mary. She's a little girl who's ill.'

'With a condition that makes her dangerous.'

'Jesus Christ,' Roma barked. 'I sometimes think you're more concerned about the people she comes into contact with than you are about *her*. What's wrong, David? Frightened what it would do to your reputation, your standing in the community, if the truth ever came out?'

'Don't be so fucking stupid. My only concern is for Kirsten.'

'Is it?'

The question hung in the air.

112

# 1.09 P.M.

Jeff Reed fed more coins into the fruit machine and hit the Start button, watching as the reels spun round.

Nothing.

He muttered something under his breath and tried again, glancing around the inside of the Oak Apple as he waited for the reels to stop turning.

As ever, the pub was busy and noisy, the volume of the jukebox a contributory factor to the sound within the building. Reed could see a group of smartly dressed men and women sitting close to it. It was they who were pushing coins into it, causing the pub to fill with the constant stream of manufactured pop shite that always seemed to dominate the charts. Reed watched them for a while.

All were in their late twenties (not unlike himself) all dressed immaculately. Talking and laughing loudly over their drinks and pub grub.

The Oak Apple attracted many customers like them at lunchtimes. There was a business estate less than five minutes' drive away and Reed had often noticed the proliferation of secretaries and other office workers who chose to spend their break in these surroundings. There were as many of them as there were locals.

At lunchtimes anyway. At night it was a different matter. Then the Oak Apple became the sole domain of those who lived on the Walton Grange Estate. Few from outside its confines had the inclination to venture on to it during the hours of darkness.

'Any luck?'

The voice startled Reed and he looked round to see the familiar figure of Julie White standing near him. She was collecting empty glasses. Her dishwater-blond hair was pulled back in a loose ponytail. She smiled warmly at him and continued jamming glasses on to the small tray she carried.

Reed looked blankly at the barmaid for a moment.

'I said, "any luck?"' she repeated, nodding towards the fruit machine.

'You're joking. My luck stinks,' Reed grunted. 'If Pamela Anderson had had triplets, I'd have been the one on the bottle.'

Julie grinned and continued with her duties, mopping the table nearest to him with a damp cloth.

'How's Nikki?' she wanted to know. 'I haven't seen her for a couple of weeks. She always used to come to the bingo on a Tuesday night, didn't she? We used to have a laugh, me and her.'

'Money's a bit tight at the moment.'

*That's a fucking understatement.*

'You should tell her to get her job back here. Maurice is always looking for staff,' Julie said.

Reed nodded, his gaze still roving around the pub. 'I'll tell her,' he said, attempting a smile.

Julie bustled off and Reed watched her as she weaved through the lunchtime drinkers, her shapely buttocks accentuated by the tight black trousers she wore.

'Out of *your* league.'

For the second time, a voice close by made him turn.

Tony Casey was grinning. He nodded towards Julie. 'Anyway, why are you staring at *her* when you've got such a gorgeous wife waiting at home for you?' Casey chided.

Reed felt his heart beat faster. 'Are you looking for me?' he said.

'Not until the end of the week. I just came in for a drink. Got a problem with that?'

Reed shook his head.

'Good,' said Casey, his smile fading. 'What the fuck are *you* doing in here anyway? If you haven't got the money to pay Max what you owe him, you shouldn't be in here boozing, should you?'

Reed reached for his pint glass, his eyes never leaving those of Casey. As he touched the rim of the glass he felt Casey's hand close over his own.

'You should be saving every fucking penny you've got,' Casey rasped, leaning closer to Reed, the pressure on his hand growing.

'We'll have the money,' Reed said.

'You'd better.'

Reed heard a faint crack and he knew that the glass had cracked.

Another second and it would shatter. Pieces of beer-soaked glass would gouge into his fingers and palm.

He tried to pull his hand away but Casey had no intention of releasing his grip.

There was another glass on the next table. Reed looked at it and thought that if he could grab it, jam it into Casey's face and . . .

*And what?*

'Better make that your last one,' Casey told him, finally easing his grip on Reed's hand.

Reed swallowed hard and looked down at the glass. There was, indeed, a hairline crack from the rim to the halfway mark.

'See you on Saturday.' Casey grinned then made his way to the bar.

'Cunt,' Reed whispered under his breath. He looked down at the cracked glass and the two inches of beer left at the bottom of it.

He held up his hand, ensuring there was no damage. It was shaking. With one final look across at Casey, he left.

'You're not going to believe it.' DS Young spoke the words as he strode along the corridor with his superior.

'Try me,' Fielding murmured.

'Work started on the first couple of confiscated computers we took from suspects.'

'And?'

'In just one of them we found two thousand six hundred images of kids.'

'Jesus Christ.'

'It gets better. The second one contained over nine thousand images. If the rest of them are like that, it's going to take for ever to go through all that shit.'

Fielding swallowed hard. 'What else?' he wanted to know.

'There're photos, video downloads, web-cams and fuck knows what else. The man hours involved to sift through it—'

Fielding cut him short. 'Is this geezer we're going to see now one of the ones who's been checked out?'

'His was the one with nine thousand on. That's why he was brought in straightaway. He's got previous too. He did eighteen months for making indecent images of children and distribution of those images. His name's George Cairns. He was married but he lives alone now.' Young handed his companion a file. Inside were photos of Jonathan Ridley and Marie Walker downloaded from Cairns's computer. Both had been stripped and posed for the camera.

Outside the interview rooms they paused, faced by two thick wooden doors.

116

'I'll go in on my own,' Fielding said.

Young held his superior's gaze for a moment then looked away.

'Give me fifteen minutes,' the DI said.

Young hesitated again then stepped back, watching as Fielding disappeared through the door of the interview room, closing it behind him.

George Cairns was sitting at the single wooden table inside the room with a styrofoam cup in front of him. He was a wiry man. Balding. He had large puffy bags beneath both eyes. He was wearing a dark-brown overcoat over the top of a crew-neck sweater and black trousers. Fielding checked his file and saw that the man was fifty-four.

Cairns looked up as Fielding entered the room, and held his cup in both hands as if to protect it.

'Good afternoon, Mr Cairns,' said Fielding, sitting down opposite him.

The older man didn't speak. He merely ran appraising eyes over the newcomer.

'I'm Detective Inspector Fielding. I'm in charge of this investigation. I'd like to ask you some questions.'

'I'm not answering any questions until my solicitor gets here,' said Cairns, the faintest trace of a Scots accent in his voice.

*Well spoken. Confident.*

'That's your prerogative, Mr Cairns,' Fielding told him. 'But if you co-operate, you'll be out of here quicker.'

'I haven't done anything wrong.'

'I'm afraid you have, Mr Cairns. Downloading child pornography from the Internet is against the law.' He pulled the two photos from the file and laid them on the table before Cairns. 'Do you know the names of either of these children?' he wanted to know.

Cairns didn't answer.

'They both lived in Kingsfield,' Fielding persisted. 'I wondered if you'd ever seen either of them around. You've lived here all your life, haven't you?'

117

'There are lots of children in Kingsfield. Why should I remember *them*?'

'The reason I ask is that both of them are dead. Both murdered. You've probably read about it in the papers.'

'So, because of my past I'm a suspect, is that what you're trying to tell me?'

'You've served a prison sentence for making and distributing indecent images of children. The computer we confiscated from your home has over nine thousand images of children stored on it. Perhaps you can understand why we were anxious to speak to you about this case.'

Cairns sat back in his chair and looked down at his fingers, splayed open on the table.

'I said I didn't want to answer any questions until I had a solicitor present,' he said quietly.

'Fair enough,' Fielding told him. 'I can call the duty brief now if you like.'

Cairns looked at the policeman then dropped his gaze hurriedly. Fielding fished inside his jacket pocket and took out a packet of cigarettes. He took one himself then pushed them towards Cairns.

The older man hesitated then took one. Fielding lit it for him.

'I never touched those kids,' Cairns said, his hand shaking.

*A little bit of panic there?*

'Forensics will tell us that for sure, Mr Cairns.'

'I would never kill a child.'

'What *would* you do to them? How far *would* you go?'

'I wouldn't kill one. I know some would.'

'Like who? Other paedophiles you know? You do know others, don't you, Mr Cairns?'

'I've met other men with similar interests to my own.'

'With interests in young children?'

Cairns nodded.

'And you don't think any of them would be capable of

118

murdering a child?' the DI muttered.

'You tar us all with the same brush, don't you?' Cairns replied, his eyes suddenly meeting those of his interrogator. 'You hate us for what we are. But you never try to understand us.'

'Tell me what there is to understand. *Make* me understand how a grown man could get any sexual excitement from looking at pictures of naked kids, or touching them.'

'It isn't just sex. Some of the people I know have genuine feelings for the children.'

'So why do they molest them?' Fielding wanted to know.

Cairns took to studying his fingers once again. 'The children are willing,' he said.

'You brainwash them,' Fielding snapped. 'Buy them things. Ingratiate yourselves with their families. Make them think you care about them.'

Fielding looked unblinkingly at Cairns and took a slow drag on his cigarette. 'You were married, weren't you?' he said.

Cairns nodded.

'Two kids of your own,' Fielding continued. 'Did you ever touch *them*?'

Cairns shot him a furious glance and jumped to his feet. 'How dare you?' he snarled.

'You wouldn't be the first father to abuse his kids. We've seen a series of web-cam downloads of fathers raping their own children. Girls *and* boys. There's nothing new there. Now, sit down.'

The older man hesitated. 'I never touched my own children,' he breathed.

'Sit *down*,' the DI said more forcefully.

Cairns finally complied.

'I wondered if that was why your wife walked out on you,' Fielding persisted. 'Did she find out about your little hobby?'

'She didn't understand.'

'Like I said, it *does* take some understanding. What was wrong with your wife? Grown women too much for you? Something the matter with straight porn? Nothing wrong with looking at birds with their legs spread, you know. We've all done it. It's nothing to be ashamed of. *I* did it when I was with *my* wife.'

'And where did *she* go? Did she walk out on you because she couldn't stand *your* little hobby? Couldn't stand you looking at other women? Is that why she left you?'

Fielding shot out both hands and caught Cairns by the lapels. He pulled the older man forward and slammed his head down hard on the table. When he shoved him away he could see that Cairns's nose was broken. There was blood gushing down his face.

'My wife didn't leave me, you fucking nonce,' snarled Fielding. 'She was *taken* from me.' His breath was coming in gasps now. He got to his feet and walked around the table.

Cairns recoiled in his seat, trying to wipe the blood from his shattered nose. 'Don't hit me again,' he whimpered.

'Shut up. You should be thankful I haven't taken your fucking head off by now. I want the names of the sites you get these pictures from. The passwords to get into them. Everything you know. Got it?'

'You can't do this,' Cairns protested, blood still pumping from his nose. It was all over his hands and the front of his sweater. Some had splashed on to the table.

Fielding leaned closer to him so that his face was no more than inches from the older man's.

'I can do just what I fucking want to you, you piece of shit.' Fielding pushed a piece of paper and a pen towards him. 'Names of the sites and the passwords to get in. Write them down now or I'll break your fucking hands as well as your nose.'

Cairns gaped at the contorted face of the furious policeman for a second longer then reached for the biro and began to write.

# 5.41 P.M.

One wall of the dining room was dominated by a massive book-case that boasted everything from tomes about the Napoleonic Wars to film books and volumes concerning philosophy and poetry.

The opposite wall was festooned with dozens of gold, silver and platinum discs. Most signed by the artists who had made them.

Kirsten Todd toyed disinterestedly with her food and gazed between the two walls, occasionally shifting on her chair. Sometimes her eyes would fall upon one of her parents, both eating in silence, seated at either end of the table.

She began building a wall around her peas with some mashed potato.

'If you're not going to eat it then just leave it, Kirsten.'

The voice made her look up. She heard the edge in her father's tone and stopped building the potato wall.

'Have you had enough?' Roma asked her.

Kirsten shrugged and prodded the potato once again.

'You can eat some more,' Todd insisted.

Roma shot him an irritable glance then reached for her wine glass and took a sip.

Another heavy silence descended.

'So, did you have a good day, Kirsten?' Todd enquired.

'You already asked me that, Dad.'

'Well, I'm asking again.'

'Yeah, it was OK.'

'Was everyone there?' Todd persisted.

121

'Megan was off. So was Tom. I think they must be on holiday. Or ill or something.'

Todd looked at Roma then at his daughter again. 'Your mum said *you* didn't feel too good at school yesterday,' he said.

'I was all right. I just fainted.' She chuckled.

Todd nodded. 'But you feel better now?' he wanted to know.

She didn't answer. She was gazing at one of the gold discs on the wall near her.

'Kirsten,' Todd said loudly. 'Are you listening to me? Are you sure you feel all right now?'

'Fine,' she told him.

Again Roma gave her husband an angry look.

'Dad, are you putting me to bed tonight?' Kirsten asked hopefully.

'We'll see,' said Todd.

'Oh, Dad,' Kirsten whined. 'I like it when you read me stories.'

'I said, we'll see,' snapped Todd, a little too forcefully. He took a final mouthful of food, dropped his knife and fork on to the plate then got to his feet. He gathered up the plates and carried them through to the kitchen.

Roma waited a moment then got up and followed him.

Todd was scraping uneaten food into the waste bin.

'Take it easy, David,' Roma said.

'I don't know what you're talking about,' he said.

'You're snapping at Kirsten and there's no need to.'

He stepped past Roma and placed the plates and cutlery in the dishwasher.

'You're acting as if you're frightened of her,' Roma persisted.

'Don't be so bloody stupid,' Todd hissed.

'Mum.'

They both turned to see Kirsten standing in the kitchen doorway.

'Can I go and play?' she asked, her face pale.

Roma forced a smile and nodded. 'If you've finished,' she said, trying to inject a lightness into her tone.

Kirsten turned and headed for her playroom. They both heard the door close behind her.

# 6.02 P.M.

Fielding was still staring at his computer screen when he heard the knock on his office door.

'Come in,' he called, glancing up to see that DS Young had entered.

The DS closed the door behind him and waited on the opposite side of the desk.

'Well, sit down, Rob, you make the place look untidy,' smiled Fielding. 'I thought you would have gone home by now. You should be with Jenny as much as you can.'

Young sighed. 'What happened with Cairns this afternoon, guv?' he asked.

'You *know* what happened.'

'He's threatening to press charges.'

'Let him. He'll never make anything stick.'

'Guv, he came out of that interview room with a broken nose.'

'Shit happens,' said Fielding, shrugging.

'If he gets a brief on it, you could be in bother. Serious bother.'

'That's *my* problem, not yours, Rob. Anyway, I've got more important things to worry about at the moment than some fucking nonce screaming police brutality.'

There was a long silence, finally broken by Young. 'Did he say anything?' the DS wanted to know.

'He gave me the password into the website where the pictures of those dead kids came from. Now, do you think with that kind of evidence against him he's going to be stupid enough to go running to a brief just because things got a bit . . . *animated* during an interview session? I doubt it.'

'But what if he does?'

'Then he does. I'll worry about that when and if it happens. Anyway, what's *your* problem? If they suspend me, you'll probably get put in charge of the investigation. Maybe even promoted. You can't knock that, Rob.'

'That isn't what I want. You know that.'

'I know,' Fielding sighed. 'Sorry.'

Another silence.

'So, do you think Cairns killed those kids?' Young wanted to know.

'No. I've seen his type before. He's a nonce. He deserved a slap but he's not a murderer. Not *this* time anyway.'

'How can you be so sure?'

'Instinct? Gut reaction? Over Twenty years' experience doing this fucking job? Call it what you like. I'd bet money it's not him.'

Young ran a hand through his hair.

'Have a look at this,' said Fielding, nodding towards the computer.

Young got to his feet and stood behind his superior, surveying the images on the screen.

'This is the site where the pictures were downloaded from,' said the DI. He clicked through a number of pages.

Children in varying states of undress. They ranged in age from eighteen months to nine years. One or two were smiling. Most looked terrified.

'Jesus,' murmured Young.

'Tasteful little number, isn't it?' Fielding observed. He clicked on to a picture of a girl no older than four who was bound and gagged. 'Caters for all tastes,' the DI continued.

'These are the worst I've seen,' Young murmured, his gaze never leaving the images before him. 'Could the ones of the dead kids have been done to order? Some *are*, aren't they?'

'It's possible. On another site somewhere there might even be shots of them taken *after* they were killed. What we've got to find out is who took them. Odds on it's the same person who killed them.'

'So, he snatches the kids, takes pictures of them to put on the web then kills them and dumps them.'

'That seems to be about the size of it,' Fielding murmured, clicking again.

Both men watched in silence as the procession of pictures went before them.

Fielding suddenly sat forward in his chair. 'That's the third kid,' he said quietly.

Young looked more closely.

The boy in the picture was around six years old. Flaxen haired. His face looked pale, his eyes puffy and red as if he'd been crying.

'That's Callum Hughes,' Fielding insisted.

The DS nodded. 'All three dead kids on the same site,' he intoned.

Fielding sat back in his seat and exhaled deeply.

'And you still reckon that Cairns had nothing to do with it?' Young asked.

'With the murders? No.'

'What about the others we pulled in for questioning?'

'Only time'll tell. Unfortunately, time's one thing we're running out of.'

# 8.27 P.M.

Nikki Reed lay back on the bed, tugging the skin-tight black jeans up over her slim hips. She fastened them then sat up, pushing her feet into a pair of ankle boots, which she zipped up.

As she stood, she was aware of her husband watching her.

Nikki smiled as she saw the appreciative look he was giving her. 'What are you so happy about?' she wanted to know.

'I was just looking at you,' Reed told her.

She moved towards the dressing table, sat down before the mirror and began applying her make-up.

Reed stood behind her, his hands resting on her shoulders. He gently massaged the soft flesh beneath his fingers, occasionally allowing the digits to glide beneath her long blond hair on to the smooth skin of her neck.

'You should have your mind on *other* things,' she told him, a note of mock reproach in her voice as she applied mascara.

'Can't I touch my own wife?' he asked.

Nikki stood up and turned to face him. He stepped forward and they kissed deeply. She felt his hands close over her tight buttocks as he pulled her to him, and she snaked her arms around his neck. Nikki's breathing became more ragged as their kiss continued and she took one of his hands and placed it on her right breast, encouraging him. Reed squeezed the soft globe gently, feeling her nipple stiffen beneath his touch.

Her right hand slid down to his chest then further still, seeking his groin and the stiffness she could feel there. Reed was also breathing faster, his heart thumping hard.

She pushed her tongue against his then allowed it to flick

over the hard edges of his teeth before she nibbled gently on his bottom lip.

When they parted, Nikki was gazing deeply into his eyes, her lips parted and gleaming. 'Let's just stay here tonight,' she whispered, squeezing his erection through his jeans. 'Forget about Macken.'

He shook his head, touching her cheek with one hand. 'We can't,' he told her.

'This *is* going to work, isn't it, Jeff?' she asked, a note of pleading in her voice.

'If we do what we said we'd do then yes.'

'But Macken's going to know who robbed him.'

'I told you, Nik. It's drug money. He can't go running to the law, can he?'

'But he might come looking for us himself.'

'Let him. Do you think I'm scared of that little prick.'

She shook her head.

'Everything'll be fine,' Reed said. 'Trust me. We'll give the money to Max Tate and . . .'

He shrugged.

Again she held his gaze. 'And what, Jeff?' Nikki wanted to know.

'It'll do for now,' he said, kissing her lightly on the lips. 'Come on, finish getting ready. I don't want that little bastard Macken turning up early and pissing off before I can get to him.'

'What if someone sees you?'

'Then they see me. Nik, you know what it's like on this estate. Nobody gives a fuck about anybody else. And who's going to help Macken?'

'He supplies to a lot of people, Jeff.'

'Yeah, exactly. That's why he'll be loaded by the time he reaches the pub tonight. Now come on.'

'I love you,' she said. 'I don't want anything to go wrong. I don't want *you* to be the one who gets hurt.'

'I won't,' he told her, glancing at his watch. 'Let's do this.'

# 9.32 P.M.

Roma sat at one end of the sofa, her legs curled beneath her, gazing blankly at the television screen.

She'd been looking at the images on it (to say she'd been watching would have implied some kind of interest in what was going on before her and that wasn't the case) for the last hour or so.

Occasionally she would pick up one of the magazines from the polished wooden table beside her and flick through it with the kind of perfunctory glances usually reserved for the publications found in a doctor's waiting room.

In the chair nearby David Todd was also reading. He held several sheets of paper stapled together.

'Another contract?' said Roma conversationally.

Todd looked up, his musings momentarily interrupted. He looked blankly at her.

'I said, is it another contract?' Roma repeated. 'Something to do with work?'

'Why?' He smiled.

'Because it's *usually* something to do with work, isn't it, David?'

He held her gaze. 'Yes, it's a contract,' he answered finally.

'Couldn't you have sorted it out at the office?' she wanted to know. 'I would have thought you'd have been glad of a break once in a while.'

'I haven't been in the office today, have I?'

'No, of course not. How could I forget? You've been sharing your valuable time with your family. Excuse me.'

She sipped at her wine, holding the expensive glass between her slender fingers.

Todd didn't like the edge to her voice but he resisted the temptation to say anything.

'How was Kirsten when you put her to bed?' Roma wanted to know.

'Fine.'

'And how were *you*?'

'Meaning?'

'It wasn't too much of an ordeal for you, was it? Putting your daughter to bed? You must have been up there with her for almost thirty minutes.'

Todd dropped the stapled sheets on to the coffee table and got to his feet. He crossed to the drinks cabinet and poured himself a Jack Daniel's.

'Do you want more wine?' he asked. 'Might help you relax. You sound like you need to.'

'I'm grand. Why should *I* need to relax? But, as you mention it, yes, I'll have some more wine.'

He carried the bottle of claret over to her and filled the glass.

'You can leave the bottle there,' she told him.

'You're not going to get drunk, are you?'

'A responsible mother and a respected lecturer like me?' she chided. 'You're fucking right I am.'

'All right, what the hell is wrong with you, Roma?'

'You have to ask?'

'Yes I do. I have to ask about every fucking thing these days. Having a conversation with you's like pulling teeth. It's hard work. Why the hell don't you just talk to me? Tell me what's on your mind without me having to play the fucking detective every time you go into one.'

He took a hefty swig from his own glass.

'What the fuck do you *think* is wrong?' she rasped.

Todd sighed. 'How many more times do we have to discuss this?' he said through gritted teeth.

'We never discussed it. *You* made a decision and I'm supposed to live with it. I don't call that a discussion, David.'

'We talked about it. Every aspect of it. It wouldn't make any sense to—'

She cut him short. 'Fuck the sense of it,' she said. 'I want to have another child.'

# 9.34 P.M.

Todd shook his head. 'We can't,' he said quietly.

'Why not, David? We're both young enough. Give me one good reason why we can't.'

'You can't replace Kirsten with another child. It's because you know she's ill. Because you know she's going to . . .' It was as if he couldn't bring himself to say the word.

'To die, David,' Roma snapped. 'I *know* Kirsten is going to die but that isn't why I want another child. Jesus, give me some credit. I know we can't replace her. A dozen children wouldn't be able to do that. She could have five or six years left before it happens. This isn't about Kirsten, it's about me.'

'You're not thinking straight.'

'And you're not listening.'

'What if we do have another child? What if it has the same condition Kirsten has?'

'The doctors said that was unlikely. Extremely unlikely.'

'Unlikely isn't good enough, Roma.'

'What do you want? A guarantee that the child is going to be perfect? Do you want the hospital to sign some sort of contract? That seems to be the only way to communicate with you, David. By contract.'

'Use your head, Roma. Try to see past your own selfishness for a minute and think about the child. What if it does have the same condition that Kirsten's got? What then?'

'We'd cope, the same as we have with Kirsten.'

'You want to go through this again? You want to watch another child die?'

132

'You bastard,' she said quietly, but there was a vehemence in her voice, matched by the glare in her eyes.

'I'm thinking about you and I'm thinking about—'

'You're thinking about yourself, as usual. *You* don't want to go through the same thing again. *You*. My God, David, you're frightened of your own daughter now.'

'Don't be so fucking ridiculous.'

'Her illness scares you. *She* scares you. I can see it in the way you are with her. The way you look at her.'

Todd didn't answer. Instead, he poured himself another measure of Jack Daniel's and downed half of it with one swallow.

'If we could be sure that another child would be . . .' He let the words trail off.

'Would be what? Normal? Is that the word you're looking for?'

'Maybe it is.'

'So, until you're sure, that's it. We have no more children?'

'We can't, Roma. It'd be irresponsible.'

'David, don't insult my intelligence by trying to turn this into a moral issue. This is all about you and the way you feel. Nothing else.'

'So you'd take the risk of having another child knowing it could turn out to be the same as Kirsten?'

'Yes. The doctors said it was unlikely—'

'The doctors aren't the ones who've got to bring it up,' Todd interrupted her angrily.

'It might be fine, David.'

'It might,' he repeated. 'No, Roma. No more kids.'

'And what if I fell pregnant? What would you want me to do? Get rid of it?'

'You won't get pregnant.'

'How can you be so sure, David? Even with the pill, with any form of contraception there's always a risk. If it happened, would you expect me to kill our child?'

'Don't make it sound so fucking dramatic. Is that the Irish

133

Catholic in you coming out? You wouldn't be killing a child, you'd be having an abortion.'

'And what if I didn't want one? Would you leave me, David?'

He downed more of his drink and turned away from her.

'You would, wouldn't you?' Roma continued. 'You'd walk away.'

'I love you, Roma, I—'

'You love me. But not enough to give me another child.'

Todd swallowed hard.

'So we just carry on the way we've been carrying on,' Roma said. 'We have sex occasionally. You check that I've taken my pill, that I'm using my diaphragm. And you pray to God that it all works and I don't get pregnant. But then, if I do, you can always whisk me off to a private clinic for an abortion, can't you? I mean, money's no object is it, David? Not to *us*. Or do you go further? Do we stop having sex? Just in case.'

'Now you're being ridiculous,' he snapped.

'Am I? Are you sure you can trust me to take the precautions you want me to take, David?'

He shot her a wary glance.

'Can you trust me?' she persisted.

Todd didn't answer.

# 9.51 P.M.

'Are you sure he said ten o'clock?'

Jeff Reed drained what was left in his glass and nodded. 'I *told* him. Ten,' he insisted, trying to catch the eye of the barmaid.

It was busy inside the Oak Apple, the loud babble of conversation competing for supremacy with the ever-thunderous sound of the jukebox.

*'How do I feel, I've been here before, I've felt this . . .'*

Nikki sipped at her drink and scanned the untidy mass of humanity filling the pub. She saw her husband look at his watch once more then glance agitatedly in the direction of the barmaid.

'How are you supposed to get a fucking drink around here?' Reed hissed, raising the empty pint glass.

Nikki looked across and saw the doors of the pub swing open. Two older men entered.

*False alarm.*

'Julie,' Reed called, trying to make himself heard above the chatter and the jukebox.

*'Retreat to a place, a place within me, I need this . . .'*

The barmaid finally finished serving two youths decked in England shirts and made her way over to Reed. He pushed his glass towards her.

'Another one of those,' he said, then looked at Nikki. 'Do you want another one?'

'No, I'm all right,' she said, her heart thudding.

'About time he brought you out with him, Nik,' the barmaid chuckled. 'I said to him the other day—'

'Just get the drink, will you, Julie?' Reed snapped.

135

The barmaid eyed him warily for a second then looked at Nikki who merely shrugged and tried a smile that never touched her eyes.

'Where the fuck is Macken?' Reed hissed, still looking around.

*'Keep it all down, bottled inside, it breaks me . . .'*

Nikki took another sip of her drink and shuffled uncomfortably on the barstool.

'You should get your job back here, Nik,' said the barmaid, setting down Reed's pint and holding out her hand for the money. 'I was saying that to Jeff the other day. Maurice could do with the extra help, especially on nights like this.'

'I wouldn't mind,' Nikki answered.

'I can have a word with Maurice if you like, or you could ask him yourself. Shall I get him?' Julie pointed towards the landlord who was busy serving at the far end of the bar.

'Just leave it,' Reed said.

'I'll talk to him another time, Ju,' Nikki assured her friend.

The barmaid nodded, smiled and moved off to serve more customers.

'Calm down, Jeff,' Nikki said, swallowing hard.

'I *am* fucking calm,' he told her, his eyes never leaving the mass of people in the bar. 'I just wish that bastard Macken would hurry up and get here.'

*'. . . to torment again and torture me like it used to . . .'*

There was a loud cheer from nearby and Nikki looked around as the sound of electronic bells added to the deafening amalgamation of sound already filling the pub. Someone had hit the jackpot on the fruit machine in the corner.

She ran her fingers through her hair and found that her hand was shaking.

'I'm just nipping to the loo,' she said, clambering down from the stool.

'Don't be too long,' Reed murmured, looking yet again at his watch.

The main doors swung open and he sat up, eyes riveted on the newcomer.

It was a large man in his early forties wearing a T-shirt that looked a size too small for him. He spotted some friends at a table and joined them.

Reed exhaled deeply once more then tapped Nikki's arm as she passed him. 'Don't be too long,' he repeated.

She shot him an irritated glance and weaved her way through the other drinkers towards the women's toilet.

As Nikki entered she saw that there were two other women inside, both in their early twenties, standing before the long mirror that ran the length of the back wall. They were applying make-up and chatting loudly. Both studied Nikki's reflection as she walked past them and into one of the cubicles.

From inside she could hear their inane chatter as well as the thud of the jukebox from the bar. She wiped the toilet seat with some wads of tissue then she slipped her jeans down and sat. The chatter of the two young women receded and she heard the toilet door close behind them as they left.

Nikki closed her eyes as she sat there, feeling as if the walls of the cubicle were closing in on her. She finished and flushed then crossed to the mirror and reached into her handbag for her lipstick. She applied it sparingly, her hand still quivering. She fluffed up her blond hair, regarded her pale reflection once more then made her way back out into the noisy bar, through the maze of drinkers to where Reed still sat waiting.

He glanced at her as she reseated herself on the barstool and sipped at her drink.

He was about to order himself another when Nikki reached out and touched his hand. 'You'll be drunk before Macken gets here,' she said.

'I'm fine. Just you worry about *that* bastard, not about me.'

He pulled his hand away then looked towards the entrance again. He checked his watch.

10.04 p.m.

'Where is he?' Reed muttered.

The jukebox was thudding out a new tune.

*'He's drunk again, it's time to fight . . .'*

Nikki finished her drink.

Reed slipped off the barstool. 'Order some more,' he told her. 'I'm going for a piss.' He fumbled in his pocket for some money and pushed a five-pound note into her hand. 'If Macken comes in, just keep an eye on him. Make sure you know where he is. Got it?'

Nikki nodded almost imperceptibly.

'Are you listening to me, Nik?' he snapped.

'I'm listening,' she said angrily. 'Just go, will you?'

Before he left he checked the entrance and his watch, once more.

The jukebox thundered out its accompaniment.

*'Tonight she'll find out how fucking tough is this man . . .'*

As Reed made his way to the toilet there was still no sign of Paul Macken.

# 10.11 P.M.

*It isn't going to work.*

As Reed stood at one of the urinals the thought kept tumbling over and over in his mind.

*It isn't going to work.*

The pub was too busy. He would have no way of getting Macken on his own long enough to take him out. To rifle through his pockets for cash and fuck knows what else.

*It isn't going to work.*

Even during the short space of time that he stood there, at least half a dozen men came in to use the toilets.

In one of the cubicles, Reed could hear the sound of vomiting. The acrid stench began to filter through the air, mingling with the stink of urine and excrement.

*It isn't going to work.*

He finished urinating then headed towards the cracked sink where he washed his hands.

Two more men entered. The silly bastard throwing his guts up was still at it. Probably would be for a while yet.

Reed crossed to the warm-air hand-drier and stood there feeling the breeze on his flesh, looking around him.

The sound of the drier seemed to fill his ears. His head.

*It isn't going to work.*

The litany was becoming painful. He could feel his head thumping with every heavy thud of his heart. There was pain at his temples and the base of his skull. It wasn't helped by the unrelenting thump of the jukebox.

*'Never again, seen it before but not like this . . .'*

He slipped one half-dry hand into the pocket of his jacket and felt the bike chain in there, still wrapped in its plastic bag.

It felt heavy. Lethal.

Reed took one last look around the inside of the lavatory then headed back to the bar and its all-enveloping noise.

*'Been there before but not like this . . .'*

Nikki was talking to the barmaid when he returned. Reed seated himself then continued with his vigil, apparently oblivious to what the two women were discussing. The occasional word reached his ears. He heard Julie say something about a man she'd been out with. He didn't catch the name.

*Didn't care.*

He sipped his drink, looking around as he heard the clack of pool balls. Another game was under way. There were half a dozen young men gathered around watching the participants who, like their audience, were in their mid-twenties or younger.

Reed narrowed his eyes as he gazed at one of them, homing in on him like a sniper on a target.

The youth was in his early twenties. Sallow faced. Dressed in designer gear.

'Do you know that kid, Julie?' Reed said suddenly.

Julie looked at him in surprise then followed his pointing finger.

'The one by the pool table with the Nike top on,' Reed continued.

'I don't know his name but I've seen him in here before,' the barmaid told him. 'Why, Jeff? Do you want to buy him a drink?' She chuckled.

Nikki smiled thinly.

'He's a mate of Paul Macken's, isn't he?' Reed said, his eyes still fixed on the youth.

'I don't know *everyone* who comes in here,' said Julie. 'I—'

Reed cut her short. 'Yeah, he is. I recognise him.'

Nikki turned to look at the youth, taking in every aspect of his appearance then she looked back at Reed. He wore a look that combined fury and determination.

'That's his fucking mate,' he murmured. 'He was with him yesterday when he was in here. I bet he's waiting for him.'

'You can't be sure,' Nikki said. 'Macken's already late. Perhaps he's not coming, Jeff.'

'He'll be here. He thinks he's got business tonight. We're not leaving until I've spoken to him.' Reed slipped his hand back inside his pocket and felt the bike chain there.

*'Never before have I ever seen it this bad . . .'*

The main doors of the Oak Apple swung open.

Paul Macken walked in.

*'Never again . . .'*

# 10.29 P.M.

Reed felt his heart pounding, the blood rushing through his veins at uncontrollable speed. He took another drink as he studied Macken.

The younger man had gone straight across to the pool table where he was greeted by a number of people standing around. Reed saw the Nike-clad youth scuttle off to the bar and return with a drink for Macken.

'I told you that was his mate,' Reed said, his eyes never leaving the gathering around the pool table.

Nikki was also watching the group of men, particularly Macken. She'd seen him before. Most people on the Walton Grange Estate knew him by sight. Many realised how he made his money. Quite a number contributed to his betterment by offering him their custom.

'You can't get near him while he's with them,' Nikki said, her voice catching slightly.

Reed didn't answer, he was still watching his quarry.

*How the fuck do you get him on his own?*

He watched as Macken potted a ball and spun the cue theatrically in his hand.

*How much are you carrying?*

All the other sounds inside the pub seemed to have receded. It was as if the only noise Reed could hear was the clacking of ball against ball as Macken played. He watched as the drug dealer moved around the pool table, occasionally stopping to speak to one or more of the other men. When he leaned forward to take a shot, the light glinted on the silver rings in his eyebrow and nose. He cursed as he missed a shot, stepping back to take a sip of his drink as his opponent played.

'He's here to do business,' Reed said. 'I'm going to talk to him.'

Nikki shot out an arm to stop her husband who was already lowering himself off the barstool.

He looked down at her hand then into her eyes. 'It'll be OK,' he told her. 'Just stay close. Do what I told you.'

She nodded and watched as he moved across the pub towards the pool table.

Reed reached the group of men and pushed one aside to get closer to Macken.

'All right?' he said.

Macken regarded him contemptuously. 'What do you want, man?' Macken asked in that high, whining voice.

'I need to talk to you. You said you'd be here at ten. I've been waiting.'

'Oh, yeah, right. I remember you. Look, I just got to finish this game, all right?'

Reed nodded and stepped back, watching as Macken bent low over the table to take another shot. Then he glanced in the direction of the bar at Nikki who was watching him.

Reed raised his eyebrows slightly and Nikki got down from the barstool and also made her way across the pub but she passed the pool table and walked out through the main doors of the Oak Apple.

Macken slammed in the black and stood up beaming. 'Check it,' he smirked.

'You ready now?' Reed asked him.

'What? Oh, yeah, right. Step into my office.' He grinned and turned in the direction of the toilets.

'No. Let's go outside,' Reed insisted. 'It's too busy in here.'

'You got the money?' Macken asked.

Reed nodded.

'Let's do it then,' said Macken, heading towards the exit. He looked over his shoulder to the other men around the pool table. 'Back in a minute,' he called. 'I got something to do. Get me another drink.' Then he disappeared out into the cool night.

There was a large car park to the side and rear of the Oak Apple. Two dozen cars were parked there in the dull glow cast by a faulty security light. Instead of its customary white brilliance, the light was sickly yellow and the shadows across the car park were deeper.

Macken led Reed towards the trees and bushes that formed the perimeter of the car park then stopped and looked around.

'Charlie, you wanted, didn't you?' he said.

Reed nodded.

'You said on the phone you had eighty to spend,' Macken reminded him.

Reed dug in his jeans pocket and pulled out a wad of notes.

'Fuck,' chuckled Macken. 'You're going to be doing some serious partying, eh? I could get you better than Charlie for that. You ever tried crystal meth? Ice? It's fucking great, man. You can—'

'Just give me what I asked for,' Reed said.

'I gotta count the money first.'

Macken held out his hand and Reed handed him the wad. The adrenalin rushing through his veins had heightened all of his senses. He looked directly at Macken, who took the money, licked his thumb and forefinger and began peeling back the notes.

He was three tenners in when he realised what was happening.

'What the fuck is this?' Macken said angrily.

The three ten-pound notes covered a wad of blank paper cut to the same size.

Reed slipped a hand into his jacket pocket and pulled out the bike chain.

He struck the first blow without removing the plastic bag.

The chain cracked across Macken's face, raising a red welt from his temple to his chin. The impact sent him sprawling.

Reed struck again, lashing out with incredible force.

The second caught the dealer across the mouth and cracked two of his front teeth. It also split his lips and blood began to pour down his chin.

By now the bag had come away and it was oily metal that Reed was slamming down on to his fallen quarry.

He hit Macken across the neck. The shoulders. The top of the head. Each blow delivered with such ferocity that it made Reed gasp with the effort.

And now Nikki appeared from the shadows.

She hurried across to the violent tableau, standing back as Reed continued to swing the chain with great power, concentrating his blows on Macken's head. As he wrenched it skyward, a chainlink caught one of the silver rings in the dealer's eyebrow and tore it free. Blood spurted from the ragged wound, mingling with the crimson fluid that already covered his face.

He was lying still now and Nikki grabbed at Reed's flailing arm. 'Don't kill him,' she gasped.

'Get the money,' Reed said breathlessly.

Nikki dropped to her knees and began rifling through Macken's pockets. She found some in his jeans. More in his inside pocket.

'Is that it?' Reed demanded, glancing back towards the main doors of the Oak Apple.

Nikki pulled out the linings of the pockets and left a handkerchief, some chewing gum, keys, several small packets of white powder and some loose change scattered across the tarmac.

'Come on,' snapped Reed, taking her by the arm.

They blundered through the trees and bushes at the back of the car park, anxious to be away from this place.

Macken lay motionless in a widening pool of blood.

# 10.48 P.M.

LONDON:

Despite the lateness of the hour, Euston station was still busy. People wandered back and forth, some dragging luggage on trolleys, some struggling under the weight of their suitcases and bags.

Others stood around gazing up at the huge electronic arrivals and departures board. A number were engrossed in conversations on mobile phones.

The man passed a middle-aged woman with two small yappy dogs. They both began barking noisily at him as he walked by and he glanced down indifferently at them as he made his way across the concourse towards the toilets.

There were more people seated in the various eateries dotted around the station. All of them were prodding disinterestedly at their purchases, some standing around drinking cups of tea or coffee.

A youth in his early twenties dressed in filthy combat trousers and a parka that looked as if only the dirt was holding it together, sat on his backside close to one of the platform entrances stuffing pieces of hamburger into his mouth and sipping from a can of Boddingtons. He belched loudly as the man passed, as if this was some kind of primitive communication system understood by only a select few.

'Any change?' he asked.

The man looked down contemptuously at him and walked past. He dug in his pocket for a twenty-pence piece and fed it into the slot outside the toilets.

The fluorescents inside cast a cold white light over everything.

He relieved himself then turned to the row of sinks, inspecting his reflection in the mirror as he washed his hands. He didn't dry them but, instead, swept them through his hair, plastering it back against his scalp. Then he wandered back out on to the concourse again and doublechecked the time of his train.

It would be leaving in eight minutes from platform twelve.

He crossed to the nearby Burger King and ordered an orange juice and some chips. As he waited for his order he was careful not to step in the large puddle of milkshake that had been spilled close to the counter.

He made his way down the ramp that led to the platform and stepped on to the waiting train. He found a seat with ease and sat down, pulling his Walkman from his bag and slipping it on.

He ate his chips and drank his orange juice then stuffed the rubbish back into the paper bag and deposited it in the waste bin.

More people got on to the train, some running as if it were just about to pull away.

The man noticed that there was a discarded newspaper on the seat just across the aisle and he reached across for it. He read the sports pages first then began flicking through it from the front.

He looked up as a woman stepped on to the train. She was in her mid-twenties, and the small child who held her hand could have been no more than eight or nine.

The woman was dressed in jeans, trainers and a white T-shirt with STAR printed on it in sparkly red letters.

The child looked tired.

The man shook his head. This was no time for a kid of that age to be up. She should be asleep in bed.

*Pretty little thing.*

He watched her as she sat down next to her mother, her eyes heavy.

The man glanced again at her as she said something to her mother then yawned.

*Definitely tired.*

The child glanced at him and he winked.

The little girl smiled and waved with one small hand.

The man waved back with his index finger.

*She was indeed a very pretty little girl.*

The automatic doors of the train slid shut and there was a slight shudder as it pulled away.

The man checked his watch. He was on time.

As the train left Euston, he glanced again at the small child sitting opposite him.

# 11.13 P.M.

KINGSFIELD:

David Todd finished cleaning his teeth and spat water and tooth-paste into the bowl. He straightened up and glanced at his reflection in the square mirror above the basin then padded into the bedroom snapping the light off in the en-suite bathroom.

Roma was sitting up in bed peering alternately at a book and the television set that was on in one corner of the spacious bedroom.

Todd walked across to her and kissed her lightly on the fore-head then he tilted the book upwards so that he could see the title.

'*The Crisis of the Self*,' he read aloud, wandering around to his own side of the bed. 'And you moan about *me* bringing work home.'

'I've got a lecture tomorrow,' she told him.

'Did you check on Kirsten when you came up?'

'I always do. She's fine. Fast asleep.'

Todd slipped off his jogging bottoms and slipped naked into bed.

Roma glanced at him and raised her eyebrows, a slight smile on her lips.

'What's funny?' Todd wanted to know.

'Nothing,' she told him. 'I was just looking.'

She put the book on the bedside table and slid closer to him, one hand sliding across his chest before moving lower towards his belly.

She leaned across him and they kissed.

Todd pulled her more tightly to him, slipping one hand up inside her T-shirt. He kneaded her breasts gently, feeling her nipples stiffen beneath his expert fingers.

Roma opened her legs, allowing him to push one thigh against her pubic mound. She pushed herself against his flesh, her breathing becoming harsher. Her hand delved lower and she felt it brush against his stiffening penis.

As their kiss continued she kept her eyes closed.

*Thinking of Harper? Wishing it was him lying beside you? The way he was this morning?*

She pulled back slightly and tugged her T-shirt off over her head, kneeling above her husband for a moment, looking down at him.

Roma took his hand and guided it between her legs, allowing him to feel the moisture there.

Todd looked into her eyes.

'Make love to me, David,' she murmured, lying beside him again.

He kissed her gently on the lips and stroked her cheek with his hand. 'Not tonight,' he whispered.

'Why not?' she said, a slight edge to her voice.

'Tomorrow.'

'Or the day after? Or the day after that?' She sat up again, the desire that had been etched on her face seconds before now transformed into anger.

'You really *don't* want to take any chances, do you? Do you want to check my pill packet? Make sure I've taken it today?' She prepared to swing herself out of bed. 'Shall I get it for you? Let you have a look? Then when you're sure I've taken it, maybe then you'll fuck me, David. If I'm lucky.'

'Roma. Just leave it. I'm tired, that's all.'

'You're always fucking tired, David. When it comes to this.' She glared at him.

'Another night,' he said, but his placatory tone only further inflamed her anger.

150

'Don't make it sound as if you're doing me a favour.'

'Keep your voice down. You'll wake Kirsten.'

Roma looked furiously at him, her eyes narrowed.

Before she could speak again, the scream filled the whole house.

# 11.14 P.M.

'*How* much?'

Jeff Reed looked wildly at the kitchen table and Nikki who sat there, the money spread out before her.

'There's got to be more than that?' he snarled.

'Count it yourself,' she said angrily.

'Two hundred and thirty-nine fucking quid,' Reed gasped.

'It was all he had on him.'

'He must have had it hidden.'

'Where, Jeff? I went through all his pockets. It's all he had.'

'He must have had the rest stuffed in his fucking sock or something.'

'It was all he had,' Nikki said, raising her voice slightly.

'Fuck,' hissed Reed, pacing the small kitchen agitatedly. 'FUCK.'

He lashed out at some plates stacked on the draining board and sent them crashing to the floor. Several shattered and pieces of china flew into the air.

'Count it again,' he said.

'Jeff, that's all there is, I told you.'

Reed wrenched a chair out from beneath the table and sat down. He reached for the notes and began thumbing through them, his hands trembling.

Nikki noticed that there was blood on his fingertips. Some had also spattered on to his shirt. Most of it was Macken's.

Reed finally sat back from the table, breathing deeply.

'I told you how much was there,' Nikki said quietly. 'Do you still want to take it to Max Tate?'

Reed shook his head slowly, his gaze never leaving the fives, tens, twenties and fifties spread out on the table. Some of the notes were held down by coins.

'What did you expect Macken to be carrying, Jeff? You said yourself, he's not a Colombian coke baron,' Nikki murmured.

'I just thought . . .' Reed allowed the words to trail off. His anger had been replaced by exhausted resignation. He rested his head in his hands and closed his eyes.

'We're fucked, Nik,' he sighed. 'That's it. End of story.'

Nikki reached out and touched one of his bloodstained hands. 'There's got to be a way out of it, Jeff,' she said.

'Yeah, right. Let's stop fooling ourselves, shall we? I was stupid to think this business with Macken could ever work. Stupid for losing the fucking money in the first place. Stupid for getting it from Max Tate to begin with.'

'We didn't have any choice.'

'And we haven't got any choice now either. We'll have to get away from here.'

'And go where?'

'London. Birmingham. Liverpool. Somewhere they can't find us.'

'But we've got no money. Nothing to live on.'

'We've got two hundred and thirty-nine quid.' He smiled bitterly.

There was a loud banging on the front door.

For fleeting seconds they looked at each other then Reed got to his feet and wandered through the living room to the hall. He paused as the banging came again.

Nikki stood watching him, her face pale. 'Macken?' she wondered.

'He doesn't know where we live,' Reed whispered. 'Anyway it couldn't be, not the state he was in when we left him . . .' He let the words trail off.

Again the banging.

He reached for the handle and prepared to turn it.

It was impossible to see through the bevelled glass who was standing on the doorstep. The fact that the street lamp outside their house wasn't working didn't help.

'Don't open it, Jeff,' Nikki implored.

'They'll have it off the fucking hinges in a minute,' he snapped. He pulled it open.

'Didn't get you up, did I?'

The voice belonged to Luke Hamilton. The big man was standing with his hands dug deeply into the pockets of his leather jacket. He made no move to step inside the house. Instead he merely nodded a greeting in Nikki's direction.

'You said you'd give us until the end of the week to get the money,' Reed protested.

'I'm not here about the money,' Hamilton said. As he spoke he pulled his right hand free of his pocket.

In the dull light of the hallway, both Reed and Nikki saw the .38 calibre revolver gleaming in his fist.

'The car's parked just outside,' Hamilton said. He gestured over his shoulder to a Datsun. Tony Casey was seated behind the steering wheel.

Reed looked down at the gun.

'Now both of you, walk to the fucking car or I'll shoot you where you stand,' Hamilton insisted.

'What's going on?' Reed wanted to know.

'You'll find out when you get there,' Hamilton told him. 'Now move it. Max is waiting.'

Kirsten was sitting up rigidly in bed, her eyes bulging wide in their sockets.

Even when Roma ran into the small girl's bedroom, she didn't move but continued to gaze blankly ahead.

Todd followed a couple of seconds later, watching as Roma crossed to their daughter and hugged her.

Only now did some of the stiffness leave Kirsten's body and she seemed to melt into her mother's enveloping embrace, tears coursing down her cheeks.

'Are you OK, darling?' Roma asked, stroking her daughter's hair.

Kirsten nodded.

'What is it?' Roma wanted to know.

'A bad dream,' Kirsten groaned, lying back down on her pillow.

Todd sat on the end of the bed and looked at his daughter. 'What was the dream about?' he wanted to know. As he spoke he squeezed her feet through the duvet.

The heat that he felt against his palms was stronger than normal body heat.

*Wasn't it?*

He sniffed the air and thought he could smell something like burning.

*Imagination taking over again?*

Kirsten took a sip from her Tweenies cup and lay still as Roma knelt beside the bed holding her hand.

'It's OK now,' she whispered. 'It's all gone.'

'What was the dream about, Kirsten?' Todd persisted.

'It doesn't matter, David,' Roma said through clenched teeth as she shot him an angry glance.

'I was dreaming about a doctor,' Kirsten said quietly. She was gazing up at the ceiling, as if fragments of the dream were suspended there. 'He was cutting me with a knife. Cutting my head.' She touched her forehead.

Todd felt the hairs rise on the back of his neck.

'Just go back to sleep now,' Roma said, running her hand over the little girl's forehead. She felt hot but not sweaty.

Todd smelled something acrid in the air.

*Burned plastic?*

He looked at the Tweenies cup. Even in the semi-darkness of the bedroom it was possible to see that there were five fingertip sized indentations in the receptacle.

'How do you feel?' he wanted to know.

'Fine, Dad,' Kirsten told him. 'It was just the dream.'

'In the dream, did you wake up before the doctor cut you?' Todd persisted.

'For Christ's sake, David,' Roma interrupted.

'I can't remember,' Kirsten said.

'It's because you're going to the clinic on Saturday,' Roma said, squeezing her daughter's hand more tightly. 'You've been thinking about it so you've been thinking about doctors and it's made you dream about them. If you were going to the zoo you'd probably have dreamed about being eaten by lions.'

Kirsten giggled.

'Or, if you'd been going to the cinema with Dad, you'd prob-ably have dreamed about being attacked by a giant bag of popcorn.'

Again Kirsten laughed.

Roma kissed her on the forehead and straightened up.

Todd was already on his feet, heading for the bedroom door.

'Dad,' Kirsten called. 'Kiss.'

Todd hesitated then moved back towards the bed and leaned forward. He planted a kiss on his daughter's cheek.

Again he felt the heat.

'Goodnight,' he said.

'I love you,' Kirsten called as he retreated from the room.

'Love you too,' he answered. Then he was gone.

As he walked back into their bedroom Roma was perched on the edge of the bed looking furiously at him. She watched as he pulled the door shut behind him.

'We should have called the doctor,' Todd said.

'She's not ill, David. She had a nightmare. That's all.'

'But she *is* ill, isn't she, Roma?'

'She doesn't need a doctor tonight, David.'

He stood motionless as if trying to choose his words. 'It's getting out of control,' he said.

'No it isn't. Once she's been to the clinic she'll—'

'She's not strong enough to handle it,' he snapped, cutting her short.

'*You're* the one who can't handle it, David. You can't accept her condition.'

'Do you blame me?' he said, trying to keep his voice low.

Roma climbed into bed, watching as he hesitated.

'She's dangerous, Roma,' he said. 'To herself and to others.'

'You're over-reacting.'

He shook his head. 'And you want another child?' he said dismissively. 'Knowing that it could be the same as Kirsten? That it could have the same condition?' A heavy silence descended.

'I'm prepared to take that chance,' Roma said.

'Well *I'm* not,' Todd said with an air of finality. He padded out of the bedroom and she heard his footsteps as he descended the stairs.

'You bastard,' she whispered.

# 11.39 P.M.

The coffee table was covered with photos. Hundreds of them. Perhaps even thousands. All stacked up in neat piles.

A catalogue of depravity.

Detective Inspector Fielding took a sip from his glass and scanned the three pictures in the middle of the table yet again.

Callum Hughes. Marie Walker. Jonathan Ridley.

There were school photos. Pictures taken on holidays. Shots of the three children smiling, playing.

In the centre of the table were the autopsy photos of them. All lying in identical positions, each picture marked with a serial number. Somewhere in among the piles of other pictures there were shots taken from the website where their small, naked bodies had been displayed for anyone who cared to look.

The crystal clock on top of the television ticked loudly. The set was on but the sound was turned down.

Fielding looked at each of the children's pictures in turn then reached for the autopsy pictures of Callum Hughes.

He studied the child's face, serene in death. No longer troubled by the suffering he may have endured before that blessed but long-premature release.

There wasn't a mark on his skin. The autopsy report gave added credence to what was already apparent merely by looking at the dead boy. The only blemishes were the two puncture marks in the crook of the left arm made by a hypodermic needle.

The same was true of both Marie Walker and Jonathan Ridley. No bruises. No cuts. No striation marks. No signs of violence.

Perhaps he should be thankful for that at least. They hadn't

158

suffered any physical torment prior to their deaths.

But what kind of mental anguish had they been forced to endure? Had they known they were going to be killed? Had they cried for their parents? Pleaded for their lives?

Fielding shook his head and looked at some of the pictures of other children downloaded from the Internet site.

He had gazed endlessly at these shots during the day and evening and now, even as the need for sleep became more pressing, he forced himself to look at them once more.

*Any links?*

The backgrounds against which the children were displayed *(there was no other word to describe it)* were different. Bedrooms. Living rooms. Kitchens. Gardens. Every location you could think of.

He looked more closely at the shots. Straining to see something he hadn't already seen. He wasn't even sure what he was looking for.

Other members of the force were poring over similar stacks of photos or had been studying videos and web-cam material all day.

Fielding sipped at his drink and regarded the enormity of the task.

Nine thousand images from just one computer. Videos to be inspected. Photographs that could eventually run into the hundreds of thousands. Every one had to be inspected, compared and examined. Somewhere in that plethora of perversion there might be more pictures of Marie Walker, Callum Hughes and Jonathan Ridley.

*There might.*

No guarantees.

And even if there were, Fielding wondered if it would bring them any closer to finding the killer.

More than once that day he had glanced at the phone number of New Scotland Yard's Paedophile Unit and wondered if he should call them. Wondered if he should seek the help of people well acquainted with the kind of horrors he now faced.

Fielding knew that the unit was housed on the fifth floor of New Scotland Yard. A tight group of dedicated individuals comprising fifteen detectives and six civilians.

There were an estimated two hundred thousand paedophiles in the country, many not even on the sex offenders' register. Ten thousand videos a year were confiscated by the unit. Studied and catalogued. Hundreds of thousands, maybe even millions, of images also passed before them during the course of a year.

Fielding lit another cigarette and stroked his chin thoughtfully.

Had the time come to call them?

He exhaled deeply.

No. Not yet.

If he could find their killer himself then he would.

He looked to the first tall stack of photos then pulled it towards him and began flipping through the images.

Some were distasteful. Many repulsive. Some monstrous.

Fielding shook his head and continued looking through them.

Behind him, the clock continued to tick loudly.

# 11.46 P.M.

Most of Kingsfield's industrial estate was in darkness.

Nikki Reed, sitting rigidly in the back seat of the Datsun beside her husband, glanced occasionally to her left or right and saw the odd security light on. For the most part, however, the buildings that flanked the roads through the estate were silent and black.

Tony Casey drove quickly and expertly to his appointed destination. Glancing in the rear-view mirror he could see his two passengers. Both looked pale. Casey smiled to himself.

In the passenger seat, Luke Hamilton gazed indifferently out of the front window, his head lolling back against the head-rest. The .38 was tucked away inside his leather jacket.

'What's all this about?' Reed asked from the back seat. His tone was strained.

'I told you,' Hamilton said without looking round.

'You're looking very nice tonight, Nikki,' Casey noted, glancing in the rear-view mirror again.

She didn't answer.

Casey's dry laugh filled the car.

He turned the Datsun down a narrow road and eased off the accelerator.

Directly ahead was a high metal fence, the top trimmed with razor wire. Two heavy gates led into a forecourt. Beyond was a two-storey building. There was a light burning in one of the second-floor windows.

A large yellow sign, lit from below by spotlamps, proclaimed CAR WAREHOUSE.

There were dozens of vehicles parked to one side of the fore-court. All secondhand.

There were more on the left-hand side but these were in varying states of repair.

The gleaming new Jag that was parked among them looked peculiarly incongruous.

Casey parked the Datsun behind a battered-looking Astra and climbed out from behind the wheel. Hamilton also clambered out then opened the rear door and indicated that Reed and Nikki should follow him.

'Through there,' Casey muttered, indicating a door that led into the building.

Reed and Nikki walked through the door into the reception area of the garage then on and up the narrow flight of stairs behind the counter. Hamilton and Casey followed.

As they neared the top of the staircase, they could see a door and hear voices behind it.

Casey pushed past Nikki, sliding his hand across her buttocks in the process. He chuckled as she opened her mouth to snap something at him. He pushed open the door and walked in, closing it behind him.

More voices, then the door opened once more and they walked into what was quite clearly an office. There was a large desk at the far end of it. A two-seater leather sofa and a couple of pot plants.

Max Tate was sitting behind the desk, sipping from a hip flask.

He was a short, bullish man in his late thirties. His dark-brown hair was receding, accentuating his prominent forehead. He wore rectangular spectacles that he had a habit of peering over the top of. His face was flabby and, when he stood up, his stomach strained against his shirt.

Reed felt his fear increase as he looked at the loan shark. He barely noticed that there was a figure seated to the right of Tate's desk.

The man was wearing a hooded sweatshirt, which hid his features. It wasn't until he turned that Reed saw his face. It was bloodied and bruised, like his hands.

Paul Macken shot him an angry glance.

'That's him,' said Macken, getting to his feet.

'Sit down,' snapped Tate. He remained behind the desk and jabbed a pudgy finger in the direction of the two-seater sofa. 'You,' he pointed at Reed and Nikki. 'You sit down too. We need to talk. Or, more to the point, *you* need to listen.'

'Max—' Reed began.

'I said *listen*, you prick,' Tate snapped, finally moving out from behind the desk and taking a step towards them.

Casey and Hamilton stood on either side of the closed office door barring any escape. Not that Reed or Nikki had even thought of that eventuality. This was it. End of the road. Nowhere to run.

'First you borrow money from me that you don't pay back,' Tate began. 'Then you steal from me.'

Reed looked puzzled.

'You robbed him,' Tate said, hooking a finger in Macken's direction. 'You took the money he had.'

Reed swallowed hard.

'You took *my* money,' Tate continued.

'I don't understand, Max,' Reed murmured.

'You turned him over tonight outside the Oak Apple,' Tate snapped, pointing at Macken. 'Knocked him about. Took his money. Took the money he was collecting for *me*.'

'Oh, Christ,' murmured Reed, the realisation hitting him with the force of a sledgehammer.

'Yeah, that's right, smart boy. He works for me. Thirty per cent of everything he sells goes in my pocket. And you took that money.' Tate sipped from his hip flask again. 'Now, before you leave here tonight I want paying. Got it?'

# 11.48 P.M.

Reed wondered if his life should be flashing before his eyes.

He'd heard that was what happened to someone about to die and, as he sat on the leather sofa looking up at Max Tate, he was convinced he had no chance of surviving.

He wasn't going to walk out of this office.

His head spun. Thoughts tumbled madly through his mind, unconnected and random. He tried to swallow but his throat felt as if someone had filled it with chalk.

Beside him on the sofa Nikki also shifted fearfully. More than once she reached for his hand and he tried to squeeze it. Tried to find the strength to reassure her that they would get through this. But, try as he might, Reed could not find that strength or belief.

'I lent you money in good faith,' Tate said, looking down at them. 'You pissed on my generosity. You didn't pay me back when you should have. But I let that go. I gave you more time. But now this.' He pointed again at Macken who was still dabbing blood from his cut lip with a sodden handkerchief.

'We didn't know that he worked for you, Max,' said Reed.

'And I'm supposed to be all right with that, am I?' said the older man. 'So what were you going to do with the money you took off him?'

'Give it to you,' Reed said, clearing his throat. 'Ask you to accept it as a—'

'A what? A fucking down-payment on the twenty grand you owe me?'

'No,' Reed lied. 'As a sign of good faith. That we were going to pay the rest of it back.'

164

'Where are you going to get twenty grand by the end of the week? How many drug dealers were you planning to roll?'

He took a step closer to them and they shrank back.

'I built up this business from nothing,' Tate said, gesturing around him. 'I worked for what I've got now.' His tone softened. 'When I had enough money I started lending to other people on the estate. I lent washing machines and TVs and stereos to start with. Then money. But that's a business as much as running this fucking garage. If people don't buy cars then I'm fucked, and if people who've borrowed money from me don't pay it back then *they're* fucked.' The harshness had returned to his voice.

Tate glared at Reed over the top of his spectacles. 'And at the moment, that looks like what *you* are. Well and truly fucked. Give me one good reason why I shouldn't break your fucking arms and legs right now.' He moved his face to within inches of Reed's.

'Just give us a bit more time, Max, please,' gasped Reed.

'I could give you until you were fifty and I'd still never see my fucking money,' Tate snarled, spittle spraying from his mouth, some spattering Reed.

He stepped back then walked towards the desk.

Reed saw Tate's hand slide out of sight as he reached for something in one of the desk drawers.

He hefted the claw hammer into view as he walked back towards the sofa.

'Please, Max,' Reed stammered.

Casey and Hamilton moved away from the office door and stood behind the sofa.

Reed felt hands on his shoulders.

'What do I start with?' Tate said evenly. 'Your toes? Your ankles? Knees? Fingers? What about your bollocks?' He swung the claw hammer through the air and it thudded down on to the arm of the sofa with a dull smack.

Reed was having difficulty controlling his breathing now. His body was trembling violently. He glanced across the room and saw Macken grinning at him.

Nikki was fighting to hold back tears of fear and frustration.

'Hold his hand still,' Tate rasped, looking past Reed to Hamilton.

'No,' Nikki shrieked and got to her feet.

'Fucking sit down, you cunt,' hissed Tate.

'No. You want paying then I'll pay you. Any way you want,' she persisted. She remained on her feet, gazing into Tate's eyes.

'Nikki,' Reed began but a hard blow across the back of his head silenced him.

'Whatever you want,' Nikki persisted.

Tate looked her up and down but the expression on his face didn't change.

He looked at Reed then at Hamilton and Casey. Only then did his features soften.

'And what can *you* offer me that I might want?' Tate asked, looking at her and smiling crookedly. He was swinging the hammer lazily back and forth beside him.

Nikki, her hands trembling, slowly unbuttoned her blouse.

'Nikki, don't,' Reed implored.

'Shut your mouth, Jeff,' Tate snapped, not taking his eyes from Nikki. 'You've got nothing to bargain with. *She* has.'

Reed felt those powerful hands on his shoulders, pinning him to the sofa.

'You said you wanted paying,' Nikki murmured, her voice catching.

Tate continued to stare at her. 'Take him home,' he said finally, nodding towards Reed.

Reed was dragged to his feet by Hamilton.

'Nikki, please don't do this,' said Reed, his voice a hoarse whisper.

'I'll be all right,' she said to him, watching as he was dragged towards the door.

'You should be thanking her, Jeff,' Tate chided. 'You'd be

crawling out of here with two broken knee-caps otherwise.'

Reed looked at Tate then at the hammer he held. How he longed to grab that tool. To slam it down on to Tate's head. To batter and strike until he split his fucking skull. To . . .

'I'll take care of her,' Tate called. He turned and looked at Macken who was gazing lecherously at Nikki.

'Enough to go around, Max?' said the dealer, grinning.

'Fuck off home, you little prick,' Tate said, watching as Macken also made his way out of the office, slamming the door behind him.

Tate turned back to face Nikki. 'Now,' he said, his voice low. 'What had you got in mind?'

# WEDNESDAY, MARCH 5TH

# 2.04 A.M.

Reed heard the key turn in the lock and jumped to his feet, hurrying across to the door.

Nikki looked at him blankly as she stepped into the living room, dropping her front-door key back into her handbag.

Outside, a car drove off.

'Are you all right?' Reed asked, looking into her eyes.

She nodded and put out her arms to him. They embraced and held each other tightly as if neither wanted to let go.

Perhaps he expected tears, he didn't know. But when they finally parted her face was set in hard lines. She sat down on the sofa and looked up at him.

'I could do with a drink,' she said, her voice low.

Reed scurried into the kitchen and returned with a glass of vodka and lemonade for Nikki and another can of beer for himself. There were already several empty on the coffee table and the floor.

Nikki drank deeply then ran a hand through her hair. Reed could see that she was trembling.

'What did Tate say?' he wanted to know.

'That he'll forget about what happened with Macken.'

'And the rest of the money?'

'He still wants it by the end of the week. He said he might be able to give us an extra couple of days but no more.'

Reed regarded her silently for a moment then sat down in the chair opposite.

'And what did you have to do to get him to agree to that?' he said finally.

'Does it matter?'

'What did he do to you, Nikki?'

'They would have crippled you, Jeff. And me too. Maybe even killed us.'

Reed got to his feet. 'What did he do?' he persisted, his tone darkening. 'Did he touch you?'

'Look, all that matters is that we got out of there alive.'

'No, that isn't all that matters,' Reed snapped. 'I want to know if he touched you.'

'What I did, I did for you,' she said, searching his eyes for some glimmer of *(of what? Appreciation? Thanks?)* understanding.

'So, you fuck Max Tate and I'm supposed to say thanks?' Reed snarled. 'You let that fat cunt put his hands all over you and you want me to be fucking grateful?'

'What did you want me to do?' she said, tears finally welling in her eyes. 'Let them hurt you? Stand by while they beat the shit out of you?' Her breath was coming in gasps now.

'Did he touch you?'

'Yes,' she roared. 'Is that what you want to hear? He touched my tits. He stuck his fingers between my legs. He asked me to suck his cock and I did. I sucked it and I swallowed his fucking spunk. Is that what you want to hear?' She too was on her feet now. 'Then he fucked me up the arse. He—'

'Shut up,' he bellowed. He struck her hard across the cheek. The blow was powerful enough to send her crashing back on to the sofa.

'They would have killed us,' she sobbed as he stood over her. She clutched at her cheek. 'They would have killed us.' Her words dissolved into more wrenching cries.

Reed sat on the edge of the sofa beside her. 'Just tell me the truth,' he said more quietly. 'Just tell me what he did to you?'

'He never touched me,' she whimpered, wiping tears from her cheeks. 'I swear to God he never touched me.'

Reed swallowed hard and put out a hand to touch her

shoulder. But his fingers hovered inches away, as if he could not bear to feel her flesh against his.

'Did he make *you* touch *him*?' he asked, forced to clear his throat more than once.

She drew her knees up to her chin and sat on the floor gazing at the far wall. 'I was trying to help,' she said quietly. 'To help us both. I love you, Jeff. That's why I did it.'

'What did you do?' He finally touched her shoulder lightly. She shook her head.

'I want to know if he hurt you,' Reed persisted.

'He said that we're going to be watched. Until the money's paid back. In case we'd thought about doing a runner, he said someone will be watching us. We won't know when but if we try to get away from Kingsfield he'll kill us.'

Reed looked down at her. 'What else did he say?'

'He just kept going on about the money. The twenty grand. How he wanted it back.'

Another long silence that was finally broken by Reed. 'Why won't you tell me what happened, Nikki?' he murmured.

'What good will it do, Jeff? What happened tonight isn't important. The money's the only thing that matters. If we don't get it . . .' She let the sentence trail off.

He rested his hand on her shoulder and gazed down at her wondering whether he should persist with his questions. Questions that were gnawing away at him like cancerous growths.

No. For now all that mattered was that she was safe.

*For now. The questions could wait until later.*

Reed slipped on to the floor beside her and held her tightly as she wept softly.

A vision of Max Tate flashed into his mind and he felt an anger unlike anything he'd felt in his life before. He saw Tate's hands on Nikki's face. Her breasts. Her buttocks. Saw fingers pushing deeply into her.

He screwed his eyes so tightly shut that white stars danced behind the lids.

'It's all right, Nik,' he whispered, through clenched teeth, his head still bowed.

He wished it was.

# 3.18 A.M.

Fielding knew that he wasn't drunk.

Work such as this would probably best have been undertaken under the influence of strong alcohol but the DI had downed his last Jack Daniel's some two hours earlier.

His head was swimming. But not with the effects of liquor.

His mind was stuffed full of putrid images. Replete with visions of torment. Bloated with replications of depravity.

*So many children.*

As he continued to sift slowly through the piles of prints, he did it with mechanical methodicalness.

Every image, despite the thousands he had already seen, seemed to sear itself into his brain. It scarred his consciousness.

He glanced at his watch, thought about going to bed. Considered returning to this seemingly endless parade of suffering in the morning.

*Fuck. Two more hours and it would be light. Why not just stay up? There'd be more of this shit to come in the following days. Lots more.*

He looked at more of the pictures.

A girl, no more than six, seated on the knee of a man with his face concealed by a clown's mask. He had his hands between her legs.

A boy of nine lying on his stomach, buttocks exposed to the prying eye of the camera.

Two girls of roughly the same age *(eight, maybe nine)* lying together on a bed. Both naked.

No smiles. Just a look of fearful bewilderment in their eyes.

Fielding knew that not all of these children had been physically harmed but what kind of mental anguish had they endured? He could only imagine and the very act almost forced a tear to his eye.

Another boy. Ten. Naked.

A girl of seven in her blue and grey school uniform. She was doing a handstand. The camera had zoomed in on her little knickers.

*Jesus fucking Christ.*

Lots of shots of little girls' knickers. Opportunist shots the paedophiles called them.

Fielding clenched his teeth.

*Jesus H. fucking stinking Christ.*

He got to his feet, needing to rest his eyes, his mind, from this unending barrage of images. The DI walked through into the kitchen, past one of his many wedding photos. He smiled at his dead wife as he passed.

In the kitchen he filled the kettle and spooned coffee into a mug then wandered back into the sitting room and scooped up a handful of the photos. As he sat at the kitchen table waiting for the kettle to boil he glanced through more of the pictures.

A girl of ten in just a pair of knickers and a vest.

A boy of five in school uniform except that his little grey shorts had been removed, as had his underpants. The boy's eyes looked red rimmed. He'd obviously been crying.

Fielding glanced at the kettle, watching the red light on it, gazing at the steam rising slowly from the spout then he continued his inspection of the catalogue of atrocities.

A boy of seven in just his socks.

Fielding continued to gaze. A single tear trickled down his cheek.

# 8.47 A.M.

Roma ran her hand over Kirsten's neatly brushed hair and smiled down at her daughter as she held open the passenger-side door of the Range Rover.

The little girl returned the gesture and clambered out of her booster seat.

As usual, parents were dropping their youngsters off at St Margaret's with various degrees of measured discipline or frantic speed.

Roma looked down at her daughter once again and handed her her red book bag and lunch box.

They set off up the driveway towards the Victorian building, Kirsten occasionally waving or calling to classmates on the way.

'Do you feel OK, darling?' Roma asked.

Kirsten looked puzzled.

'After what happened last night, I mean,' Roma elaborated.

'It was only a nightmare, Mum,' said Kirsten, shrugging her shoulders. 'I went straight back to sleep when you and Dad went back to bed.'

Roma thought how much she would have appreciated the chance to drift off to sleep after the incident. It had not been so easy for her. She had lain awake for another two hours at least. Tossing and turning while her husband slept fitfully beside her.

When the alarm had sounded so stridently that morning, Roma had been forced to use all her willpower to drag herself from beneath the duvet.

Now she yawned as she walked, sucking in deep breaths of petrol-tinged air in an effort to clear her head.

Up ahead she saw Louise Barton and her children, and Kirsten suddenly ran on ahead to catch up with her friend. Chloe Barton turned and smiled at her and the two girls began chattering.

'Morning, Louise,' said Roma, stifling another yawn.

'Late night?' Louise asked smiling.

'I couldn't sleep. That's all.'

'Mum.'

She looked down at Kirsten.

'Can I go and see Chloe's new puppy today?' said the little girl.

'That's up to Chloe and her mum,' Roma said gently.

'I'll pick her up and take her back to ours,' Louise grinned. 'You look as if you could do with the rest.'

'Thanks but there's no chance of that. I've got a lecture to give at ten,' Roma said wearily.

'Can Kirsten come for tea, Mum?' Chloe asked, bouncing up and down on the balls of her feet like some manic jack-in-the-box.

'Of course she can,' Louise said chuckling.

'Thanks, Louise,' Roma said. 'What time do you want me to pick her up?'

'I'll bring her home,' Louise said, still smiling.

Roma kissed Kirsten, kneeling before her as she spoke. 'You be a good girl for Louise, OK?' she said.

'I will, Mum,' Kirsten assured her.

Roma kissed her daughter again and then watched as she raced off towards the classroom. Roma waved a greeting to the young teacher who was standing by the doorway, touching each child gently on the head as they entered. She waved back.

Roma turned and walked back down the drive with Louise.

'I saw David in the paper again today,' Louise said. 'He's quite a celebrity, your husband.'

Roma smiled humourlessly. '*He'd* like to think so,' she said. She climbed behind the wheel of the Range Rover. 'Are you sure about Kirsten coming round for her tea?'

Louise nodded, heading off towards her own car. 'Don't worry about her,' she called. 'You go and deal with your students. See you later.'

The two women exchanged goodbyes and drove off in opposite directions.

Roma glanced at her watch and then at the dashboard clock. She'd be at the college in ten minutes.

# 10.03 A.M.

'Come out, come out, wherever you are.'

Detective Inspector Fielding paced agitatedly back and forth in front of the large noticeboard that was attached to the rear wall of the incident room.

The board was covered with photos.

*So many photos.*

Some were of Jonathan Ridley, Callum Hughes and Marie Walker. On his desk there were piles and piles of others.

Elsewhere in the room, four video recorders turned simultaneously, displaying a montage of images on the television screens they were hooked up to. Fielding glanced from one screen to the next. Each had a police officer seated at it, a notepad in their hand.

The videos showed the same appalling images that Fielding had come to know only too well in the past couple of days. The fact that these were moving pictures only served to make them *more* repulsive.

A girl of six being raped by her father. A boy of nine being sodomised by a man in his late fifties. Two girls, no older than six, jumping in and out of a small paddling pool. Both of them naked.

DS Young was standing close to the board running his expert gaze over the photos too. Many were of the three murdered children. Others were indistinct blurs. Shots of portions of their bodies blown up and enhanced. Increased in size three, sometimes four times. Young stroked his chin thoughtfully. It seemed that the larger the pictures became, the more difficult it was to make out what they were. The harder they looked, the less they saw. He too glanced at the video images every now and then.

'Over twenty thousand images downloaded from four computers so far,' he said wearily. 'Five more to check.'

'At least we've got a start now,' Fielding said defiantly. 'The photos of the dead children all came from the same website and were downloaded less than two weeks ago.'

'Then if we find who created the site, we'll be able to track down the bastard who took those pictures. And you believe the photographer is the killer?'

Fielding shrugged. 'We know that two, probably three, of the kids were murdered in the same place,' he said. 'Or at least *photographed* in the same place.'

Young continued to gaze at the mass of photographic material. 'We don't *know* that,' he protested. 'We're just assuming.'

'And it's a reasonable assumption, I'd say. The poses, the backgrounds and the ages of the victims are all very, very similar. Let's stick with that assumption at the moment.'

He perched on the edge of his desk. 'Forensics says there were no signs of violence on the kids apart from the needle marks,' the DI mused. 'How the fuck could that be?'

Young looked around at his superior. 'You mean there would have been some bruising when they were snatched?' he asked.

'If a kid's about to be pulled into a car or a van or some kind of vehicle they're not just going to go, are they? They'd put up some kind of struggle.'

'Unless they were threatened.'

'No. They'd still struggle. They'd try to run. There'd be *something* to show that they'd been taken against their will and yet, not one single scratch on any one of them.'

'They knew their killer?'

'They were all from different backgrounds. None of them knew each other. It's unlikely.'

'But not impossible.'

'Nothing's impossible, Rob, but I'm not clinging to it.'

He crossed to the noticeboard, jabbing a finger at each of the three photos of the naked children. 'Anything strike you as strange about the poses they're in?' the DI said.

'They're all naked. All laid out on the floor. All lying on their sides, stomachs or backs.'

'Yeah, right. There isn't one where any of them are sitting up. And look at their eyes. In every one the pupils are dilated.'

'What are you thinking, guv?'

Fielding crossed to one of the phones on his desk and punched a number. 'Donna,' he said when the phone was answered, 'it's Fielding. Could you come up to the incident room, please? And bring your files on the three dead kids.'

He replaced the receiver and went back to staring at the plethora of pictures that festooned the noticeboard. A collage of death.

There was a knock on the door and Donna Thompson walked briskly in. The pathologist was dressed in a charcoal trouser suit, her hair pulled back into a loose ponytail. She cast a fleeting gaze in the direction of the television screens as if to look too long would taint her with something indescribable.

'Sorry to disturb you,' Fielding said as she joined the two policemen. 'Listen, I know we've been over this before but is there no way of estimating time of death on the three victims?'

'I can give you approximate times, I think I did, but nothing exact.' She shook her head.

'No bruises. No cuts. No contusions. No signs of violence,' Fielding murmured. 'And no fingerprints?'

'The killer wore gloves,' Donna emphasised.

'No sign of sexual interference,' Fielding said.

'Where's this going, Alan?' Donna wanted to know.

'We're not looking for a paedophile,' said the DI.

Both Young and Donna stared at him.

'This bastard's got no interest in kids,' he continued. 'Except as commodities.'

'Meaning?' Donna asked.

'He doesn't touch them. He gets no sexual pleasure from them. But he knows that others do. They get their kicks from looking at the pictures *he's* taken. He's providing a service. Lots of paedophiles like looking at pictures of kids when they're passive, right? This bastard takes their pictures when they're at their *most* passive.' Fielding looked at his colleagues. 'That's why there were no signs of struggle. He takes their pictures *after* he kills them.'

# 10.37 A.M.

Roma pushed the last of the books on to the passenger seat and closed the door of the Range Rover.

As it swung shut she saw the figure of Peter Amerton loom into view. He was a tall, slightly built individual with thick glasses perched on a hawk-like nose. Approaching his fifty-sixth birthday, Amerton had been lecturing in English literature for more than thirty years and had been a fixture at Kingsfield College long before Roma ever took up her own post there.

Amerton regarded her indifferently for a moment, locking his Fiat, which he'd parked beside her Range Rover in the college car park.

'I didn't see you there,' Roma told him.

'I move silently and without fear of detection,' Amerton said, forcing a smile. 'Perhaps you should do the same.'

Roma eyed him warily for a moment then turned to walk back towards the main doors of the college.

'I was wondering if you had a minute, Roma,' Amerton asked.

'I've got some papers to go over but I think I can spare you *some* of my precious time.' She smiled.

'It might be best if we spoke out here. Besides, what I have to say is of no consequence to anyone else anyway.'

'You're starting to sound mysterious, Peter. Why don't you put me out of my misery? What do you want to talk about?'

'I'm not sure which term one would best apply to it. Irresponsibility. Lack of morality. Perhaps even selfishness.'

'What *are* you going on about?' Roma demanded, her tone darkening.

184

'What a tangled web we weave when first we practise to deceive,' Amerton said smugly.

'You don't have to quote Sir Walter Scott at me, Peter. If you've got something to say, just say it.'

'I salute your knowledge, Roma.'

'Just get to the point, will you?'

'You have a directness your compatriot Brendan Behan would have admired,' Amerton grinned but, again, the gesture didn't touch his eyes. 'I'm talking about your involvement with one of your students. One of *my* students, too, as it happens. Michael Harper.'

Roma merely held his gaze. 'What are you saying?'

*As if you need to ask.*

'If you *are* sleeping with him, as I suggest you are, then I would, if I were you, be more, how can I put it, *discreet*.'

'What makes you think I'm sleeping with Michael Harper?'

'You might teach psychology, Roma, but even a layman has certain observational powers.'

Roma chuckled. 'If I am, what business is it of yours?' she enquired.

'As I said, there are certain factors to be taken into consideration, not least of which is your professionalism. Or should I say lack of it. How can you view Harper's work with impartiality if you're involved with him?'

'What gives you the right to speak to me like this?'

'I have the welfare of a student at heart.'

'The only thing you have at heart is your own job. What are you going to do if it's true? Go straight to the head of the college? Report me?'

'Is it true?'

'That's none of your business, Peter.'

'Have you considered the ethical implications? I doubt it.'

Roma turned away from him. 'I've got work to do,' she said. 'More important things than standing here arguing with you about nothing.'

'There are always your husband and child to consider as well.'

'Keep your theories to yourself. No one wants to hear them anyway.'

'If you don't want to attract attention then don't behave like a bitch on heat when Harper's around.'

Roma spun round. 'You pompous bastard,' she snarled and for a fleeting second she thought she saw Amerton recoil. 'You stay away from me. And don't you dare accuse me of something like that again.'

*Hit a nerve?*

Amerton watched as she stalked towards the main doors of the college, the sound of her heels clicking loudly on the tarmac.

As she disappeared inside, a slight smile creased the corners of his mouth.

'Alan, I've told you before, there *is* no physical evidence.'

Donna Thompson sat on the edge of the desk in the incident room looking around at the bank of television screens still displaying their images.

The officers watching the montage were still taking notes. Due to the nature of the material they were being forced to view, they were replaced every fifteen minutes.

'Just run over, once more, what you got from each body,' Fielding persisted.

Donna sighed.

'Indulge me,' he said, raising his eyebrows.

She flipped open the files on the three murdered children and glanced at her notes.

'There were no fingerprints on any of the bodies,' the pathologist began. 'The killer wore gloves at all times. The bodies were dumped at different locations, not the places where they were killed. No signs of violence. No marks on the corpses except the puncture wounds in the crook of the right arm. The lethal dose of heroin was administered through these puncture marks.'

'Where did you take prints from?'

Donna looked vague.

'Which parts of the bodies?' Fielding elaborated.

'Are you saying I could have missed something, Alan?' Donna asked somewhat guardedly.

'I'm clutching at fucking straws,' the DI said. 'It's a hobby of mine.'

Donna smiled. 'I can check the body of the Ridley boy again

if you want me to,' she said. 'The other two kids have been buried, as you know. If you want me to go to work on them again you'll need exhumation orders and Christ knows what else. You'll also need—'

'Yeah, I know what I'll need,' said Fielding, cutting her short. 'Forget about the other two. Concentrate on the Ridley boy. He was the most recent. There might just be something that didn't turn up the first time around.'

'Like what?' Donna enquired.

Fielding was gazing blankly at the television screens, looking at the images but not taking them in.

'Check under his finger- and toenails,' he said quietly.

'I did that. All I found was mud from the bank of the reservoir where he was discovered.'

'Check again.'

Donna looked at Fielding then cast a curious glance at DS Young who merely shrugged.

'And I want you to run fingerprint tests again,' Fielding told her.

'Where? I tried everywhere before. There wasn't an inch of his body that I didn't inspect.'

'How about inside his mouth. His lips and maybe teeth,' Fielding said, looking straight at the pathologist. 'Your first report didn't mention those.'

'Why would he touch the kid's lips?' Young wanted to know.

Fielding shrugged. 'I'm not sure,' he said. 'To alter the expression perhaps?'

'He would have kept his gloves on,' Donna offered.

'Probably. But dust them anyway.'

She sucked in a deep breath and got to her feet. 'You're the boss,' she said, heading for the door.

Fielding turned once more to look at the television screens.

# 11.42 A.M.

Nikki Reed stood at the sink rinsing scraps of food from plates, occasionally glancing out into the small back garden.

Every now and then she would stop, let out a deep, almost painful sigh, then continue with her task.

Behind her, her husband sat at the tiny kitchen table gently tapping a cigarette packet against the formica top, gazing at his wife.

The only thing that broke the silence was the music coming from the radio.

' '. . . I don't want to say I'm sorry, 'cos I know there's nothing wrong . . .'

Reed ran appraising eyes over his wife. The tight-fitting Levi's that hugged her taut buttocks, the short-sleeved T-shirt that showed so obviously that she wore no bra beneath it.

*Max Tate would have approved.*

Reed felt the knot of muscles at the side of his jaw pulsing angrily once again.

'If you want to help you could dry these things,' Nikki said, without looking round.

Reed got to his feet, tugged a teatowel from the plastic hook on the back door and began drying a plate.

The radio continued to provide its accompaniment to the funereal atmosphere.

'. . . Don't be afraid, there's no need to worry, 'cos my feelings for you are still strong . . .'

Nikki continued washing up, looking down into the soap suds. In fact, it seemed to Reed, she was looking anywhere except at him.

'Nikki . . .' he began.

'Jeff, don't,' she said flatly.

'You don't know what I'm going to say.'

'I know *exactly* what you're going to say. You want to know what happened with Max Tate.'

*'I can see it in your eyes, there is something, something you want to tell me . . .'*

'Just drop it, for Christ's sake, Jeff,' she said. 'I got him off our backs for a while.'

'I want to know *how*. What did you have to do for that cunt to persuade him to back off?'

She shook her head, her tousled blond hair falling across her face like a veil.

*'. . . see it in your eyes, there is something, that you hide from me . . .'*

Reed took a step closer to her. 'Just tell me,' he said, his mouth inches from her ear.

'And what are you going to do?' she snapped. 'Go round there and sort him out? What if he *did* touch me, Jeff? What can you do about it?'

She turned and looked straight at her husband.

*'Is there a reason why there is something, something you want to tell me . . .'*

They locked stares and she saw the fury in his eyes. Pure, undiluted, impotent rage. There was nothing he could do. They both knew that.

'And when do you go back to him?' Reed asked. 'He already owned us. Now he's got a ready-made whore who—'

She slapped him hard across the face.

Reed felt the anger rise quickly within him and he shot out a hand to grab her wrist, as if expecting another blow. As he pulled her closer to him, he saw the tears in her eyes.

The loud banging on the front door startled them both.

Nikki shook free angrily. 'I'd better go,' she said sniffing. 'It might be Max Tate.'

Reed turned away from her furiously.

She padded through the living room to the hall and paused for a moment before opening the front door.

She recognised the figure standing there immediately.

'Hello, Nikki,' said John Dawson smiling.

She embraced her brother warmly.

# 12.23 A.M.

John Dawson sat on the edge of the sofa next to his sister, the mug of tea cradled in his large hands.

He was in his early thirties. His skin looked tanned and healthy next to the pale flesh of his sibling. Several tattoos adorned each arm, hidden for the most part by the sleeves of his black Nike sweatshirt.

Dawson had listened intently for over thirty minutes as Nikki and Reed had spoken to him. Asked him how he was, what he'd been up to.

*The usual shit.*

All their questions had been answered with the minimum of effort. Information imparted only where he thought it necessary. They knew he'd been in London. Working. He was still doing well for himself. Making a crust, as he liked to put it. He moved around the country a fair bit.

*Blah, blah, blah.*

He'd seen something behind their eyes as they spoke. Felt a tension in the air. The longer the conversation went on, the more it seemed to Dawson that the oxygen was being sucked from the small room. He had glanced around once or twice while they had talked but, for the most part, he had watched their faces and gestures. Over the years, he had grown to understand as much about people from what they *didn't* say as the words they gave voice to.

Dawson sipped at what was left in his mug and shrugged. 'So what do you want me to do?' he said, looking at each of them in turn.

'Help us,' Nikki said.

Dawson nodded. 'You owe this Tate geezer twenty grand, right?' he said. 'And he wants paying. And he's going to hurt you if you don't settle up.'

'He'll kill us,' Reed said flatly.

'Whose idea was it to knock over the dealer?' Dawson asked.

'Mine,' Reed told him almost apologetically.

'You never were very expert in that area, were you, Jeff?' Dawson smiled.

'Maybe not,' Reed snapped. 'I mean, you're the man when it comes to stuff like *that*, aren't you, John? What was it the first time? Two years for GBH? Then what, three and a half for assault with a deadly weapon?'

Dawson put the mug down on the table before him. 'Shit happens,' he said, a slight smile playing on his lips. 'You still haven't told me what you want. Why you phoned me?'

'We thought you might be able to help us with some of the money,' Nikki said quietly. 'If you lend it to us we would pay you back.'

'Where the fuck do you think I'm going to get twenty grand before the end of the week, Nikki?' Dawson scoffed.

'Not all of it. Just enough to give us some breathing space.'

'And what makes you think I'd *have* that kind of money?'

'You've always got money, John.'

'I work for it.'

'Doing what?' Reed asked.

'That's *my* business, Jeff.'

'So, are you going to help us or not?' Reed wanted to know. 'You must have some friends you've worked with before who'd know how to help.'

'I work on my own now,' Dawson said. 'I don't move in the same circles.' He sat back on the sofa. 'Twenty grand by the end of the week. Maybe early *next* week if you're lucky. I haven't got it to give you.'

'Can you give us *anything*?' Nikki said imploringly.

'How about my expertise?' He looked piercingly at Reed. 'Will that do?'

'Your expertise got you sent down twice,' Reed chided.

'Yeah, but not for dogshit charges like receiving stolen goods or shoplifting. That *was* what you did your six months for, wasn't it, Jeff?'

The two men regarded each other for a moment.

'What can we do?' Nikki persisted.

'You've got no money,' Dawson intoned. 'How bad do you want it? How desperate are you?'

'We've told you.'

'So you're prepared to do anything to get it?'

'If you've got an idea then for fuck's sake just tell us,' Reed snapped.

'I've got an idea, Jeff. But I'm not sure *you've* got the balls to go through with it.'

'What is it?' Reed demanded.

'This is shit or bust,' Dawson said. 'No fucking half measures. No pissing about with little fucking drug dealers. This is *proper* business. If it works, you're sorted with Tate. You'll never see him again. You can get out of this fucking dump. Get out of the country if you want. But if you fuck it up you'll go down for fifteen years. That's your choice.' He looked at each of them in turn. 'Now, do I keep talking or not?'

# 2.17 P.M.

The flat smelled of perspiration and a stronger, muskier scent.

Roma Todd rested one hand on each of Michael Harper's spread thighs and looked up at him.

Harper's breath was coming in ragged gasps and their intensity increased as Roma bent her head forward slightly and allowed her tongue to glide over the swollen head of his erection. Beneath her fingers, the muscles in Harper's thighs tightened as she continued with her ministrations, allowing her lips to engulf his stiffness. She rested her head there for a moment longer then began to move it gently up and down his already slippery shaft.

Harper gripped her shoulders, one of his hands straying to the back of her neck but Roma pulled away slightly, looking down at her saliva glistening on his erection.

He whispered something that she didn't catch and, for interminable seconds, she merely gazed at his penis and the gradually tightening flesh of his scrotum. Then she licked from the base to the tip of his shaft and felt his erection twitch as she traced the outline of the pulsing veins.

She allowed one hand to slip from his thigh and, with eager fingers, she sought her moist cleft. As she pushed Harper ever closer to his release, she gently teased the sensitive folds of flesh between her legs, her index finger probing deeper.

Again she closed her lips over his penis and again he murmured something as she began to build up both speed and pressure with her mouth.

'Don't stop,' he breathed imploringly.

Roma knew he was very close to release and she could already taste the salty fluid seeping from the tip of his penis. Her fingers moved more urgently between her legs. She could feel the moisture coating the digits.

Roma moved her head away once more and heard Harper let out a frustrated groan. But this time she pushed him backwards on to the bed so that he was lying prone before her. Then she clambered up so that she was gazing down at him. At his throbbing shaft which, moments later, she took in one hand and rubbed so gently, one thumb gliding over the tip as she moved purposefully over his groin and lowered herself until her sex was just above his erection.

She sank down slowly, her eyes screwed tightly shut, gasping as she felt every inch of him slowly penetrate her.

Harper also gasped as the sheer pleasure overcame him, intensified seconds later as she began to ride him expertly, grinding her pubic bone against him as she felt his penis swell inside her.

She looked down at him and saw his face contort. Felt his body arching off the mattress as if trying to hurl her off then, with a grunt, he filled her with his oily white fluid and she felt its warmth inside her.

'Jesus,' he whispered, his breath coming in gasps.

A single bead of perspiration ran down her body from the hollow of her neck, between her breasts and to her navel.

She smiled at him as he gazed up with wide eyes, his mouth hanging open as he gasped for breath.

The sensations gradually subsided and she leaned forward to rest her arms on his chest.

'Fuck,' he murmured.

Roma smiled again. She felt him softening inside her and, finally, his flaccid penis slipped from the sticky embrace of her muscles.

'That was fucking amazing,' he said, his heart still pounding. He curled her light-brown hair around one index finger and looked into her eyes.

'I wonder what Professor Amerton would have said if he could have seen us?' Roma smiled.

Harper looked bemused.

'He thinks there's something going on between us,' she elaborated. 'He told me this morning. Practically warned me off.'

'What did you say?'

'I denied everything and told him to keep his fucking nose out of my business. I don't know how convincing I was. I don't really care.'

She rolled off and lay beside him.

'How does he know?' Harper asked.

'He doesn't. He's just guessing.'

'Fuck. What if he finds out that there *is* something between us?'

'It's not your problem. I've got more to lose than you have. I've told you that before. If it doesn't bother me, why should it worry you, Mike?'

He shrugged. 'I suppose you're right,' he conceded.

'Anyway, if things do get too complicated we just stop seeing each other.'

'Just like that?'

'Why not? At least that way no one gets hurt.'

'*I* get hurt, Roma. Or doesn't that matter to you?'

She leaned across and kissed him gently on the cheek. To Harper, the gesture seemed more maternal than passionate.

'I couldn't care less if Amerton suspects what's going on between us,' she said, propping herself up on one elbow.

She kissed him again. This time on the lips and he responded, his tongue seeking hers, flicking past the hard white edges of her teeth. They were both breathing heavily when they parted.

'What time do you have to pick up your daughter?' he asked, glancing at his watch.

Her hand slid down his chest and across his belly towards his stiffening penis. 'Not yet,' she murmured.

# 2.58 P.M.

DI Fielding gazed into his coffee cup as he stirred it.

Opposite him DS Young was spooning sugar into his own cup, his eyes flicking back and forth between photos of Marie Walker, Callum Hughes and Jonathan Ridley.

'Put them away,' said Fielding, nodding in the direction of the photos. 'We're on a break, remember?'

Young smiled and slipped the pictures into the inside pocket of his jacket.

'Cheers,' said Fielding, raising his cup. He glanced around the café in which they sat. Red-check tablecloths and small vases of fresh flowers on each table. There was a pleasing smell of freshly baked pasty in the air. Two waitresses stood talking quietly behind the till, all their customers having been served. It was relatively quiet inside the café anyway and the two policemen had chosen a table in a far corner beneath a copy of Constable's *The Haywain*.

'This is very civilised, isn't it?' Young commented. 'Afternoon tea?'

'Civilised,' Fielding murmured. 'That sums up Kingsfield, doesn't it? At least until these murders started.' He sipped more of his coffee then looked across at his subordinate. 'How's Jenny?' he asked. 'The baby's due soon, isn't it?'

'Less than two weeks.'

'What do you want? Boy or girl?'

'Well, as the old cliché goes, as long as it's OK I don't mind but, if I'm pushed, I'd rather have a girl.'

'Really,' Fielding said smiling. 'Most guys want a boy. So they can play football with him, and all that crap.'

'That doesn't bother me.'

'You want a daddy's girl?'

Young smiled but it faded rapidly. 'Sometimes I wonder if we're doing the right thing, guv,' he muttered.

Fielding looked puzzled.

'Having a kid,' the DS elaborated. 'Bringing a kid into *this* world. I think that's struck me even harder because of what's been happening lately.'

'I can see your point, Rob, but if you kept thinking about all the bad things you'd never have kids. No one would.'

They sat in silence for a moment then Young spoke again. 'Do you think the parents of those three dead kids ever wished they'd never—'

Fielding cut him short. 'No,' he said. 'They had seven, eight years with their children. And I know it's not right, you shouldn't bury your kids, but at least they had *some* happiness together.'

The DI stared down into his cup as if hoping to find his next sentence there.

'Did *you* ever want kids?' Young asked tentatively. 'If you don't mind me asking.'

'We talked about it. Every couple must do, I suppose. We might have got around to it sooner or later. But I don't have to think about that any more, do I?' He attempted a smile but couldn't manage it.

Young was about to say something (something about how sorry he was that Fielding's wife had been killed in that accident. Something about respecting his strength for being able to go on) when the ringing of Fielding's mobile phone broke the silence.

The DI reached for the Nokia and pressed it to his ear.

Young watched his face as he listened to whoever was on the other end of the line.

'You're sure?' the DI said. 'Yeah. That's great. Thanks.' He switched off.

'That was Donna,' Fielding said, that old fire burning once more in his gaze. 'She just completed another examination of the Ridley boy's body.'

'And?'

'She found two fingerprints on the inside of Jonathan Ridley's upper lip. She's sent them down to Hendon for analysis. If the bastard who killed him has ever been printed, they'll have a confirmation for us by tomorrow.'

# 3.37 P.M.

The puppy was a cross-breed. Predominantly Labrador but with some greyhound in it – it had that lean look to it.

Louise Barton didn't know much about dogs except that they needed lots of attention, cost a fortune in vet's bills and, in this young state, were prone to leave puddles of urine any- and every-where around the house and garden.

She watched the dog bounding about near the conservatory, chasing the small rubber ball that was being thrown for it.

Her daughter and Kirsten Todd were laughing happily as they ran around the garden with the animal, displaying equally bound-less energy.

Louise opened the freezer and gazed at the vast array of food, trying to decide what to give the girls for their dinner. She settled on pizza and chips. Always a winner with seven-year-olds. She smiled to herself.

She laid the table in the kitchen, glancing occasionally at the portable TV. There was a quiz show on and Louise happily answered questions as she went about her task. Occasionally she would shake her head in disbelief when a contestant answered wrongly.

With everything prepared, she poured two glasses of orange squash for the girls and made herself a coffee, then placed all three on a tray and carried them out into the garden.

The sun was struggling out from behind a bank of cloud and it had some warmth in it. Louise sat down on the wooden bench on the patio and watched the two girls chasing the dog around. She sipped her coffee and glanced around the garden. The grass needed cutting. The flowerbeds needed weeding. Jobs for the weekend, she mused. She'd mention it to her husband when he got home that evening.

'Come on, girls,' she called. 'Time for a rest.'

'Oh, Mum,' Chloe protested.

'Come and have a drink,' Louise insisted. 'Sam looks like he could do with a break too.'

She looked down and saw that the dog's water bowl was full. The animal lolloped over towards her and began lapping at the cool water. The two girls followed, somewhat reluctantly, and sat down at the wooden table where they both drank thirstily.

'Kirsten asked her mum if *she* could have a dog,' Chloe said.

'What kind of dog, Kirsten?' Louise asked.

'Any kind, really,' Kirsten told her. 'My dad says they're expensive though.'

Louise nodded. 'That's true,' she agreed.

*Not that your father couldn't afford to keep one. How much did the local paper say his company profit was last year? Four or five million?*

'Mum says that somebody should be with it all day if it's a puppy,' Kirsten continued.

Louise nodded again. 'I spoke to your mum earlier,' she said. 'She'll pick you up about six.'

'Can't Kirsten stay tonight, Mum?' Chloe pleaded.

'Not tonight. It's a school night. You know no one stays on school nights. I'll have a word with Kirsten's mum, and she can stay one weekend. If she wants to.'

Kirsten nodded eagerly and Louise smiled.

The dog finished lapping at its water and wandered across to the table where the two girls sat. It moved close to Chloe who stroked its head.

'You stroke him,' she said to Kirsten.

She got down from her seat and moved towards the dog.

It sat where it was for a moment, watching her, then it began to growl.

'Sam, that's not very friendly,' Louise said grinning.

Kirsten drew nearer.

The dog's lips slid back to reveal its teeth and the growl became deeper as it fixed its eyes on Kirsten.

The smile on Louise Barton's lips faded.

Kirsten was standing two or three feet from the dog now, one hand extended towards it.

The animal got to its feet, the hair along its spine rising. The growl became a bark.

Kirsten took a step back.

Again it barked but, even in that act of defiance, it backed away from Kirsten, teeth still bared.

'Sam,' snapped Chloe.

The dog barked again and moved even further back.

Kirsten stood motionless.

Louise got to her feet, worried that the puppy might attack Kirsten. It was barking furiously now, its body quivering, still moving away from Kirsten. Finally it turned and ran off down the garden.

Chloe began to run after the fleeing animal but Louise restrained her.

'Leave him,' she said, holding her daughter close to her and glancing at Kirsten.

'Why was he growling like that?' Chloe whined.

'He just needs to get used to strangers,' Louise said, still looking at Kirsten. 'That's all.'

Kirsten shrugged and sat down again.

At the bottom of the garden, the dog continued to bark.

# 3.41 P.M.

'It still sounds fucking crazy to me.'

Jeff Reed poured himself another measure of Jack Daniel's and slumped back on the sofa.

'Maybe it does,' John Dawson said. 'But what choice have you got?'

Nikki looked from her husband to her brother and back again. They had been talking for more than two hours now. To her it seemed as if they had been saying the same words over and over again and still she felt she could not appreciate the gravity of what she had heard. Could not fully accept it.

First she and her husband had listened. Then, when Dawson had finished speaking, they had each reacted in their own individual way.

With shock. Disbelief. Amazement. And fear.

Every emotion had run through Nikki's mind with dizzying speed and only now was there some semblance of clarity.

'Do you think it could work?' she asked, even though it was a question she had already voiced more times than she could remember that afternoon.

Dawson shrugged. 'There's no reason why not,' he told her, also aware that he had spoken the litany ad nauseam in that small living room.

'Well, I'm not sure,' Reed admitted.

'It'll work if you've got the balls to do it and to do it right,' Dawson said. 'Do as I tell you and there won't be any problems.'

'You sound like you've done it before,' Reed challenged.

'It's not rocket science,' Dawson intoned. 'It's common sense. And bottle. If you haven't got the bottle then forget it. Both of you.'

He looked at his sister who swallowed hard.

'What do *you* stand to gain out of this?' Reed asked.

'The joy of having helped my sister and beloved brother-in-law.' The sarcasm in Dawson's words irritated Reed.

'Come on – how much?'

'Thirty per cent,' Dawson said.

Nikki ran a hand through her hair and exhaled deeply. '*If* we do it. *If* it works,' she murmured.

'It had better work, for *your* sakes.' He took a drag on his cigarette. 'Now are we going to sit around here all fucking day and night talking about this or are we going to do something? What's your answer?'

'I thought we already gave it,' Nikki said quietly. 'We don't have any choice.' She looked at her husband.

'Hold on—' Reed protested.

'No, fuck it, Jeff,' snapped Dawson, interrupting him. 'You *don't* have any choice. You've got nothing left to bargain with. In less than a week Max Tate's going to come looking for that money you owe him and if you haven't got it then you'd better let me know now where you'd both like to be buried. That is if they ever find your fucking bodies once he's finished with you.'

Reed downed what was left in his glass and wiped his mouth with the back of his hand.

'We've got to do it, Jeff,' Nikki insisted.

'And if it goes wrong? If we get caught?'

'Either Tate gets you or the law do,' Dawson said. 'It's not much of a choice but beggars can't be choosers, can they? If you don't pay Tate then he *will* kill you. If you do this right, there's a chance you'll get away with it. No one will get hurt and you'll be sorted. That's your odds, Jeff. Slim and none. Now what's your answer?'

'And you'll help us?' Reed persisted.

'I've fucking said I would, haven't I?'

'I say yes,' Nikki offered.

'Just like that?' Reed chided.

'No, Jeff,' she retorted. 'Not just like that. I know what's at stake, same as you do. I know what could happen. I know what *will* happen if we fuck this up. I also know what will happen if Max Tate doesn't get his money.'

Reed looked at Dawson.

'In or out, Jeff?' Dawson wanted to know. 'No more pissing about.'

Reed nodded. Slowly at first then almost madly. 'All right,' he said, his voice barely audible.

'Thank Christ for that,' Dawson said wearily.

'How do we decide—' Nikki began but Dawson cut her short. He reached inside his jacket and pulled out a piece of crumpled newspaper. It had been torn from a national. He smoothed it out on the small table in the middle of the room.

'Read it,' he said, pushing it towards his sister.

She cleared her throat and picked up the scrap of paper, her hand trembling slightly. 'It says he's a millionaire,' she began.

'*Multi*-millionaire,' Dawson corrected her.

'He's head of a record label. Lives in Kingsfield,' Nikki continued. 'He's got a wife and daughter.'

'What's his name?' Reed asked.

'David Todd,' Nikki said.

Dawson eyed them both evenly. 'It's his kid we're going to snatch,' he told them.

# 6.19 P.M.

'You're quiet,' said Roma Todd, glancing at her daughter.

Kirsten was sitting in the passenger seat of the Range Rover gazing absently out of the side window.

'I'm just tired,' said the child, without looking round.

Roma reached across with one hand and felt her daughter's forehead. 'Do you feel OK?' she asked.

'Just tired.'

'You did take your tablets this morning, didn't you?'

'Mum, I just feel tired. And I'm not in a very good mood.'

Roma suppressed a grin as she turned the vehicle into their street. 'Why's that?' she asked.

'I don't think Chloe's dog likes me,' Kirsten said miserably. 'He kept growling at me and he wouldn't let me stroke him.'

'Well, he's only a puppy, darling, and they get nervous around strangers.'

Kirsten shrugged, still gazing out of the side window.

Roma brought the vehicle to a halt outside their house and they both clambered out, Kirsten trudging dejectedly towards the front door.

'What time will Dad be home tonight?' the little girl asked as Roma opened the front door.

'He didn't say,' she answered, watching as Kirsten took off her shoes and placed them neatly beneath the staircase. 'Why?'

'I wanted to ask him about having a dog. He said he'd think about us getting one.'

'He's probably *still* thinking about it. He's got a lot on his mind.'

*He always has, hasn't he?*

Kirsten wandered into the sitting room and put the TV on while Roma started to make herself a coffee in the kitchen. She stood watching the kettle for a moment then changed her mind and retrieved a wine glass and a bottle of red. She poured a measure and drank it.

David had said he'd be home around eight. She wasn't going to hold her breath. But the fact that there were no messages on the answerphone made her hopeful that he might actually arrive when he'd promised.

She took her wine into the sitting room and seated herself on the sofa close to Kirsten. The little girl was lying with her head on a cushion gazing distractedly at the television screen.

'Why didn't Chloe's dog like me, Mum?' she said pitifully.

'Dogs are funny sometimes. Like people. They can't like everyone, can they? I mean, *you* don't like everyone you meet, do you now?'

'Most people.'

Roma grinned and rested one hand on her daughter's leg. She felt the heat immediately.

The skin was pale and looked cool but Roma could feel tremendous warmth in it. As if Kirsten were running an abnormally high fever. She looked down at her daughter who was looking at the TV, untroubled by her mother's touch.

Roma pulled her hand away as slowly as she could, her fingertips tingling.

'Are you *sure* you feel OK?' she asked, attempting to mask the concern in her voice.

Kirsten merely nodded.

'You'd better get your pyjamas on,' Roma told her.

'Oh, Mum.'

'Do as you're told.'

Kirsten got to her feet and hurried out of the room. Roma heard the sound of her footfalls on the stairs as she scurried to get changed. She regarded her own fingertips closely. They were still tingling from where they had touched Kirsten's flesh.

Roma rubbed them gently and as she did she noticed that her hand was shaking.

# 7.23 P.M.

The room was small and cramped by the self-assembly units that had been crammed around the sofa bed. There were bookshelves on three walls, one of them mounted at such an obtuse angle that a scented candle barely balanced on it. The others held a few books but mostly cheap ornaments.

'Will you be all right in here,' Nikki asked as she pushed open the bedroom door and peered in.

'I've slept in worse places,' John Dawson told her, managing a smile. He was unpacking the black holdall that he'd arrived with, placing T-shirts and jeans on the bed before finding temporary resting places for them in the chest of drawers close by.

'Thanks,' Nikki said with mock indignation.

'I didn't mean it like that,' her brother explained.

'Places like prison, you mean?'

'Some prisons. Some places on the outside are worse than the nick.'

'And you'd know?'

He smiled again as he continued to unpack.

'Why didn't you get in touch before, John?' she wanted to know. 'You must have got my messages. Known how badly I needed to talk to you.'

'If I could have found the time I would. I told you before, I was busy.'

'Doing what?'

'Earning some money.'

'Shacked up with a girl?'

'Why is that so important to my little sister?' He placed the last of his clothes in the drawer then zipped up the holdall and placed it at the bottom of the sofa bed. 'You've got more important things to worry about than whether or not I've got a girl-friend.'

She nodded.

'Come here,' he murmured.

She crossed to him and he embraced her.

'I'm scared, John,' she said, holding him tight. 'Scared of the situation we're in. Scared of what we've got to do. Scared of what could happen.'

'Don't worry about it.' He held her close to him. 'If I ask you something, will you tell me the truth?'

She nodded.

'How the fuck did you get into Max Tate for twenty grand?'

'It just seemed to build up.'

'Did Jeff's gambling have anything to do with it?'

He felt her shiver slightly. It was answer enough.

'He's a fucking prick,' Dawson snapped.

Nikki pulled back and looked into her brother's eyes. 'He's my husband and I love him, John,' she said. 'What did you want me to do? Just walk away from him? Some of it was my fault too. I wanted things. Things for the house. For myself. It wasn't all Jeff's fault.'

Dawson looked at her expressionlessly. 'He's weak, Nikki,' he said. 'And if this is going to work, we can't afford that.'

'He'll be fine.'

'I hope you're right. Because *I'm* not going down for him or anyone else.'

She nodded and turned towards the door. 'Dinner'll be ready in a minute. I'll call you.'

He heard her footsteps as she descended the stairs. Then after a moment he sat on the end of the bed and unzipped the holdall once again. There was another smaller black canvas bag inside and Dawson carefully loosened the drawstring around the top of it.

Everything he needed was in there.

He re-tied the string then zipped up the holdall and secured it with a small padlock. He didn't want prying eyes to discover what he had inside.

Not yet.

# 9.16 P.M.

'If I could have got home earlier, then I would,' said David Todd apologetically. 'I'm sorry, Roma.'

'It's OK, really,' she told him, legs drawn up beneath her on the sofa. She sipped at her red wine and regarded her husband evenly.

He'd poured himself a Glenfiddich and was seated opposite her, sipping from the crystal tumbler. The TV was on but the sound was off. Their voices were all that disturbed the peacefulness inside the living room.

'No scenes? No arguments?' Todd asked, a slight smile on his lips.

Roma shook her head.

'Not tonight anyway?' he continued.

A long silence passed between them, finally broken by Todd. 'Was Kirsten all right when you put her to bed?' he wanted to know.

'She *seems* fine.'

'But?'

'Like I said, she seems fine.' Roma got to her feet and poured herself another glass of wine. 'She's been talking about us getting a dog again. Chloe Barton has one so . . .' She let the sentence trail off.

Todd shook his head. 'It's not the right time, Roma. Maybe after we hear what the doctors say.'

'What, you mean if they say she's got a chance of living another year or two then it might be worth spending the money?'

'That wasn't what I meant.'

Another silence descended.

'I might have to go to New York for a few days at the beginning of next month,' Todd finally announced. 'There's some
stuff that needs sorting out over there. Maybe you and Kirsten
could come too. Go shopping, see some sights while I do what
I have to do.'

'I've got lectures, David, and Kirsten's got school.'

'It was just a thought. You're always moaning that I'm never
here, that we don't spend enough time together as a family. I
thought—'

She cut him short. 'You can't buy us off, you know,' she
chided. 'Shopping trips to New York. It won't work, David.'

'What won't work?' he snapped irritably.

'Flying her halfway across the world isn't going to make Kirsten
better, is it?'

'There might be doctors in the States who could help her.
Experts—'

'There *are* no experts on her condition. You know that. We
probably know as much about it as most of the doctors she's
seen.'

Todd downed what was left in his glass and poured himself
another.

'If you have to go to New York, David, then go. Don't think
you need my approval or my blessing.'

'I know I wouldn't get them. Even if I wanted them. Which
I don't. I work every hour God sends for this family and I never
get any thanks for it.'

'Is that why you do it, David? To earn our gratitude?'

He shook his head and refilled his glass, angrily taking several
large swallows. 'Fuck you, Roma,' he said.

She smiled humourlessly. 'But you won't, will you, David,'
she said quietly. 'You *won't* fuck me.'

He put his glass down and crossed to her, pulling her roughly
to her feet. He pressed his mouth to hers and she tasted the
whisky on his lips. Simultaneously he pulled at the stud of her

jeans, tugging it free, pulling the zip down. Todd pushed one hand inside the smooth cotton of her panties, stirring her pubic hair. His other hand sought her breasts. He squeezed each in turn through the material of her T-shirt then he pushed her backwards.

'Get off me,' she protested.

She fell on to the sofa and he knelt before her, tugging at the legs of her jeans, pulling them over her bare feet and moving closer.

Todd slid his trousers off to reveal his erection. He undid his shirt, tugging so hard that a button flew off and landed on the carpet nearby. He grabbed for her knickers and tore the flimsy material, snapping the elastic.

Both of them were breathing heavily as Roma spread her legs, as if challenging him to enter her.

He moved closer, the swollen head of his penis nudging her cleft. 'You want it?' he snarled, angrily.

He licked the tips of his index and middle finger and rubbed them gently over her labia, lubricating her. Preparing her. He pushed hard into her, gritting his teeth for a second as his penis was finally enveloped by the warmth of her sex. He thrust and continued his short, sharp movements, his breath coming in gasps.

She raked her fingernails down his chest, grazing him, breaking the skin in three places as she thrust back against his penetration, forcing him deeper. Todd grabbed her wrists and slammed her hands back against the sofa, pinning her beneath him.

Roma felt his penis stiffen even more inside her, saw his face contort. 'Go on,' she said, knowing he was close to release. His grip on her wrists tightened as he held her beneath him, pinned by his weight and strength. He was glaring down at her with anger in his eyes. Thrusting into her with something approaching fury.

As he climaxed he moved his hips backwards, pulling free, his erection slipping from within her, his white fluid spurting across her belly and pubic hair.

He sank back on his haunches, his breath ragged.

Roma looked down at the semen streaked across her flesh then at Todd. When he looked up he saw the contempt in her eyes.

'That's what you wanted, wasn't it?' he gasped.

'Not quite,' she breathed, slipping her fingers into his seed and rubbing it into her skin. She pulled a tissue from her pocket and wiped it off then she pulled up her jeans and headed for the door. She tossed the sodden tissue in his direction.

'I'm going to have a shower,' she told him. 'Wash it away. That's what you want me to do, isn't it, David?'

She closed the door behind her, leaving him breathless on the floor.

'Fucking bitch,' he hissed.

# 10.29 P.M.

They'd stolen the car an hour earlier. It had been parked in a road a couple of streets away from the Oak Apple.

Reed had suggested taking one from the car park of the pub itself but Dawson had merely shaken his head. It had been he who had hot-wired the old Renault and driven it across Kingsfield to where they now sat. The lights of the town were visible behind them. The town lay in a slight hollow, overlooked by the rising ground upon which the surrounding houses were built.

With the vehicle light turned off, the orange tip of Dawson's cigarette was the only illumination within the gloom of the Renault. There were streetlights set at regular intervals along the road but the two men had parked in the enveloping blackness between them.

Lights burned in the windows of a number of houses. Figures could occasionally be glimpsed within them. But, for the most part, the street was quiet.

Dawson wound down the window and flicked his cigarette butt out into the street. 'You can smell the money,' he murmured, glancing up and down the street.

All the houses were large, approachable by driveways. Many had gates at the top of these tarmac or gravel tracks. Some were protected by high hedges, others by fences. Beyond them, however, it was possible to see well-manicured lawns and immaculately kept flowerbeds.

'Nikki would love to live in one of these,' said Reed.

'If what we're planning works, she'll be able to,' Dawson told him.

'Yeah, *if*.'

'You know, Jeff, one of the reasons you were always small-time was because you always *thought* small. Burglaries. Nicking stuff from shops. You never had the balls for anything bigger.'

'Sorry to disappoint you, John,' Reed sneered. 'I forgot you were the fucking specialist.'

Dawson continued gazing out of the window at the large houses all around them.

'If you'd been *that* good, you wouldn't have got caught, would you?' Reed continued.

'Maybe, but look at it this way. *I'm* not the one who owes a loan shark twenty grand. *I'm* not the one who's pissed away his money at a bookies. *I'm* not the one who's going to get his fucking head kicked in if I don't come up with the cash.' He looked at Reed. 'Am I?'

Reed didn't answer.

'And just remember this, Jeff,' Dawson continued. 'I'm doing this for Nikki. Not for you. I'm helping *her*. I couldn't give a toss if they nail *you* to a wall by your bollocks.'

The two men sat in silence for long moments. It was Reed who finally spoke.

'I thought things took weeks of planning,' he said, shifting uncomfortably in the passenger seat.

'What things?'

'Kidnapping.'

Dawson shrugged. 'We're grabbing a kid, that's it,' he said. 'No big deal. We take her to the place I mentioned, send the ransom note and wait for the money.'

'And what if he doesn't pay?'

'Then he'll get his daughter back in fucking pieces, won't he?'

'And we're looking at a murder charge.'

Dawson shook his head and exhaled wearily. 'You worry too much, Jeff,' he said. 'He's going to pay. Anybody would.'

'And what about the law?'

'We let them know that if the law are involved then the kid dies.'

'How long do we give them?'

'Forty-eight hours. That's long enough. He can afford it. Any of the bastards living around here could. Rich cunts.' He hawked and spat into the road. 'They've all got money to burn. Todd more than most.' He glanced down the street towards the white painted house with the leaded windows. On the roof of the double garage beside it, there was a weather vane. It turned slowly in the gentle breeze.

'But the kid'll have bodyguards and—'

'Don't talk shit. He owns a record company, he's not the Sultan of Oman. There might be a nanny. That's it. No bodyguards. Even if there are we can handle them, can't we?'

Reed remained silent.

'Jeff. I said, we can handle them, can't we?' Dawson insisted.

Reed nodded, the gesture almost invisible within the black interior of the car.

'Don't you bottle this,' Dawson said menacingly. 'When the time comes I don't want you hesitating. If you fuck up then *I'm* in the shit too and I won't let that happen. Got it?'

Again Reed nodded. 'Don't worry about me,' he said.

They sat gazing at the house for a moment longer. Dawson lit another cigarette and sucked on it, blowing out smoke in a long blue-grey stream.

'How did you find out about Todd anyway?' Reed wanted to know.

'Newspapers. TV. Does it matter?'

'I just wondered.'

'And now you know.'

Dawson reached forward and started the car, the sparks from the stripped wires creating a bright spark inside the Renault.

'We need to be back here early tomorrow,' Dawson said, pressing down on the accelerator. 'Get a good look at the kid. See how she's transported about. Who drives her. That kind of shit.'

'When do we take her?'

'When the time's right.'

He guided the car back down the road in the direction of Kingsfield.

Reed glanced over his shoulder in the direction of the Todds' house.

# 11.27 P.M.

Roma entered the room quietly. She stepped over a couple of books that lay on the floor, moved past the toy chest and the mountain of stuffed animals that regarded her silently.

Kirsten didn't stir. Roma could hear her low breathing as she moved across the room towards the window. She eased it shut and locked it then turned to the bed and tucked in one loose end of the duvet.

From the bedside table, a porcelain doll watched her with lifeless eyes as she headed back towards the door as quietly as she could.

'Mum.'

The sound startled her and she spun round.

Kirsten was still lying down but her eyes were open. Roma could see them glistening in the shaft of light spearing through the gap in the half-open bedroom door.

'Sorry, darling, I didn't mean to wake you up,' Roma said quietly. 'Go back to sleep.'

'I heard shouting,' Kirsten said.

Roma hesitated. 'It was probably just the television,' she answered.

'It sounded like you and Dad.'

*Are you going to tell her the truth?*

Roma moved away from the door and headed back to her daughter's bed. She sat gently on the side of it and began smoothing a hand over Kirsten's hair.

'What did you hear?' she wanted to know.

'Shouting. Like you and Dad were arguing.'

221

'You were probably just dreaming.'

Kirsten didn't look convinced. 'Does Dad love me?' she said, slowly.

Roma was temporarily taken aback but did her best to hide the surprise.

'Of course he does,' she answered, attempting to suppress the note of incredulity in her voice. 'We both do. You know that. We both love you more than anything in the world. Why do you ask?'

'I just wondered.'

Roma tucked the duvet around her daughter's neck.

'I like it when he puts me to bed,' Kirsten continued. 'When he reads me stories.'

'He does it as often as he can. But you know he has to work. He doesn't always get home in time to do it.'

Kirsten nodded.

'Are you going to go back to sleep for me now?' Roma asked, kissing her daughter on the forehead.

Again the little girl nodded.

Roma tucked her in once again, kissed her on the forehead and got to her feet.

'What shall I dream about, Mum?' Kirsten called as her mother reached the door.

Roma hesitated.

*Dream that we are a happy, normal family.*

'Dream about your friends at school,' she said finally. 'Dream about the seaside.'

Kirsten pulled the duvet tighter around her neck as Roma pulled the door closed.

'Sleep tight,' she whispered.

'Good night, Mum.'

'I love you.'

Roma stood with her back to the bedroom door for a moment, almost unwilling to walk back across the landing to her own room.

She knew that her husband was still downstairs. Perhaps she should go down and tell him what Kirsten had just told her. But, she reasoned, that would only lead to another argument.

*Another one Kirsten might hear?*

Wearily, Roma padded back to her own room and climbed into bed. She lay back and waited, in vain, for sleep to come. Every now and then she could hear Todd moving about in the kitchen or sitting room below her.

An hour later he was still down there and Roma was still awake. She glanced at the luminous green hands on the clock and, once again, wished that sleep would envelop her.

It didn't.

THURSDAY, MARCH 6$^{TH}$

# 7.58 A.M.

Nikki Reed knocked once then pushed the bedroom door open, careful not to spill the mug of tea she held in her other hand.

The room was empty. The sofa bed had been made and folded up.

Of her brother there was no sign.

She hesitated a moment then turned and made her way back downstairs.

Her husband was in the kitchen, pouring milk into a bowl. He sat down at the small table and began eating.

'Did you hear John go out this morning?' she asked, pushing a couple of slices of bread into the toaster.

Reed shook his head. 'He comes and goes when he wants,' he muttered.

'And you don't know where he is?'

'Probably planning another crime of the century,' Reed sneered. 'How the fuck should *I* know where he is, he's your brother.'

Nikki regarded him warily for a moment. 'I just thought that with today . . .' her voice faltered then trailed away.

'What do you mean? You thought that as we're going to kidnap some millionaire's daughter today, he might have been around to talk about it. Is that it?'

She buttered her toast and sat down opposite her husband. 'Look, I'm as nervous about this as you are, Jeff,' she said irritably.

'Are you? I doubt it.'

'What's that supposed to mean?'

'Well, big brother's taking care of everything, isn't he? Why the fuck are any of us concerned?'

'He's trying to help us.'

'Help us straight into fucking prison.'

'If anything goes wrong, *he's* in trouble too.'

'He's already *been* in trouble, hasn't he? He's done time. No one knows what he's been up to in the last few years. He turns up here every now and then, out of the blue, and that's it.'

'He's here this time because we asked him to be.'

'And he's sticking around because there's money in it for him.'

'So what? If it gets Max Tate off our backs then isn't it worth it?'

Reed shrugged. 'Why do we need your brother to keep Max Tate off our backs?' he snapped. 'You could do that yourself, couldn't you? Go and visit him. See what he wants you to do for him.'

'Fuck you, Jeff. Don't bring that up again.'

He regarded her angrily for a moment then continued eating, gazing into the depths of his cereal bowl.

'The kid won't be hurt, will she?' Nikki said finally.

Reed looked vague.

'When you take her, you won't hurt her,' she persisted.

'You heard what your brother said. Forty-eight hours. Her family will get forty-eight hours to pay the ransom. After that . . .' He shrugged.

She swallowed hard. 'Did you see her last night?' she asked eventually.

Reed shook his head. 'We just watched the house,' he told her.

'What's it like?'

'Big. Expensive.' A slight smile creased his lips. 'I told your brother it was the sort of place you would have loved to live in. I wish I could have given it to you.'

He scraped the last of the cereal from the bowl then got to his feet and rinsed it under the tap.

Nikki chewed her toast slowly.

'I'm going out,' Reed said. 'I need some air.'

'Where are you going?'

'Just down to the shops to get a paper. I won't be long.'

She heard the front door close behind him.

# 8.03 A.M.

John Dawson lit a cigarette and blew out a stream of smoke. He walked slowly around the room as he spoke, his companion remaining motionless in the doorway. 'I'll need it for two days, maybe three, tops.'

The other figure in the room didn't speak.

'Same as last time,' Dawson continued. 'Same deal. Same money. You got no problem with that, have you?'

The other figure shook its head.

'I don't want to be disturbed,' Dawson said. 'I want to be able to come and go without anyone seeing me or getting in my way. You told me that this place was going to be empty for another six months, right?'

Again the other figure nodded in compliance.

'And most of the places nearby are going to be empty too? So I'll have the privacy I need?' Dawson insisted.

He smiled as the figure signalled in affirmation.

'I don't want to see *you* either,' Dawson added. 'Not until this is over.'

Another nod.

Dawson stopped and sat down on one of the two rickety wooden chairs in the small basement.

The dwelling consisted of a small living room which, as well as the wooden chairs, contained a portable single hotplate electric hob in one corner. It was perched on a stainless steel worktop close to the sink. The surface was stained and rusted, and the sink itself was the colour of excrement, especially around the plughole.

A threadbare grey carpet covered the wooden floor and also extended through a narrow arch, and into a tiny bedroom barely large enough to accommodate the camp bed within. There were no sheets on the stained mattress, just a striped pillow at one end. The wallpaper had been painted over with a dark-green paint that was peeling in a number of places revealing the flowered pattern beneath. There were patches of damp on the skirting boards and also on some parts of the wall.

'It's going to need some work when someone finally moves in,' Dawson said conversationally. He got to his feet and followed the figure outside.

'Keys,' he said curtly, extending his hand.

The figure dropped a bunch into his outstretched palm and turned to walk away.

'You haven't *seen* me,' Dawson said, not taking his eyes from his companion. 'You don't *know* me.' He closed his fist around the keys. 'I'll be in touch when it's over.'

He walked up the five steps that led to street level then turned and looked back at the other figure.

'You stay here for a minute, give me time to walk away,' he instructed.

Dawson slipped the keys into his jacket pocket then set off briskly down the street. When he came to the end he turned and looked back in the direction of the house he'd just left. Like most of the others in the thoroughfare, it was empty. Some of the buildings were practically derelict.

He reached into his pocket and took out his mobile. As he walked he jabbed digits.

It began to ring.

As he waited for it to be answered, he spotted a bus pulling up at the bottom of the road. Dawson sprinted towards it and hauled himself up on the running board. He ambled down the vehicle and found a seat alone. As he sat, the phone was answered. He recognised Nikki's voice immediately.

'It's me,' he said. 'I've just been sorting something out. Yeah, everything's fine. We'll go ahead today, just like we said. Get Jeff to meet me in twenty minutes on the top level of the multi-storey near the multiplex in Kingsfield. Got that?' He switched off.

# 8.25 A.M.

Detective Inspector Fielding carried the styrofoam cup carefully along the corridor to his office, trying not to spill any of the strong coffee as he walked.

Once inside, he sat down at his desk and regarded the drink warily for a moment before sipping it.

*Christ, it was strong.*

Fielding forced himself to drink more. He needed the caffeine to jolt his mind into action.

He'd had trouble sleeping the previous night. A number of things had caused this wakefulness. The pressures of the case. Anxiety about the source of the fingerprint found on Jonathan Ridley's body.

And thoughts about Kate.

Most of the time he could cope with these but, every now and then, the realisation that she was gone for ever became almost unbearable. Last night, lying alone in their double bed, he had found himself reaching out for where she should have been.

Perhaps if she were alive she would make this case easier to bear. She would have listened to him as he poured out every dark and oppressive thought clouding his mind. She would have sat patiently while he unburdened himself of some of the horrors he had witnessed. But she *wasn't* there. He had no one's company but his own.

He drank more coffee, winced and added another sachet of sugar. It didn't really help but he persevered.

His desk was groaning with the sheer weight of material on

it. Photos of all kinds but mainly the pictures of the three dead children which had been discovered on the website.

On each one the child had been photographed on what looked like a white sheet pinned up against a dark background. It was almost impossible to make out what was behind them although Fielding had asked for the images to be enhanced as much as possible. There could be something that might at least lead them to a location.

*Just one little break, that would be enough.*

He wondered too if the fingerprint would yield anything worthwhile.

If the owner of the print had been arrested before then there was the possibility of a match. The fingerprint had been with the specialists at Hendon for nearly a day. Surely they would come back with something?

*And if they didn't?*

If the perpetrator had been printed then there was a chance of finding him. If not . . .

Fielding sipped at the creosote-like coffee again and found that the foul taste was hardly noticeable any longer. The more he stared at the pictures of the murdered children, the less everything around him seemed to matter.

He hardly heard the knock on his office door.

DS Young finally tired of waiting and walked straight in. 'You all right, guv?' he asked, looking at the wan expression on his superior's face.

'Yeah,' Fielding said. 'I'm just tired.' He finally looked up at Young. 'You got anything, Rob?'

'The three photos are being worked up in the lab. They should be ready in an hour or so.'

'What about the owners of the computers they were found on?'

'Nothing to tie them to any of the murders. They all say they were checking out the site and just found the pictures there.'

Fielding sat back in his chair and sighed.

'What about the fingerprint from the Ridley boy?' he wanted to know.

'Nothing yet.'

The DI got to his feet. 'It's all a fucking game, isn't it?' he complained. 'And there isn't a thing we can do about it except wait. We either catch the bastard or we get ready to pin another dead kid's picture on the wall.'

Young didn't speak. There was nothing else to say.

# 8.49 A.M.

'What if she's already gone?' Jeff Reed tapped the steering wheel of the stolen Astra agitatedly and glanced once again at the house.

Dawson didn't answer. His gaze was fixed on the home of David and Roma Todd.

Reed fumbled for a cigarette, his hand shaking. He dropped it and made to retrieve it from the floor of the vehicle.

'Leave it,' snapped Dawson.

'I need a fucking fag,' Reed told him.

Dawson dug in his jacket pocket and shoved a pack of Rothmans towards his companion.

Reed lit one and sat back in the driver's seat.

The street was busy with traffic. Those leaving for work late, early morning shoppers and, of course, the school run. They had already seen a number of vehicles pass with children in them.

'If you hadn't gone missing this morning we could have been here earlier,' Reed complained. 'Made sure we didn't miss her. Where the hell were you anyway?'

'That's my business.'

'You like your little secrets, don't you?'

'It was business. Now forget it.'

Reed sucked on the cigarette, rolling the window down a little to allow some smoke to escape. 'How long are we going to sit here?' he wanted to know. 'People in places like this remember strangers, you know. We don't exactly blend in, do we?'

'She's coming out,' Dawson said quietly, his eyes never leaving the front door of the Todd residence. 'Get ready.'

'What do you want me to do?'

'Follow her. Keep a couple of car lengths back. All we need to know is where she's going. Her route.'

Dawson watched as Roma helped Kirsten into the passenger seat of the Range Rover then walked around and climbed in herself. A moment later, she guided the vehicle down the driveway on to the road and swung left.

'All right, go, but take it easy,' Dawson said.

Reed moved the Astra smoothly out of its parking space and into the road.

Ahead, the Range Rover stopped at a junction then turned.

'Give her a minute,' Dawson said. 'Let a couple more cars get between us and her.'

'What if we lose her?'

'We won't if you don't panic.'

'I'm not panicking. Do *you* want to fucking drive?'

'Turn now.'

Reed swung the Astra right. 'Where the fuck is she?' he said agitatedly.

'She's just up ahead,' Dawson reassured him. 'Will you just calm down?'

The traffic moved steadily. Dawson sucked slowly on his cigarette and kept his gaze fixed on the vehicle ahead.

'What if she knows?' Reed said.

'Why should she? What reason has she got for thinking she's being followed? Just take it easy.'

As they moved through the leafy streets Dawson and Reed saw more and more cars filled with noisy children.

'We're about the only fucking car that hasn't got a kid in it,' Reed hissed.

'There's plenty of other traffic going this way. Just keep your eye on that Range Rover.'

There was another turning up ahead. The traffic slowed down as it approached another junction.

Roma turned the Range Rover when a gap in the traffic appeared. The cars behind moved forward, waiting to turn. A young girl on the back seat of the car in front of the Astra peered straight at Dawson and Reed.

'Come on, come on,' muttered Reed, trying to avoid eye contact with her.

The next car found a space in the traffic. Then the next.

Reed edged the Astra forward again, waiting for his turn.

A woman stepped in front of the vehicle pushing a buggy, a child of seven or eight trotting along dutifully beside her.

Reed hit the brakes. 'Get out the fucking way,' he bellowed.

'Shut it,' snarled Dawson.

'I could have hit her.'

'Calm down,' Dawson rasped.

The woman looked into the car then continued walking.

'Go now,' Dawson told him, seeing a gap in the traffic.

Reed swung the Astra to his left on to a dual carriageway. He pressed his foot on the accelerator.

'Slow down,' Dawson told him. 'I can see her from here.'

The large edifice of St Margaret's School was looming ahead of them. Both men saw the Range Rover turn into the gravel driveway.

'Just drive past,' Dawson instructed. 'Park over there.' He jabbed a finger at a side road and Reed did as he was instructed.

'What now?' Reed asked.

'We wait for the mother to come out. Then we follow her. I want to know where she's going. The kid's in school until three, we know that. It gives us plenty of time to get things sorted.'

'If she takes the same route *back* to the house when she picks the kid up, where the fuck do we grab her? It was main roads all the way.'

Dawson nodded. 'If she does use the same route then the best place to snatch her'll be outside her house.'

Reed swallowed hard.

Moments later, the Range Rover emerged from the driveway of St Margaret's.

'Go on,' Dawson said, and Reed sent the Astra off in pursuit, once more.

'It looks like she's heading back home,' Reed noted, aware that the Range Rover was returning the way it had come.

Dawson remained silent, watching the vehicle ahead like a hawk.

Indeed ten minutes later it swung back into the drive of the house and both men saw Roma climb out and go inside.

'Now what?' Reed said. 'We can't sit here all fucking day. One of the neighbours'll get suspicious.'

Dawson reached into his coat and pulled out his mobile phone. He tapped out the required digits and waited. It was answered almost immediately.

'Nikki, it's me,' he said.

Reed looked across at him.

'Yeah, we followed her to the school. Her mother dropped her off and then came back to the house. No. It won't be a problem.' He was aware that Reed was still staring at him. 'We'll be back in a couple of hours. There's some stuff we need to do.' He switched off.

'Did she want to speak to me?' Reed enquired.

'Why should she?' Dawson said.

The two men regarded each other warily for a moment then Dawson looked at his watch.

'It's just after quarter past nine now,' he said. 'We've got less than six hours until the kid comes out of school. In the meantime, let's get things sorted. We're only going to get one crack at this.'

As the Astra pulled away, he took one more look at the house.

# 9.24 A.M.

As Roma waited for the kettle to boil she dialled the number she wanted.

She cleared the breakfast things from the kitchen table, the mobile wedged between her ear and shoulder. There was no answer. She allowed it to ring. Ten. Eleven. Twelve times. Still it wasn't answered.

Roma put the phone down on one of the worktops and pushed bowls and plates into the dishwasher. She made herself a cup of tea and wondered how long to leave it before calling again.

She carried her tea and the mobile into the sitting room and flicked distractedly through the daily paper. Waiting. She had a lecture to give that afternoon at twelve o'clock but until then she was free.

She knew how she wanted to spend that time.

Roma sipped from her mug, finished skimming through the paper then dialled again.

Still no answer.

Where the hell *was* Michael Harper?

Roma was sure he didn't have a lecture that morning (*he'd have said wouldn't he?*) and even if he did he'd be up by now.

*Wouldn't he?*

She wondered if she should drive to his flat in Western Way and surprise him.

As she sat waiting for the phone to be answered she decided against it. She wondered about trying the number of the flat but then chose not to.

*You don't own him. He's entitled to do things without you knowing. Entitled to be places without telling you.*

She pressed End Call and made her way upstairs where she reapplied her lipstick and swept a brush through her light-brown hair.

She'd try his number again later. If she didn't see him then so be it. There was always the following day. Roma wandered back downstairs, pulled a notepad from a drawer in one of the kitchen cupboards and began scribbling down her shopping list.

Every so often she would glance at her mobile phone.

Perhaps *he* would ring *her*.

'How many fucking cars are we going to steal?'

Jeff Reed looked irritably at his brother-in-law, waiting for an answer. 'We dumped the Astra. Why couldn't we have held on to it?'

'Because the police will be looking for a stolen Astra by now, won't they?' Dawson told him condescendingly. 'Just like they'll have been looking for a stolen Renault last night. That's why we dumped that too.' He regarded Reed evenly. 'We take one more. That's the one we drive when we snatch the kid.'

'Great,' Reed murmured. 'Kidnapping *and* nicking cars. If they catch us—'

'They're not going to catch us,' snapped Dawson, cutting him short. 'Not unless you fuck things up.'

'Why me?'

'Because you're acting like some kid on his first job.'

'Sorry I can't be Mr-fucking-Cool like you, John, but I'm not used to this shit.'

'No, I know. I told you before that you were small-time, Jeff.'

'Oh, shut up, both of you.'

Nikki wandered into the living room and looked at them. 'Stop arguing,' she insisted. 'I'm nervous too, John.'

'Everything'll be fine,' Dawson reassured her. He looked at Reed. 'As long as we keep calm.'

There was a long silence finally broken by Nikki. 'So what now?' she wanted to know.

'We've got somewhere to take the kid once we've snatched her,' Dawson began. 'That was the most important thing. That's sorted.' He dug in his pocket and produced a set of keys that he dropped in the middle of the small table. 'Keys to the kingdom.' He grinned.

Reed looked at the keys then at Dawson. 'Are you sure this place is safe?' he wanted to know. 'How do we know no one's going to see us?'

'Because we're going to do it right. You're going to do as you're told.'

There was an uneasy silence. Then Reed said. 'So we snatch her and get her back to this "safe" place. Then what?'

'We let the parents know she's all right,' Dawson informed him. 'If they think she's been hurt or killed they're not going to pay the ransom. They're not going to cough up for a dead kid, are they?'

'And how the fuck do we contact them?'

'By phone,' Dawson continued. 'We leave them a mobile. All contact between us and them will take place on that one phone.'

'The police will trace the calls,' Reed insisted.

'As long as we're not on the line for more than forty-five seconds we're OK. They can't run a trace in that time, even if they're ready and waiting. It won't take that long to give the instructions.'

'And if they agree?' Nikki wanted to know. 'How do we know they won't mark the notes or something? I've seen things like that done in films.'

'Because we'll specify that in the instructions,' Dawson told her. 'If they don't follow orders to the letter then their fucking kid dies. They're not going to piss about with her life.'

'And what if they call our bluff?' Reed demanded. 'What if they say they're not going to pay?'

'Let them,' Dawson said flatly.

'The police could be waiting for us when we pick up the money,' Nikki insisted.

'They'll think about it,' Dawson agreed. 'But they won't dare put the kid's life at risk. Not when they know we mean what

243

we say. But we've got to be prepared to go through with whatever we say we're going to do. If we say we're going to cut off her finger, then we do it. If we say we're going to break her arm, then we do that.'

'Jesus Christ,' murmured Reed.

'Do you want to get out of this fucking mess with Max Tate or not?' Dawson snapped. 'Do you want to pay him his twenty grand?'

Reed nodded.

'You called me because you wanted my help,' Dawson continued. 'I'm giving it. You don't want it, you don't like what's got to be done, then sort things yourself. I told you before, Jeff, I'm doing this for Nikki, not you. Now, if you don't want to do it then say so now. I'll get the fuck out of here and you can speak to Max Tate about what you owe him.'

He looked first at Reed, then at Nikki, then at the set of keys in the middle of the table.

'We don't have a choice, Jeff,' Nikki said, looking at her husband. 'We've *never* had a choice.'

She reached out and picked up the keys, closing her hand around them.

Dawson smiled.

# 11.49 A.M.

Fielding brought the Mondeo to a stop and turned off the engine.

There was an old Capri a couple of spaces to his right. Both the front and rear windscreens had been smashed in and the two front wheels were missing.

The DI swung himself out and made his way towards the main entrance of Robson Court. He didn't even bother trying the lift, he just took a deep breath and began the climb up the cold, urine-reeking stone steps that would take him up to the fifth floor.

When he reached number 56 he banged loudly and waited.

There were sounds of movement from inside then the door opened a crack.

'Open up, Clive,' Fielding smiled. 'I said I'd be back for a chat, didn't I?'

Muttering something to himself, Clive Fowler slipped the chain off and pulled the door open, allowing the policeman inside.

'You haven't cleaned up since the last time I was here,' Fielding observed, looking around the small living room.

The television was on, some soap opera. The sound turned down to a bare minimum.

'This is harassment, you know,' Fowler protested.

Fielding crossed to the TV and switched it off. 'You said that last time,' he muttered. 'Sit down, Clive.'

Fowler did as he was told.

'You said you'd have some information for me by the end of the week,' Fielding reminded him.

'I never said that. I told you before, I don't know anything about these murders.'

'What do you know about a website called Slamming?'

'Never heard of it.'

'Liar.'

'I've never been into it.'

'Bullshit.'

Fielding lit a cigarette, walked slowly around the small living room, then moved across to the computer on the MFI desk in one corner. He switched it on and it whirred into life.

'You can't touch that, it's private property,' Fowler protested, getting to his feet.

'What's your password for getting in?' Fielding wanted to know.

'I told you, I've never used that site,' Fowler insisted, taking a step nearer.

The computer screen was lit up now.

'So, if I was to open any of these files I wouldn't find anything you didn't want me to?' the DI asked, studying the screen. 'How about one of these with the name of a fish on it. What would happen if I opened up Cod?'

He gripped the mouse and guided the arrow to the appointed file.

'Just leave it, will you?' Fowler blurted.

'I've seen all these before, Clive,' Fielding said, his tone darkening. 'On eleven other computers this week. On eleven computers belonging to blokes like you. Now, you get me into that site I want or I'll wedge this mouse so far down your throat you'll be able to click your password with your fucking tonsils.'

Fowler hesitated.

'How did you find out about it?' he wanted to know.

'Hard work,' Fielding said, wearily. 'How did *you* find out about it?'

'You hear things. Information gets passed on.'

'Did you know there were pictures of dead kids on it?'

'No. I swear on my mum's life that I didn't.'

'With a little bit of checking I might get to believe you, Clive. Who did *you* tell about it? About the site?'

'Guys in chat rooms.'

'How does the stuff get on the site?'

'People put it on themselves. Anybody with a camera and a scanner can do it. But I don't know who put the pictures of those three kids on there, Mr Fielding, I swear.'

The DI regarded Fowler contemptuously for a moment. He was about to speak again when his mobile rang. He pulled it from his pocket and pressed the Call button.

'Guv,' said the voice at the other end of the line. 'It's Young.'

'What you got, Rob?'

There was a crackle of static on the line.

'Hang on a minute, you're breaking up,' said Fielding. He looked at Fowler. 'It must be the shit in the air.' The DI stepped out on to the parapet outside the flat. 'Go on, Rob.'

'We've just had a call from Hendon about that fingerprint that was taken from the Ridley boy's lip.'

'What about it?'

'They've made a positive ID.'

Fielding felt his heart beat faster. 'So the geezer *had* been printed,' he said. 'Has he got previous?'

'Plenty.'

'Give me a name, Rob.'

'The fingerprint belongs to a man called John Dawson.'

247

# 2.36 P.M.

'Where the fuck is she?' Jeff Reed looked at his watch then up and down the road outside the Todd house.

'She might not have left yet,' John Dawson murmured. 'It only took her fifteen minutes this morning.'

He too checked his watch and glanced at the front door of the house across the street.

Reed began drumming his fingers on the steering wheel of the stolen Nissan. He sucked hard on his cigarette then tossed the butt out of the open window.

There was still no sign of movement in the driveway of the Todd residence.

'We give it another five minutes then we drive to the school,' Dawson said.

'Why?'

'We can follow her from there when she's picked the kid up.'

'She might not even be *at* the school.'

'Look, the kid's got to be picked up, right? If her mother's not home then she must be there already or at least on her way.'

'And what if she doesn't pick the kid up in the afternoons? Perhaps there's some fucking nanny or something that does it. You know what these rich bastards are like.'

'Then if there's a nanny we'll take the kid from *her*.' Dawson looked defiantly at Reed. 'If the mother's not at the school to pick up the kid, *someone* will be.'

'We didn't plan this properly,' Reed sighed, shaking his head.

'And what would you have done?' Dawson snapped. 'Staked out the house for a week first? You haven't *got* a fucking week,

248

Jeff. You've got no time at all. It's *got* to be done this way.'

Dawson glanced at his watch again. 'That's it,' he said. 'Drive to the school.'

'And what if we miss her coming back?'

'Just drive.'

Reed started the engine and guided the Nissan towards the end of the street where he turned left. 'This is bullshit,' he rasped. 'We haven't got a clue where the kid is.'

'She's in school until three, you dummy,' snapped Dawson. 'It's the *mother* we can't find but she's not important. The kid's the only one that matters to us.'

Reed drove on, the needle on the speedo nudging forty-five.

'Slow down a bit,' Dawson told him. 'We don't want to get pulled for speeding.'

As he spoke he glanced on to the back seat.

His black holdall lay there like a sleeping dog, the top partially unzipped.

Reed guided the Nissan down the stretch of dual carriageway that led to St Margaret's.

'What do I do when we get to the school?' Reed wanted to know. 'I can't park outside, can I?'

'Just swing it into a side street like we did this morning. We'll watch for the mother's car. It shouldn't be too hard to spot.'

'I hope she's driving the same one.'

Dawson shook his head.

A number of the vehicles ahead of them drove straight through the open gates into the grounds of St Margaret's. Reed took a left and found a gap among the vehicles parked in the side street nearby. He swung the Nissan around so that they were facing the gates of the school.

'The kid'll be out soon,' Dawson said, his eyes never leaving the gateway.

Reed switched off the engine then lit another cigarette and drew hard on it.

\* \* \*

Roma could feel the beginning of a headache gnawing at the base of her skull. She gently rolled her head on her shoulders as she drove through the open gates that led to St Margaret's.

The lecture that afternoon had gone well although she hoped that the indifference she herself had felt had not communicated itself to her words.

She had tried ringing Harper before she entered the lecture theatre and also when she left the college but on both occasions his mobile had been switched off.

*Stop thinking about him.*

She brought the Range Rover to a halt, reversed it into a space outside the school and sat behind the wheel. She could see Louise Barton parking up and realised that she wouldn't be able to escape without a quick word. Louise waved and started across to the Range Rover. Roma tried to forget about her headache and climbed out to greet her friend.

Already the first children were beginning to stream out of the main doors of the building.

# 3.03 P.M.

'There.'

John Dawson jabbed a finger in the direction of the Range Rover. 'That's her. Let's go.'

Reed twisted together the wires dangling from the steering column, waiting for the engine to burst into life.

It whirred loudly then died.

'Come on,' snapped Dawson.

The Range Rover was already moving away. Dawson could see the small figure of Kirsten Todd in the passenger seat.

Reed twisted the wires again, hissing angrily when he got a shock from the bare metal.

'For fuck's sake!' snarled Dawson.

'I'm trying,' Reed told him angrily.

The engine turned over again then died.

Reed tried a third time.

Dawson could see that the Range Rover was held up at the junction but would soon be off.

The engine fired and Reed stepped hard on the accelerator. It roared into life.

'Come on, move it,' Dawson shouted, his gaze fixed on the Range Rover.

The Nissan moved off into traffic six or seven cars behind its target.

'Don't let her get too far in front,' Dawson instructed.

'What the fuck do you want me to do?' Reed snapped. 'Shunt these other cars out of the way?'

The Range Rover nudged out on to the dual carriageway and sped up.

Other cars followed. Reed coaxed the Nissan forward, pressing harder on the right-hand pedal to prevent the car stalling.

Intimidated by the weight of traffic, some of the other drivers hesitated as they tried to find a gap that would allow them on to the carriageway.

Dawson was still watching the Range Rover. It was approaching a roundabout. He knew that Roma would take a left there, which would lead her home.

'Fuck this,' snarled Reed. He swung the Nissan out of the line of traffic, almost clipping the bumper of a BMW in front.

'What the fuck are you doing?' Dawson snarled.

'We'll be sitting here all day,' Reed told him, guiding the Nissan up to the junction.

He saw a gap and pulled out, slipping seamlessly into the traffic. Dawson glanced irritably at him.

'You told me not to lose her, didn't you?' Reed hissed, over-taking another car.

The Range Rover was turning left now. Reed followed. The Nissan was about a hundred yards behind.

'Don't get too close yet,' Dawson said, reaching over to the back seat. He grabbed the holdall and pulled it on to his lap, digging his hand inside.

He pulled something free that Reed couldn't see properly. All he knew was that it was black.

'Put that on when I tell you,' Dawson instructed and dropped the black object into his lap.

Only then did Reed realise it was a ski-mask.

Dawson took out another for himself and stuffed it into the glove compartment of the Nissan then he pushed his hand into the holdall again. He pulled out a Nokia mobile phone and checked that the battery was fully charged then he slipped his hand back into the holdall a third time.

His fingers closed over the butt of a 9mm Beretta automatic pistol.

# 3.10 P.M.

Kirsten turned the pages of the *Animal Hospital* magazine slowly, running her bright-blue eyes over every detail.

'Mum, they've got rescue dogs in here,' she said excitedly. 'You can adopt them.'

Roma smiled. 'I know, I looked at some of them while I was waiting for you to come out of school,' she said.

'I'll show Dad. Oh, look at that one, he's so cute.' She pushed the magazine towards her mother who nodded, keeping her eyes on the road.

'I'll have a better look when we get home, sweetie,' she said, turning right.

Roma glanced in the rear-view mirror and noticed a Nissan close behind her.

'It would be good to adopt a rescue dog, wouldn't it, Mum?' Kirsten said, still poring over the magazine. 'There's one here called Bob. Ahh, look at him. He's only got three legs.'

Roma laughed.

'It's not funny, Mum,' said Kirsten indignantly.

'Well, I suppose he wouldn't need so much exercise if he only had three legs.'

'That's cruel.'

Roma grinned at her daughter as she turned the wheel. Another couple of minutes and they'd be home.

Dawson pulled on a pair of black leather gloves, slotting his fingers together to ensure that they fitted tightly.

The road ahead and behind them was clear. The Range Rover

was less than twenty yards ahead now.

Dawson pulled the Beretta free and worked the slide, chambering a round.

'What the fuck are you doing?' Reed said, his breath ragged.

'What do *you* think?' Dawson snapped. 'She's not going to hand over her kid just like that, is she?'

'Don't kill her,' Reed blurted.

'You just keep your fucking eyes on that Range Rover. She's nearly there now.'

He looked behind. The road remained clear.

'Put your mask on,' Dawson instructed, steadying the wheel with one hand as Reed did as he was instructed. Just his eyes and mouth were visible through the slits in the material. Dawson did the same, his breathing harsh inside the tight nylon covering.

Reed closed in.

Fifteen yards.

Dawson had the Beretta shoved into the waistband of his jeans.

Ten yards.

He looked behind once more. Road still clear.

The inside of the car smelled of sweat.

Five yards.

'Now,' shouted Dawson.

Reed floored the accelerator, sending the Nissan hurtling up alongside the Range Rover and then sharply across it where it screeched to a halt.

Roma stamped on the brakes, shooting out her left arm to prevent Kirsten slamming into the dashboard.

'Jesus Christ,' she gasped. 'What the hell are they doing?'

She saw both men clambering out of their car. Saw one rushing towards the passenger door, the other towards her side of the vehicle.

Before she could hit the central locking the passenger-side door was wrenched open.

Roma screamed as one of the men scooped Kirsten into his arms and ran back to the Nissan with her.

The little girl also screamed as she was bundled into the passenger seat of the vehicle.

Roma saw the second man approaching her and she was aware that he was carrying something in his right hand. When he swung it up towards her head she saw that it was a gun. She felt every muscle in her body tightening except those in her bladder. Something warm and wet began to flood between her legs as she lost control.

The pistol was inches from her face.

'Take this,' snarled Dawson, pushing the Nokia towards her. He shoved it into her lap, on to the sodden material of her jeans.

'We'll contact you with it. Understand?'

She was crying now, her eyes darting back and forth from the barrel of the pistol to her daughter held firmly in the Nissan. Roma could hear muffled screams and knew that they were Kirsten's.

'Listen to me,' Dawson rasped, his voice distorted by the ski-mask. He pressed the cold metal against her cheek. 'Are you listening?'

She tried to nod but it was as if her neck muscles had gone into spasm.

'We'll call later with details. On *that* phone.' He pushed her head towards the Nokia. 'Don't lose it or the fucking kid dies.'

He pushed her hard, sending her sprawling across the passenger seat.

By the time she had hauled herself upright, he was running back towards the waiting Nissan. Roma saw him jump in through one of the rear doors. He dragged Kirsten through the gap in the front seats so that she was sitting beside him in the back then, as Roma began to clamber from the Range Rover, the Nissan sped off. She saw the gun pointing at her daughter's head.

Roma, tears pouring down her cheeks, stumbled and fell into the road, scraping flesh from her hands. She landed heavily and lay still for a moment. Then she was aware of voices coming from both sides of the street, and of footsteps moving towards her.

She tried to rise but her head spun. She felt sick. Sobbing uncontrollably she remained on her knees as if in an attitude of prayer.

She glanced towards her car and saw the Nokia on the floor in front of the driving seat.

Hands were reaching for her now. Words floated around her like wraiths. They were deafeningly loud then suddenly vague. The world began to spin.

She blacked out.

# 3.32 P.M.

'There's no mistake?'

Detective Inspector Fielding sat at his desk, his eyes fixed on the image on his computer screen.

'None at all,' DS Young assured him. 'Dawson's the man. The print taken from the Ridley boy's lip is definitely his. Hendon confirmed.'

Fielding looked away from the screen to glance across at Donna Thompson.

'Are you satisfied with that?' he asked.

'They're the experts, Alan,' the pathologist said. 'All fingerprints fall into four main categories. Arches, loops, whorls and compounds. I found twinned loops on the inside of Jonathan Ridley's upper lip. Hendon confirmed they belonged to John Dawson. You need eight points of reference for fingerprint evidence to stand up in court. Hendon found fourteen.'

'So if we catch this bastard we've got enough to send him down,' Fielding murmured, looking at his screen once more.

'Even without any other evidence, the print will be enough to convict him,' Young said.

Fielding nodded. He allowed his gaze to move over the image of John Dawson that was on his screen. Below the unsmiling face were arrest details and all manner of personal information.

'According to this, he finished a stretch for assault with a deadly weapon two years ago,' Fielding mused. 'But nothing since. He's either kept his nose clean or he's been careful.'

'GBH and assault,' Young interjected. 'Not the kind of apprenticeship you'd expect in a case like this, is it, guv?'

257

Fielding shook his head. 'I agree with you, Rob, but the print's his,' the DI said. 'It looks like he made the jump. But you're right. Kicking the shit out of someone or going for them with a knife is a world away from murdering kids. What the hell made him start that?'

A heavy silence descended.

Fielding tapped one of the keys on his computer and read some more of Dawson's details.

'He was born in London. Lived there most of his life, when he wasn't inside. One sister, Nicola.' Fielding looked up at Young. 'It might be an idea to run *her* name through the system too but there's no hurry.' He continued to scan the report.

'You said that you thought whoever killed the kids was doing it for reasons other than personal gratification,' Young interjected.

'I'm even more certain of it having seen this,' Fielding agreed.

'Could Dawson have been working *with* someone?'

'Or *for* someone?' Fielding murmured. 'I said I thought those kids were treated like commodities. Perhaps he was paid to kill them and photograph them.'

'Done to order?' Young wondered.

'It's possible. But who the fuck would pay for stuff like that?'

'We're not going to find that out until we catch Dawson are we, guv?'

Fielding glared at the image of John Dawson on his screen.

'I'm going to get you, you bastard,' he said, his eyes never leaving the screen. The image of John Dawson stared blankly back at him.

He was still studying the expressionless features when the phone on his desk rang. He waited a moment then reached for the receiver.

'Fielding.' The colour visibly drained from his face. 'When? Where? Right.' He put down the phone and looked at Young.

'What is it, guv?' the DS wanted to know.

When Fielding spoke, his voice was a hoarse whisper. 'Another kid's been taken.'

He looked back at his computer screen.

# 4.57 P.M.

She was blind.

Kirsten Todd could see nothing. All she had been aware of since the man in the mask had grabbed her was hands on her body. Pushing. Shoving.

She had heard voices occasionally. More than once they had shouted at her.

One had yelled as he forced the black hood over her head and pushed her on to the back seat of a car. He had wound something sticky around her wrists until it hurt. She'd tried to tell him but he'd ignored her.

They had shouted words at her (bad words) that she knew she should not repeat. Words she had heard adults shout when they were angry. Words she had sometimes heard her mother and father use when they were sure she couldn't hear.

Kirsten had not even tried to struggle after the man in the mask had pushed her into the car. She had been frozen with fear. Uncomprehending. Terrified.

The hands that had touched her skin had been rough. She had kept still when those hands were upon her. She'd obeyed when the harsh voices had instructed her to lie down or to sit up. And, finally, to walk.

It had been difficult with the hood over her head and with her wrists bound. More than once she'd stumbled. The second time, she had fallen on to concrete and scraped her knees. It had hurt enough to make her cry. One of the harsh voices had told her to shut up. She'd tried but the tone had only succeeded in making her more desperately upset.

She had heard whispering then. The odd word here and there. Then another voice, a woman's voice, had spoken to her more kindly. Told her that she didn't need to cry. Softer hands had held her arms as she walked and Kirsten had managed to stop sobbing.

Then she had felt strong arms sweep her up into the air and she heard footsteps on stairs.

The smells had changed too. From the petrol stink of the car and the sweat on those around her to the damp smell that now filled her nostrils.

Kirsten had been pushed on to what felt like a bed. Nothing like her *own* bed though. This one was uncomfortable. There were springs sticking up through the mattress. She could feel them against her legs as she shuffled, trying to get comfortable. They had begun to wind the sticky stuff around her ankles too but then stopped. She had cried out again when they had ripped it off, tugging the soft hairs on her flesh away in the process.

Her throat was dry, her eyes were puffy and swollen and she was having difficulty breathing but still the hood remained in place.

She wondered where her mum was. Wondered how long it would be before she was back in those safe and welcoming arms.

The harsh voices spoke more frequently now but she heard little of what they said. Some of the words made no sense to her. Many were bad words. Even the lady's voice said bad words.

Kirsten moved up the bed slightly and rested against the wall. She drew up her knees and rested her hooded forehead against them.

And she wondered again where her mum was.

# 6.23 P.M.

'Shit.'

DS Young stepped away from the vending machine as a stream of boiling water spurted from the nozzle over the styrofoam cup.

Further down the hospital corridor his superior looked up, shook his head and then continued to gaze at the door opposite.

Young pushed more coins into the machine and eventually wandered back down the corridor with what passed for two coffees. He handed one to Fielding who looked at the dark-brown concoction and raised his eyebrows questioningly.

'How much longer have we got to wait?' the DI said, leaning back.

'The nurse said that Mrs Todd was sedated.'

'I remember what she said, Rob,' Fielding snapped. 'But that was over two hours ago. Fuck knows where her kid is by now. The quicker we can talk to her and get some details, the quicker we can start trying to find the girl.'

Young nodded and chanced a sip of his coffee. He winced and swallowed hard.

There was a plastic bin close by. He dropped the full cup into it and rubbed his hands together.

'No point in talking to the husband?' the DS offered.

Fielding shrugged. 'Take a statement later but what the hell's *he* going to tell us? He only got here himself half an hour ago, didn't he? Besides, he's been in London all day. I think we can discount him as a suspect.'

Fielding got to his feet and began pacing the corridor slowly.

261

'Do you reckon it's the same bloke who took the other kids?' Young asked.

'Didn't the first reports say there were two men? Anyway, this isn't our man's style, is it? The other three kids were snatched while they were on their own, not taken from under their mothers' noses.'

'A kidnapping?'

'It's possible.' Fielding looked at his watch. 'Come on, for Christ's sake,' he muttered under his breath.

He turned as he heard the door being opened. A tall nurse with dark-brown hair emerged and regarded the waiting policemen indifferently.

'You can see Mrs Todd now,' she said. 'She should be allowed home in a short time but—'

'Thank you,' said Fielding, interrupting as he headed for the door. He handed the nurse the styrofoam cup as he passed her. She took it and threw it into the bin.

The hospital room was small. Other than the bed, it contained a cabinet and a couple of plastic chairs. On one sat David Todd.

Roma was lying on the bed, barefoot but still dressed in her crumpled clothes. Her face was ashen, her hair scraped back from her face. She looked drained, and was dark beneath the eyes as if someone had been shading the skin there with charcoal.

The two policemen introduced themselves, showed their ID cards and stood at the bottom of the bed.

'I know this is hard for you both,' said Fielding. 'But we need your help and the more you can give us, the better it'll be for your daughter.'

Todd regarded the two policemen suspiciously for a moment then exhaled. He touched his wife's hand gently.

'Are you up to this?' he asked her.

Roma nodded.

'I need you to tell me what happened,' Fielding said. 'In as much detail as you can remember.'

Roma cleared her throat and recounted the events that had happened more than three hours earlier.

*Hours? Days? It didn't seem to matter any more.*

Fielding listened, nodding occasionally. Young made the odd jotting in a small notebook he had pulled from his jacket pocket.

'What about the phone he gave you?' Fielding said.

Roma motioned a shaking hand in the direction of the Nokia on the bedside table. 'He told me that he'd contact us with it,' she said softly.

'Did he say when?'

Roma shook her head.

'Dust it, for what it's worth,' Fielding said, glancing at Young. 'Chances are it was nicked anyway.

'Can you tell me anything about either of the men?' he continued, returning his attention to Roma.

'She told you, they were both wearing masks,' Todd snapped.

'Their build,' Fielding persisted, his gaze still fixed on Roma. 'Were they tall, short? Fat, thin?'

'I didn't see anything unusual about either of them,' Roma said. 'I've told you everything I can remember.'

Fielding nodded.

'So what do we do?' Todd wanted to know.

'We wait for them to call,' Fielding said.

'Is that it?'

'There's nothing else we *can* do, Mr Todd. Not at the moment. We have to treat this incident as a kidnapping.'

'And what if it's not? What if our daughter ends up like those other kids? The ones that were murdered.'

'The m.o. is different,' Fielding explained as calmly as he could. 'At the moment there's no need to think that your daughter is anything other than the victim of a kidnap. There's no evidence to suggest the cases are linked.'

'Oh, thank God for that,' said Todd acidly. 'And there was me getting worried. As long as it's only a fucking kidnapping we can all relax, can't we?'

'Calm down, Mr Todd. I understand how you feel—'

'You haven't got a fucking clue how I feel,' Todd snarled.

Fielding raised his hands in supplication. 'No, you're right, I haven't,' he conceded.

'That's just the standard police cliché in this situation, isn't it?' Todd barked. 'Is that what you said to the parents of those murdered kids? That you understood how *they* felt.'

Fielding shot the other man a furious glance.

'Stop it,' Roma said, sitting up. 'For God's sake. This isn't doing Kirsten any good, is it?'

'Perhaps if you'd been a bit more careful this wouldn't have happened,' Todd rasped at her.

'What the hell is that supposed to mean?' she snapped. 'Are you blaming *me* for what's happened?'

'They could have been watching the house for weeks,' Todd said. 'They probably knew you always took the same route to the school when you were picking Kirsten up.'

'*Did* you always use the same route, Mrs Todd?' Fielding interjected.

'No,' Roma told him. She glared at her husband. 'It wasn't even always me who picked Kirsten up. A friend of mine sometimes did it for me if I was busy.' She kept her gaze on her husband. 'If you weren't so keen on getting your face in the papers all the time then maybe they'd have taken someone else's child. You're so happy for everyone to see how much money you've got, aren't you, David? That's what made Kirsten a target. Perhaps *you're* the one who's to blame.'

'No one's to blame,' Fielding interrupted, looking at each of them in turn.

An uneasy silence descended.

It was broken by the strident ringing of the Nokia.

# 6.39 P.M.

For long moments, no one moved.

All eyes turned to look at the mobile, regarding it as if it were some kind of venomous serpent.

Roma looked at the phone then at her husband.

'Answer it.' It was Fielding's voice that broke the spell.

Roma reached for the Nokia with shaking hands but Todd stepped around the bed and snatched it up before she could get it.

He pressed the Call button, aware that Fielding was standing close to him.

A number showed on the Nokia.

'Odds on the phone they're calling from is nicked too,' said the DI quietly.

Todd raised the phone to his ear. 'Hello,' he said, his voice cracking.

Silence.

'Hello,' he repeated.

'Who's this?' the voice on the other end of the line wanted to know.

'David Todd. Who am *I* talking to?'

Fielding touched Todd's arm and shook his head gently.

'Hello,' Todd continued.

'You're talking to the man who's got your fucking kid. Now shut up and listen.'

Roma sat up on the bed and moved closer to her husband.

'What do you want?' Todd asked.

'I said *listen*, you cunt,' the voice rasped.

265

Todd clenched his jaws together hard. 'Go on,' he said.

'One million and you get your kid back unharmed. Got that? One million pounds. Do you understand?'

'I understand.'

'You'll deliver it no later than midnight this Saturday.'

'I can't get that sort of money in such a short time, I—'

'You can do it, you rich cunt. You'd *better* do it or your kid'll be coming back to you piece by piece.'

Todd swallowed hard.

'We'll ring again,' the voice told him. 'Tell you where to drop the money and if I see one copper then the kid dies. Got that? You try to fuck us over and the kid dies. In fact, unless you do exactly what you're told, the kid dies.'

'How do I know she's not *already* dead?'

Silence.

'I said—'

The voice cut him short. 'You're not in any fucking position to bargain, cunt,' the voice rasped. 'Don't try to play games. And if the law are listening to this, you can tell them to fuck themselves too.'

'No one's listening,' Todd said, trying to control the emotion in his voice.

There was another silence, then, 'Dad.'

'Kirsten,' Todd gasped. 'Hello, darling. Are you all right?'

'Dad, please help me.'

'Kirsten!'

'She's still alive,' the voice told him. 'Satisfied?'

'Yes,' Todd answered.

'One million by midnight on Saturday. Wait for the next call.'

The line went dead.

'Midnight, Saturday,' murmured Fielding. 'That gives us over forty-eight hours.' He looked at Todd. 'You're sure you can get the money together in that time, Mr Todd?'

Todd, who was now sitting on the end of the bed with his head bowed, nodded. 'I can try,' he said.

Fielding looked at Young and something unspoken passed between them.

'With all due respect, Mr Todd, I hope you can.'

Todd got to his feet and began pacing the small room.

'And he didn't specify how it should be paid?' Fielding continued. 'No drop points? No note denominations?'

'He just said he'd ring again to tell me where to leave the money,' Todd said.

'Guv, if we're working on the assumption that the phones the kidnappers are using to communicate are both stolen, then we've got a problem,' Young offered. 'As soon as they're *reported* stolen, the signals to both of them will be cut off. We might not have forty-eight hours. It could be less.'

'The kidnappers will know that,' Roma interjected.

'They *should*,' said Fielding. 'We'll have to assume they've made some kind of contingency plans.'

'And if they haven't?' Todd demanded.

'It's in their own interests to have things worked out, Mr Todd.'

'He said no police,' Todd insisted.

'I'm sure he did. We'll keep as low a profile as possible.'

Another heavy silence descended.

'Could it be the same men who killed those other children?' Roma wanted to know.

'It's possible,' Fielding said. 'I'd be lying if I said otherwise but at the moment I think it's unlikely.'

'The peaceful little town of Kingsfield,' sneered Todd. 'Murderers and kidnappers. All of human life is here, isn't it?' He looked contemptuously at Fielding.

'Shall I set up a trace for the next call, guv?' Young wanted to know.

'It's not worth it, Rob. They won't be on long enough,' sighed Fielding. He looked at Roma. 'The nurse said you can go home soon, Mrs Todd. If I were you that's what I'd do.'

'So we can sit in the comfort of our own home while we wait to find out if our daughter's been murdered or not?' Todd snapped.

Roma looked first at her husband then at Fielding. He could see the tears forming in her eyes.

'If Kirsten isn't returned to us by Saturday night she'll die,' Roma murmured.

'If you do as the kidnappers say then she'll be safely returned, I'm sure of that,' Fielding said. 'If you follow instructions—'

'It's got nothing to do with the money!'

Todd rounded on his wife. 'Roma, no,' he snapped.

Again Fielding and Young exchanged telling looks.

'They have to know,' Roma said forcefully.

'Know what?' Fielding enquired.

Roma sucked in a deep breath, trying to fill her lungs. As if what she was about to say could only be communicated in one exclamation.

'Kirsten is ill,' she said. 'Very ill.' She wiped her eyes as the first tears began to trickle down her cheeks. 'She's had a condition since she was born. She needs to take medication every day otherwise the condition will accelerate.'

'What kind of condition?' Fielding wanted to know.

'It's a deficiency of the pineal gland. It's just a small area of the brain. It was called the "third eye" by ancient civilisations. The philosopher Descartes called it the seat of the human soul.'

'Forget the lecture, Roma,' chided Todd. 'Just tell them what's wrong with Kirsten.'

'I *am* telling them,' she snapped. Her tone softened again as she faced Fielding. 'It produces a hormone called melatonin, which is released in the dark during sleep. Melatonin regulates body rhythms, most notably the day and night cycle. It's also been shown to inhibit the growth of some tumours, and may play a part in inhibiting cancer. It also helps the immune system. If the pineal gland doesn't work properly then the sufferer is more prone to conditions like hypertension, epilepsy and Paget's Disease, as well as cancer itself.' She managed a weak smile that never touched her eyes. 'Sorry to sound like a walking encyclopaedia but I've been studying everything about Kirsten's illness ever since we knew what was wrong with her.'

'And your daughter takes medication for this condition?' Fielding said slowly.

Roma nodded. 'Without it she'll die.'

'All right, that's enough,' Todd said wearily.

'No it isn't,' Roma told him. She wiped her face once more, her voice a little stronger as she continued. 'Problems with the pineal gland are not uncommon but our daughter has complications which may or may not be linked to that.'

'Roma, please,' Todd said through gritted teeth.

'They have to know,' she snapped.

Fielding and Young looked intently at her.

Roma sniffed back more tears and cleared her throat. 'Have you ever heard of Molitor's Fire?' she said quietly.

Fielding shook his head slowly and gazed even more intently at Roma.

'It's extremely rare,' she said. 'We were told that there haven't been more than six thousand recorded cases in the last eight hundred years.'

'Is it a disease?' the DI wanted to know.

'I don't know if that's the right word,' Roma told him, attempting a smile that she couldn't quite manage. 'Over the years other terms have been used to describe it. A judgement. A curse.'

Fielding's brow wrinkled. 'You're losing me, Mrs Todd,' he confessed.

'Molitor's Fire is named after a man called Ulrich Molitor,' Roma explained. 'He was one of the earliest writers on witchcraft. He lived in Germany in the fifteenth century. I suppose you could say he was one of the first witch-hunters to examine the psychological nature of witchcraft.'

'Jesus Christ,' snapped Todd. 'Just get to the point will you?'

Fielding looked at Todd to silence him.

'Molitor was a doctor of law at the University of Constance when his first book was published,' Roma continued. 'He hated women. He blamed them for all of the witchcraft cases he witnessed. He said that it was women copulating with the Devil that populated the earth with demons. It was a woman who finally accused *him* of witchcraft. He was sentenced to be burned alive for heresy.'

Fielding nodded sagely, the furrows on his brow deepening as Roma continued.

'He was tied to the stake, the kindling around him was lit but his body wouldn't burn,' she said evenly. 'Witnesses said that as he appealed to God to prove his innocence, his body seemed to absorb the flames. That they were sucked into his flesh, into his very bones. When they couldn't burn him, they strangled him.'

'I'm still not with you,' Fielding confessed. 'What has this got to do with your daughter?'

'The first recorded case of Molitor's Fire was in the early sixteenth century,' Roma explained. 'A young girl was accused of witchcraft because things she touched became charred and burned. Even people. As time went on and medicine advanced, people realised that witchcraft wasn't to blame, but the condition still remained a mystery. People who had it didn't live long. It was unusual to find anyone with it surviving into their twenties. They were usually locked away where they could do no harm to others. The most recent recorded case was in Peru in 1946. A girl of ten was diagnosed with brain cancer in the area of the pineal gland, and one of the side-effects was the appearance of Molitor's Fire.'

'So it *is* a disease?' Fielding said.

Roma nodded. 'For want of a better word,' she agreed. 'Even the doctors who treated Kirsten didn't know what they were dealing with. They tried to run tests, to discover the true nature of what was wrong with her. To find out what Molitor's Fire really was.'

'What did they say?'

'The disease attacks the skin,' Roma began.

'Of the carrier?' Fielding interrupted.

'No. Not at first. Of those *touched* by the carrier,' she corrected him. 'Anyone afflicted with Molitor's Fire draws oxygen from the skin of the person they come into contact with. If I had the disease and I was to touch you then your skin would calcify. Burn. The oxygen is sucked from the flesh so quickly that the place where contact is made has the appearance of a burn. The sufferer eventually . . .' Her voice cracked and she paused for a moment. 'The person with the disease finally burns themselves. It happens very quickly. From the inside outwards. Doctors think that some cases of spontaneous human combustion could well have been carriers of Molitor's Fire.'

'And you're saying that's what'll happen to your daughter if she's not treated within the next forty-eight hours?'

'Her condition will deteriorate rapidly if she doesn't have her medication. What I'm telling you is that the men who kidnapped her are in as much danger as she is.'

# 7.59 P.M.

'How did you find this place?'

Jeff Reed looked around him as Nikki spooned food on to his plate.

John Dawson was already eating and seemed more interested in his food than in answering Reed's question. He pushed rice and curry into his mouth with all the haste and enthusiasm of a man who hadn't eaten for days.

'Does it matter?' he said finally, wiping his mouth with the back of his hand before taking a long swallow from the can of Carlsberg beside him.

'Actually it does,' Reed said irritably. 'If we're going to be here for two days, how do we know we're not going to be seen? There are plenty of other houses around here.'

'Most of them are empty,' Dawson told him, stuffing more rice into his mouth. 'The others have been converted into flats. The people in them mind their own business. They couldn't give a fuck what's happening down here.'

'So how *did* you find it?' Reed persisted.

'A contact. Right?'

'Does he know what's going on?'

'What do *you* think? Do I look like a cunt? Yeah, I said to him, "I'm kidnapping a kid and I need somewhere to hide for a couple of days, but don't tell anybody, will you?"' He looked scathingly at Reed.

There was a portable TV set up in one corner of the room. Its barely discernible picture was constantly broken up by static and Dawson got to his feet to adjust the aerial. He twisted it one way then another in an effort to get a clear image. He finally got sound but little else. Muttering to himself he returned to the small table and sat down.

Through the beaded curtain he could see into the bedroom where Kirsten Todd was still huddled on the worn and battered bed.

'Shall I give the kid something to eat?' Nikki asked. 'She must be starving.'

'She can have this,' Dawson said, pushing his plate across the table. 'I've finished with it.'

Nikki looked down at the scraps then at her own plate. She picked out some pieces of meat with a fork and some fresh rice and scraped it on to a side plate. She crossed to the sink and filled a glass with water then carried both into the bedroom.

Kirsten heard footsteps approaching her and she shrank back even further against the wall.

'It's all right,' said Nikki, sitting on the bed beside her. 'I thought you might be hungry.'

Kirsten remained motionless.

Nikki put one hand on the little girl's arm and squeezed gently.

'I want Mum,' Kirsten said faintly, her voice further muffled by the hood that was still over her head.

'You'll see your mum soon enough,' Nikki told her.

'When?'

'Soon. Here, eat some of this.' She pushed the fork into a piece of curried chicken and reached for the bottom of the hood, preparing to lift it up.

'What the fuck are you doing?'

The voice startled Nikki and she looked around to see Dawson standing in the doorway glaring at her.

'I'm giving her something to eat,' Nikki told him.

'You were taking her hood off,' Dawson snapped. 'Leave it.'

'How's she supposed to eat with it on?'

'I couldn't give a fuck but the hood stays on. Unless you *want* her to see all our faces. Think about it. That's the kind of stupid thing I'd have expected your old man to do.' He hooked a thumb over his shoulder. 'I thought *you* had a bit more sense.' He tapped his temple with one index finger.

'Can I have a drink, please?' Kirsten said from beneath the hood.

Nikki looked at Dawson who hesitated a moment then held up one finger. He disappeared into the other part of the basement flat then returned carrying a roll of gaffer tape. Nikki watched as he crossed to the bed and knelt beside the little girl.

'You listen to me,' he said, leaning close to her. 'I'm going to take this hood off you, right? Now, when I do, I want you to keep your eyes closed. Tight as you can. Understand?'

Kirsten nodded.

'If you open your eyes,' hissed Dawson, 'I'll cut them out and post them to your fucking father. Got it?'

Kirsten began to cry softly.

'Shut up,' snapped Dawson. 'Now, I'm going to take the hood off, right? Are your eyes shut?'

Kirsten merely sniffed.

'Are they shut?' Dawson repeated, raising his voice.

The little girl coughed. 'Yes,' she told him, fighting back more tears.

'Keep them shut,' he told her.

He tore off a long strip of gaffer tape and held it in one hand then with the other he pulled the hood free. With one swift movement, he slapped the tape across Kirsten's eyes and wound it around her head twice. Satisfied that she couldn't see he backed away.

'Now you can feed her,' he said to Nikki as he retreated from the room.

Nikki pushed a forkful of rice and curried meat towards Kirsten who recoiled slightly.

'Eat this,' Nikki said.

'What is it? It smells funny.'

'Just eat it.'

Kirsten opened her mouth and chewed tentatively. 'I don't like it,' she said, almost apologetically. 'Can I have a drink, please? Can I have apple and blackcurrant?'

'Just drink this,' Nikki said, trying to inject a note of authority into her voice.

She held up the glass of water and allowed the little girl to slurp from it. Some of the liquid dribbled down her chin and on to her school blouse.

'Can I go home soon?' the little girl asked.

Nikki got to her feet, hesitated a moment then slipped silently from the room.

# 8.32 P.M.

DS Young brought the Mondeo to a halt just behind the BMW and watched as David Todd slid from behind the steering wheel then hurried around to the passenger side. He helped Roma out but she shook free of the arm he offered her as they walked towards the front door of their house.

'What is it with these bloody people?' Fielding murmured, watching them intently. 'They've been at each other's throats for the last two hours. Their kid's been kidnapped, she's ill, likely to die, and all they've done is snipe at each other.'

'Could be the stress of what's happened,' Young mused.

Fielding shook his head. 'No. There's more to it than that,' he said with an air of certainty.

'Gut feeling?' The DS grinned.

Fielding also managed a smile.

'How do you want to play this, guv?' Young asked.

'One of us needs to be in there with them. Especially when that next call comes. I'll take care of that.'

'What do you want me to do?'

'Get our people to check out the prints that were taken from the mobile the Todds were left. See if you can find out if it's been reported stolen yet, that kind of thing. Go through the statements. Get some information on the parents. Backgrounds and stuff.'

'Do you want someone watching the house?'

'We can take care of that ourselves. The fewer uniforms around here the better.' He ran a hand through his hair. 'Another thing, Rob. It might not hurt to have a word with the girl's doctors. See what they can tell you about this . . . disease she's got.'

'I thought Mrs Todd told us all we needed to know.'

'She might have forgotten something.'

'By the morning?' Young asked.

Fielding nodded and swung himself out of the car, slamming the door behind him.

'Guv.'

Young's voice made him turn.

'What Mrs Todd said back at the hospital,' the DS began. 'About what's wrong with her daughter. Do you believe it?'

'Why should she lie, Rob?'

'It just seems . . .' The sentence trailed off as if the DS couldn't find the word he was searching for.

'Incredible?' Fielding added. 'Weird? Frightening?' He paused for a moment. 'It sounds like poetic justice to me. Kidnappers snatching a kid that might cause their death.' He raised his eyebrows. 'They say God moves in mysterious ways, don't they? Perhaps he's having a laugh this time.'

'Do you believe in God?'

Fielding smiled humourlessly. 'Like the man said, "I think that God's a sadist, but probably doesn't even know it." Does that answer your question?' He lit a cigarette, took a couple of drags then made his way slowly up the short driveway towards the front door of the Todds' house. Behind him he heard the Mondeo pull away.

Fielding found the front door slightly ajar. He knocked then stepped into the spacious hall, careful to wipe his feet on the mat.

'Come in,' said Roma, appearing from the sitting room. She beckoned him towards a door on his left and he stepped through, casting a swift glance around. The place was immaculate. There could be no doubting that it was the abode of people to whom money was no object. That the word 'struggle' had no place in their vocabulary. At least, not when it came to financial matters.

'Would you like a drink?' Roma asked, pouring herself a glass of red wine.

'Whatever you're having,' Fielding smiled.

'I thought you lot weren't supposed to drink on duty,' Todd offered.

'It's not set in stone, Mr Todd,' Fielding said, taking the glass from Roma.

'So, what do we do now?' Todd wanted to know.

Fielding shrugged. 'Wait,' he informed them. 'That's all you *can* do.' He glanced at the Nokia lying on the coffee table in the centre of the room. 'When they're ready, they'll call.'

'And what will *you* be doing?' Todd asked acidly.

'Everything we can, Mr Todd. I want these men caught as much as you do.'

'I doubt that,' Todd snapped. 'After all, it's not *your* daughter they've got, is it?'

Fielding looked at the other man evenly, aware that the more time he spent in David Todd's company, the more he disliked him. The professional side of him said that Todd was understandably stressed by what was happening and was venting his anger on the nearest target.

The other side of him thought that Todd was an irritating prick.

Roma poured herself another glass of wine, aware that her husband was watching.

'Take it easy, Roma,' Todd said quietly.

She met his gaze. 'I'm going to have one more then I'm going to have a shower,' she said defiantly. 'If that's OK with you, David?'

Todd shot her an angry glance and poured himself another Jack Daniel's.

Fielding gazed into the bottom of his glass.

'What if they don't call tonight?' Todd asked. 'How long are we supposed to sit around here waiting for them?'

'They'll call because they want the money. They're not stupid. They know you've got to arrange for that. If they want the ransom within forty-eight hours then you'll hear from them soon enough.'

Todd seemed unimpressed. He sat down on the edge of a chair, glass in hand, and stared at the Nokia as if willing it to ring.

'Is that usual in these circumstances?' Roma wanted to know. 'For kidnappers to want a ransom delivered so quickly?'

'I wish I knew, Mrs Todd,' Fielding said. 'This is the first time I've been involved in a case like this.'

'How reassuring,' chided Todd, getting up to refill his glass.

'You'll have to excuse my husband, Detective Inspector. He hates anything that stops him from being at work. This is more of an inconvenience to him, you see.'

'Shut up, Roma,' snapped Todd. 'You're making yourself look ridiculous.'

Fielding shuffled uncomfortably in his seat.

'Perhaps if you laid off the wine a bit more often then you'd see that,' Todd continued.

Roma refilled her glass and headed for the door.

'I'm going to have a shower,' she announced. 'Excuse me, Detective Inspector.' She closed the door behind her and Fielding heard her footfalls on the stairs.

A funereal silence gradually descended within the room. The odd car drove past outside but, apart from that, nothing disturbed the painful solitude.

Fielding looked at his watch then again at the mobile.

# 10.21 P.M.

Nikki heard the sound first.

A low whimpering that she detected over the crackling of the portable television.

It only took her a second to realise that it was coming from the direction of the bedroom. She looked at Reed then at Dawson who never took his eyes from the TV screen.

'Shall I see to her?' Nikki said hesitantly.

'She's crying,' Dawson said flatly. 'What's the big deal?'

Nikki got to her feet anyway.

'Let her get on with it,' Dawson insisted.

'We don't have to treat her like an animal,' Nikki said.

'Do you know what that kid is?' Dawson asked. 'She's your ticket out of here. That's it. Nothing more. She might as well have pound signs stamped on her forehead. She's a means to an end.'

Nikki glanced at her husband then disappeared into the bedroom where she approached the bed slowly.

'Are you all right?' she asked.

Kirsten continued to whimper quietly. 'I need the toilet,' she said.

Nikki hesitated a moment then returned to the other room.

'She says she needs the toilet.'

'Then get her a bucket.' Dawson chuckled.

'Can you take her, Nik?' Reed asked.

Dawson remained immobile in his chair, still gazing at the fuzzy picture on the screen.

Nikki turned back towards the bedroom.

'Keep her eyes covered,' Dawson reminded her.

She crossed to the bed once again, but this time she reached out gently and touched one of Kirsten's arms. 'Come on,' she said quietly. 'Come with me.'

Kirsten got off the bed and allowed herself to be led out of the bedroom and into the tiny toilet next to it.

There was a cracked porcelain bowl without the benefit of a seat or lid and a small washbasin. Nothing else. The room was less than six-feet square and it smelled strongly of damp.

Nikki pulled the masking tape from around Kirsten's wrists and backed away from her.

'Can you manage?' she said.

Kirsten nodded and, feeling around, lowered herself blindly on to the cold porcelain. Nikki stepped out of the room allowing the little girl at least a small measure of dignity.

'You should stay with her,' said Dawson as Nikki appeared in the sitting room again. 'She could fall, crack her head or something. She wouldn't be much use to us then.'

'Yeah, perhaps you *should* watch her, Nik,' Reed interjected. 'I mean, she might have a gun or a knife hidden somewhere. She might jump the three of us when we're not expecting it.'

Dawson looked directly at Reed, anger in his eyes. 'This isn't a fucking game,' he snapped. 'If anything happens to that kid, we're *all* fucked. If she hurts herself, like I said, then we lose our bargaining power.'

'Then when the fuck are we going to ring her parents?' Reed wanted to know. 'We snatched her to get money. When does that happen? When do they pay up?'

Dawson leaned forward and grabbed the mobile phone lying on the table. He tossed it at Reed.

'You ring them now,' he snarled. 'You want the fucking money. You tell her old man where to drop it. What denominations you want it in. How you want the notes stacked and bound. What he's supposed to carry it in and where you want him to leave it. Go on, big shot, make the fucking call.'

Reed looked at the phone in his hand then at Dawson.

'Make the call,' said the other man defiantly. 'All you've got to do is press the button and talk to the kid's father. Simple as that. Go on.'

Still Reed hesitated.

'For Christ's sake stop it,' Nikki interrupted angrily. 'Both of you.'

'Go and see to the kid, Nikki,' Dawson said without looking at her.

She hesitated then walked out of the room, heading back towards the damp bathroom.

'Give me the phone,' Dawson snapped, holding out his hand.

Reed passed it to him willingly, watching as he jabbed the digits.

'Let's get this sorted,' Dawson snarled. 'Once and for all.'

# 10.36 P.M.

When the Nokia rang no one moved to pick it up.

Fielding, Roma and Todd gazed at the mobile for interminable seconds then Todd finally reached for the phone and raised it to his ear.

'Hello,' he said falteringly.

Silence.

'Hello,' Todd repeated, trying to inject a note of defiance into his voice.

'Is that David Todd?' the voice at the other end asked.

'You know bloody well it is.'

Fielding leaned forward and raised a hand slightly, as if to dampen Todd's tone.

'Time to talk,' the voice informed him. 'Are you listening?'

'Go on.'

'One million by midnight on Saturday, right?'

'You told me that.'

'*Before* midnight on Saturday.'

'Just tell me where you want me to drop the money off.'

'Patience. It's not as easy as that. Have you got a pen handy? You'll need to write this down.'

'Wait a minute.' Todd looked at Roma. 'Pen and paper,' he whispered, cupping one hand over the mouthpiece. She pushed a pad and a Bic in front of him. 'All right, go on.'

'The money's to be paid in tens and twenties,' the voice told him. 'Nothing bigger. Got that? One million in tens and twenties. And you can tell any coppers who might be sitting there with you or listening in to this that if they try marking the cash with fucking dye then the deal's off and your kid ends up dead. Got that?'

'A million in tens and twenties,' Todd repeated, glancing at Fielding who nodded. 'Where do I leave it?'

'You'll get a call tomorrow to tell you that.'

'Is Kirsten still all right?'

'She's OK.'

'Let me speak to her again.'

'Or what? You're not going to pay the money? Don't fuck me around. You know what'll happen to the kid if you do. Get the money and wait for the call.'

Roma suddenly lunged forward and grabbed the phone, dragging it from her husband's startled grip.

'Listen to me, please,' she said. 'Our daughter is ill. She needs medication. Without it she'll die. Please—'

'Who the fuck are you?' the voice snarled.

'Please, let me leave some of her tablets somewhere. You can pick them up. Give them to her.'

'If your old man pays up, you'll have her back in time.'

'She needs the medicine now,' Roma protested.

'And *we* need the fucking money.'

The line went dead.

Roma slumped back on to the sofa.

'The kid's ill,' Dawson said. 'So they reckon.'

'What's wrong with her?' Reed asked.

'Who cares? By twelve o'clock on Saturday night it won't matter anyway.'

'What did they say?' Nikki asked.

'They'll pay,' Dawson smiled. 'What else are they going to do?'

'No, about what's wrong with her.'

Dawson shrugged. 'They didn't say,' he said dismissively. 'I didn't ask. Does it matter?'

'What if it's something serious?' Nikki wanted to know. 'She

285

could be diabetic. She might need insulin or something like that.'

'That's not our problem.'

'It will be if she goes into a coma or dies,' Nikki insisted.

Dawson looked straight at her. 'If her old man doesn't pay up, she'll die anyway,' he said quietly.

# 11.23 P.M.

'I think I should leave you two good people alone now.' Fielding got to his feet.

'I thought you said one of you would be here at all times,' Todd protested. 'In case the kidnappers ring again.'

'They won't ring again tonight,' the DI assured him.

'How can you be sure?' Todd said defiantly. 'Especially as you've got no experience of this kind of case. How do you know what they'll do?'

Fielding regarded the other man evenly for a moment. 'They told you they'd call with details of the drop point,' he said slowly. 'If they said they'll call tomorrow then that's when they'll call. I'll be back here tomorrow morning. I can leave a plain-clothes unit outside the house overnight, if you like.'

'It's a bit late for that, isn't it?' Todd said acidly. 'I mean, a little like shutting the stable door after the horse has bolted.'

Fielding looked at Roma and tried a smile. 'I know this is a stupid thing to say,' he began, 'but try and get some sleep. They won't ring again until tomorrow. I'm sure of that.'

'I'll see you out,' Roma said, walking with him towards the hall.

At the front door she paused. 'What are the chances of getting her back alive, Detective Inspector?' she asked, her voice cracking. 'Honestly.'

'If you do as they tell you then the chances are good. I can't say any more than that. I won't raise your hopes, Mrs Todd.'

'I appreciate your honesty.'

'I'm glad someone does. Goodnight.'

287

He stepped out into the chilly night and heard the door close behind him. He thought about calling a patrol car to pick him up then decided against it. The walk would do him good. Clear his head. He should be home in an hour. Fielding dug his hands into his jacket pockets and set off.

He looked back once and saw the outline of a figure silhouetted against the curtains in the sitting room of the Todds' house. Then, like a fading dream, it vanished from sight.

Todd poured himself another drink and slumped in the chair, looking at the Nokia on the coffee table.

'He's trying to help, David,' Roma said, seating herself opposite him on the sofa. 'They all are.'

'Am I supposed to be grateful? They're doing their jobs. If they were doing them properly they'd have some idea where the hell Kirsten was now. Why the fuck aren't they tracing the calls?'

'Fielding told us. They can't trace calls on a mobile.'

There was a long silence, broken by Todd. 'What the hell were you doing snatching the phone off me the way you did?' he wanted to know.

'I thought they needed to know that there was something wrong with Kirsten.'

'You should have told them the truth. They'd have probably brought her back and forgotten about the money.' He exhaled almost painfully. 'Jesus, of all the kids they could have taken. Why Kirsten?'

'Because they know we've got money. They know we can pay what they want.' She sniffed back tears and poured herself another glass of red wine.

'I'll ring the bank first thing in the morning,' Todd said wearily. 'Arrange to pick up the money. They don't need to know what it's for.'

'You sound ashamed, David. As if what's happened is a slight on your character. As if paying them is a sign of weakness. And you'd never want anyone to think you were weak, would you, David?'

'Don't be so bloody ridiculous,' snapped Todd.

'You don't want to pay them do you? You don't want to *lose* a million pounds of your money. Do you?'

He met her gaze and held it.

'Everything in life is a competition to you, David,' Roma continued. 'Everything has a price, doesn't it? Everything can be bought. Even your own daughter's life. But when you pay that money, you lose that contest with the kidnappers. That's how you see it. I know how your mind works.'

'You're drunk,' he said dismissively.

'I wish I was. Maybe I'd wake up in the morning and all this would be over. Finished. But it won't be, will it?'

Todd got to his feet. 'I'm going to bed,' he said wearily. 'If you've got any sense you'll join me.'

Roma didn't answer, she merely refilled her glass and looked across the room at a framed photograph of Kirsten.

The image of her daughter smiled back at her. Roma felt the hairs on the back of her neck rise and the feeling that she might never see that smile again crept insidiously over her once more.

# 11.36 P.M.

John Dawson dragged himself to his feet and stretched. 'I'm going for a walk,' he said. 'Watch the kid while I'm gone.'

'Are you sure you trust us to do that?' Reed muttered.

Dawson looked at his brother-in-law silently for a moment then headed for the door. 'I won't be long. I need some air,' he said and let himself out. He closed the door behind him and they heard his footsteps receding as he climbed the short flight of stone steps that led from the basement flat to the street.

'How's the kid?' Reed asked.

'I think she's asleep,' Nikki told him, moving quietly towards the bedroom. She peered in to see Kirsten lying on the bed.

'I hope it's nothing more than that,' Reed mused. 'I wonder what *is* wrong with her?'

Nikki didn't answer. She sat in the chair opposite Reed, chewing agitatedly at the skin around the nail of her left index finger.

'What your brother said was right, Nik,' Reed told her. 'Whatever's wrong with the kid won't matter by Saturday night. Once we've got the money—'

'And what if we *haven't* got the money?' Nikki interrupted. 'What if all we've got is a dead child? We don't know what's wrong with her, Jeff. It could be serious. What if she needs medication? We need to know what's wrong with her and if there's anything we can do to help.'

'And how the fuck do we do that?'

'Ring her parents.'

'Don't be so fucking stupid. What difference would that make?'

290

We'd know if there was anything we could do to help her.'

'No way, Nik.'

'We've got to do something, Jeff. If she dies while she's with us, the police might hold us responsible for her death. They might class that as murder.'

Reed shook his head.

Nikki was already reaching for the mobile on the table.

'Don't, Nik,' Reed said, getting to his feet.

'Go and look at her, Jeff,' Nikki said defiantly. 'I mean it. Go and look at her. She looks half dead *now*.'

Reed crossed to the beaded curtain that hung at the doorway to the bedroom and parted it. He could see Kirsten's shoulders rising and falling shallowly as she breathed. Her mouth was slightly open and the breath was rasping in her throat. He moved closer and saw that her skin was the colour of rancid butter.

Reed reached out one hand and touched her forehead gently. The skin was hot. There was no perspiration but she felt as if she'd been sitting in front of a fire for the last few hours.

As he stepped back he smelled something that reminded him of burning plastic. He wrinkled his nose and returned to the living room.

'What do you want to do?' he asked.

'Ask if there's some kind of medicine she has to take. They could drop it off somewhere and one of us could pick it up. Give it to her.'

Reed nodded. 'Do it,' he said, watching as Nikki began dialling.

Roma just stared at the Nokia when it started ringing. For interminable seconds she remained frozen. As if every muscle in her body had been injected with novocaine. Then suddenly she shot out a hand and snatched up the mobile.

'Hello,' she said, her voice a hoarse whisper.

'Is there anyone with you?' the voice at the other end wanted to know.

Roma frowned. Surprised that it was a woman's voice.

'Any police?' Nikki asked.

'No. I'm alone,' Roma told her. 'What do you want? Kirsten's all right, isn't she?'

'You tell me. You say she's ill.'

'She is. Very ill.'

'She needs medication?'

Roma shifted the phone to her other ear.

'If we tell you where to drop her medication off, we'll pick it up and give it to her,' Nikki said.

'Why would you do that?'

'We don't want her to die either. She's no good to us dead. Put the medicine in a carrier bag with instructions on when she has to take it. I'll tell you where to leave it.'

'Thank you.'

'If you tell the police . . .' Nikki tried to inject some steel into her voice. 'If you tell them then she's dead.'

'I understand. Where shall I leave the medicine?'

'You know the multiplex in the town centre? There are rubbish bins outside the main entrance. Leave the bag with the medicine inside the one on the right-hand side tomorrow morning at ten. Just drop it in and walk away. One of us will be watching you so don't try anything.'

'Ten o'clock tomorrow morning,' Roma repeated. 'Thank you.'

'And take the phone with you,' Nikki added finally.

The line went dead.

Roma still had the phone pressed to her ear when Todd appeared in the doorway of the sitting room.

# 11.46 P.M.

'What did they want?'

Roma looked at her husband then at the phone.

'I heard the phone ring,' he told her.

'They want to help Kirsten,' she said.

'They can help her by letting her go.'

'They want me to drop off some of her medication. They say they'll pick it up. Give it to her.'

'And you believe them?'

'Why should they lie, David? They told me that Kirsten's no good to them dead. Even the Detective Inspector said that.'

Todd reached for the phone that was on the antique table near the sitting-room door.

'What are you doing?' Roma asked, getting to her feet.

'I'm calling Fielding.'

'You can't. They said if they saw any police they'd kill her.'

'They're bluffing.' He picked up the phone. 'They tell us in one breath that they'll kill Kirsten and in the next that they don't want her dead. This is all part of their plan.'

'Put the phone down, David,' Roma said, moving closer to her husband. 'You can't reason with these people. This isn't a fucking business deal you're negotiating. It's our daughter's life. Let me drop the medicine off.'

Todd hesitated, the phone still gripped in his fist.

'And where are you going to drop it?' he wanted to know.

'Where they told me. Outside the multiplex in the middle of Kingsfield.'

'When?'

'Tomorrow morning. Ten o'clock.'

He swallowed hard then gently replaced the phone, his breathing shallow and ragged.

'What about the instructions for the money drop?' Todd wanted to know. 'One of us has to be here in case they ring for that.'

'They told me to take the phone with me.'

'What else did he say?' Todd asked.

'It wasn't a man. It was a woman that called.'

'Jesus. How many of them are involved in this?' He walked to the front window and eased the curtain back slightly, peering out into the darkened street beyond.

Was someone, even now, watching the house? Police? Kidnappers?

*Cops or robbers?*

He almost smiled. Almost.

'What did you tell her about Kirsten's illness?' Todd enquired without turning round.

'Just that she needed medication urgently.'

'Nothing about the . . . *nature* of it?'

'What did you want me to do, David? Warn them that they're in danger too?'

He shook his head.

'I'll come with you,' he said finally.

'You can't. You've got to pick up the money from the bank,' she reminded him.

Todd turned to face his wife.

'You can't do this alone, Roma,' he told her. 'You know the kind of people we're dealing with. You need someone with you. The police—'

She cut him short. 'All I've got to do is drop the medicine off. I won't see them or get close to them.'

'How can you be sure? How can you trust them?'

'I don't know if I can, but what option do we have?'

Her words hung in the air.

# 11.58 P.M.

Jeff Reed was slumped on the worn sofa gazing distractedly at the flickering picture on the portable TV when he heard he door of the basement flat open.

Nikki, who was sitting in one of the chairs, tucked her legs beneath her and glanced in the direction of the door.

John Dawson walked in and looked at each of them in turn.

'Short walk,' Reed said.

Dawson ignored him and dropped on to the end of the sofa, also staring at the fuzzy images before him. 'Is the kid asleep?' he asked.

Nikki nodded.

'Let's just hope she wakes up, eh?' Dawson chuckled, lighting a cigarette.

Nikki and Reed exchanged glances. It was Nikki who broke the silence. 'I rang her mother,' she said.

'You what?' Dawson snarled, peering at his sister, the unlit cigarette stuck to his bottom lip.

'The kid is sick,' Nikki continued. 'You said yourself she's no use to us dead. So I—'

'You fucking what?' Dawson hissed.

'She needs medical help,' Reed interjected.

'You rang her fucking mother,' Dawson continued. 'You spoke to her?'

'The police can't trace the call, you said that yourself, John. I—'

'You stupid bitch, Nikki.'

'Hey, watch it,' snapped Reed.

'Fuck off,' Dawson answered, getting to his feet. Again he glared at his sister. 'You fucking stupid bitch.' He enunciated each word carefully and slowly as he looked at her. 'It doesn't matter whether or not they can trace the call. The fact is they heard your voice. They now know that there's a woman involved too. Up until then, as far as the law were concerned, this job had been done by two men. But now you've gone and fucked it up.'

'The kid needs help or she's going to die,' Reed said angrily. 'What the fuck would *you* have done?'

'I wouldn't have called her mother for a cosy little chat. What did you say to her?'

Nikki told him.

'Jesus fucking Christ,' snarled Dawson. 'The law'll be everywhere tomorrow when she makes the drop. As soon as you go to pick up the stuff they'll grab you.'

'They won't dare,' Nikki protested. 'Not after what's been said about us killing the girl if they interfere.'

Dawson shook his head. 'Stupid,' he muttered, shooting Nikki a derisory glance. 'You only had to wait another two days. Less than that.'

'The kid might be dead before then,' Reed reminded him.

Dawson shook his head once again then wandered into the tiny kitchen. He returned with a can of Carlsberg. Flopping back down on to the end of the sofa he tore the ring pull free and drained half the contents in two huge swallows.

'You drive her,' Dawson said, looking at Reed. 'Get the medicine or whatever the fuck the mother's leaving and get out of there as quick as you can. Got it? If you see *anything* at all that looks wrong, any sign of what might be law, get out, whether you've got the stuff or not.'

'What about you?' Nikki wanted to know.

Dawson took another swig from the can then wiped his mouth with the back of his hand.

'I'll stay here with the kid,' he said quietly.

FRIDAY, MARCH 7^TH

# 1.09 A.M.

Luke Hamilton brought the car to a halt and switched off the engine.

'No lights,' Tony Casey remarked, looking at the house in Eastly Road. 'Perhaps they've done a runner.'

Hamilton glanced at the dashboard clock. 'They're probably in bed,' he mused. 'Like anyone else with any sense would be at this time of night.'

Casey looked at him then back at the house and the others that flanked it. Uniform in their design and construction, the only things that distinguished one from another were the different coloured doors and curtains. Here and there attempts had been made to brighten up gardens and even front porches (there were a number of houses sporting hanging baskets) but, for the most part, Eastly Road, like the rest of the Walton Grange Estate, remained neglected.

'Shitholes,' said Casey, casting a derisive eye over the houses. 'Why do you think Reed and his missus wanted to get out?'

'They should have thought more carefully. Especially before they got themselves twenty grand into debt with Max Tate.'

'Yeah, well it's payback time now.'

'I wouldn't mind some payback from Reed's missus,' grinned Casey. 'No wonder Max wants to see her again.'

'Then we'd better do our job and take to him.'

Hamilton hauled himself out of the car and headed towards the short path that led to the front door of the house, closely followed by Casey.

They waited a moment, listening for any sounds from inside,

then Hamilton lifted the knocker and slammed it down hard three times.

No answer. No sounds of movement.

He tried again with more urgency and more force.

Casey stepped on to the small patch of unmown grass that constituted a front lawn, and cupped his hands to his eyes, peering through the glass into the sitting room.

'I can't see anything,' he said.

Across the street several lights flashed on as Hamilton's assault on the door continued. He still pounded, oblivious to the disturbance he was creating.

'They would have come by now if they were here,' Casey said, rejoining his companion.

Hamilton waited a moment then hammered on the door again.

Still nothing.

'They've fucked off,' Casey said, through gritted teeth.

'They wouldn't dare,' Hamilton said.

'Oi! You!'

The voice came from behind them. From across the narrow street.

There was a man standing on the front step of his house, dressed only in a pair of tracksuit bottoms and a crumpled white T-shirt.

Hamilton and Casey looked in the direction of the shout then Hamilton banged once again on the door.

'Are you deaf or something?' the man across the street shouted. 'It's one o'clock in the morning. What the hell do you think you're doing? People are trying to sleep.'

Casey made his way down the path watched by the man who had now been joined by a woman in a long housecoat.

'Do you know them?' Casey asked, hooking a thumb in the direction of the Reeds' house.

'Who are you?' the man wanted to know.

'I said do you know them?'

'Are you police?'

'No,' smiled Casey. 'We just want to know where they are. They owe us some money.'

The man took a step back.

'I haven't seen either of them for a couple of days,' said the woman beside him.

She saw that Hamilton had now left the front door of the house and was making his way back to the parked Datsun.

'If you see them, you tell them someone was looking for them,' Casey said, also retreating towards the car.

'Who?' the man wanted to know.

'They'll know,' Casey called, sliding into the passenger seat.

The Datsun moved away at speed, disappearing into the night.

# 2.17 A.M.

Kirsten shivered and drew her legs up closer to her chest.

With the gaffer tape still wound tightly around her eyes she fumbled for the single blanket on the bed and tried to wrap it around herself. She lay still on the lumpy mattress wishing she was back in her own bed. Wishing she was with her parents.

Thoughts of home and her family brought tears and she cried softly, the salty liquid dampening her cheeks.

She had no idea where she was. Who the people were who were keeping her here or what they wanted. She shivered again and wiped her face on the rough blanket as best she could.

For fleeting seconds she wondered if she should try to pull the tape free. Ease it away from her eyes so that she could see. It was silent in the room (or wherever she was). Perhaps if she just had a tiny peep from beneath the tape blindfold . . .

Kirsten decided against it and pulled the blanket more tightly around her, wanting to drift off to sleep. She wanted to wake and find that all this had been some horrible dream.

The room smelled of damp. She hated the smell. But, most of all, she hated having the tape wrapped around her eyes. She wondered who had done it. Perhaps the same man who had taken her from her mother's car. The lady whose voice she heard every now and then seemed kinder. She had at least offered her food. It hadn't been very nice food but the lady had tried to get her to eat it. Perhaps she should ask her to remove the tape. Just for a while. She *would* keep her eyes shut if the lady asked her to. She would promise and she never broke promises.

Kirsten lay still beneath the blanket and tried to sleep. She sniffed back more tears and, as she did, she detected another smell in the room. A smell she recognised. It was perfume. The kind she smelled when the lady was close to her.

She kept as still as she could, wondering if there was someone in the room with her. She could hear no breathing but, the more she listened, the more she became convinced that she could hear very small movements.

Kirsten was convinced she was being watched.

'Is she asleep?'

Kirsten recognised the voice. It was one of the men who had taken her from her mother.

'I think so,' the lady's voice said, softly. 'She's restless though.'

'I'm not surprised,' said the man. 'Come back to bed.'

*This wasn't the voice of the bad man who had threatened to cut her eyes out. This man's voice was different.*

'I just wanted to make sure she was OK.'

'You mean you wanted to make sure she hadn't died.'

Kirsten shuddered slightly.

'Leave her,' murmured the man's voice. 'She'll be all right. She'll be better when we get that medicine for her.'

'I hope so,' the lady's voice told him.

'By Saturday it won't matter anyway.'

'It will if she dies.'

'She won't.'

Kirsten felt her heart jump.

*Medicine.*

Were they taking her home? Was she going to see her parents again? She wanted to ask them but, instead, she remained still on the mattress.

'We'll get the money and it'll be over,' said the man's voice.

Kirsten wondered what money they were talking about.

'We pay Max Tate and that's it,' the man continued.

*Who was Max Tate?*

'Come on,' the man's voice insisted. 'Leave her, Nik.'

*Nik? There was a girl at school they called Nik. It was short for Nicola. Sometimes they called her Nikki.*

Kirsten listened as the two people who had been watching her left the room.

# 2.19 A.M.

Roma lay on her back staring at the ceiling, unable to sleep.

For the last hour or more she had tossed and turned in the large bed, unable to find the oblivion that she sought so desperately. Not even half a bottle of red wine had aided her in that quest.

Beside her, Todd also rolled around. He too finally slumped on to his back and exhaled deeply.

'David,' Roma murmured.

'Can't sleep,' he said, his voice raw.

'That's not really surprising, is it?'

'I keep wondering what's happening.'

'What they might be doing to Kirsten?' she said.

'No, not that,' Todd said irritably. 'I don't *want* to think about that.' He swung himself out of bed and sat on the edge for a moment, head bowed.

Roma also pulled herself upright, leaning back against the padded headboard. She reached across and switched on the bedside light and a warm glow enveloped the area around the bed. Beyond, in the large bedroom, the shadows were dark and threatening.

'We should tell the police about tomorrow,' Todd said. 'About you dropping off Kirsten's medicine.'

'We can't, David. If the kidnappers see any police . . .' She stopped speaking as if finishing the sentence was too much.

'And what if something goes wrong?'

'There's no reason why it should. I'll leave the medicine where they tell me to and I'll walk away. They'll give it to Kirsten.'

'And she'll be OK for another few days? You know she needs more than tablets this time, Roma. It's gone too far.'

'As soon as we get her back—'

'What if we *don't* get her back?' interrupted Todd, angrily. 'Let's face facts, Roma. Our child could be dead by this time tomorrow.'

'If we pay them what they want—'

Again he cut her short. 'You can't reason with people like that,' Todd hissed. 'They're fucking . . . savages.'

'We're not trying to reason with them, David. We're trying to buy them off.'

'You still have to face the fact that she could die, even if the ransom is paid. She could die and she could . . .' He stopped speaking.

'Kill them too? Good. If our daughter's going to die because of those bastards then I hope they *do* die with her. I *want* them dead, David. For what they've done to Kirsten and for what they've put us through. I want them to die in fucking agony.'

He looked at her, the shadows on her face making her seem even more gaunt. Only in her eyes and her tone was there any fire.

'And if she *does* die. What then, David?' Roma wanted to know. 'What about us? Do we go on? Just the two of us?'

'Where's this going, Roma?'

'If Kirsten dies do you still refuse to allow me to have another child?'

'I've never *refuse* you another child, don't be so bloody stupid.'

'You don't want another child. You're afraid to have another one. In case it has the same condition as Kirsten.'

'The clinic told us that if we had another child there was a chance that it would be affected in the same way as Kirsten. You know that. You heard what they said.'

'A chance, David. Not a certainty. There's also a chance the baby would be fine.'

'Would you want to risk it? Think about the child, Roma,

not just yourself. Do you want it to have to go through everything that Kirsten's had to go through? Operations. Medication its whole life. Wondering what the hell makes it different to other kids.'

'Kirsten's never asked about her condition.'

'And if she does, what are we supposed to tell her? That she's unlikely to live past twenty? That if she doesn't receive regular medication she'll die? That she could be a danger to others?'

'According to you, that won't matter after tomorrow night. It wouldn't matter to you if she *did* die would it, David?'

He glared at her.

'Then you wouldn't have to worry about her any more,' Roma continued. 'You wouldn't have to be ashamed that she isn't like everyone else's child. That she isn't perfect. You wouldn't have to be afraid of her any more.'

'You know, Roma, at least when you're drunk I can tolerate some of the crap you come out with,' Todd said derisively. 'Why don't you get drunk now. I think I like you better that way.' He got to his feet and stalked across to the bedroom door. He hesitated, thought about saying something else, then slammed it behind him and padded across the landing.

Roma lay motionless, gazing into the dark shadows that surrounded the bed.

# 2.23 A.M.

Nikki jerked awake at the sound.

Not a scream. Not as piercing as that. More a protracted groan that dissolved away into a series of racking sobs.

She swung herself out of bed and, wearing just the long T-shirt that she slept in, she padded through the small sitting room, past the sleeping form of her brother slumped on the sofa, and on to the bedroom beyond.

Kirsten was hunched against the wall, still whimpering.

Nikki hesitated in the doorway for a moment then crossed to the little girl and sat down beside her, snaking one arm around her shoulder.

Kirsten recoiled, her breathing becoming more rapid, tears still coursing down her cheeks from beneath the tape.

'It's all right,' Nikki said softly. 'It's all right.' She pulled Kirsten closer to her.

'I had a bad dream,' Kirsten murmured, her voice cracking.

'It's all right now. Don't worry.'

'Can I have a drink of water, please?'

Nikki gave the little girl one more reassuring hug then moved swiftly into the tiny kitchen and returned with a glass of water that she held close to Kirsten's lips. The little girl sipped at it then moved her head away.

'Thank you,' she said quietly.

Nikki started to get up.

'Can you just stay for a minute?' Kirsten asked. 'Please?'

Nikki hesitated a moment then sat back down on the lumpy mattress.

'Just until I go back to sleep,' Kirsten told her.

'You lay down then,' Nikki told her. 'Are you warm enough?'

Kirsten nodded but Nikki pulled the blanket over her anyway and tucked it around her.

'My mum does that,' Kirsten said as she settled her head on the grubby pillow. 'She tucks me in. Sometimes my dad does.'

Nikki perched on the edge of the bed and looked down at the little girl.

'Have you got any children?' Kirsten asked.

'No.'

'Would you like some? Is that why you took me away from my mum and dad?'

'No. That wasn't why we took you.'

Nikki got to her feet again.

'Please don't go yet,' Kirsten implored. 'Just stay until I go to sleep. You said you would.'

Nikki sat on the bed once more. Kirsten moved closer to her.

'I have bad dreams sometimes,' the little girl told her. 'I can't always remember them though.'

'Everyone has bad dreams.'

*Some people live them.*

'Do you?'

'Sometimes.'

'What do you think about to help you get back to sleep again? My dad says that I should think about nice things. About my friends at school or going on holiday or going to stay with my grandma and grandad.'

'Think about nice things then and you'll go back to sleep.'

'What do *you* think about?'

'I think about nice things too.'

*Money. Being free of bastards like Max Tate.*

'Did *your* dad used to read you stories when you were a little girl?'

Nikki swallowed hard. 'I never knew my dad,' she confessed. 'He left home when I was two. I can't remember him.'

'Where did he go? To heaven?'

'What makes you say that?'

'My Grandad Frank left my dad before I was born, and Dad says he went to heaven. Perhaps that's where *your* dad went.'

'Perhaps,' Nikki murmured. 'You said you thought about your friends at school to help you sleep. Have you got lots of friends?'

'I like nearly all the people in my class. Chloe's my *best* friend though. And Daisy. And Megan.'

Nikki looked down at Kirsten.

*Are all their parents as loaded as yours?*

'Did you have lots of friends when you were at school?'

'Quite a few.'

'Were they all girls?'

Nikki smiled weakly. 'When I got older,' she said brightly, 'I had more friends who were boys.'

Kirsten giggled. 'There's one girl at my school with the same name as yours,' she announced.

Nikki stiffened.

'Nikki,' Kirsten continued. 'The teachers call her Nicola.'

'What makes you think my name's Nikki?'

'I heard one of the men call you Nik. That's short for Nikki, isn't it? Is he your husband?'

Nikki got to her feet. 'You go to sleep now,' she said with an air of finality.

Kirsten nodded. 'Thanks, Nikki,' she called.

'How does she know your name?'

Nikki stepped back in surprise as she heard the words. She looked directly at John Dawson who was glaring alternately at her then at Kirsten.

'Did you tell her?' he demanded.

'What woke you up?'

'You, talking to your little friend. So, did you tell her your name?'

'She heard it,' Nikki explained.

'What else does she know?'

'Nothing.'

'Don't get close to her. Don't make friends with her. She's a means to an end. That's it. Besides, if you get too friendly you might start telling her things she shouldn't know.'

Nikki made to push past but Dawson gripped her arm and leaned closer to her.

'Stay away from her,' he said forcefully.

Nikki shook loose and made her way back to her bedroom.

Dawson stood in the doorway, his gaze fixed firmly on the motionless form of Kirsten Todd.

# 8.13 A.M.

'We *should* tell the police.'

David Todd fastened his tie, glancing in the bedroom mirror at the reflection of his wife. She was still wrapped in the towel she had wound around herself when she emerged from the shower.

'There's no *need* to tell the police, David,' Roma said, drying herself. 'I follow the instructions they give me. Leave the medicine where they tell me and that's it.'

'Someone should be with you in case something goes wrong.'

'Nothing will go wrong as long as I do what they tell me.'

Todd watched in the mirror as she dropped the towel and pulled on her pants and bra. He finally turned to face her.

'You might be in danger,' he said quietly. 'Be careful, Roma.'

She smiled at him. 'I'll be OK,' she said, trying to reassure herself as much as her husband.

They were both startled by the ringing of the doorbell.

Todd hurried down the stairs and opened the front door.

DI Fielding nodded a greeting and Todd stepped aside to usher him in.

'I hope I'm not too early,' Fielding said as Todd showed him through into the large kitchen. 'I didn't want to disturb you.'

'We didn't really get much sleep last night,' Todd said, a slight edge to his voice. 'You're not disturbing us. Where's your colleague?'

'He's got his own duties to perform. He'll be here later. What time are you picking up the money, Mr Todd?' Fielding wanted to know.

'The bank said they'd have it ready for me as early as possible. I leave for London as soon as I'm ready. It'll take me a couple of hours in the traffic. I should be back here by lunchtime. I'm doing *my* bit, Detective Inspector Fielding.'

'Meaning what, Mr Todd?'

'Well, you haven't exactly set the world alight with your investigation so far have you?'

'Neither phone that's being used by the kidnappers has been reported stolen,' Fielding said evenly. 'That means they were probably acquired illegally and the chips have been changed. They're untraceable. Also, the background checks that we ran on you and your wife don't indicate any involvement in this situation with your daughter. As far as we're concerned, neither of you are implicated in the kidnap.'

'How dare you?' snapped Todd.

'It's routine, Mr Todd. Parents are often the first suspects in cases such as this.'

'I could report you for this. You come into my house and accuse me of being involved in the kidnapping of my own daughter, I—'

'No one's accusing you, Mr Todd,' Fielding said quietly. 'As I said, investigation into the backgrounds of the parents is routine.'

Todd clenched his jaw furiously.

They both heard footfalls on the stairs.

'Excuse me,' Todd said bristling, and left the room.

Roma entered the kitchen, her hair still damp. She was dressed in a black polo neck and a pair of tight-fitting jeans flared over black ankle boots.

'Would you like some coffee?' she asked Fielding.

He accepted, watching as she poured him a cup and pushed it across the worktop towards him.

'Any toast? Croissants?' she continued.

'I'm fine, thanks,' Fielding told her.

'It's no problem,' she insisted.

'Please, Mrs Todd. I know it's a ridiculous thing to say but just relax. This is more than I usually have for breakfast anyway.' He smiled and sipped at the coffee, watching as she poured herself a cup and sat down on one of the high stools opposite him.

'Does anyone at your college know what's going on?' Fielding asked.

Roma shook her head. 'I rang in and told them I wasn't feeling too good,' she said. 'Didn't know when I'd be back. They were fine about it.'

*Tell him about the phone call.*

She sipped her coffee, holding the cup with both hands to stop it shaking.

'My colleagues are due to speak to your daughter's doctors today. Try and find out a little more about her condition.'

'I told you all you need to know,' Roma snapped.

'I realise that, Mrs Todd. But there might be things you left out. Things you forgot. That'd be understandable in the circumstances. You've got enough to think about already.'

'What are you expecting Kirsten's doctors to tell you?'

Fielding shrugged. 'Like I said, the more we know, the better,' he explained.

'It won't help her. No matter how much more you know.'

*Dropping her medicine off for the kidnappers to pick up.* That'll help her.

Fielding sipped his coffee.

'Tell him.'

The DI turned when he heard Todd's voice behind him. 'Tell me what?' he asked.

Roma glared at her husband furiously.

'Tell me what?' Fielding repeated, his tone darkening.

'After you left last night, the kidnappers called again,' Todd announced. 'They want us to drop some of Kirsten's medication off so they can pick it up and give it to her.'

'Why the hell didn't you call me?' Fielding demanded.

Todd opened his mouth to speak but Roma beat him to it. 'I didn't want you involved,' she said, looking at Fielding.

'It's my *job* to be involved, Mrs Todd.'

'They said if they saw any police they'd kill her.'

'They won't see any,' Fielding assured her, pulling his mobile from his jacket. He jabbed in the number and waited. 'Rob, it's me. I want you at the Todds' place in thirty minutes. And bring Ray Griffin with you.'

He put the mobile back in his pocket then looked at Roma. 'Now, tell me what they said.'

# 8.41 A.M.

'Make sure you're close enough, so that as soon as she drops the stuff, you pick it up. Get it and get out.' John Dawson looked first at his sister then at Jeff Reed. 'There'll be law around somewhere, so be careful,' he continued.

'Even though they know what might happen if they tell the police?' Nikki protested.

'Yeah. The police might not try to jump you there and then, so get the stuff and get the fuck out of there without being followed. Quick. If anything looks even remotely dodgy then get out anyway.'

'And leave the medicine behind?' Nikki said.

Dawson merely held her gaze.

'If you don't trust us to do this then come with us,' Reed said.

'So all three of us can get caught?' Dawson sneered, shaking his head. 'You set this up. You two see it through.'

'You'll be there when the money's dropped though, won't you?' Reed challenged.

'Fucking right I will,' Dawson hissed. 'I don't trust you to pick up a million without any help. Besides, the money matters to me. The kid's medication *doesn't*.' He took a drag on his cigarette. 'You know, if you get caught, they're not going to knock off ten years just because you suggested this shit with the kid's medicine. You're still kidnappers.' He grinned. 'Even if you have got feelings.' Dawson chuckled. It was a hollow sound.

'What are you going to do while we're gone?' Reed demanded.

'Keep an eye on the kid,' Dawson told him, taking another

316

drag on his cigarette. 'But don't worry about me. You just concentrate on what *you're* doing.' He got to his feet and crossed to the black holdall that lay behind the sofa. From inside he withdrew something that Reed couldn't make out at first. Only when Dawson put it on the table did he recognise the sleek outline of the 9mm Beretta automatic.

Nikki glanced at the gun and swallowed hard.

'Take that if you want,' Dawson said.

'We won't need it,' Nikki assured him.

'You sound very sure of that, Nik,' Dawson chided.

'You keep the fucking thing,' snapped Reed. 'You might need it to control the kid.'

Dawson held his gaze for a moment then a slight smile creased his lips. He took the automatic from the table and stuck it into his belt.

'Once you pick up the medicine, make sure you're not being followed,' Dawson said. 'Drive round in circles for a few streets. If the same car's on your tail then the law are following you.'

'And what if they are?' Nikki wanted to know.

'Just don't bring them back here.'

'They wouldn't dare follow us, not while we've still got the kid,' Reed said defiantly.

Dawson raised his eyebrows. 'Be careful anyway,' he repeated. He watched as they both got to their feet. Nikki slipped the mobile into her jacket pocket.

'I'll call her in ten minutes,' she said. 'Tell her where to drop the stuff.'

'I thought she already knew,' Dawson said.

'I don't want to be predictable, John,' Nikki retorted. 'I'll give her another location to drop it off at.'

Dawson smiled, watching them as they made their way towards the door.

'Don't fuck it up,' he called.

The door slammed behind them.

Dawson sat back on his chair, listening to the sounds of their footsteps on the stone steps that led to street level. For long moments he rocked lazily back and forth on the back legs of the chair then he got to his feet and crossed, again, to the black holdall.

There were things inside he would need.

# 8.44 A.M.

The tracking device was smaller than a child's thumbnail. Ray Griffin prodded it gently with the tip of his ballpoint, moving it slightly on the slippery worktop.

Griffin was a small man with greying hair and a moustache. He wore thick bi-focals that he removed occasionally in order to chew on one of the arms. He had a ready smile and, when he spoke, his voice had a soothing quality. It seemed that nothing in the world could hurry him.

'It's got a range of one mile,' Griffin said in his relaxed tone. 'That's it.' He brushed a fleck of imaginary dust from the sleeve of his navy blue jacket. Beneath it he wore an open-necked shirt and black trousers.

'What if they find it?' Roma asked, watching as Griffin prised the plastic circle from inside the lid of the medicine bottle free and slipped the tracking device carefully behind it.

'They won't,' Griffin assured her. 'I can superglue the top back inside the cap. Even if they suspected there was a bug inside they'd never get it off.'

'It's our best chance, Mrs Todd,' Fielding told her. 'You drop off the medicine as you agreed. We'll follow the signal the tracker gives off. It'll lead us straight to them.'

'And then what?' Roma demanded.

'We'll deal with that when it happens,' Fielding said.

'Won't they be expecting something like this, guv?' DS Young wanted to know.

'These are amateurs, Rob. There's no reason to think they'll suspect anything.'

319

'Like I said,' Griffin interjected. 'Even if they *suspect* there's a bug, they won't be able to find it.'

'I hope you're right, Ray,' Young said.

Griffin screwed the cap back into place and set the bottle of tablets on the worktop. He pressed a button on the small receiver he was holding and it emitted a low beep. 'It's working,' he said smiling.

'What time did they say you had to make the drop?' Fielding asked.

'Ten,' said Roma, glancing at her watch. 'Outside the multiplex in the centre of Kingsfield.'

She looked up as the Nokia rang twice. She snatched it up.

'Have you got what your daughter needs?' said the voice at the other end.

'Yes,' Roma replied. She nodded towards Fielding.

'Right, then you'd better let *us* have it,' the voice told her. 'Where are you now?'

'I'm at home.'

'Get in your car and drive towards Kingsfield. We'll give you instructions as you get near the drop-off point.'

'You told me to drop the medicine outside the multiplex,' Roma protested.

'Change of plan,' the voice snapped. 'Just start driving. We'll be in touch again soon.'

The line went dead.

'They've changed the drop point,' Roma said, her mouth dry.

'That's not a problem,' Fielding said. 'I'll be following you in one car, DS Young will be in another. We'll both be tracing your movements by phone *and* with the help of the tracking device. Just do as they say. We'll be close to you at all times.'

Roma nodded and dropped the bottle of tablets into her jacket pocket. She picked up her car keys and the Nokia and headed for the front door, followed by the three policemen.

'Just do as they tell you and your daughter will be fine,' Fielding said, doing his best to sound reassuring.

Roma slid behind the wheel of her Range Rover and started the engine.

'Give her three minutes,' Fielding said, watching as the silver car disappeared around a corner. 'Then follow her.' He looked down at the small unit in his hand which was giving off a low rhythmic beep every second. 'This had better fucking work, Ray,' he said, looking at Griffin.

'It will,' Griffin assured him. 'Just don't let her get more than a mile away or you'll lose the signal.'

Fielding looked at his watch once again then all three men climbed into their cars and, one by one, drove off.

# 9.47 A.M.

She knew that someone was in the room with her.

Kirsten sat up on the bed moving her head from side to side, aware of a presence but unable to pinpoint it.

She wondered if she dare pull the tape away from her eyes for a second, just long enough to see who was close to her. She decided against it.

Perhaps the lady had brought her something to eat or drink. The lady was nice to her. The lady spoke to her.

Kirsten felt nervous. She didn't like this silence.

There was a creak. The sound of a floorboard as weight was put upon it. She jerked her head in the direction of the sound.

No. This wasn't the lady. The lady would have spoken to her by now.

She hoped it wasn't the man who said bad words to her. Who shouted at her. Who threatened to hurt her.

Kirsten sucked in a deep breath which rattled in her throat.

She heard a low click. A whirring sound. It seemed to be moving around her, moving with the footsteps.

Kirsten thought she was going to cry.

'I need to go to the toilet,' she said, anxious to break this silence.

The whirring sound stopped.

'Soon,' said a voice that she immediately recognised. It belonged to the bad man. The man who shouted. Who threatened. But it sounded different this time. 'You can wait a little while, can't you?' There was no hard edge to it now. No menace.

Kirsten nodded, hesitantly, still not sure whereabouts in the room he was. 'I'm hungry too,' she said.

'I'll get you something in a minute,' John Dawson told her. 'Can you just be patient for a little bit longer?'

Again she nodded. He sounded nice now.

'Would you like a drink of water?' he wanted to know.

Kirsten nodded. She felt a weight on the bed beside her and realised that he had sat down next to her. A glass was pushed into her hand and she sipped from it. Dawson took it gently from her then stood up.

'Where's the lady?' Kirsten asked.

'She's gone out for a little while,' Dawson told her. 'I'll look after you until she gets back. You just sit quietly for a minute.'

Again Kirsten heard the click and the low whirring.

Dawson held the camcorder before him, moving around the bed slowly, tracking with the device. He moved smoothly, watching Kirsten then looking at her image on the screen.

'What are you doing?' she asked softly.

'Just sit quietly,' he said, his voice little more than a whisper.

Again he moved back and forth, allowing the camcorder to capture every inch of her body as she sat against the wall on the small bed.

'Your name's Kirsten, isn't it?' he said quietly, still recording.

She nodded.

'You *can* talk to me, you know,' chuckled Dawson. 'I won't hurt you. Tell me your name.'

'Kirsten.'

'Have you got any middle names? Some of the little girls I know have got middle names too.'

'Danielle. That's my middle name.'

'That's a pretty name. Do you like it?'

She nodded.

'I think that if a little girl has a pretty name then *she's* pretty too. Do you think that's true? Do people tell *you* you're pretty?'

'Sometimes.'

The whirring noise stopped.

Dawson crossed to his holdall and pulled it open. He took out a 35mm camera and checked that there was film loaded into it then he pressed the Nikon to his eye and took three or four pictures of Kirsten.

'You just sit there like that,' he murmured.

'I really do need to go to the toilet, please,' Kirsten said.

'OK,' Dawson breathed. 'Hold my hand. I'll take you.'

Kirsten hesitated.

'It's all right,' he told her gently. 'I said I won't hurt you. Come on.'

He took her small hand and guided her from the bedroom towards the tiny toilet. He pushed open the door and helped her on to the cracked plastic seat.

'Can you manage?' he wanted to know.

Kirsten nodded.

'I'll be outside if you need me,' Dawson informed her.

As he walked out he left the door open so that she was clearly in his view.

Once again he reached for the camcorder.

# 9.49 A.M.

The centre of Kingsfield had yet to become busy. Roma guided the Range Rover along streets not yet crowded with shoppers.

In addition to the main street there was also a sizeable covered shopping centre where most of the serious trading was done, and an outdoor market that bustled with life on a Tuesday and a Thursday. A number of the car parks were still half empty.

As she drove she glanced about her, gazing at every car that passed with suspicion and dread.

Was she at this very moment being watched? Were the kidnappers sitting in the car ahead?

She drove past the multiplex, turned the car around the roundabout at the bottom of the gentle slope and drove back up, the Nokia lying on the passenger seat beside her. Her own mobile was on the dashboard in front of her.

It was that which rang first.

Roma snatched it up.

'Any contact yet?' Fielding wanted to know.

'Nothing. Where *are* you?'

'Close by. We can see you. Just keep driving. As soon as you hear from them, let me know.'

He hung up.

Roma turned left and headed down slowly past a garden centre towards another roundabout. As she turned the Range Rover, Kirsten's tablets, wrapped in a plastic sandwich bag, slid across the seat.

Roma felt hot. She wound down the window to let in some

air. She could feel the perspiration on her back and face despite the coolness of the morning.

She drove back up the road, the multiplex ahead of her again now.

*They're not going to make you drop the medicine there, they told you that.*

She looked around. If not there, then where?

There were so many places. So many vantage points where they could be stationed.

A car pulled in behind her and she studied it in her rear-view mirror. There was a woman driving, a man in the passenger seat obviously giving instructions.

*Was that them? Would the phone ring any second?*

The car turned off to the right into a large pay-and-display car park.

Roma drove on.


Jeff Reed looked at his watch. 'Call her,' he said. 'It's time. Let's get this over with.'

Beside him in the passenger seat of the stolen Datsun, Nikki hesitated. 'We told her ten o'clock,' she said.

'Just do it, Nik.' He gripped the wheel tightly, glancing around the car park.

There were vehicles parked all around them. Immediately ahead was a large branch of John Lewis. Beyond it lay the shopping centre.

Still Nikki wavered.

'Call her,' Reed snapped.

Nikki began to dial.

# 9.58 A.M.

The Nokia rang once.

Roma grabbed it and pressed it to her ear. 'Hello,' she said breathlessly, careful to keep the car under control as she wedged the mobile between her ear and shoulder.

'Park your car and go inside the shopping centre,' Nikki told her.

'Where shall I park?'

'Where you like. Just leave your car and take the medicine inside. Take the phone too. When you're inside I'll tell you where to drop the stuff.'

'Is my daughter all right?'

'The quicker you drop her medicine off, the better she'll be.'

The line went dead.

Roma swung the car into the first available space, tucked the Nokia into the back pocket of her jeans and reached for her own mobile. She dialled Fielding's number with shaking hands and waited.

'They want me to take the tablets inside the shopping centre,' she told the DI when he answered.

'Leave your own phone on,' Fielding told her. 'Whereabouts are you?'

'At the bottom end of the centre, down by Marks and Spencer, I'm just about to go in.'

'Put your phone in your pocket; if they're watching, you don't want them to see you using it. We've got a good signal from the tracking device so don't worry.'

Roma pushed the glass door and stepped inside, the sound

327

of her heels clicking on the floor. As she walked she looked around, wondering where they were watching her from. Wondering how many of them there were. She felt weighed down, the Nokia in her back pocket, her own mobile in her jacket and, in her other jacket pocket, Kirsten's tablets.

She walked on.

Fielding reached for the two-way in the Datsun.

'Puma One, come in,' he said into the handset. 'Rob, are you receiving?'

There was a crackle then he heard Young's voice.

'Puma One, receiving,' said the DS.

'She's inside the shopping centre,' Fielding told his subordinate. 'They haven't told her where to make the drop yet. My guess is they'll leave it until the last minute.'

'Maybe we should have used back up on this, guv.'

'The kidnappers are as nervous as Mrs Todd. I don't want them panicking. If they think she's being tailed by undercover guys they might do a runner. As long as they pick up the medicine we've got them anyway.'

'As long as this bloody tracker works.'

'It'll work. What's your position?'

'I'm just passing the multiplex, heading across the traffic lights towards the centre now.'

'Just keep driving round until I tell you they've made the pick up.'

'Got it.'

'Where shall I tell her to go?' Nikki said, looking at Reed.

'What's the most crowded part of the centre?' he asked, tapping agitatedly on the steering wheel.

'The open area in the middle where the fountains are.'

'Too obvious, besides the fucking law could have dozens of plain-clothes people watching her.'

'So where?'

'I'm thinking,' Reed hissed irritably. He tried to swallow but it felt as if his throat were full of chalk.

'I know,' Nikki said. She dialled again.

Roma walked slowly, her eyes scanning every face. She expected every figure that walked towards her to stop her. To ask her for the tablets. To tell her not to turn around or contact the police. To . . .

The Nokia rang.

She dragged it from her back pocket and pressed it to her ear.

'Yes,' she said, moving quickly past a mother who was trying to pacify her screaming two-year-old.

'There's a Starbucks about halfway down, close to a set of exit doors,' Nikki told her. 'Head for there.'

'I'm almost there now,' Roma told her.

'Leave the medicine in the waste bin opposite. Drop it in and just walk away. If anyone else goes near that bin or near you then we'll assume they're police and the deal's off. Do you understand?'

'Yes. Listen, please don't hurt my daughter. I'm doing what you told me to do.'

'Drop the medicine in the waste bin and walk away.'

Again the line went dead.

'Drive round now, Jeff,' Nikki said, sitting back in her seat as Reed jammed the car into reverse.

He pulled out a little quickly, almost colliding with a Mondeo whose driver gestured angrily to him.

'Come on,' Nikki urged.

Reed spun the wheel and guided the car out of the space. He headed back the way he'd come, the perspiration soaking through his T-shirt.

# 10.04 A.M.

There were two of them. Both teenagers. Barely fourteen.

The assistant in HMV had been watching them surreptitiously ever since they entered the video department of the store, looking as they picked up DVDs and video cassettes. Occasionally replacing the goods in the racks, sometimes holding on to them for a minute or two. Wandering up and down the aisles, sometimes alone or sometimes together.

He had watched the two boys on the bank of closed-circuit TV screens beneath the counter as they had wandered through into the Soundtracks and Easy Listening section of the store. He had seen one of them pick up two CDs and slip them inside his Kangol fleece.

It had been then that he'd pointed them out to a colleague, suggesting it might be a good idea if she called the police and had them waiting for the thieving little shits when they walked out of the store. Uniformed officers usually patrolled the shopping centre, as well as the white-shirted security guards entrusted with keeping order within the shopping area.

Now he watched as the boys made their way back through the DVD section, loitering beside the racks.

He saw one of them pick up two of the slim boxes and slip them inside his jacket then both of them made for the escalators that would take them back to the ground floor.

The assistant's colleague assured him that the police were already on their way.

The boys were halfway down the escalators now, trying their best to look nonchalant.

330

They stepped off the moving stairway and headed for the main entrance.

As they passed through it, the alarm, triggered by the security tags on the stolen merchandise, erupted into life.

Both boys ran.

Roma reached into her pocket for the tablets and slipped them into the top of the waste bin.

Several people drinking coffee at a nearby table watched her with passing interest as she turned and looked around, waiting for someone to approach.

For interminable seconds she stood there then she moved off briskly, not looking back. Somewhere behind her she could hear an alarm.

There was a man walking towards her, unshaven and scruffily dressed.

*Was this him? Was this one of the men who held her daughter hostage?*

He passed her and headed into a nearby sports shop.

Roma walked on.

Reed stopped the car, watching as Nikki climbed out and made her way through the doors that led into the shopping centre.

Starbucks was just ahead of her. She could see the waste bin and she quickened her pace to reach it.

The uniformed policeman rounded the corner, stepped in front of the bin and didn't move. He was looking in the other direction as if searching for something or someone in the jumble of shoppers now starting to fill the shopping centre.

Nikki hesitated, her pulse racing. She reached for the mobile.

'What have you done?' she rasped into the mouthpiece.

'What are you talking about?' Roma's voice answered. 'I left the tablets where you told me to.'

'And what about the copper?' Nikki hissed. 'That's it. Deal's off.'

She turned on her heel and headed back outside to the waiting car.

Reed looked at her in bewilderment as she scrambled into the passenger seat.

'Move it, Jeff,' she said urgently. 'She set us up.'

'What do you mean?'

'There was a copper waiting,' Nikki told him.

He snatched the mobile from her. 'Fucking bitch,' he bellowed into the mouthpiece. 'You just killed your own kid. Fucking stupid bitch.'

He hurled the mobile furiously out of the window then guided the car away towards the road.

Roma turned back towards Starbucks, her breath coming in gasps. She ran towards the bin where she'd left the tablets.

As she drew nearer she saw the uniformed constable standing there, still gazing at the mass of shoppers coming his way.

She wanted to run to him, tell him to move away from the bin, ask him what he was doing. Demand that he tell her why he was standing there.

She didn't have to.

The uniformed man spotted his target.

The two teenagers came hurtling towards him, crashing into people, weaving in and out of the shoppers.

The constable stepped in front of them and grabbed them both.

CDs, DVDs and video tapes spilled from their jackets and clattered to the floor. The boys struggled helplessly for a moment then gave up. Another uniformed officer and the assistant from HMV were making their way through the crowd towards them.

*A fair cop.*

Roma put both hands to her head in despair. She hurried across to the waste bin and dug her hand inside, her fingers closing on the plastic bag the tablets were wrapped in.

Oblivious to the stares of onlookers, she sank slowly to her knees, tears coursing down her cheeks.

# 12.42 P.M.

'There was nothing we could do about it, Mrs Todd,' Fielding said irritably. 'I didn't want that to happen any more than you did. If they'd picked up the tablets we'd have followed them straight back to where your daughter's being held.'

Roma poured herself another glass of wine and swallowed half of it in one despairing swallow. 'Only now that won't be happening, will it?' she said angrily.

'If there was anything that could have been done to prevent it—' Fielding began.

'Forget it,' she snapped, cutting him short. 'They'll kill her now. I know they will. They think I double-crossed them.'

'They won't kill your daughter,' Fielding said, trying to inject calm into his voice. 'They need her alive to collect the ransom. You *know* that.'

'Tracking device,' Roma said under her breath. She picked up the bottle of tablets and hurled them across the kitchen. 'What fucking use is it now?'

Fielding said nothing. DS Young stepped back and lowered his gaze.

'When will your husband be back?' the DI asked.

'What does it matter?'

'The important thing is that the money drop goes ahead without any problems,' Fielding reminded her. 'If they get their money, you'll get your daughter back unharmed. We tried something today and it didn't work.'

'And it might have cost Kirsten her life,' Roma shouted. 'I haven't heard anything from them for nearly three hours.

333

Nothing since we got back here to the house. She could be dead already.'

'They need her. They're not going to kill her. They'll wait now. They know that if they wait until midnight tomorrow they'll get paid. There's no *need* for them to contact you.'

'Sorry to interrupt, guv,' Young offered. 'But it seems that after what Mrs Todd told us about her daughter's condition, we really should be concerned about the bastards who took her too.'

Fielding looked at his subordinate, his eyes cold. 'Our only concern is the girl,' he said. 'They can take their chances as far as I'm concerned.'

Roma glanced at him and took another sip from her wine glass.

An uneasy silence settled over the room finally broken by Fielding.

'Do you want to call your husband, Mrs Todd?' he asked. 'Make sure he's picked up the money?'

Roma shook her head wearily. 'He'll have got it,' she said. 'He would have rung if there'd been a problem. He should be on his way back by now.' She sat forward, head cradled in her hands.

Fielding and Young exchanged helpless glances.

'They can't hide for ever,' Fielding said. 'Kingsfield's not a big place. We'll find them.'

Roma ignored his declaration for a moment.

'What if they're not even *in* Kingsfield?' she wanted to know.

'We'll *find* them,' Fielding repeated, a note of defiance in his voice.

The knock on the front door broke the silence. Roma sucked in a deep breath, as if steeling herself to make the walk from the kitchen, then went to answer it.

Fielding looked at Young who was sipping coffee from a china cup, looking as if he were terrified of dropping the expensive crockery. He finally set it down on the worktop. 'What now, guv?' he wanted to know.

'We wait,' Fielding told him.

Roma returned with a battered Jiffy bag which she laid on the kitchen table.

She pulled at the seal but staples had been hammered haphazardly into it then covered with brown masking tape. The address had been scrawled in black marker pen on the faded brown exterior. Muttering to herself, she reached into a nearby drawer and pulled out a knife, hacking the Jiffy bag open.

There was a loud crack as the videotape inside fell out and hit the worktop.

Fielding now crossed to Roma's side and saw the white label Sellotaped to the front panel. Written on it, in the same spidery hand as that on the front of the bag, were two words:

*PLAY THIS*

'Don't touch it,' Fielding said, realisation finally sweeping over him. He pulled a handkerchief from his pocket and lifted the videotape, inspecting it.

'Who delivered it, Mrs Todd?' Young asked, joining his superior.

'A courier,' Roma told him. 'I had to pay the delivery charge on it.'

Fielding glanced down at the Jiffy bag and saw that there were no stamps on it.

'It's from them, isn't it?' Roma said, her voice a hoarse whisper.

'We'd better find out,' Fielding muttered.

All three of them headed for the sitting room.

# 12.45 P.M.

Roma sat on the sofa facing the television screen. Young seated himself in one of the chairs and Fielding held the tape before the video recorder.

The colour had drained from Roma's face and she had her palms pressed together before her mouth in an attitude of prayer.

Fielding pushed the tape into the machine and backed off.

Roma pressed the Play button on the remote.

On the television screen there was nothing at first. A moment or two of blank leader, and then a vision.

Kirsten sitting on the battered single bed, the tape still wound tightly around her eyes.

Roma let out an involuntary gasp and began quivering, her own eyes bulging in their sockets.

'Jesus,' murmured Young.

Fielding stroked his chin.

'Say what I told you to say.'

The voice came from off screen. The camera never left Kirsten or the bed.

Roma was crying softly now as she watched transfixed.

'Say it,' the voice repeated.

'Mum, help me, please,' Kirsten said, trying not to cry.

'And the rest,' the voice snapped.

'You tricked them,' Kirsten faltered.

'Say it,' snarled the voice.

Tears were coursing down Roma's cheeks and she moved closer to the screen, dropping to her knees like a supplicant at some vile altar.

336

'They told you what would happen if you tricked them,' Kirsten continued.

'Oh, please God, no,' Roma gasped.

The figure that moved into shot was dressed in black and kept his back to the camera.

There was a jerky movement and the lens was pointed downwards, blurrily out of focus for a moment. Then the image swam into horrific clarity.

A knife, about six inches long and serrated on one side, came into view.

'No,' Roma wailed.

Fielding moved to turn the video off but Roma snatched the remote from him.

'I want to see her,' she said, her cheeks sodden.

The figure moved towards Kirsten, back always to the camera, and reached for one of her arms. He pulled it towards the small bedside cabinet and pushed her hand down on to the scratched wood.

Kirsten was trying to pull away, her own tears now flowing freely.

'Please don't,' she wailed.

Roma was sobbing uncontrollably now, unable to tear her eyes away from the vision before her.

'Don't fuck with us,' the voice snarled. 'You were warned.'

The figure gripped Kirsten's wrist in a vice-like grip and flattened her hand against the wood of the bedside table. The camera followed, the movements jerky and sometimes out of focus.

Fielding shook his head slowly, also unable to look away. Hypnotised by the vile images, held by them like a fly in a web awaiting an approaching spider.

'Mum,' Kirsten's plaintive scream rose like a plea to the heavens.

The knife blade was against the base of her little finger.

'Mum, please help me,' screamed the little girl.

'Watching?' said the voice. 'Remember this. How easy it is.'

Roma shook her head.

The knife cut through the little girl's finger easily, the severed digit skidding across the wood, propelled by a gout of blood.

Roma bellowed at the top of her voice, feeling the pain that she saw her daughter endure. It was a shriek of pure suffering, and Kirsten echoed it on screen.

Fielding again reached for the remote.

The camera wavered over a blurred shot of Kirsten's severed finger.

Off screen, the voice spoke again. 'You fuck with us once more and I'll cut her throat. Wait for the next phone call.'

The screen went black.

Roma fell forward, sobbing helplessly.

Young lowered his gaze.

Fielding ejected the tape, careful to hold it in the folds of his handkerchief. He handed it to Young. 'Get that back to forensics as quick as you can,' he said. 'Get it dusted and copied. Take the bag it came in too.'

Young nodded and hurried to complete his instructions.

Fielding knelt beside Roma wondering if there was anything he could say.

Realising that there wasn't, he just held her.

She continued to cry hysterically.

# 2.58 P.M.

The bleeding had stopped. Most of the blood on the dressing was congealed. A dark, rusty stain that had soaked the gauze.

Nikki sat on the edge of the bed beside Kirsten, looking down at the little girl as she struggled to hold the plastic beaker of water and drink from it.

It slipped slightly and some of the clear fluid splashed on to her. Kirsten whimpered quietly and Nikki reached forward to hold the beaker for her, watching as the little girl drank thirstily.

Nikki glanced around in the direction of the doorway where Reed was leaning, glancing alternately at Kirsten then at the bloodstained bedside table. He drew in a deep breath, held Nikki's gaze for a moment then retreated back into the other room.

John Dawson was sitting on the sofa flicking through the *Sun*. There was a can of Carlsberg beside him, balanced on the threadbare arm.

Reed sat down opposite him, regarding his brother-in-law silently.

The basement flat had been quiet for the last few hours, but it had taken a long time for Kirsten to stop screaming.

*Too long.*

Reed shuddered as he remembered the high-pitched keening wail of agony she had uttered when her finger had been severed. It had gone on for what had seemed an eternity, only to be replaced by relentless sobbing and begging for her mother.

*Always her mother.*

Nikki had bandaged the stump where the digit had been, cleaning it first with Dettol.

*More screams.*

She had sat with the little girl until the screaming died away. Even stroked her hair as she cried. Kirsten had finally fallen asleep a couple of hours later, her whole body shuddering spasmodically every now and then.

Reed closed his eyes but every time he did he saw the knife carving through the tiny finger. Just as he'd viewed it through the camcorder, watching with shaking hands as Dawson had performed the act.

The three of them had said little to each other. It seemed to Reed as if he and Nikki were surprised at their own acceptance of what Dawson had done. While Dawson himself seemed unmoved by the entire episode.

*Big fucking hard man.*

Reed studied him a moment, distaste in his eyes.

'What?' Dawson said, looking up and catching Reed staring. 'What are you looking at?'

'Nothing,' said Reed acidly.

'I told you at the beginning, Jeff, this kind of thing takes balls. If you haven't got them then walk. Go and see Max Tate now and tell him he can sing for his fucking money.'

'Or go and give myself up to the law and hope I get off with a lighter sentence?'

Dawson chuckled. 'I don't know who you're more scared of,' he said smiling. 'Tate or the fucking police. At least the police will only lock you up. Tate will kill you. *Both* of you.'

'Perhaps that's what we deserve after what we've done.' Nikki appeared in the doorway, looking at the two men. It was her words that made them turn.

'It's a bit late for the morality trip, Nik,' Dawson said disinterestedly. 'What do you want to do? Hand the kid back? Hope everyone forgets about what's happened? Hope that the law will give you a pat on the back and drop the kidnapping and conspiracy charges. Not to mention demanding money with menaces, being accessories . . . I can go on if you like.'

340

'Forget it,' snapped Reed.

'So, beating the shit out of a drug dealer and robbing him was different, was it?' Dawson chided.

'At least he could defend himself,' Nikki countered.

'Not against your old man here. You just picked the wrong pusher, didn't you?'

'That was different,' Nikki insisted.

'Not as far as the law are concerned. Don't *you* go soft on me too, Nik,' Dawson said, looking at Reed disdainfully.

'Just ring them,' Nikki said. 'Arrange the money drop and get this over with.'

'There's still plenty of time,' Dawson said, returning his attention to the newspaper.

'If *you* don't then *I* will,' Nikki said, reaching for the mobile phone.

'Leave it,' Dawson rasped. 'I said, there's plenty of time.'

'You sound like you're enjoying this,' Reed ventured.

Dawson chuckled throatily. The sound echoed around the basement flat. A hollow, emotionless accompaniment to the low whimpering coming from the small bedroom where Kirsten huddled.

'I'm thinking about the money,' Dawson said. 'Perhaps you should be too.'

# 4.23 P.M.

One million pounds had never looked so worthless to David Todd.

Piled on the coffee table before him, he regarded the bundles of notes disinterestedly, his face pale, his eyes blank.

'They should be destroyed,' he murmured. 'Shot down like diseased fucking animals. Tortured first. Made to feel the pain that Kirsten felt.' He let the words trail off and slumped back in his seat.

'They will pay, Mr Todd, when they're caught,' Fielding assured him.

'You mean *if* they're caught,' Todd replied. 'You're no nearer to finding them, are you?'

'The video could prove to be a very good lead,' the DI said. 'Once it's been dusted for prints there's no telling what we might find. If it's studied closely there could be things in it that help us pinpoint the location.'

Todd got to his feet and crossed to the drinks cabinet.

'Things in it,' he sneered. 'The torture of my daughter, *that's* what's in it, Detective Inspector.' He poured himself a large measure of Jack Daniel's, downed half of it in one swallow then refilled the crystal tumbler. 'Something *you* weren't able to prevent. Something you were indirectly responsible for.'

'What happened earlier today was completely unforeseen,' Fielding snapped. 'If it could have been avoided, it would have been. Do you think I *want* harm to come to your daughter? I'm doing my job.'

'That's it, isn't it? To you it's a job, to me it's my daughter's fucking life. I don't think you're up to it, Fielding. You or your men. I think it's time you called in help from New Scotland Yard or Special Branch. Someone used to dealing with this sort of situation.'

'It doesn't work like that,' Fielding told him, trying to keep his voice calm.

'Jesus Christ,' Todd shouted. 'You said yourself that you'd had no experience of anything like this. How the hell are we supposed to trust you to find Kirsten when you tell us that?'

The Nokia was on the table beside the money. Todd jabbed a finger in the direction of the mobile.

'I *want* them to ring,' he said. 'I *want* them to take that fucking money. I want this over.' He drained what was left in the glass.

Both men turned as the sitting-room door opened and Roma walked in.

She crossed straight to the sofa and sat down on one end.

'I thought you were supposed to be resting,' Todd said. 'Didn't you take those tablets the doctor gave you? You should be sleeping, you—'

'Stop telling me what I should be doing, David,' she said wearily. 'I don't want to sleep. Not now. Not when I think what they could be doing to Kirsten.'

'They won't do anything else to her as long as you follow their instructions, Mrs Todd,' Fielding interjected.

'And we're supposed to take *your* word for that, are we, Fielding?' Todd snapped. 'The expert.' He snorted derisively.

Fielding shot him an angry glance but then seated himself in one of the large chairs in the sitting room. He saw Roma looking at the money piled up on the table before her.

'All that money,' she muttered. 'I'd give everything we had just to have her back. They could ask for the rings on my fingers and I'd give them gladly just for Kirsten to be returned safely.'

Fielding thought about saying something but decided against it. The images on the videotape were still vivid in his mind and he had little doubt that the same was true for Roma. It would have been like him watching a tape of his wife's death. Helplessness, anger and frustration welled up inside until he feared he would explode. The feelings were obviously ten times worse for the two other people in the room.

'Why are you still here anyway?' Todd wanted to know. 'Shouldn't you be out doing your job? Trying to find our daughter?'

'Someone should be here with you, Mr Todd, for when the kidnappers call again.'

'So you can fuck up the money drop as well?' Todd snarled.

'Leave it, David,' Roma sighed. 'This isn't helping Kirsten, is it?'

The silence that descended on the room was broken by the ringing of Fielding's mobile.

He got to his feet, excused himself and wandered out into the hallway as he answered it. Todd glared angrily at him as he stepped out of sight.

'Guv, it's me,' Young said.

'What have you got, Rob?' Fielding wanted to know. 'Give me some good news for Christ's sake.'

'Well there's news all right. Forensics took two usable prints off the videotape.'

'Have they been ID'ed?'

There was a pause.

'Rob, can you hear me?' the DI continued. 'The prints.'

'We've got positive ID on both of them. They belong to John Dawson.'

'Jesus,' Fielding murmured. 'Are you sure?'

'Positive. Forensics got a fourteen-point match on them.'

A crackle of static on the line.

'So the murders and this kidnapping *are* linked,' Fielding mused aloud.

'What are you going to do, guv?'

'I'm going to break it to the Todds that the man who's holding their daughter captive has already murdered three kids.'

# 5.13 P.M.

'I'll call them at seven.'

John Dawson stuffed several chips into his mouth and chewed noisily.

Reed and Nikki looked at him, then at each other.

'I'll tell them where to make the drop.' He swilled down the chips with lager.

'So we're finally getting the money?' Reed asked, a note of excitement in his voice.

Dawson nodded. 'When it's done,' he said, still eating, 'you take the money you owe to Max Tate then you get the fuck away from here. As far as you can, as quick as you can. Got that?'

'Fuck him. Fuck Max Tate. Why should he have that money?' Reed hissed. 'After what we've been through why should he get twenty grand of it? We're running anyway. After tonight, the police are our problem, not Max fucking Tate.'

Dawson shrugged. 'Your decision, Jeff,' he muttered.

'What do you reckon, Nik?' Reed enquired. 'Fuck Tate?'

'Where are we going to go?' Nikki wanted to know.

'Anywhere you like,' Dawson told her. 'You'll be able to afford it. But don't start spending the money yet because you can bet your arse, no matter what they've said or what we've threatened to do to the kid, the law will have marked those notes somehow. They'll be watching out for them. Don't spend anything for at least six months.'

'And how the fuck are we supposed to manage that long?' Reed protested. 'That was the whole point of snatching the kid. To get money that we hadn't got.'

'Fair enough,' Dawson said. 'You spend what you like. Go out and buy a fucking Jag if you want, but I'm telling you this: if you get caught and the law turn up on *my* doorstep, I'll know who sent them and I will fucking find you.' He glared at Reed.

'What about the girl?' Nikki wanted to know.

'They can pick her up after we've got the money,' Dawson said. 'After we're safely away from here we'll let them know where she is.'

'How are you going to do this, John?' Nikki asked. 'Where are you going to get them to drop the money?'

Dawson shrugged. 'You know this town better than I do,' he said. 'Any suggestions?'

Reed stroked his chin thoughtfully. 'The cemetery?' he offered.

Dawson burst out laughing. 'You've been watching too many films, Jeff,' he chided.

Reed looked angrily at his brother-in-law.

'We get them to split it,' Dawson suggested. 'Three different places. It'll be harder for them to cover. Each of us pick up just over three hundred grand then we all meet up and we're sorted.'

'And how much do *you* take?' Reed wanted to know.

'I told you at the beginning, thirty per cent. Three hundred thousand. That's a bargain, Jeff. Without my help you'd have been nailed to Max Tate's wall by now. Remember that.'

'What time are you going to get them to drop it off?' Nikki asked.

'Ten o'clock tonight.'

'And when do we tell them where the girl is?'

'Who gives a fuck? As long as we get the money that's all that matters. Besides, the longer they spend trying to find *her*, the more time it gives *us* to get away.'

'But she needs her medication, John, and she needs it quick.'

'I told you not to get too attached to her, didn't I?' Dawson said. 'Once we're gone from here, forget about her. Like I always said, she was a means to an end. Nothing more.'

'She'll die without that medicine. I won't let that happen.'

'And there's me thinking Mother Teresa was dead,' laughed Dawson. He wiped his mouth with the back of his hand. 'My little sister. You always did have a soft side, didn't you? You must have to have married Jeff.'

'Fuck you,' Reed snapped.

'After my fish and chips, Jeff,' Dawson smirked. He belched loudly and continued eating.

'Are you going to tell them where the girl is?' Nikki persisted.

'*You* tell them. You're the one who's so concerned about her.'

'I will,' Nikki said and she disappeared into the small bedroom.

Kirsten was lying on her back on the bed, her breathing shallow, her skin waxen and sheathed with perspiration.

Nikki crossed quickly to her and placed a hand on her forehead.

The skin was very hot yet still pale. Nikki touched her fingertips to Kirsten's cheek.

Searing pain shot through her hand and she pulled away sharply, staring down at her fingertips. The skin was bright red. As if she had touched a hotplate.

There was a strong odour in the room that seemed to be growing more intense by the second.

Nikki recognised it as the smell of burning.


They had listened to him in silence as he'd told them the news.

Fielding had paused every so often, waiting for an interruption, a question. Anything. But both Roma and David had remained silent as he had relayed to them what DS Young had told him earlier. Silent.

*Speechless.*

Fielding knew that the same thought had been going through both their minds.

*How can this get any worse?*

But it just had.

He took their mute reaction for shock and he could hardly blame them. He said he would leave a car outside their house with a plain-clothes officer in it while he returned to the police station in Kingsfield.

Still they sat saying nothing, merely nodding.

He let himself out, glad to be away from the choking silence.

He had reached the front door when Roma emerged from the sitting room, her eyes red-rimmed but her face set in determined lines.

'Detective Inspector,' she said. 'I want to come with you. I need to see that videotape again.'

'I wouldn't advise that, Mrs Todd,' he said.

'I have to see it.'

'Why?'

'I have to be sure.'

'Of what?'

'I think I know where Kirsten is.'

# 6.28 P.M.

The incident room at Kingsfield Police Station echoed to the screams of Kirsten Todd.

For the second time that day Roma watched as her terrified daughter's little finger was cut off. Heard her shrieks of pain and distress. Her sobs of agony.

And again Roma cried although as she did she kept her eyes fixed on the screen, studying every detail of the monstrous images before her. She forced herself to watch the horror through eyes that were already puffy and bloodshot.

Finally Fielding reached for the remote and lowered the sound to a whisper.

*If a scream of agony can be heard as a whisper.*

Behind Roma, his back to the screen, her husband kept silent, his head bowed.

DS Young stood close to him, wondering if he should place a hand on the man's shoulder.

*Make some gesture of comfort.*

He decided against it.

Donna Thompson sat on one corner of the desk near the television set also transfixed by the tape. More than once she averted her eyes.

There were a dozen uniformed and plain-clothes officers scattered around, all silent, all watching the tape. Even when it finished they stood motionless, as if some filmic gorgon had glanced out of the screen and turned them to stone.

Fielding switched the tape off and slapped the lights in the room back on.

Roma wiped her eyes with a tissue.

When Fielding looked at her, she nodded.

'Come through into one of the interview rooms,' he said, putting a hand on her shoulder.

She got to her feet and followed him, watched by the waiting police officers.

David Todd turned to follow but then decided to let her go. The Nokia was lying on the desk and he dare not leave it unattended. One of them had to be nearby to answer it when it rang.

Fielding held open the door to the interview room and stepped back to allow Roma in. She sat down at the small table and the DI seated himself opposite her.

'I feel like a suspect,' she said, trying to force a smile.

'Mrs Todd, what did you see on the tape?' he wanted to know.

'Apart from my daughter being tortured?'

'I'm sorry.'

'No. *I'm* sorry. This is a room where confessions are made, isn't it, Detective Inspector? Well, perhaps I should make one now.'

'Did you recognise anything on the tape?'

'There are some flats in Western Way. About a dozen of them. They're used by students mostly. Some of the students I lecture live in them. I recognised the flat because they're all decorated the same. Same colour. Same carpets. Same lampshades. Everything.'

'How do you know that, Mrs Todd?'

'Because I've been in one of them and I know the others are almost identical. I know because I'm having an affair with the man who leases them.' She cleared her throat. 'He's one of my students. His name is Michael Harper.'

'Does your husband know about the affair?'

'Not yet, but then it doesn't really matter any more, does it? I either lose a husband or a daughter, and I won't lose my little girl.'

'As far as you're aware does Harper know John Dawson?'

'I don't know his friends, Detective Inspector. Our relationship . . .' she smiled humourlessly, 'isn't like that.'

Fielding got to his feet.

Roma also rose.

'Please let me come with you,' she said imploringly. 'When you find Kirsten she'll need me.'

'Your husband will have to know, Mrs Todd, you realise that?'

'Like I said, it doesn't matter any more.'

'I need you to take me to Harper. Now.'

Roma nodded and swept out of the room pursued by Fielding.


Three unmarked cars. Two regulation police vehicles.

Six men in plain clothes. Two uniformed policewomen and five uniformed constables.

Two civilians.

The small convoy set off for Western Way at an even thirty miles an hour. Radio contact was maintained for the first ten minutes.

As the vehicles drew nearer their target, radio silence was initiated.

# 6.58 P.M.

John Dawson picked up the mobile and dialled. It was answered almost immediately.

'Hello,' said David Todd's voice.

'Have you got the money?' Dawson wanted to know.

'I've got it.'

'Then listen carefully. Write this down if you have to but make sure you get it right because if you don't, your fucking kid is dead. What I did to her on that tape is nothing compared to what I'll do if you try and fuck me over, got it? And if you like, I'll send you a tape of *that* too.'

'Just tell me what you want, you animal.'

'Hey, you watch your fucking mouth, rich cunt. Or do you want to hear her scream again?'

'Just tell me what to do.'

Static on the line.

'Can you hear me?' Dawson said, holding the phone away from his ear momentarily.

'. . . line . . . breaking up,' burbled Todd into the Nokia.

'Where the fuck are you?' Dawson wanted to know.

'In a car. Why? . . . does . . . matter where . . . am?'

More static.

'I can just about hear *you*, you'd better hope, for your kid's sake, that *you* can hear *me*.'

'I can hear you. Go on.'

'This is where you'll take the money. You take it there and you leave it.'

'When do I get my daughter back?'

'When I've got the money. Now shut up and listen.'

* * *

In the back seat of the Mondeo, which was driving along Western Way, Todd pressed the Nokia more tightly to his ear, straining to hear what Dawson said to him.

He finally put the mobile down and lay back against the upholstery, his face pale. 'They want the money left at three separate locations,' he said.

'What time do they want to take delivery?' Fielding asked.

'Ten o'clock tonight.'

'It might not matter by then,' the DI said, then he turned to Roma who was seated next to him. 'Which house?'

'Number twelve,' she said hoarsely.

He stepped on the brake and brought the car to a halt, slipping out hurriedly from behind the wheel.

Roma clambered out of the other side.

'Stay inside, Mrs Todd,' the DI snapped.

'I have to see him,' Roma protested. 'I have to know if he's involved.'

Fielding nodded then ducked down again and looked into the back seat where Todd sat alongside DS Young.

'Stay here,' said the DI, and both men watched as Fielding, closely followed by Roma, climbed the steps to the front door.

# 7.10 P.M.

'What the fuck is wrong with her?'

Dawson stood in the doorway of the small bedroom and watched as Kirsten's body first went rigid, then spasmed, then stiffened again.

Nikki moved closer, aware of the smell of burning growing stronger.

*Where the hell was it coming from?*

'She needed that medicine,' Nikki said.

'Well, if they hadn't fucked us around she'd have had it, wouldn't she?' Dawson snapped.

'She'll die,' Nikki gasped helplessly. 'She's been like this for five or six minutes. I think she's having a fit.'

'And then what happens to the money if she dies, big shot?' Reed added furiously.

'They won't know she's dead,' snarled Dawson, rounding on him. 'They don't know anything until *we* tell them. If she dies, she dies. As long as we've got the money it doesn't matter. We'll be long gone before they ever fucking find her.'

'No,' Nikki muttered. 'There must be something we can do for her.'

She retreated into the kitchen and returned with a large glass of water.

As she approached the bed she saw that Kirsten was now lying motionless. Only the gentle rising and falling of her chest signalled that she was still alive.

'What the fuck is that?' murmured Reed, pointing at the bed.

Beneath Kirsten's legs, the blanket was scorched as if a blow torch had been held against it.

'And there,' Dawson said, jabbing a finger in the direction of the pillow case. It was dark brown, almost blackened, beneath her head.

'Give her the water,' Dawson said.

'No, don't touch her,' Reed insisted.

Dawson took the glass from Nikki and approached the bed. '*I*'ll give it to her,' he snarled.

They watched as he knelt beside the bed, prodding Kirsten's arm then pulling more forcefully at it.

'Hey,' he said loudly, leaning close to her ear.

She didn't move. Her breathing was low and guttural, rasping in her throat.

*A death rattle?*

He reached towards her, preparing to sit her up. 'She'll be all right once she drinks this fucking water,' he insisted.

He slid one arm beneath her neck.

Fielding jabbed the button on the panel and waited. 'Is there anyone else who could let us in?' he asked Roma.

She ignored his question, stepped in front of him and pressed the buzzer herself.

'Hello,' said a voice.

'Mike, it's Roma,' she said into the grille. 'Let me in. It's important.'

There was a loud electronic click as the door was unlocked from inside.

Fielding looked at Roma who stepped into the hallway ahead of him.

# 7.21 P.M.

John Dawson roared in pain.

As he cradled Kirsten in his arms he felt sudden, searing agony in his left forearm. It spread rapidly to his shoulder and he pulled back quickly. In his haste, he dropped the glass and it shattered on the floor beside him.

He staggered backwards, his left arm held before him. The material of his shirt was burned through to the flesh. The skin beneath the ragged hole was bright red, already blistered in places.

Kirsten stiffened once again and let out a low gurgling sound, her right hand lolling backwards against the wall.

All around the spot she had touched, the paint bubbled.

Holding his arm Dawson stared at her, his expression a combination of pain and bewilderment. He finally dragged his gaze from Kirsten and studied the burn on his arm, groaning as he touched the bright red flesh.

Nikki too stared at the injury. She could not find the words to express her feelings at what she'd just witnessed.

Reed was looking alternately at Kirsten then at Dawson, his face pale.

'I didn't even touch her skin,' Dawson murmured, looking at a large blister that had risen on his flesh. 'What the fuck is wrong with her?'

The smell of singed flesh now permeated the room, mingling with the odour of burned material.

'She's going to die!' Reed said frantically.

'Like I said,' Dawson told him. 'They won't know that. As

long as we collect the money and get out of Kingsfield, it'll take them days to find her.'

Kirsten rolled over on to her side.

They all saw that the back of her blue cardigan and skirt were burned. The sheet beneath her looked as if it had been smeared with crushed charcoal.

Nikki took a step towards the little girl who had begun to cough violently.

'Stay away from her,' Dawson said. 'She's a fucking freak.'

He spun round and headed back into the living room where he reached for the black holdall.

From inside it he pulled the 9mm automatic.

Fielding had barely stepped across the threshold of Michael Harper's flat when he asked the question, 'Do you know a man called John Dawson?'

Harper looked in bewilderment at Fielding, then at Roma.

The DI fumbled in his jacket and pulled out his identification. He flipped the slim leather wallet open and pushed it towards Harper.

'I've never heard of him,' Harper protested.

'You leased a flat to him,' Fielding continued. 'How long ago?'

'Look, what the hell is going on here? I don't know what you're talking about.'

'I told him about the flats you lease, Mike,' Roma interjected.

Harper retreated, pulling the door of his living room closed.

'Where's Dawson?' Fielding persisted.

Still Harper looked bemused.

'A child has been kidnapped,' the DI snapped. 'Mrs Todd's child. She's being held in one of the flats that *you* lease, Mr Harper. I have reason to believe that one of those same flats could have been used before in connection with the murders of three other children in Kingsfield. If that's true then you're an accessory. Now, I want to know where John Dawson is. There isn't much time.'

'I don't know anyone called Dawson, I swear to God,' Harper protested. 'I leased a flat to a guy called Blake a few days ago.'

'Have you done so before?' Fielding asked.

'Once or twice.'

'Was it definitely the same man?'

'Yes. He said his name was Blake. George Blake.'

'What number flat?'

'Twenty-nine, it's just around the corner. The basement flat.'

'Is there anyone in there with him?' Fielding demanded.

'I just lease the flats. I don't ask how many people are going to be in them. As long as they're not wrecked I don't give a shit.'

Fielding was already reaching for his mobile, jabbing a number.

'Rob, it's me,' he said. 'Number twenty-nine, the basement flat. Close off the area around it but don't go in yet. I don't want them to know we've found them.'

He switched off and turned for the door. 'I'll need to speak to you later, Mr Harper,' he called.

'I didn't know what was happening,' Harper shouted. 'None of this has got anything to do with me.'

Roma walked slowly towards him, her eyes never leaving his.

He opened his mouth to speak but never got the words out.

She struck him, catching him across the cheek with a stinging blow that almost knocked him off his feet.

'Roma,' he said.

He heard the front door slam.

'I didn't know,' he shouted after her.

She was already gone.

# 7.32 P.M.

'She doesn't seem to be in any pain herself,' Nikki said, kneeling beside the bed and looking at Kirsten's face.

The little girl was breathing more evenly now, her eyelids flickering constantly.

Dawson and Reed stood on either side of the bed looking down at the child. The Beretta was tucked into the waistband of Dawson's jeans, hidden beneath the folds of his sweatshirt.

'Kirsten,' Nikki whispered.

'Don't get too close to her,' Reed said.

Nikki reached out to wake the child.

'Nikki, don't,' Dawson warned. 'You saw what she did to my arm.'

Nikki hesitated for a moment then moved her hand closer to the little girl again. She prodded her gently with the tips of her fingers, wincing as she felt the incredible heat against her flesh.

'Kirsten,' she said, a little more forcefully. 'Can you hear me?'

The little girl rolled on to her back, her eyes suddenly jerking open.

'Is there anything we can do to help you?' Nikki wanted to know.

Kirsten shook her head slowly.

'What will happen to you if you don't have your medicine?' Nikki persisted.

'That's pretty fucking obvious, isn't it?' Dawson said, again looking at his scorched flesh.

The little girl mouthed something that Nikki couldn't hear.

Nikki leaned closer, trying to pick up the faint, whispered words.

359

Dawson reached backwards for the automatic.

'Keep away from her,' he snarled.

'Kirsten,' Nikki murmured, now bent over the bed.

The little girl flung up her arms and locked them around Nikki's neck, pulling her down.

Nikki felt incredible pain everywhere that Kirsten touched her. Strands of her hair ignited and burned with incredible speed. Tiny wisps of smoke rose into the air. She felt as if someone had strapped a blazing collar around her neck.

The flesh there seared black in seconds. Welts appeared, became blisters, then burst, spilling their pus on to flesh that was already charcoal.

Nikki screamed and tried to pull away but Kirsten held her with a strength far beyond her size.

Reed tried to pull the little girl's hands away but he too was burned as he touched her skin, both palms turning a vivid red.

Dawson was already pulling out the gun. 'Let her go, you fucking freak,' he roared at Kirsten but the child's eyes had closed once more.

Still she clung to Nikki who was screaming in pain now, huge lumps of burned flesh peeling off like calcified tendrils from her neck, face and upper chest.

A choking, acrid stench filled the room and grey smoke formed a shroud-like pall over the two grappling figures.

'Fucking freak,' Dawson roared again, and aimed the pistol at Kirsten's head, his finger tightening on the trigger.

The little girl suddenly released her grip on Nikki who fell forwards across the bed. With lightning speed, Kirsten shot out a hand and grabbed Dawson's testicles.

The pain was unbelievable and he let out a high-pitched cater-waul of agony that bounced off the walls of the flat and rose to the very heavens themselves.

The pain was so savage that he jerked violently on the trigger of the 9mm, his only concern to drag that hand from his groin.

It felt as if someone had clamped his genitals in a red hot vice and was swiftly tightening it.

The sound of the weapon's discharge in such confined surroundings was deafening.

Moving at a speed in excess of fifteen hundred feet a second, the bullet struck Nikki in the back of the head, stove in a portion of her skull then tore through her brain and exited from her forehead, carrying a reeking flux of pulverised bone, blood and brain matter.

'No,' roared Reed as blood jetted from the remains of Nikki's skull.

'Get her off me,' Dawson screamed, the suffering now almost unendurable.

He felt his scrotum burning. Felt the flesh pucker then melt. Felt first one, then both testicles swell under the incredible heat and pressure. The left one burst, spraying blood and fluid over Kirsten's crushing hand.

Dawson toppled backwards, the gun falling from his grip and skidding across the floor.

There was a smouldering hole where his genitals used to be. Lying in a foetal position he screamed frantically as the pain seemed to flood his entire body. It was as if someone had injected liquid fire into his veins.

Reed looked on with bulging eyes, the gun close to his feet.

Kirsten herself was thrashing madly from side to side, as if someone had driven a cattle prod into her and was pushing it deeper into her small body.

The entire room reeked of burned flesh and fresh blood, and resounded with Dawson's screams as he tried to drag himself across the floor, over the broken glass that cut his hands and arms. But he didn't care, all he wanted was to be away from this child, whatever the fuck she was. All he wanted was for the intolerable pain to stop.

His screams continued, deep and torn from the depths of his being. They deafened Reed as he stood transfixed.

'Kill her,' shrieked Dawson. 'Kill the fucking kid.' His voice had a terrible high-pitched intonation now as he continued to crawl. 'Look what you've done.' There were tears of pain and anger coursing down his face.

Reed finally snatched up the automatic and held the gun in one wavering hand. He drew a bead on Kirsten's head, his finger tightening on the trigger.

'Kill her,' Dawson screamed.

Reed's quivering finger tightened on the trigger, his gaze moving back and forth from Kirsten to Nikki who was still sprawled across the child's body.

'Do it,' Dawson sobbed.

For interminable seconds, Reed steadied himself. Somewhere close by he could hear the sound of footsteps, of hammering on the door and the windows. It was as if all the sounds in the world were spinning around him like some malevolent tornado.

'Kill the cunt,' bellowed Dawson, still crawling. Still bleeding.

Reed swung the pistol down just as Dawson looked up at him.

'Fucking bigshot,' Reed whispered, tears welling in his eyes too.

He fired twice.

Both of the heavy grain slugs hit Dawson in the face, blasting away most of the right side of his head. It was as if he'd been struck by a red-hot sledgehammer. The bullets blew his skull to confetti with terrifying ease.

Reed dropped the gun and turned as the door exploded inwards.

The first of the uniformed men hurtled in, Fielding close behind them.

# 8.48 P.M.

It was like a charnel house.

Even more than an hour later, as Fielding sat on the edge of the worn sofa in the small basement flat, the air was thick with the stench of death. And burning.

The DI got to his feet and walked slowly into the bedroom from where the three bodies had been removed, two to be taken directly to the morgue, the third to the hospital.

Jeff Reed was in custody at Kingsfield police station. He hadn't spoken a word since his arrest.

*Wouldn't? Couldn't?*

Fielding didn't really blame him. He looked at the blood-soaked bedroom. The burned sheets. The bullet holes. He shook his head slowly, knowing, but still not fully comprehending, what had happened in this tiny room.

Perhaps it was beyond the reasoning of any man.

*Any* sane *man?*

He turned as he heard footsteps.

DS Young approached slowly, almost reverentially, as if reluctant to disturb his superior's thoughts.

'You shouldn't be here, Rob,' Fielding told him. 'You should be at home. There's nothing more we can do until the morning anyway. Forensics have already been over the place. I was just about to leave myself.'

'You wanted to know about the little girl,' Young said, his voice barely more than a whisper.

'When did she die?'

'Half an hour ago. Her parents are still at the hospital.'

Fielding shook his head.

'Jesus Christ,' he murmured. Then he looked at his subordinate. 'Go home, Rob. Go home to Jenny. Go home to your pregnant wife, sit with her, hold her.' He smiled. 'And when your kid's born, you make sure you're always there for it, and when it gets older, you spoil it every chance you get.' He shrugged. 'You just never know.'

Young hesitated.

'Go on,' Fielding told him. 'Go home. I'll see you tomorrow.'

'Goodnight, guv,' Young murmured. 'I'm sorry it turned out like this.'

'Me too, Rob.'

Young left. Fielding heard his footsteps on the stone steps that led up to street level. Heard his car start and move off.

The DI stood alone in the tiny flat for a moment longer then he too wandered to the door and stepped over the threshold.

He closed the door tightly behind him.

THREE MONTHS LATER

Detective Inspector Alan Fielding dropped the stalks of the dead carnations into the Tesco bag he'd brought with him then set about polishing the headstone.

When he'd finished he carefully placed fresh flowers in the vase that stood on the plinth at the front of the stone then got to his feet.

'I'll be back in a few days,' he said in the direction of the headstone. 'See you, darling.'

Carrying the bag of dead flowers, he made his way back along the gravel path towards the main driveway that ran through the middle of Golden Hill Cemetery.

It was a beautiful, windless afternoon and birds were singing in the trees. Fielding saw others visiting the graves of lost ones. He watched an old woman kneel before a headstone and cross herself before hauling herself upright again.

In the newer part of the necropolis, a young woman was laying a small bunch of daffodils on a plinth in the section devoted to those who had been cremated.

*Dead parent?*

He often wondered about the others who visited. Who exactly they were paying their respects to.

It seemed strange to Fielding that two days earlier he had been attending the christening of Rob Young's baby boy, and now here he was attending to the grave of his departed wife. If he had been a philosophical man he might well have reflected on the cyclical nature of life and death. But he wasn't.

He dropped the Tesco bag into a nearby waste bin and headed back towards his car.

'Detective Inspector.'

He heard the voice and turned.

Roma Todd raised a hand in greeting and walked towards him.

'Mrs Todd,' he said smiling.

'I've been putting flowers on Kirsten's grave,' she told him. 'I still come nearly every day.'

'So did I to begin with.'

'I didn't know you'd lost someone.'

'My wife. Nearly two years ago now.'

They walked in silence for a moment.

'I read about your husband in the paper,' Fielding said. 'It said he was moving to America.'

'New York,' she elaborated. 'Expanding his empire. He didn't really need an excuse to leave me after he found out about the affair. His pride couldn't take a blow like that. Going to live in New York was the easy way out for him.'

'I'm sorry anyway. For . . . everything that happened.'

Roma put a hand to her stomach and winced slightly.

'Are you OK?' Fielding wanted to know, seeing her expression.

She smiled and nodded. 'I should know what to expect,' she told him. 'It's my second time.'

Fielding looked puzzled.

'I'm pregnant,' she explained.

The policeman slowed his pace slightly, glancing first at Roma's belly then at her face.

'Is the baby . . . ?'

'Tainted? Cursed? Dangerous?' she replied, a slight edge to her voice. 'The same way Kirsten was?'

'You said that there was a possibility a second child could inherit the same symptoms,' he said slowly.

'A possibility. Nothing more. It's a chance I'm willing to take.'

They walked a little further, back to their waiting cars.

Fielding unlocked his. 'I'd better get back to work,' he said. 'It was good to see you, Mrs Todd.'

'Can I ask you something?' Roma said. 'They say that it gets easier as time passes.' She sniffed. 'When you've lost someone. They say time is a great healer. Is that true?'

'No,' Fielding said flatly. 'They lied.'

He slid behind the wheel and started the engine.

Roma watched as he pulled away then she got into her car. She sat for a moment then pulled open her jacket and looked down at her belly as if trying to see beyond the flesh to the child inside.

She pressed her fingers gently against the skin.

All around her navel the flesh felt hot.

She swallowed hard then started the engine of the BMW and carefully guided the vehicle into the road.

She opened the window slightly.

There was a faint smell of burning in the car.

'The innocent won't fear the judgement day.'
The Scorpions

'What's gone and what's past help
Should be past grief.'

Shakespeare, *The Winter's Tale* Act III, Scene II

**Other bestselling Time Warner Books titles available by mail:**